Captain
of the
Sands

Keith Dewhurst

Captain of the Sands

JONATHAN CAPE
THIRTY BEDFORD SQUARE LONDON

First published in Great Britain 1982
Copyright © 1981 by Keith Dewhurst

Jonathan Cape Ltd, 30 Bedford Square, London WC1

British Library Cataloguing in Publication Data

Dewhurst, Keith
Captain of the sands.
I. Title
823'.914[F]   PR6054.E94/
ISBN 0 224 01619 9

Printed in Great Britain by
Butler & Tanner Ltd, Frome and London

This Novel is Dedicated to the Memory of
JOHN KNOWLER
in Gratitude and Respect

Contents

CONTENTS

Part One

High Top

All hushed and still within the house;
Without—all wind and driving rain;
But something whispers to my mind,
Through rain and through the wailing wind, Never again.
Never again? Why not again?
Memory has power as real as thine.

—EMILY BRONTË

Chapter 1

The Fair at Low Crags

My father bought the cow-in-calf at Low Crags cattle fair on a wet and soggy Tuesday in July. It was the first and last time that he walked me with him, and for me it was a dream come true, because at every Christmas, when the story-tellers and fiddlers had vanished into the frost-sharp darkness and he sat sentimentally fuddled on the settle, or after a day stacking peats when he was unexpectedly satisfied with his work, or once when he wagered a guinea on a cock-fight and won, my father had clapped his arms round me and wetly kissed me, and said that he worked the farm for me, and that his proudest day would be when we went like two men together to the cattle fair on the old upland drove road from Scotland. "You'll make 'em respect you," he'd say. "My son. My lad. My son." I knew that the fair was held in a big, flat, sheltered meadow, and in my mind I saw white clouds sail across the sky. I saw tents and streaming flags, canvas pavilions, and men of a most proud and deliberate cunning. They clapped their hands and ordered music to excite the senses. It was heathenish music, all blare and crash and dangerous majesty. Yet the men respected my father, and were grave to me.

Low Crags fair inspired more dreams than even my mother's winter stories, when the wind moaned and my eyes smarted from the peat fire we never let die, and I lay on the bracken-filled mattress and she knelt with her face next to mine, now kissing me and now telling again the stories that my uncle William had told her, about the worlds he'd seen on his voyages—worlds that I've seen for myself now, and as I shall write in these confessions, not one of them as noble as the Low Crags fair in my mind.

Uncle William was my father's brother. I'd never met him but I knew he was a brave, warm, smiling giant. I worshipped him because I knew that he would never blame me when I made mistakes. I worshipped my father, too, but I was afraid that I would not live up to him.

When he muttered one supper-time that he expected he'd better go to the fair tomorrow, my mother said, "Yes," and then, "You should take our Tom. He's twelve. It's time he went."

"What about you?" my father said.

"What about me?"

"On your own up here."

"Big Field's stone-walled. The beasts can't get out, can they?"

"It's not that at all," my father said. "You know very well it's not that."

His features always seemed big to me, bigger than any other man's. His nose was big and the lobes of his ears and the hairs in his nostrils. When he walked he put his feet down very heavily for a man of medium height. His shoulders sloped. He held his head at an angle, and his mouth was set in a tight, long-suffering grimace.

"What I mean," he said, "is that I'm thinking about *you*. That's what I'm thinking about."

My mother got up and took the trenchers to the bakehouse sink.

My heart pounded. I imagined the talks I'd have with my father as we walked across the moors to the fair. I thought that away from my mother, away from women's silliness and the things they make you do, away from all that he would speak as man to man. He would be my equal. He would confide in me. He would ask my help in his problems.

My mother came back to the parlour. Her clogs squeaked on the sanded floor.

My father was silent. He stared at oatcake crumbs on the table and crushed them with his finger.

My mother looked at him. His head moved as though he were

4

talking to himself, but his lips were tight. His face had an exasperated flush.

My mother's smile was nervous, and she blushed herself, but her chin was up, and when she went out of the open door to feed the scraps to the fowls, the evening light shone through her hair that had once been russet but now had patches of grey.

"Come on, Sukie. Come on, Prince. Come on, Brownie love . . ."

My mother's shoulders were stiff. She was wearing coarse grey worsted, and beyond her the moor fell away from our yard and rose again to encircle us at the horizon. It was freshly green and sprinkled with dots of white flowers.

I turned to my father. His eyes accused mine. "Do you see now what distresses her?" he said. "It's whether you can behave like a man or not."

I looked away. I was intensely aware of pricks and itches of sweat on my body and of the wooden hardness of the stools and table. My limbs seemed fixed and heavy. My eyes stung with embarrassment and yet seemed to dilate. The lime-washed walls glowed with light. There was pink in them, and blue in the shadows. I stared at the strange mottled pattern of the scales on one of the hen's legs, and I heard larks sing as they rose above the moor.

I tried to speak, but my voice was thick in my throat. Then I managed to breathe and I said, "I won't let you down. I won't."

"It's four days' walking."

"I'll keep up."

"What if you don't?"

"I will. I promise I will."

He sighed and rapped his fingers on the table and swayed the upper part of his body like a man pulled by a rope.

"It's folk, though, in't it?" he said. "It's folk. Important men that have to be talked to."

I felt tears in my eyes. He dursn't trust me, I thought. He works this farm for me but he dursn't trust me. He could have sailed away like Uncle William, the younger son, but for my ungrateful love he had stayed, even when the farm was so poor and remote that no one could have thought the worse of him for selling it. The nearest house was a mile away—Jack O'Slattocks's, where Jack lived with his mother, both of them fuddled on their own ale and cackling like two old crones. A mile beyond Jack O'Slattocks's the folds became deeper and kinder. There were thick oak-woods and the path became a lane, with looms clacking and people strolling from cottage to cottage to visit one another.

That lane led to the valley and, after eight miles, the town. We would walk there and back when we had a piece of cloth to take to market. It was not far, in summer especially when all the ways were passable, but it did not count for much in our feelings. Our feelings looked to ourselves and to the moors. In the spring young salmon darted like sun-dazzle in the high, brown, gushing brooks, and in winter darkness we carded the wool and made rush-lights from the fat of the beast killed for salting. We sat by the fire and heard outside the sleet and dashing hail, and my mother would say how good my father was to us, and how he was always the first to go out on a bad night. She would coax him to tell me again how on the worst night in living memory Uncle William and my father, young men both, had gone out because they loved their dog. They found her frozen dead where she had scented six feet deep in the drift the sheep still dimly alive.

My father dismissed the story, because his invariable way was to punish himself. The work was never well enough done. The peats were always cut too raggedly, the rain would batter down the oats, my mother and I did not understand that to do a piece of work properly was the most important thing in life. Why didn't we help him? Why did we just throw muck all over the yard? Useless to protest that we did not, or that the yard was earth, slippery and foul for most of the year, dry and dusty on that evening when my mother stood there with the hens pecking round her skirts and the moors rolling and swooping away as far as the eye could see.

"Are you coming in, then?" said my father to her back. She shrugged, a petulant jerk of her shoulders; she looked like a little girl.

My father laughed in a forced, surprised, uneasy way and said, "Well, if Low Crags means that much, he'd better walk with me, hadn't he?"

My mother came back into the house. My father smiled and held out his hand, but she ignored it. "There's things need doing," she said.

My father sat with his mouth in a hard line. Then he sighed and said, "Some of us are to blame for that as well, I suppose," and went out.

We went to bed early in silence, and at first light, after a break-fast of porridge and small beer, my father and I set off. My mother held me to her, then laughed and pushed me out of the door. The sky was grey and pink, and mist hung damply in the hollows. We sent back the two black dogs and kept Betty, the brown-and-white bitch, with us.

It was brisk walking over the tops as the sun warmed away the mists and made rocks gleam where water drained across them. Once Betty startled a blackcock, which whirred up in front of us and shed sparklets of dew from its plumage. Alas, in the north and west there were dull, dark clouds that as we walked towards them filled the sky. When the sun shone we had felt fresh; these clouds were cold and yet we sweated.

After two hours the first blobs of rain fell, and we were soon soaked. We ate our dinner on the move and at dusk came to an inn, where we took our supper in a low-ceilinged room full of men and the smell of sweat and damp and stale beer. My father had said nothing all day, and now when men commented on the weather, all he said was, "Oh, I knew it would. I knew there'd be rain if I brought him," jerking his thumb at me and setting his mouth in a defeated smile. He seemed unsure of himself at the inn. He hung about in the rain for several minutes before going in at all, and when we ordered two black puddings but were given only one, he refused to complain.

I went to sleep in a corner near the fire. My clothes dried but my arm was flea-bitten.

The next day we came down from the tops and walked along sloping hillsides where trees loomed out of the grey damp. Occasion-ally we passed other travellers: packmen, farmers driving a beast they had bought, and old men who muttered to themselves as they walked and seemed not to see us. One of them lay like used rags at the edge of the track, and Betty sniffed at him and whimpered, but my father called her to heel and tramped on. I looked at him but he refused to meet my eye, and since whenever I spoke he was angry or sneering, I kept silence. Sometimes he would quicken his pace, so that I had almost to trot. My legs ached. I had a pain in my side. At midday we came to a hamlet of six or seven houses. There was a company of soldiers. In the wet the pipeclay of their crossbelts had run a grubby white upon their scarlet coats. They had three or four women with them and a cart for the baggage.

"Is this Low Crags?" I said.

"Don't be daft," my father said.

I couldn't understand why he ignored me. I thought that there must be secret dangers from which he wanted to protect me. There were pressgangs, or witches, or old women who came out of their hovels and offered boys cans of milk that contained sleeping-draughts, or perhaps there were rope bridges across ravines. What-ever the dangers, my father had known but not inflicted them upon my mother or me. He had kept the knowledge of terror to himself. I loved him for it. I touched his damp sleeve. He grunted but did not check his heavy stride.

In the late afternoon the light became greyer and thicker, and we could scarcely see the difference between the mizzle and the shadows. The track climbed to open moorland again, and in the last sheltered dip, among the last straggling sentinels of trees and hedgerows, we came abruptly upon an inn. It was low and dark, and smoke drifted across it from three or four open fires. There were rough shelters under some of the hawthorns, and men and horses, and about a hundred beasts with their brown and black heads very miserably down in the rain. They were tethered to pegs stuck in the churned-up ground and guarded by boys younger than I, barefoot boys, dirty and shining-eyed, who carried long sticks and were wrapped round with pieces of cloth instead of shirts and breeches. Against the wall of the inn a man sat with his chin on his chest and his lap full of vomit. Betty went to sniff at him, but my father called her off, and I followed him into the inn.

The room was dark and full of what seemed quarrelling men, and I felt afraid and stopped to rub the smoke from my eyes. A man grabbed me, and pushed his face near mine, and spoke a sing-song gibberish. I looked at my father but he was walking away. I tried to wrench free but the man's fingers dug in. Half his nose had been eaten away by some disease. I started to cry. The man laughed and shoved a drinking-pan at me. I swallowed. It was like fire. I gasped and choked. Six or seven men screamed with laughter, at which my father turned.

"You damn blasted . . . You stupid . . . You fool boy."

He dragged me outside, and in the drizzle, with shaggy northern ponies standing round us, he knocked me down and then lifted me and hit me across the head. I was covered in mud and muck. Cold slime had run up my sleeve.

"Don't you dare tell your mother," he said. "You tell your mother I hit you and I really will."

I sobbed. He hit me again, a mean, embittered jab with a single forefinger that jolted my cheekbone. Then he went back into the inn. I didn't know what to do. I looked round for the dog but she was nowhere to be seen. I tried to touch one of the ponies. It shied away. I wished that everything could be different and forgotten. I took off my coat and wiped it on the inn wall. Muck cakes when it dries, I said to myself, and then I can rub it off with twigs. If I can stay outside until it cakes, nobody will see me. When they do see me they won't be able to see how stupid and disgusting I am, and so my shame will be forgotten. I suddenly felt very safe, alone in the vague rain with only the ponies near me.

Then my father came out of the inn. He gave me a pot of small beer and one of the oatcakes that my mother had prepared for us. He rubbed me with a handful of straw that he must have gathered from the floor. He held me by the shoulder. There were tears in his eyes.

"My boy," he said. "My son. My little lad . . ."

"Is this it?" I said.

"Is it what?"

"Low Crags."

"Where d'you think it is?" he said, and walked towards the groups of tethered beasts. I ran after him. His head was thrust down and forward.

Some of the Scots drovers spoke to him but he would not answer. The Scotsmen watched him pass. In those years after the Jacobite rebellion they were forbidden to wear their kilts and tartans or to carry weapons. They were a strange mixture of softness and violence. They were elaborately polite, and yet a sneer lurked in their smile, and a cringe in the deference of their greeting. They were dirty and many of them had marks of disease. They talked their own language among themselves, and when their English was not thick with drink, it had a soft and most beguiling lilt.

Their beasts were sturdy and rough-haired, and even I could see that they had been driven south at a shrewd pace, which meant that by grazing on the way they had not lost too much weight.

My father walked among the beasts, and the little boys guarding them affected to ignore him, but when he had walked two or three times past the same animal, the boy signalled with his stick to another, who ran to the inn and returned with the stocky man who had grabbed me and made me drink his spirits. He, too, ignored us, but he was smiling and muttering to himself, and as my father passed the beasts for a seventh time, took off his bonnet and said, "Well now, chentlemen, and which ish it to be?"

His rotted nose was horrible but his eyes had a twinkle. He was stubbly and fair-haired, and his leggings were tucked into what looked like a pair of old military boots.

My father gave him a glance and, clearing his throat, said, "How much is the cow-in-calf?"

"Chust the one," said the drover. "Chust the very one."

"How much?" said my father.

"Och and it's hard as an English soldier you are."

My father spat into the mud.

"It's a good wee beasht. It's chust the beasht I'd choose for a lassie's dowry," said the drover, but he had grasped that my father was not a man to enjoy the elaboration of business, so they very soon agreed upon a price and struck palms upon it, and my father delved in his bundle for some guineas. Then the drover unpegged the beast, and with Betty at heel and me holding the rope, we squelched to the hedgerow shelters.

We paid an old man a halfpenny to tether the cow, a penny for broth from his cauldron, and twopence to sleep under his tarpaulin. He and my father never spoke, but as we supped our broth a woman came up and said something to my father. "No," he said, "certainly not; and I don't want you near us, neither." He turned his back on her. She stood in the fire-glow, and beyond her, other lights showed through the damp. She looked as though she had been struck and winded. She had a plain but stubborn face.

"Listen," she said, "listen, you . . ."

She picked up a clod of mud and threw it. Some spattered across my father's shoulder. He turned and got up and swung his fist at her but missed because she ducked. He swung again. This time he hit her and she sat down in the mud.

"Call yourself a woman?" my father said. "Call yourself a worthwhile creature?"

He threw his own handful of mud, and some of it flicked across her face. Then he sat down again and took up his broth.

The old man's eyes danced from one to the other of us. "See that, son?" he said to me. "See that?"

The woman picked herself up. People shouted at her from other shelters along the hedge. Her nose was bleeding. She sniffed and wiped the mud off her face. I wanted to help her and I half rose, but my father said, "Where are you going?" and the old man cackled.

"But why did you hit her?" I said. My father ignored me. He held the bowl to his face and supped. When I looked up again, the woman had gone.

The old man followed my glance into the darkness and then turned to my father and said, "Not changed much, have you?"

"No," said my father. "Nor ever will."

The old man sighed. "I had fine women in my day," he said.

· "I had a good conscience," said my father. He smiled to himself as though no one understood him, and lay down to rest. When later I stirred in my sleep, I was sure from the set of his body next to mine that he was still awake, and staring into the damp-filled darkness.

Chapter 2

High Top in the Snow

Next morning was drier, and between the dark clouds and the horizon there was a strip of bright, colourless sky. We set off at a slow pace so as not to tire the cow, and Betty loped sometimes in front of us, and sometimes around the cow's heels to keep her moving. I'd soused my face under the inn pump and squatted down in the field to defecate, and at the top of the hill I cast a backward look. Steam rose from the animals, and there were already two Scotsmen arguing in the yard. So much for Low Crags, I thought, yet even my disappointment bred new daydreams and romance. I wove a story about the Scots drover—how he fought for the Pretender and slew an English soldier for his boots—and I wondered about the sad, mysterious woman and the old man. My father might talk about him, I thought, and so I said, "Where does that old man live?"

"Old man?"

"The one we sheltered with.'

"He lives there," my father said. "He's had fine women, but he still goes round fairs and lives in hedgerows." He strode on in silence. Then he gestured, stabbing the air with his finger. "I've seen plenty of them," he said. "Scores and scores of useless people. One year you can't find 'em and it means they've died."

12

When we reached High Top he told my mother that my clothes were mud-stiffened because the weather had been so vile that I kept slipping and falling with the cow's rope in my hand.

"At least he held on," she said.

"Aye," he said, and was grudgingly obliged to praise me, at which her smile was joyous.

Then three weeks later came a great misfortune: the cow was delivered prematurely of a dead calf. I can hear to this day the cow's dazed bellows and see my father with his arm half inside her as he grunted and heaved at a mucus-dripping thing that looked like a calf but was hunched up and frozen even though it was warm: a thing that the cow tried to lick to life while my father set to milk her with his hands running blood and slime. It was a fine August night, and we went out of the byre and looked at the stars. My father shook his fist at them.

It was the last vigorous gesture of his life, because although he accomplished his autumn tasks, although he collected the peats in September and in October took me to the shepherds' meeting, where we sorted and marked our own sheep, although at Martinmas he worked hard in pouring rain to get the beasts into the byre for the winter, although he talked often about what tune he'd have the fiddlers play for my mother at Christmas, although he seemed unaltered, he was not. His health was failing. He would be unusually tired and complain of aching limbs. Then he would be his true self for days at a stretch until he was overcome by nausea that would pass in a morning.

One evening my mother vomited without warning, and thereafter she, too, had days of lassitude followed by weeks of energy. More often than not, the task of spreading hay for the beasts in the byre fell upon me. Then my father had the running flux from his bowels. He lost weight. It was an effort for him to spread the threshed oats for drying.

I was to walk to the apothecary, but the next morning my father felt fresh and eager again, and told me not to go. I thought that my mother would argue with him, but she was too tired, and when I said, "Don't you think I *should* go?" my father said, "You should do as I say," and in that moment the course of all our lives and deaths was set.

A week later, on one of the last afternoons of November, I was picking rushes by the stream that ran near Jack O'Slattocks's. I felt a chill even in that weather, and looking up, I saw the landscape disappear into grey, and out of the grey advanced whirls of hail-stones. A magpie swerved among them. I started homewards over the hill. The hailstones made shapes and spirals; they were like pictures of the wind, and yet when they struck me they vanished. They were just wet. The grass ahead had a faint silver whiteness that when I reached it was merely damp. The gullies were still black. I was cold, and the hail stung, but the path was easy. As I reached the brow and looked down at our farm, the hail stopped. The sky broke into very fresh, clear blue. Low clouds were luminous with hidden sunlight. The dead bracken was a vivid orange. I was elated by the beauty of the harsh place where I lived, and I ran the last few hundred yards down the slope and burst shining-faced into the house.

My father was on the stone floor spewing blood, and my mother wrestled to lift him but she was too weak. Together we half dragged, half carried him to bed, where his eyes stared without seeing and he babbled and shouted about his childhood and once cried out, "Don't hit me! Don't hit me!" Then he fell peacefully asleep, only to wake minutes later, crying, "William! William, you bastard!" Sweat streamed from him. He rolled and threw himself about, and my mother wept because she did not have the strength to hold him. We put cold cloths on him, and when I went into the yard to soak them anew, the sky was like lead and the hills were dark, and I saw the white shapes of the wind again, but this time they were soft and blurred and obscuring. This time it was a snowstorm.

When I went back, my father was open-eyed and alert. He knew where he was and he spoke clearly, although his voice was faint. "Best fetch the apothecary," he said.

"It's snowing," said my mother, "he can't go in that."

"I can reach Jack O'Slattocks's," I said, "and then Jack can go."

But I hardly reached a hundred yards. Big flakes whipped and whirled in all directions. The air was thick and grey. I passed the yard-post, but soon after I fell down for the first time. When I stood up and looked round I couldn't see where I was. The house had disappeared. The wind tugged at my breath. Flakes hit my eyes and exploded into every colour. They dazzled me. I fell again. I sobbed and scrabbled at the snow. The grass inside it was like wet iron spikes. I followed my own footsteps back to the house. By the yard-post they had already begun to fill in, but I knew my bearings, even though I came to the byre door instead of the house.

Next morning the house was full of light from the snow outside. My father was feverish and then abruptly lucid. He glanced round the room for the apothecary, and when he did not find him his eyes sent venom into mine.

In that instant I knew that I hated him, and it was a strange relief to me. I felt full of energy but I had no way to release it. I could not run into the yard because of the snow drifts. I was numb and cold. I crouched near the fire in the parlour, where the light was unnatural because one mullion was blocked by a drift outside. I was floating. I was under the sea or gliding in a mist. Hours passed. Even the darkness shone white from the drift. The peats glowed. I heard my mother's clogs on the stair.

"Tom," she said. "Give us a light, Tom." I lit a rush light. She slumped on the settle and said, "I think he's dead."

"Don't you know?" I said, surprised at my own maturity.

"Will you go and look?"

"No. I don't want to."

"Are you feared?"

I shrugged. Yes. Yes, I'm feared. But I took the light and went. He lay with his eyes and mouth wide open. In the struggle she had ripped off his shirt to wipe his sweat, and his naked chest was very white. I put my ear against it. He was perceptibly cold. There was no heartbeat. I thought of the linnets I'd caught and held in my hand. I'd felt their hearts pumping; their whole bodies had quivered. I shut my father's eyes by pulling down on the lashes, first the right eye and then the left, because I did not know a surer way. His expression was a cry of fear and surprise. He looked coarse but vulnerable. I pulled the blanket up and over him. Then I went down to my mother and said, "Yes. He's dead."

"Is he cold?" she said.

"Yes."

"I think I fell asleep." She wept, slowly and exhaustedly.

"Do you want to eat?" I said. She shook her head.

I cut a chunk of the salted beef and ate it in my hands. Then I took another light through into the byre and fed the beasts. My mother sat where I'd left her. The rush light wiped out her lines. She looked young. I sat down on the floor with my head in her lap, and when she stroked my brow her hand was hot.

I settled myself more cosily against her, and the next thing I remember is waking up in the hard, strange, snow-light of the day and feeling achesome and cold all over. The rush lights were out, but the fire smouldered. My mother slept with her mouth open. Her breath was harsh and troubled. I stood up, all stiffness and bewilderment. The wind howled and drove the blizzard through the yard, and then I remembered my father upstairs and I ran to the door and opened it. The wind blew snow in and made the smoke swirl. My mother woke up. I shut the door, and so without our knowing it, began our ordeal, when the blizzard blew five days and nights together, and even after it had stopped we could not leave the house because the snow lay under dull skies for another week.

Huge drifts changed the shape of the moors and half buried the house itself. Where the yard should have been, snow sloped up to the roof and covered all the windows. From one small back window in the loft room where my father lay, we glimpsed the sky, but when we opened the front shutters it was to see the inside of the drift packed against the glass. We could walk through to the byre and did so to relieve ourselves among the animal muck, and sometimes to cling to the beasts for warmth, because the peat store was outside and what we had in the house burned up after six days.

We had food but lost our desire for it. We were cold and light-headed. We had no sense of time. My mother was often delirious. When the blizzard stopped, the silence was a dream in which we lived like children who make their pretend house under a table. We would open the shutters and marvel at what the wind had imprisoned in the drift: specks of soil and grass, and above our heads a mouse, his frozen fur like spikes against the rimy pane. We ate tiny portions from the smallest plates and drank ale from a thimble, and my mother called me Will, which was my uncle's name, and sometimes John, which was my father's, but never Tom, which is my own.

"Do you remember, Will, do you remember when I was a girl at Waterfoot and you and your brother, John, walked over the moors to see me? You'd stride and stride and, oh, I remember one day when I was young and light. We gathered primroses. John put his foot in the brook. We laughed but he sulked all day. Then the hillside was purple. You put your hand down my bodice. We met in the dark. I trembled. You made my whole body tremble. Under the old trees near the washing-stones you kissed me good-bye.

"Your brother John still walked over, didn't you, John? Of course you did. We sat in the parlour with the clock. Tick tock. I'd hear my own heartbeat. I'd hear looms three or four houses away but not a word said except your sighs and grumbles; not one of my questions asked.

"Where is he? How can you be so like him and so different? What if he's drowned in the sea? Then one day after a long silence you said, 'I've talked to your father. He says I mun ask you. Will you wed me?' I said, 'Yes.' I had a sorrow every day. It stirred in me every day like a child. I'd forget and then my sorrow moved and made me gasp. I was big with it. I carried it like Tom. Help me. Stop this pain. If you didn't look like Will I'd never have wed you, would I? Who else could I have wed, though? Who else?"

Once her strength returned in full and she swept out half the byre, but then the fever raged again and I laid her on my bed, where she talked about the family Bible and gifts of hot spices that my uncle William brought her, and about practical jokes she'd played as a girl.

Her features had shrunk, which made her eyes seem larger and more beautiful. She was frail and I wanted to protect her and discover properly her elusive strength. By now the thaw had begun, and water seeped in through the mullions and around the doors and we heard the suck and whisper of the melting drift. The light was greyer and dirtier, and my mother lifted her head and looked at me directly (although I knew she did not see me) and said, "Tom, where's your uncle? I want to lie by him."

"My uncle?" I said. "My uncle's at sea."

"He's dead upstairs," she shouted, and sat up in bed to cuff me. I felt tears in my eyes.

"I'll move him," I said, "I'll just have to move him," and went with dread to where my father lay. I pulled back the blanket. He was yellow and stiff, and his open mouth screamed in agony, but the cold seemed to have preserved him. He lay across the bed, and what I had to do was heave him straight. I retched but swallowed back on it and breathed the cold air. Then very quickly I thrust my arms under his body, and as I did so, I knew the impossible weight of him, and then I felt the underside where all the liquid had drained burst open like bad fruit, and there was a stench of rot and faeces and my hands went through mush and grasped his backbone. I screamed in revulsion and pulled away. The mush squelched and spilled out, and his body sank into the straw. I retched again and grabbed the blanket to wipe my hands. The room was full of his stench.

I threw the blanket over him and ran out.

My mother seemed much weaker. She mumbled to herself, so I ignored her, but she knew I was there. I was shivering. I ached for the snow to melt. "Tom," she said, "Tom. I must lie by him."

I did not know what to do, so I lay down beside her and took her hand in mine. I was afraid to speak.

"Where have you been?" she said. "What was it? Why did you leave me?"

I did not reply I shut my eyes. Help her. Please help her.

"Why did you leave me?" she said. "Why don't you speak? Tell me. Surely to God you can tell me now."

I sobbed and clenched her hand. I remembered Low Crags and the old man and the drover and the woman who threw mud at my father. "Don't shout," I said. "I'm here. Don't shout." I was afraid and confused. I felt sick. Icicles hung from the roof beam and down the cold chimney. They dripped. "Listen," I said. "It won't be long. It's melting. Listen."

As we listened we fell asleep, and I awoke shivering in darkness. Her fingers were like clamps around mine, and I knew that she was dead. Gasping and frightened, I freed my hand and sat on the settle. I heard the drifts collapse and the snow dribble away. I fell asleep again and awoke in daylight. There were voices in the yard. I was so weak I could hardly walk, but I went to the door and opened it. A mess of snow and water sploshed in.

Jack O'Slattocks and Mr. Sutcliffe and my father's cousin Crabtree and some others were in the yard. They looked dark and pinched in the dirty thaw. I was happy, but I did not want to speak to them. The cold made me gasp. They wrinkled their noses at the stench that came through the door, and Sutcliffe said, "Bleeding Jesus . . ." I stood in the portal and let them go past me into the house and make their own discoveries.

Chapter 3

The Reading of the Will

For a week I lay in bed at Crabtree's cottage with the fever still on me. I saw strange creatures in the shadows. I wrestled with imaginary chains and tried to buffet Crabtree even though I knew he wept for me. He was a tall, gawky man with big hands, big feet, and a big jaw. He was famous throughout the valley for his clumsiness and his indulgence in cock-fighting and all manner of sports, especially the wrestling, at which he would throw a swaggering opponent with ease and then fall over his own feet, injure himself, and have to be assisted to the alehouse. Assistance or not, he laughed so much at his own lapses that he hadn't an enemy in the world. His wife was tiny. She had a little pointed face like a dormouse's and a little mob cap and bright eyes, and it seemed that whatever time of day or night I half awoke, her hands would pitter-patter a cool cloth across my face, and she would argue in a whisper with poor, kind, hopelessly eager Crabtree.

"Where's them cloths, husband? Where's that bowl of water?"

"Here," he said, and let go of the bowl before she had time to grasp it, so that water splashed everywhere.

"God bless us," she said, "you're all thumbs, Crabtree. You're like a big door with no knobs on."

"That's a good one is that, Mrs. Crabtree. A door with no knobs on."

"Oh, fetch some more water," she said.

"The bowl's broke," he said, and I could not help laughing and crying in my pain.

"God bless his little heart," said Mrs. Crabtree, dabbing at my tears, and Crabtree said, "See? See what I mean? If he can laugh he's mending."

He stood up, very pleased with himself, and cracked his head on the low ceiling.

"What's that?" he said. "What's happened? What have I done?"

"You big gatepost," she said.

"I am," he said, "I know I am," and when he went for fresh water it seemed to my sick fancy that Mrs. Crabtree prayed aloud to God to keep me with them, for I was the little lad they'd always wanted and where else would I be lodged with love?

Then one day I opened my eyes and knew that I was cured. I was weak but my head was clear and the air was sharp in my nostrils. Crabtree was sitting on a stool. When he saw that I was awake he opened his mouth. I smiled. He realized that I was recovered and tried to speak but all that came out was a wheezing laugh. He rushed to the door. It was shut and he collided with it. "Mrs. Crabtree!" he shouted. "Mrs. Crabtree!" and jumped up and down with excitement like a scarecrow dancing.

Mrs. Crabtree appeared and squeaked and scurried all over the loft, and clapped her hands and kissed me. Then they both went downstairs and heated some broth, and sat and watched me sup it, and Crabtree wheezed and rocked with glee, until a thought struck him and he stopped in mid-gesture, so that his arms hung in the air.

"Er—" he said, and jerked his head at me, "I must tell him, mustn't I? It's my duty, isn't it?" Mrs. Crabtree sniffed, and Crabtree put his clumsy hand on hers and said, "Now, then, Mrs. Crabtree. Now, then. I thought you was a British Grenadier." Mrs. Crabtree sat up straight and found a tight little smile, and her eyes were brighter for the tears held back in them.

"What's happened, Tom, is that we've had the funeral," said Crabtree. "I know it was your right to be there, but we couldn't wait, not with their bodies in that state." He looked uneasily at Mrs. Crabtree. She patted his hand. "Anyhow," he said, "they're both where they'd want to be: in the one grave together. I'll walk you up there when you're able."

I imagined the churchyard on the shoulder of the moor, and the earth around the farm door scoured black by the thaw, and the house cold with no fire in it—a sharp, waiting cold, the past years gone but the spring still far away.

"What about the beasts?" I said. "Who's seeing to them?"

"They were starved, Tom. We had to kill two, and Jack O'Slattocks walks over to feed t'others. I reckon you mun pay Jack for that."

I laughed because I could not imagine myself having money to pay a grown man.

"Not that it's our place to say owt about paying," said Crabtree. "It's not. It's your place is that, Tom, after Mr. Sayer's read the will."

They stared at me, as though waking with a clear head had made me a different person. I did not know how to respond. Mrs. Crabtree sniffled.

"Now, now, Mrs. Crabtree," he said, "face your front."

"But who will take him?" she said. "Who will take him for himself?"

Crabtree blushed and shifted his limbs about. Mrs. Crabtree watched him and then smiled as she might at an awkward child. Crabtree grinned.

"Crabtree," she said, "you're as daft as a sheep. Don't just sit there. Remember Mr. Sayer."

Mr. Sayer was the family lawyer. Crabtree had promised to tell him when I threw off my fever, and set off at once for the town, where Mr. Sayer said that sooner than wait for me to get stronger he would ride out to read my father's will.

Snow fell again as Crabtree trudged from farm to farm to inform our relatives, and next morning grubby patches survived in the hollows. But the sky was blue and the wind keen, and my family arrived with shining and invigorated cheeks that seemed ill-suited to their ritual gloom.

My father's cousin James Derker and his wife, Kitty, were the first. James wore a coarse brown wig and a fustian coat. He had the same stocky figure as my father but was more bellowing and comical, and would trumpet the praises of his thin, sallow, simpering Kitty as though she were not in the room.

"How are you Tom, lad? Broken-hearted? I'm sure you must be.

I know how I'd feel if I lost my Kitty. Well, how would you be, Crabtree, if *you* lost a beauty like my Kitty?"

Mrs. Crabtree offered him a pickled herring. "You know damn well they give me wind," he said, and Kitty sniffed like a person accustomed to more refined hospitality.

Poor Mrs. Crabtree ran into the kitchen, and Crabtree blundered after her because he thought that if there was an embarrassment it must be his fault.

James sighed like an abused philosopher. "Hopeless," he said. "I knew we'd be too early."

"Ssh," said Kitty, and nudged his arm.

"Eh?"

Kitty rolled her eyes in my direction.

"What's up?" said James. "You've not got that nauseousness again, have you?"

Kitty glared, and her lips said "Tom" without uttering a sound.

"Ah!" said James, and he tapped the side of his nose. He clasped his hands behind his back and shouted at me as though a high wind were sweeping through the room. "We may not have seen all that much of you these last few years, Tom, but what we have done is think about you. My father was like yours, Tom. A man that went down in the world, God rest his troubled soul."

Kitty blew her nose.

"Don't you fret about nauseousness," said James, "because if you was a princess I'd buy you five tigers."

Kitty simpered. I saw that her teeth were broken. She and James had two sons, who always bullied me.

"What I mean to say," said James, "is that I know what Tom's suffered because I've suffered the same. My father lost his farm. He became a charcoal burner. So I've had a long way to climb, Tom, a very long way indeed, but with the help of a guardian angel I've done it."

James patted Kitty's wrist. She squirmed with modesty. James sighed admiringly.

"Of course," he continued, "the higher I've climbed, the more of a view I've had. What I see now is more money in cotton than there is in worsteds. People in this valley call me mad but I don't think I am. I want to pack up and risk Manchester."

James stared at me in silence. I was not sure where Manchester was, so I did not reply.

"It needs money," said James, "and it needs setting myself up with an apprentice. He'd live in the house, wouldn't he, Kitty?"

"He'd live like family," said Kitty.

"Mind you," said James, "he'd have to pay for his indentures, and if he'd no coin he could pay with saleable assets."

There was another silence. James stared at me very seriously.

"What thought have you given the matter?" he said.

"Matter?" I said.

"Your future, Tom. What's to become of you."

It was the question I feared the most, but I was saved from answering it by the arrival of Crabtree's mother, who was as tall and angular as her son but thinner, white-haired, and very rheumaticky. She had a shawl over her head and a shrunken, toothless mouth.

"Well, how are you, Mrs. Crabtree?" said James, and since she was deaf they shouted happily at each other for a quarter of an hour until my mother's sister, Aunt Annie, and her husband, Dawson, arrived with my grandfather Hartley and many cheery greetings. When they saw me they sighed, and James jerked his head at the men, who withdrew, leaving me with Kitty and Aunt Annie.

"How's Tom?" said Aunt Annie. She was broader-hipped and more bustling than my mother, but her eyes were the same. She held my hand and said, "Lovie, we must talk about where you'll live." I smiled.

Kitty stared at the ceiling above our heads. In the side kitchen the others continued their conversation in loud voices until the sound of horses' hooves in the lane restored everyone's pious expressions. James, who had earlier complained bitterly about having to wait for Mr. Sayer, the lawyer, was now the first to greet him with an unctuous hand-shake. "You know Crabtree, of course," he said, as though it weren't Crabtree's house at all.

"I know everybody," said Mr. Sayer. "And their faults," he added with a foxy little smile as he entered the parlour and stared at me very hard and shrewdly.

I had never met Mr. Sayer—if my father went into his chambers my mother and I were left to wait in the street—but I knew that he had been an orphan, that he had married money, and that he now owned one of the town's first brick-built houses. He was always mentioned with such respect that I had imagined him to be a calm and wise old man.

I saw now that he was far from that. He was slight but young and vigorous. His grey eyes demanded attention. His smile was quick and dangerous, and his wig was the finest I'd seen. He slipped off his cloak. His coat and breeches were black, and there was linen at his wrist and throat.

"My apologies," he said, and held out his hand to me, "you're the one I don't know. Mr. Tom Derker, I presume."

I blushed. Mr. Sayer drew me to the table and invited the ladies to sit down. He waved his hand at his servant. "Well, Mr. Featherstone, where are we? Where's the dreaded parchment?"

Mr. Featherstone was an ugly-looking youth with a cudgel stuck through his belt. He put a writing-box in front of Mr. Sayer. Mr. Sayer produced a key from his waistcoat pocket, opened the box, and riffled through his papers. We all watched in silence. Mr. Sayer took a rolled-up document from the box. James Derker cleared his throat.

"Trouble, James?" said Mr. Sayer.

"Eh?"

"Trouble with your throat?" said Mr. Sayer.

James was not sure how to answer. He slapped his chest and said, "It's most inflammatory weather."

Mr. Sayer's eyes twinkled into mine. Then abruptly he began to read. " 'I John Derker of High Top Farm in the parish of Hepton in Waterfoot in the West Riding of the County of Yorkshire on this seventh day of March anno Domini 1749 being of sound body and mind declare that this is my last will and testament. Item. To my wife Mary Derker . . .' "

Mr. Sayer read the will in a brisk monotone—one bed, one best bed, one settle, inscribed, three stools—and then said, "It's very simple, Tom. High Top and everything therein passes to you." Aunt Annie pressed my hand.

"Unhappily," said Mr. Sayer, "there are three impediments. The first is that the deceased left debts."

"I knew it," said Dawson, and James sighed heavily.

"I don't know what you think," said Mr. Sayer, raising his voice for the benefit of old Mrs. Crabtree, "but in my opinion there should be a sale of goods and chattels. The expense pays for itself."

James shrugged like a man of far-flung enterprises. "What's a few shillings?" he said, and no one challenged him.

"Good," said Mr. Sayer. "I take it that I can leave the arrangements to Mr. Featherstone and his brother, as I usually do?"

Mr. Featherstone stuck out his chest. His puffy eyes gleamed. The men nodded at him. He was a dog to whom they threw a bone. For themselves they wanted juicy meat.

"The second impediment," said Mr. Sayer, "is that High Top's mortgaged."

"What?" said James. "High Top's what?"

"It's mortgaged," said Mr. Sayer, "to William Derker, younger brother of the deceased."

"By God!" shouted James, and banged his fist on the table.

There would have been pandemonium had not Mr. Sayer checked it. "Now this I'll not listen to," he said, "for you were all asked to help John Derker and you all refused. Where else could I turn but to his brother?"

"Eh?" said my grandfather, white-stubbled and pretending to be deaf.

Mr. Sayer would have repeated his question but Dawson interrupted. "For God's sake," he said. "What else is there?"

"Don't you raise your voice," boomed James, "for I won't have more strains on Kitty's health."

"I'll wager you won't," said old Mrs. Crabtree.

"You speak for yourself!" shouted James. Mrs. Crabtree snorted and banged her stick on the flags.

"The third impediment," said Mr. Sayer, "is that the liabilities on the estate leave Tom with neither a penny-piece nor a stick of furniture to his name; and since the will makes no provision for a guardian, we must ask what's to become of him."

Mr. Sayer looked round the table. His glance was not met. My heart pounded. I prayed that James would not speak, and yet his silence was unbearable. Finally Aunt Annie said, "We've the room to take him, haven't we, Dawson?"

"We have," said Dawson, "for who can you turn to if not your own flesh and blood?" He turned to Mr. Sayer and said, "Will you manage High Top yourself, sir?"

"I will," said Mr. Sayer.

"I'd not refuse a lease on the grazing," said Dawson.

James gasped like a winded wrestler. Kitty sneered, and my grandfather muttered to himself. Then little Mrs. Crabtree blurted out, "Why can't Tom live with us? Eh? Why can't he?"

"By heck," said Crabtree.

"You big daft sod," said his mother.

They would all have spoken at once, but Mr. Sayer stopped them. "Tom," he said, "I'm your father's executor. I'll not decide before I've heard your opinion."

They all stared at me. My voice caught in my throat, but I knew now that my dream would come true.

"Uncle William," I said. "Can't I live with Uncle William?"

Dawson laughed roughly and said, "This lad's as stubborn as his father." Aunt Annie sniffled. Mr. Sayer's eyes looked steadily into mine. He was neither ashamed nor frightened of his own opinion, nor of what might be said to him. I trusted him and was convinced that he understood me.

"Your uncle's at sea, Tom. A letter might not find him for months. When it did, he might not want you."

"He will," I said. "I know he will."

He smiled at my vehemence and said, "Mr. Crabtree, if I write to Captain Derker, will you give Tom a home pro tem?"

"Pro what?" said Crabtree.

"Of course we will," said little Mrs. Crabtree, not sure whether to laugh or cry.

Mr. Sayer nodded. "Then it's settled." He closed and relocked his writing-box.

The men were stunned; they had got rid of me and yet none of them had won anything for himself.

"Will you take more ale, sir?" said Dawson.

"Mr. Dawson," said Mr. Sayer, "if my time was my own I'd sit here all day." He got up. "Tom," he said, "I expect the best of you." He bowed to the ladies, nodded to Mr. Featherstone to pick up the writing-box, and went.

Chapter 4

Uncle William

Poor Mrs. Crabtree. Of all of them, she would have been most like a natural mother. Mr. Sayer had written to the owners of Uncle William's ship, and they had sent the letter across the oceans; while we awaited a reply Mrs. Crabtree pretended that we were a family who would live together always, at the same ages, just as we were.

Like my real mother she helped me with my letters, and neither she nor I dreamed that an education begun so haltingly on wind-howling winter nights would be completed in a fine gentleman's library on the other side of the world. In the better weather we watched Crabtree at the wrestling, or sat outside to card the wool, and eventually Mr. Sayer received a reply to his letter.

Uncle William grieved for my father and mother and said that he would most joyfully be my guardian and friend. Unfortunately he had neither a home of his own nor a wife with whom he might leave me. "I am consoled in this," he wrote, "by the knowledge that a young man will find his character, his situation, and his God more readily upon the ocean than elsewhere; it has been my own life's element, and Tom and I might thereon know each other quickest."

To this end he proposed, if Mr. Sayer agreed, to make me a ship's apprentice and take me with him on his next voyage. Mr. Sayer did agree, and on a thundery-sullen August afternoon he and his servant, Featherstone, came with their own mounts and a pack-pony to take me to Liverpool.

We jolted up our lane to go over the tops, and from where I sat in front of Mr. Featherstone, I took one backward look. Crabtree's hands dangled like hopeless, loosely-knotted ropes, and his wife blew her nose on her apron. Poor Mrs. Crabtree. I loved her, but I never felt between us the blood-entanglement that drew me now to Uncle William.

I turned forward again and felt the breeze on my face, and soon we came to the watershed and on the Lancashire side wound down the steep shoulders of the moor to Rochdale, a woollens and worsted town with pack-ponies in the market-place and many new brick houses among the local stone. Then we crossed a river and rode through undulating country of lanes and hedges and weavers' cottages to a long, straggling village called Heywood, and to Bury, another active town. But the moors were still our horizon, and the roads still bad, and it was not until we reached Bolton that we saw a wagon.

Bolton was a bleak, exposed place, with half-timbered buildings as well as stone, and two broad, dirty streets. It was a cotton town, where Mr. Sayer had business with a merchant. It being market day in Manchester, the merchant was away, but there was a pile of stuffs awaiting us and the apprentices loaded our pack-pony; Mr. Sayer explained that he intended to invest the goods in Uncle William's voyage.

After Bolton we turned our backs upon the moors. There were pleasant fields and foliage and little sandy bluffs above the streams. Then we saw the coal pits, and it was not the muddy, ransacked earth or the grimy men and women or the hiss and clank of the pumping-engines that amazed me, but something else that I had never seen before: the steam. It drifted so romantically into the trees, and yet its smell was stale and sulphurous.

Around Leigh and Newton there were stretches of reeded, marshy wastes and strange, flat lakes called meres, and then the country became lush again and Mr. Sayer said that the craftsmen who occupied the hamlets here were not weavers, as in our part of the world, but watch- and instrument-makers, and that they supplied the greater part of Europe.

We put up for the night at Prescott, a town surrounded by coal pits, and in the morning my excitement quickened when I saw what in the dusk and my tiredness I had missed: the road that we had now to join was a turnpike, broad and clear, with a gravelly surface.

There was a steady flow of wagons and pack-horses, and after two hours we topped a rise and halted. Below us there were cows in the fields, and hedgerows of honeysuckle and wild roses, and beyond them windmills, and then houses, spires, and towers packed together. Mr. Sayer gestured and said, "Liverpool!"

I levered myself up on the pommel, as though being six inches higher would enable me to see Uncle William. Mr. Featherstone laughed and spat. There was a thin blue veil of smoke over the town, but it dulled neither the gleam of the river nor the white of the sails upon it, and golden clouds rolled over the green land on the other side.

"Which is ours?" I cried. "Which ship is ours?"

"The *Margaret*?" said Mr. Sayer. "None of them. She'll be in the dock, loading."

He urged his horse downhill, and we were soon in narrow, smelly, ill-paved streets that contained more bustle than I had imagined possible. People bumped against our horses, and it was difficult for Mr. Featherstone to control the pack-pony. When we halted I thought that it was because we had been stopped by the number of people and barrows in the street, but Mr. Sayer dismounted and motioned us to do the same. Mr. Featherstone took the reins of all three horses in his hands and set off for the docks on foot, and Mr. Sayer led me into an alley. We stepped over a drunken woman, who stank of urine, and emerged into a small, peaceful square built round an old church and its graveyard. Men in rich coats talked and laughed with each other and strolled in and out of large, beautifully bow-windowed houses.

"What are those?" I said. "Are they rich men's palaces?"

Mr. Sayer laughed. "They're coffee-houses," he said. "We'll try The George first."

I followed him in and felt ashamed of my poor clothes, for although the rooms were plain, the wood of the tables and chairs was finely turned and varnished, and I saw white china in use, and quiet corners in which men sat to read the news-sheets.

Mr. Sayer glanced this way and that. "I can't see him," he said.

But I could, for there was no mistaking my father's hunched shoulders and neck and determined set of head. If I had not been so happy I would have been frightened to see a dead man strangely alive again.

"Uncle William!" I said.

He turned, and I saw that he was bigger than my father, and that his face was more open; it was more human and vulnerable and at the same time amused and experienced.

"Good day," said Mr. Sayer.

Uncle William looked from one to the other of us, and I heard for the first time the loud, unfeigned, slightly wheezing delight of his laughter. He had seen himself in my stance and shape, and then realized from my face what astounded me: I could not step forward to embrace Uncle William because there was a man between us.

He was on his hands and knees to scrub the floor of the coffee-house, and he was black. His face was black and his fingers and arms were black, although the palms of his hands were horribly pink. His lips were thick and ugly, and his eyes popped out. His limbs were thin, and his head was bald and wrinkled. Uncle William prodded him with his boot. The black man looked up. Uncle William jerked his head. The black man laughed at himself. He crawled out of distance and then stood up and shambled away. He was the strangest creature I had ever seen. I was both fascinated and repelled.

Uncle William flung out his arms, but they banged into the backs of the men at his table, and he shrank a little with the shyness that in my father had been morose but in him was clumsily appealing. The men he had buffeted smiled.

"Well, Tom," he said, "if you're a man at all, shake hands like one!"

He held me at arm's length and looked me over. There were tears in his eyes. I felt a whole world of love and sympathy in the hand that gripped mine. I felt safe at last.

"I've done the right thing," he said, "I know it."

"So do I," said Mr. Sayer.

Uncle William stood, and for a moment took Mr. Sayer's hand as well, and held us both in a trance of happiness. He stared above our heads and said, "Amen!" in an intense whisper, and again, "Amen!" Then he laughed and said, "God bless us, where's that serving-wench gone?"

He thrust us into chairs and waved his clay pipe about and ordered us a fish apiece, poached. He asked questions about the journey, and the health of our relatives, and when he saw me still staring at the black man, he laughed again and squeezed his arm around me.

"By God, Tom," he roared. "By God, I know that if he was a fish you'd throw him back, but you'd best get used to the sight, for where we're bound there's none else."

"Where are we bound?" I said.

"Africa," said Uncle William, and looked past me at far-away things. I was spellbound.

Mr. Sayer smiled in his brisk, chiding way. "Tom Derker," he said, "do you not remember what the *Margaret* is?"

I blushed and felt foolish.

"Of course he remembers," said Uncle William, and my heart thanked him, for I could never forget what was uttered with such pride by the family—boomed out in awesome style by James Derker, said softly and wryly by my mother, and by me, who did not understand it, repeated to myself in an impressed whisper to see how it would sound—the fact that my splendid, jowly, humorous, strong uncle was the captain of a slave ship.

Chapter 5

The Man with the Ravaged Face

Africa or the ice-walls of the north, it was not our destination that filled my mind. It was the living nearness of Uncle William. He coughed, and laughed, and blew clouds of tobacco smoke, and when our fish was served he stole flakes from our plates and explained in a voice loud enough for the dead in the old churchyard to hear that we had been given graining, a Liverpool fish, peculiar to the River Mersey, and one that if it resembled anything at all resembled a dace, but had a straighter back. He insisted that I drink chocolate, which I had never tasted before, and then marched us into the street, where he talked at the top of his voice and saluted innumerable passers-by.

Only once was his flow of geniality checked, when he caught sight of a tall, handsome, ravaged man in a shabby officer's coat. The man was evidently in wait for Uncle William, because he stepped into his path with eyebrows expectantly raised. But Uncle William gestured as if to say, "Not yet," and the man slipped back. I looked at Mr. Sayer, but he seemed not to have noticed. Then we turned the corner into a wider street, and Uncle William said, "There we are. Smallshaw's."

"What?" I said.

"The owners," said Mr. Sayer. "Messrs. Smallshaw and Hill Company Limited."

We entered the central passage-way of a long, low, dirty red-sandstone building. There were storerooms on one side, and on the other a counting-house, where the clerks sat in the front and the partners at the rear, behind a barricade of desks and ledgers and shelves. The ceiling was low and the floor flagged. There was a rancid candle-smell and a coal fire and everything was polished but old and much-used. Mr. Sayer went straight to the back, and Uncle William sat on a high stool and chaffed the clerks.

They had a quick wit in reply, and so did Mr. Smallshaw Junior, who now appeared from the back of the room in his waistcoat and shirt-sleeves. He had watery blue eyes that roamed everywhere. He shook my hand, laughed at a clerk's joke, and immediately deflated the man by pointing at his ledger and saying, "I'll tell you what is comical. There's a mistake in your second column." He then explained to me my articles of apprenticeship, and I signed. Mr. Smallshaw shook my hand again, and entered my name in the ledger that referred to the *Margaret*. The entire ship's company was listed, with each man's rank and wages set against his name. Mr. Smallshaw tapped the page.

"I see McBride's your surgeon again," he said.

"He's the best," said Uncle William. "He keeps more folk alive than any other."

"He's an old devil," said Mr. Smallshaw. "Did you hear about him yesterday?"

Uncle William had not heard. Mr. Smallshaw told the story.

"Well," he said, "McBride was passing the Customs House when they came out on to the steps for the auction, and what made him listen was that he noticed there was a new auctioneer. A young feller. They were giving him his chance. . . ." Mr. Smallshaw smiled and went on. "So the young feller calls the first lot, and it's a woman as old as your granny. Very black and decrepit, and there's no bids at all, at which the young lad got most offended. 'Come on, sirs,' he says, and puts his hand on the old bag's shoulder. 'Don't take advantage. Be honourable. What am I bid?' McBride can't resist it. 'For Jesus Christ's sake, son,' he shouts, 'knock her down quick or she'll be dead!'"

As uproarious laughter subsided, Mr. Smallshaw nodded at the ledger and said, "Still no Second Mate, I see."

There was immediate silence. Uncle William sucked at his pipe. "Now, Mr. Edward," he said, "you're well aware that I've asked for Henry Dingwall."

"Henry Dingwall is not to be trusted," said Mr. Smallshaw, "for reasons known to us all."

"He's the best man for your Gambia River business," said Uncle William, "but if it's one of those quarrels between you and your father, I'll not insist. I've too much respect for you both."

Mr. Smallshaw flushed and his eyes glinted. But he made a joke about how Uncle William was more a member of the family than the family itself, and they praised each other very amicably until Mr. Sayer reappeared with Mr. Smallshaw Senior, who had the same round face and pudgy body as his son but was bowed and white-haired. He shook my hand and peered at me over the top of metal-rimmed spectacles. Then he sniffed like a rabbit. Sniff. Sniff, sniff.

"What's that smell?" he said. "What can it be?"

"It's tallow," I said.

"Good," he said. "Good boy. So think on. Never use wax when money's saved on tallow. Eh, Derker? Eh?"

"True enough, Mr. Smallshaw," said Uncle William, and Mr. Sayer smiled deferentially.

"Now that you're all crewed up, Derker, we can take tea with the ladies. Eh, Edward? Eh?" Mr. Smallshaw gripped Uncle William's arm and shuffled towards the door. His son shook his head.

"He's no Second Mate," he said.

"Henry Dingwall," said the old man. "It was promised two year ago by Mr. Hill."

"Mr. Hill's dead," said his son.

I thought that old Mr. Smallshaw would explode. He went red. He stamped his foot and shook. He gasped for breath. His son was angry but implored him to be calm and to write Henry Dingwall's name in the ledger.

"Write it yourself," said old Mr. Smallshaw, and hung his head. He was exhausted. He grimaced and pouted. "I wish your mother was alive," he said. Uncle William sighed heavily. Young Mr. Smallshaw smiled to himself and led us upstairs, for like most Liverpool merchants the Smallshaws lived on the floors above their counting-house.

In the parlour, which was cold because it was used only when there were guests, we met young Mr. Smallshaw's wife, his unmarried sister, on whom the family face was a flat, warm-hearted blur, his baby daughters, one as thin as her mother and the other two fat and fair, and a Welsh skivvy. Old Mr. Smallshaw tried to join us, but his breath failed him. He kept a chair at the turn of the stairs for just such situations, and sat on it throughout the half-hour. The skivvy ran up and down with tea, and Uncle William stood at the door so that he could boom down to Mr. Smallshaw what people were saying about him.

Young Mr. Smallshaw stood with his back to the empty fire, and his womenfolk gleamed with pride. They pretended to be outraged by Uncle William's stories of the way dogs always cock their legs up against brand-new sedan chairs, or the time old Mrs. Smallshaw ate radishes and couldn't stop belching, and they were delighted by his comical amazement at whatever people wore, or bought, or painted themselves with, or believed would bring them good fortune.

When we took our leave we went to a slop-shop, where Uncle William bought me some sea-clothes and tried on every item of head-gear himself, pulling faces, clucking like a hen, and imitating different sorts of women. Then we walked towards the river breeze and the masts that rose above the roof tops.

At the Old Dock the bustle increased. There were sailors with their hair in tarred pigtails, smells of sugar and tobacco, and wagons and horses and mounds of merchandise everywhere. At the outermost dock we found Mr. Featherstone and the horses. Uncle William nodded when he saw that the pack-pony had been unloaded, and pointed to the quayside. All I could see were masts and people. "There she is," he said, "there's the good old *Margaret.*"

I scrambled aboard and marvelled that so large an object could be made entirely of wood. I stood on the maindeck, and her two masts soared above me, and her rails and cordage were all round me. I soon learned that she was indeed a solid ship, a snow, square-rigged with a big fore-and-aft trysail on her mainmast; but she was not large. She was of some hundred and fifty tons' burden, and as few as eight or ten men could handle her. She had deep bulwarks, a small forecastle where the hands lived in blasphemous confusion, and one big hold the length of the ship. Under the quarterdeck there was a state-room, where Uncle William lived; and on either side of an alley, six or eight small cabins, some partitioned by wood and some by canvas. Uncle William had a commode that doubled as a dining-chair, but everyone else relieved themselves at the heads, a sort of lattice at either side of the bowsprit.

That day, ropes and canvas lay in tangles, the hatch was open, and ragged dockers swarmed everywhere. There were piles of kettles and kegs, and a relay of men carried buckets to and from a water-cart. At the quarterdeck rail stood a dark young bearded officer with a tight mouth and a watchful eye. He raised a hand to acknowledge Uncle William and then pointed beyond us, to the quayside. The man with the ravaged face was there, his hands clenched at his sides, his head thrust vulnerably forward. Uncle William beckoned to him. The man smiled, and as he did so, his face seemed most finely moulded, and his expression gave out a pure light.

Uncle William introduced the bearded officer. "This is the First Mate, Mr. Partridge," he said, "and you can trust him with your life." Mr. Partridge nodded, but I felt afraid of him. His glance seemed to me to say that he disliked me because I was the master's nephew.

Most of the inside timbers of the ship were tarred or whitewashed, but Uncle William's state-room was panelled. The din of loading was muffled, and the light had a curious opaqueness. I went to the stern windows and stared at the other vessels and the shipyards and town beyond; it was an odd angle, near the water, and looking at things from below. When I turned round, Uncle William and Mr. Sayer had spread various papers over the table and the shabby man stood on the threshold. Uncle William shrugged, a big, open gesture that admitted as much embarrassment as it concealed.

"Well, Henry," he said, very gravely and sincerely, "they'll take you. Old Smallshaw's kept his word."

The shabby man laughed, an attractive, throaty bubble. His hair was full of grey streaks, and there was something of a woman in his forehead and soft eyes. His body was like a spring; it was lean, with a barely suppressed tension.

"They'll pay three pounds a month," said Uncle William.

"Accepted," said the man, with another laugh.

"Mr. Sayer," said Uncle William, "this is Mr. Henry Dingwall, my oldest acquaintance and Second Mate of this ship." Then he indicated me. "Thomas Derker. My nephew, and Ship's Apprentice." He made it sound like a fanfare. I was so proud that I laughed.

"Thomas Derker," said Mr. Dingwall, in his light, refined, ironic voice. "Your servant, sir." Then he said, "William, my sea-chest's in pawn," as jaunty now as on the quayside he had been desolate.

"Then sign for an advance," said Uncle William, which Mr. Dingwall did, and went off with a brisker step.

Mr. Sayer watched him go. "Is that man truly capable?" he said.

Uncle William sighed. "The fact of the matter is," he said, "that God's purpose for my life is that I should bring Henry Dingwall to his eternal salvation."

Because he was not ashamed of them his words seemed inescapably true. Water lapped round the stern, and there were thuds and shouts overhead. Uncle William laughed, half in astonishment at himself, and his eyes engaged mine. "It's a holy debt, Tom," he said, "for I wasn't like you when I left the moors. I was wild and bitter." And in his rumbling voice, with much coughing and sucking at his filthy pipe, he told us the story of himself and Henry Dingwall.

"It begins with your grandfather, Tom, who built High Top and died there before you were born. He was a stern man, like our John —very like him, in fact—and I quarrelled with him. I'd not be disciplined, so I ran away to Liverpool and shipped before the mast. I took the first ship I saw and she was Africa bound, so Africa chose me, I reckon, to test me and to show me God's will. What did I think I wanted? I don't know. Must I call it revenge? Or is the word *defiance*, Tom? Shouting at God, 'Look here, and if You don't like what You see, strike me dead!'

"Well, on the Slave Coast disease struck dozens dead but not me. I drank and gambled and took what women I wanted and in a grog-shop in Old Calabar I killed a man. He was a Dane, poor blue-eyed devil. I put my knife in him and blood came out of his mouth, but I went unpunished because our captain, Bully Riley, cared for nothing except profits at the end of the voyage. He's retired now. I daresay you've met him, Mr. Sayer. He has long white hair like a saint's. That's for me, I thought. A captain's share of the profits, and then, who knows, I'll become an owner and sit at home while others break their hearts in that hot sun.

"So I put my one good shirt on and I went to Mr. Manesty in the coffee-house—he was there today, Tom, a very cultured-looking man reading the news-sheets—and he said, 'Who are you?' and I said,

'William Derker, one of your seamen, and I'll work in your counting-house for two-thirds the proper wages!'

" 'Done!' he said, and I worked the ledgers for two years, during which I taught myself navigation from books and waited for my chance, and God bless us, it came as I knew it would. The chief clerk was a man named Harrison and he had a sick wife, but instead of appealing to Mr. Manesty he falsified the books and stole. So I betrayed him. I did. I'd no compunction because I knew what must follow: Mr. Manesty offered me advancement. He had a ship called the *Falcon*, whose master was new to the Africa trade, and so I was asked to sail with him as supercargo.

"It was the chance I'd schemed for, but it fell out strangely because —well, you've guessed, Tom, haven't you? I think you've understood. The master was Henry Dingwall, and we loathed each other. We were mortal enemies from the start. Or immortal friends, Tom, put it how you will. Why did I hate him? Because he was handsome, damn it, and because he was a gentleman born.

"Look at me now, sweaty at the thought of it, and that's how I was then, all perspiration and bad temper, but Henry was as cool as a nobleman.

"Well, the fact is that his father was Sir Cadwalader Dingwall of Whittern Hall, Herefordshire. He owned thousands of acres, and— I know, I see it in your face, Tom. Why was such a man in the Africa trade at all? That's what I asked myself, and the answer is that he's a flawed man, is Henry, flawed from start to finish. He was educated by a tutor, and bought a commission in the Royal Navy. He was flag-lieutenant to Sir John Norris, and you can see him, can't you? See him in his gold braid and see him hob-nob with important men, and in the smoke of battle, Tom, you can see him with his little smile and no fear at all.

"Aye, God bless us, and you can see him at the card tables, or I can, because that's where he staked his life and lost. He lost so much that even his father wouldn't support him any more. Henry couldn't pay, and when a gentleman can't pay, that's the end of him.

"Henry resigned his commission and took command of the *Falcon*, and from the first day he met me, he laughed at me. Not openly, but inside, behind his eyes, so that when we reached the Sherbro River I said, 'Be damned to you. I'll go ashore!' which I did.

"I had two African wives and I lived like a tyrant. If my servants displeased me, I sold them. I dealt very shrewdly, and I thought many a time that I should stay there until I'd made my fortune. At the time it was hard to explain why I didn't. Afterwards, I knew that it was God who directed me—what I'd felt was conscience, and the person who'd made me feel it was Henry, and that's why I returned to the ship.

"Henry commanded us as naturally as I breathed. He had dignity. That's the word. He was reconciled—you'll know what I mean, Mr. Sayer—reconciled to life itself, as well as to the snakes that twisted and turned in his own guts. Or so I thought.

"We spoke little, although we sat often in silence and listened to the noises of the ship while Henry read his books. They were Greek and Latin, were some of them, and Henry—how shall I say?—Henry seemed to me to be at peace."

For a moment Uncle William seemed lost. Then he sighed deeply and resumed his story.

"I wanted that peace, Tom. I wanted it, Mr. Sayer, because I was ashamed of what I'd done, and of my daily life. When we reached Antigua, in the West Indies, I went ashore and sought the chaplain to the English garrison. I confessed my remorse. I groaned aloud at the memory of what I'd done, but the chaplain—well, it may sound comical but the fact is that he was very henpecked, and it was his wife who told me what books to read. No more than a sparrow of a woman, but that's how they are, isn't it?

"Anyhow, what matters is that in these books, and in the fact of having spoken, I found God. I suddenly knew that I was saved, and it happened one morning, actually, as I watched them get the sugar on board. It was like a voice that said, 'God has made Christian Englishmen his imperfect instruments in the world, and it's their duty to do their utmost. We mustn't question such things as the slave trade. We must conduct them properly, that's what we must do, and try to convert heathen souls.'

"I was sublime with it, Tom. I could have walked back to Liverpool on the ocean. I talked most earnestly to Henry, and he replied in kind, even if he never would join me in prayer or in the study of particular texts. Then one day he met the chaplain's wife, and all that laughter burst out. He went red in the face and had to fight for breath.

"After that he was drunk every day. He'd hardly drunk at all before, and I'd virtually stopped, but he was awash by midday. Had he despaired before? I don't know. All I thought about before was myself, whereas now I knew that I'd offered my life to God and that His task for me was to bring back to the fold the soul of Henry Dingwall.

"Make no mistake, though. I'd no illusions. I knew that we must be separated before coming together again, and so did Henry, because I'd traded well, Mr. Sayer. I'd sold the slaves dear and bought sugar cheap, and I'd come to live simply, as I do now, with all that I own in one sea-chest.

"I made my peace with the clerk I'd wronged, and although I say it myself, I won the respect of every shipowner in Liverpool. Mr. Manesty knew it, for when Smallshaw and Hill wanted a new master he recommended me, and so the next season I got my own ship, and, God bless us, my voyage was a success.

"Not so that of Henry Dingwall. Henry's voyage was a disaster. He behaved like a madman—and perhaps he was, who can say? He left Africa only half loaded with slaves, and threw dozens of muskets and trade goods into the sea. He took no precautions against sickness because he was drunk in his state-room for days on end, so that the ship was a pest-house. Half his slaves died, and when he bought his sugar the price was too high. The voyage showed a loss, and after that not one owner looked at him. He couldn't even get taken on as a supercargo.

"He advertised himself as a tutor, but he was dismissed for drinking, and to get money he worked as a dock labourer. Oh, he was a famous talker in the taverns, which is where I'd sometimes see him. He ignored me, of course. When he was very drunk he'd wash the feet of stupid black pot-boys, and sometimes, they say, he smeared himself with mud and danced on the foreshore.

"What's certain is that he was badly beaten up in brawls, and I thought: He'll be found knifed; but no—he smartened himself up and got taken as mate aboard an Irish coaster, and he seems to have stayed sober for a year or two, until he suddenly got drunk one day and ran her aground. After that I heard no more of him for a long while.

"Then one day after I'd made three African voyages as master, I was told by Smallshaw's that this ship we're aboard now was building and they'd like me to command her. She was on the stocks in Fearon's shipyard, where I saw this creature that laboured in the mud. It was Dingwall. He pretended not to know me and walked out of the yard.

"I followed. I caught up and spun him round, and I saw in his eyes that he was ready. He was in despair, Tom. He was ready to be brought unto the Lord. 'Henry,' I said, 'let us pray!' He did not kneel but he did say 'Amen!' and he came to my lodgings and together we defeated the devil brandy.

"When he saw apparitions with whips and branding-irons I held him in my arms. I argued and prayed and pleaded, Tom, and I said to old Mr. Hill that if ever there was a man for the Slave Coast it was Henry Dingwall, because he'd only been there a month or two before he could speak their languages as well as you or I talk English. I convinced Mr. Hill, and that's why I promised Henry that if he stayed sober in Liverpool until I returned from Africa, I'd make him once again an officer.

"Where did he take work? In a bakery. If his desire for a drink became very strong, he walked for miles to distract himself, and he deliberately lost his money at dice or cock-fighting. They say that he shouted Greek poetry out loud as he worked, and ate handfuls of sugar to slake his craving for sweetness. He slept in an outhouse behind the ovens, and the baker's wife was charmed by his manners, so she mended and ironed his clothes.

"By the time I returned he no longer wanted a drink, not even when I told him that Mr. Hill was dead and Smallshaw's might not honour their promise. They did, of course, because I made it an issue between the two of them, and the old man won't let his son have all the say—not yet, anyhow. Oh, I know I took a risk, but it was for God's purpose, not for mine. It was to bring Henry to the Father's side."

When Uncle William finished there was silence. The state-room was darker and the dockside noise seemed far away. I had never heard a grown man speak so honestly to a boy about his sins and failures. I was both awed and proud, and sure that Mr. Sayer felt the same, because when he did speak, it was very quietly. It was time for him to leave. He and Uncle William resolved their business in a sentence or two, and we went on deck.

Mr. Sayer looked out of place on the ship, and when he had shaken our hands he had to be helped up on to the quay. He looked back, and his eyes twinkled at his own awkwardness. Then he nodded curtly at Uncle William, as men do who understand the business between them, and his worsted cloak swirled as he walked to Mr. Featherstone and the horses. I hoped to see him mount, but there were wagons in the way. I felt lonely. Then Uncle William put his arm round my shoulder and by a shared impulse we walked.

We walked off the ship, and along the docks that flanked the river until we came to where the town ended, and on a low, grassy spit I stared out across the water and told Uncle William how my father and mother had died. I told him about Low Crags and my mother's delirium, and about the children in Crabtree's lane who jeered at me and said, "Go on. Were your mam and dad both rotten? Did you eat them? Why don't you tell? What did it taste like?"

Then I wept. I sobbed aloud and hot tears ran down my cheeks, and when Uncle William tried to speak, but could not, I knew that he, too, was weeping. He touched my shoulder and shrugged helplessly and walked down to the water. Mud sucked at his sea-boots. The light was fading and there was a mist across the moon. The far shore was black and bulky. We looked at the seagulls and at a coaster that beat against the ebb, but what we saw was the mess of snow in the yard at High Top. Then the breeze made us shiver and we walked back to where lights flared along Strand Street.

We ate in one of the taverns, where, like two men who have worked side by side on the moors all day, we said little but were each of us content. Then on the quayside the stench of Uncle William's pipe mingled with damp rubbish-smells, and the thud of his steps was like my father's; but never his understanding, nor his roistering humour, which exploded again when we reboarded the *Margaret*.

Uncle William gripped my wrist and peered through the darkness. "God bless us!" he said. "That watchman's asleep!"

Although the crew made the ship ready by day, their pay did not start until we cast off, so at night they went ashore or were not to be relied on, and Smallshaw's hired a watchman. He was a scrawny old fellow, slumped now on the bottom step of the companion-ladder with his chin firmly on his chest.

Uncle William stood over him and barked like a big dog. "Woof! Woof! Woof!"

The watchman fell off the ladder and rolled on deck, shouting, "Get off! Get off, you daft bugger!"

"If this was Africa," said Uncle William, "you'd be run through with spears."

"It's not Africa," said the watchman.

"Go home!" said Uncle William. "I'll take the watch myself!"

"I'll not go without my money," said the watchman.

"How about this on account?" said Uncle William. He picked the watchman up and threw him on to the quay.

"Amen!" shouted Uncle William. Mr. Partridge came out of the stern cabins. He was in his shirt-tails and carried a pistol. The watchman shouted at them both. "Go back to your dreams!" boomed Uncle William. Then he laughed and sent Mr. Partridge away and showed me how to sling a hammock. He was a giant and a wizard, and I fell asleep to the muffled pacing of his feet.

Chapter 6

The Leaving of Liverpool

Loading resumed at daybreak, as it was Uncle William's hope to leave the dock on the afternoon tide. He sent me to Mr. Bruce, the Third Mate, who was in charge of stowing the hold. Mr. Bruce was a tall, eager, big-hipped young man who loped along with his neck stuck forward. He told me to stand where the dockers were stacking the last kegs of spirits, and tell him if they stole any. The dockers were big, rough men who chaffed and jostled me. I was afraid of them, and yet I wanted them to like me, so I smiled. When they saw me do so, they deliberately smashed a keg and produced pannikins to drink the stuff there and then.

"That's stealing," I said.

The dockers ignored me. I did not know what to do. Then one of them looked at me and gestured obscenely.

"Get off, cowcack," he said. "Most of you ran down your mother's leg."

The others laughed, and my anger sent me to Mr. Bruce. When we returned, the dockers were hard at work. Mr. Bruce blushed and thrust his chin out even farther. He was so agitated that he stammered.

"W-w-which one was it?" he said.

I was not certain who had actually contrived to smash the keg, but I pointed to the man who had jeered at me. The man repeated his gesture.

Mr. Bruce smiled ruefully and lashed him across the face with a knotted rope. The man spat. Mr. Bruce lashed him again. The man's mouth was bleeding.

Mr. Partridge appeared at the open hatchway. "Keep them at it, Mr. Bruce," he said, as though the cut mouth and rope did not exist, and stalked out of sight.

"Come on, now," said Mr. Bruce. "B-b-bend your backs." He had broken into a sweat. The dockers went back to work. One or two of them laughed. "They think a keg of spirits is w-w-worth a bruised face," said Mr. Bruce, and I kept to myself the knowledge that but for their insult I would have been afraid to act. I did not know then that when they came to hear of it, most of the ship's crew would judge me by that action and behave accordingly. I was thankful that the dockers ignored me, and when they had finished their work, at about midday, I went on deck again.

A boy of my own age danced up to me and said, "D'you want a fight, then, eh? Is that what you want?"

"What?" I said.

"Come on, then. I'm ready. Come on."

He slapped me in the face. I stared at him. He was wiry, with red cheeks and curly black hair. He jumped up and down and waved his arms at me.

"Come on," he said. "What's wrong with you?" He slapped me again and stuck out his tongue. I kicked his shin. "Ow!" he said. "Oh, Moses! What d'you do that for?" He hopped about and stamped his foot.

"Peter Case," said Mr. Bruce. "What's your antics this time?"

"It's me and him. Captain wants us in the state-room."

Mr. Bruce nodded. "Thank God," he said. "At least we can finish this work w-w-without you boys."

"I'm Tom," I said. "Did he say you were Peter?" Peter was limping horribly.

"I'm your number-one apprentice," he said, "and don't you forget it." He jabbed me in the wind-box and darted away as though he had never limped at all. I gave chase. We dodged around an irate docker and dashed towards the state-room. On the very threshold I caught

Peter up and tripped him. He fell on the deck at the feet of Uncle William and young Mr. Smallshaw, who were toasting each other and the voyage in fortified wine.

I giggled and so did Peter. Uncle William picked us up by the scruffs of our necks and held us at opposite arms' lengths. "Now, then, you boys!" he said. "Now, then!" and suddenly banged our heads together, which put us painfully in our places, and we were ignored until Mr. Smallshaw produced a cake that his wife and sister had baked especially for me. Then with a flicker of his cold eyes he asked Peter to sign a copy of the ship's manifest, or rather, to put his X to it because he could not write.

My surprise at such an invitation showed in my face, because Uncle William chuckled and explained that Peter was the orphan of a common seaman who had died on the Sherbro River. Uncle William had paid for Peter's indentures, and between voyages Peter worked as a pot-boy at The Sailor's Block tavern. He slept on the kitchen table and saved his few shillings to buy sacks of nails and cheap beads, trading goods that Uncle William and the owners had accepted as part of the *Margaret*'s cargo. This gave Peter a stake, however small, in the profits of the voyage, an interest that of the other twenty-six souls aboard only Uncle William shared.

Mr. Smallshaw said that his father, who was, alas, too frail to come down to the quay any more, had chuckled loud and long at Peter's enterprise. "Proper Liverpool!" he had said. "Terriers that won't be kept from a bitch!"

Peter sniffed and said, "Thank you very much," as though it were no more than his due.

Mr. Smallshaw suggested that it was time for him to go on to the quay, and indeed, when we returned to the deck we saw that the carpenter had gone round with his mallet and pegs to secure the hatch, and Mr. Partridge and the bosun, Taffy Owen, a big, honest man with his head sunk in his shoulders, were standing upon it to get a superior view as the last of the seamen arrived, the worse for drink.

Mr. Partridge jerked his head and the bosun went forward and got hold of the drunkest man and walked him off the ship. The man's friends shouted and waved their fists. "We're coming with you, Job, lad, don't you worry!"

One of them did go with him, and another hesitated.

"What's your name?" said Mr. Partridge.

"Mossop," said the man, and fell over.

Mr. Partridge watched him. Mossop crawled to the fo'c'sle.

"Peter Case!" shouted Mr. Partridge. "Run up to the slop-shop and tell Melia I want two more men."

All this took place amid last-minute bustle, in which the bosun sent up the duty watch to break out our topsails, and Mr. Smallshaw and Uncle William chatted on the quayside, with never a word said between them about Henry Dingwall or any other disagreement. Then Mr. McBride, the surgeon I had heard discussed in the counting-house, arrived with his daughter, a big, florid girl, and kissed her good-bye.

Mr. McBride was Irish. His voice was harsh, his face flat, battered, and weathered, and his nose puckered. He looked about him to see how much work still needed to be done, and shook his head. "Where's Dingwall?" he said. Mr. Partridge shrugged and Mr. McBride laughed. His eyes were a distant pale grey.

Then, to the interest of the watchers and workers and odd wives and trollops on the quay, Peter returned with Melia, the owner of the slop-shop. They were followed by a porter, who wheeled two men on a barrow. The men were dead drunk, drunker by far than those Mr. Partridge had seen off, but they were not insubordinate, and so they were tipped aboard and some clothes thrown after them, and Mr. Partridge paid some money and Uncle William and Mr. Smallshaw shook hands with the owner of the slop-shop, and one of the harbourmaster's officers came up to report on the state of the tide.

Uncle William and I had actually said farewell to Mr. Smallshaw and come aboard, when Mr. Dingwall arrived with a black porter, who stumbled beneath the weight of his sea-chest. The porter stowed the chest in Mr. Dingwall's cubby-hole, and Uncle William said, "To the forehead, if you please, Mr. Dingwall." Mr. Dingwall went to the bows, where he stood like a great admiral, and Mr. McBride laughed at the sight of him.

Then the ship responded as the dock gates were opened and more water surged in. "Cast off!" shouted Uncle William, and when that was done he shouted, "Brace round, Bosun!" and the crew heaved the braces. I marvelled as the top-yards came round, so that the breeze first cracked the sails and then gently swelled them, and the *Margaret* eased away from the quay and slowly, at the pace of the people on the quay walking to keep up with her, cleared the gates and stone piers of the Salthouse Dock and glided into the estuary, where the ebb tide picked us up and a fresher breeze ruffled our hair, and under full topsails we went down to the Black Rock, where as dusk fell we hoisted in our yawl and longboat and anchored in the channel.

Next morning a pilot boat came out with our gunpowder, fresh vegetables, and a crate of live fowls. For three days we were employed in braiding cordage to lash down the boats and the anchors. We rigged the jib-boom and bent the mainsail to its yard. I became used to talk and laughter in our partitioned cabins, to the slow swing of the ship in the tide, to the shipping in the river, the low green hills on either side, and the spires that poked above the blur of the town. Then on August 19th, the wind having freshened, we weighed anchor, and as our fiddler played most sturdily, we slipped down the Formby Channel and out into the Irish Sea.

Chapter 7

Coming South

It took us two weeks of tacking and close-hauling in squally weather to be clear of British waters: to round Anglesey, to beat past the Isle of Man, and, often in sight of the Welsh coast and the sunlight and storm-clouds upon its mountains, to clear somewhere off our starboard bow the southern tip of Ireland. We knew when we had done so because instead of jumbled seas we faced head-on the massive Atlantic swell. I had felt queasy since we left the Mersey. Now I was vilely sick and dizzy, and I did not know which was worse: the lurch of breath out of my body when the ship plunged into the long trough between the waves, or the crash and judder when she half rode and half sustained the impact of the crest. Sometimes her head was down and water seethed through her. It knocked men over and flooded our quarters, which because we dared not open the ports soon stank of wet clothes and vomit. I felt better on deck, where I huddled weakly like one of those land-birds that the wind blows unaccountably to sea.

Then one day my nausea vanished and I had sea-legs. I leaned into the ship's roll, I swarmed aloft like a monkey, and I was ravenously hungry and pleased with myself. Uncle William's response was to announce that I must buckle down to some serious schooling. "I know you boys," he said. "You'd waste all your time listening to sailors' yarns." He taught me arithmetic, navigation, and spelling. Sometimes Peter Case joined in; his declared ambition was to be richer than the Smallshaws, and he knew that it would be more attainable if he could write his name. Uncle William showed Peter how sounds become letters, and he smoothed my jagged hand into a copper-plate. Every day he discoursed for an hour or two upon a selected Bible passage, often illustrating his meaning with one of the very sailors' yarns that he derided, but of which he was nevertheless the master spinner.

Prophets and apostles acquired the tobacco-spitting horsesense of Liverpool slave captains, and the rationality of God's universe was not unlike that of a well-commanded ship, or even a farm on which wise husbandry doubled nature's bounty. This led us to my dead father's stubbornness, and how he always believed that a living could be wrested from where it could not. But when I expected Uncle William to condemn my father, he did not. He smiled, and sighed, and quoted another text to show that love must reign.

Weeks of that voyage live in my memory as an image of the state-room: Uncle William is braced against the battering swell, my books skid down the table, and outside there is glaring sunlight and white foam—headache weather, Uncle William called it, neither north nor bloody south. Then it changed, and we knew that we had come a long way south, because the sea eased and the nights were warm and gentle. We saw the islands of the Grand Canaries come and go in the haze, and we set a new, south-easterly course, on which the sunshine was warm and the swell smooth, and the trade winds caught us and blew us towards Africa; but I still felt in my heart an unease, like that of the headache weather, even when I skylarked with my fellow apprentices, Peter Case and Mark Baker.

Mark was a fat boy with short breath. He had been articled to a wig-maker but ran away, for which the magistrates ordered him to sea. The three of us shared a cabin so small that in the bad weather our hammocks bumped together. Mark reckoned that he could piss the farthest and fart the loudest, which caused famous fights between himself and Peter. Peter would lose his temper and pummel Mark's flab without effect. Mark would then blunder into Peter, knock him over, and lie on top of him like a gasping human turtle until Peter capitulated. Then the two of us would attack Mark, or we would all giggle for minutes on end at what seemed to us the weirdness of the grown men. We raced each other to the foretop and we plagued the life out of the cook, Joseph Fielding. We invented a secret language based on Mr. Bruce's stammer, and yet our high spirits often ended in silence, because just as every soul on board watched Mr. Dingwall to see what he would do, so Mark and Peter watched me.

I thought at first that it was because I was the Master's nephew. I knew from one of Mr. McBride's gruff confidences that many of the men were suspicious of me because I had had the docker whipped. Most apprentices ignored what they saw and peddled information; they told the officers about the men and the men about the officers. I seemed committed to the officers, and so the men ignored me. But in my heart I was committed to nothing except love for Uncle William, and I wanted the men to respect me; when we came to the Tropic of Cancer I saw my opportunity.

Uncle William invited all those of us who had not been south of the line before to pay for grog all round to avoid a ducking. I had no money. Uncle William said that he would pay for me, or that a few pence could be deducted from the good-conduct bonus that the owners were in any case not obliged to pay me. I said that I had not yet earned my bonus and would prefer the ducking. I realized well that Uncle William's sermons were as often as not intended to show me how to tackle my problems, but at the time he blustered a bit before giving his approval. Inwardly he must have been pleased.

Mark and Peter were certainly full of excited questions before and after a seaman named Donovan and I were ducked from the main yard-arm and came up spouting. Donovan declared the ocean most warm and refreshing. I was afraid that the men would drag me a long way through the water, but they did not, and afterwards they were much more cheerful and open towards me. Uncle William set me fewer school exercises, and when the men replaced the fore-topgallant sail to make the old one into an awning, I worked with them.

They were boastful and loudmouthed, and their laughter was easily turned to quarrelling. They joked about the Manx seaman, Taylor, sticking his third leg up the backside of a young Maltese named Salinas—"More like Salt-in-His-Arse," said Mossop—and bragged of what they would do when they got among the grog and the black women. They had a lewd triumph when one of the ship's cats came on heat. Our tattered black tom mastered her before our eyes, on the sail that we had spread flat to render with resin and oil. The men whistled and howled and the cats squirmed with ecstasy and greasy inconvenience. Even Mr. Partridge smiled thinly.

Peter Case and I worked next as labourers for the carpenter, Matthew True, a tall, gentle, grey-haired man, light on his feet and quietly spoken, who sucked in his mouth as he studied the work and without looking at me muttered praises that were both kind and mischievous. "If you was to ask me, I'd say you've done well. I would. There's some very wild men in that fo'c'sle. They piss in their sea-chests and don't care nothing for nobody." True joked about the wild men, but he must have known that they were not the real cause of my unease, and never had been.

Our task was to fit up the state-room as a shop, and build shelves on which to display samples of our goods: lengths of cotton, kettles, basins, rolls of tobacco, linen handkerchiefs, jugs, pint mugs, nails, beads and bangles, knives, and cheap raw spirits, some of which were in kegs and some in great butts in the hold. When he had finished the shelves, not without Uncle William's lengthy reminders of what they had or had not done differently the previous season, True made a grating to replace the solid hatch-cover. This gave us light and air when we set to in the hold itself.

What a dusty, smelly, confused scene it was, half gloom and half bright shafts of light from the grating. Men shoved and heaved at chests full of muskets for barter, and the gunner, Davy Morgan, short and stout, a mean man with a big, greying head, a pugnacious smile, and an odd, deliberate gracefulness, extricated his cannons from the rest of the gear and lifted them on deck by block and tackle. When enough space had been cleared, Matt and Uncle William marked out the boundaries of the slaves' rooms with a piece of chalk, and for my benefit explained how we would build first the bulkhead that would separate the men slaves from the women. Some of the timber we had shipped with us, and the rest slowly accumulated as the cooper, James Lees, broke up the water and bread and spirit butts that we emptied during the voyage.

Uncle William stood where the bulkhead would be and explained how in the event of a mutiny the men slaves would have to break the chains in their own room and pass through the women's room to reach the grating. If they forced that and climbed to the open deck, they would still face the barricado that would be built behind the mainmast to shut off the wheel, quarterdeck, and stern cabins from the rest of the ship. "But we reckon we'll keep 'em here," he said, shrugging to indicate the bow-end room, and looked at Matt True.

True's preparations were as ordinary as beaming up on a loom. He whistled and sighed as he considered the wood. "Aye," he said, "they'll not break this." James Lees sawed away, and dust danced in the light from the grating.

Uncle William looked at me. "What do you think?" he said.

"They'll be in the dark," I said.

"They will"—Uncle William laughed—"and all the more secure for it!"

He watched me closely, and as soon as he saw in my face the admission that the cause of my unease was Africa and the slave trade, he turned and said that it was time for our Bible study in the state-room. On deck we halted for a moment and stared at the sultry ocean. Then we smiled because there was a glitter of flying fish.

Our text was from the Gospel According to St. John, Chapter 6, Verse 68: "Then Simon Peter answered him, Lord, to whom shall we go? thou hast the words of eternal life." It reassured me. Uncle William and Mr. Partridge and Mr. Dingwall and Matt True were such good men that they would never do devil's work. No Englishman would. Africans may have been savages with smaller brains than Englishmen, but being Englishmen, we did not enslave other nations. It was their own cruel world that enslaved them, not ours. We merely traded in people who were slaves already, and to judge from what I heard in the state-room, the trade was like the cloth market at Halifax, where there were some fine men and some who could not be trusted—or so my father and Crabtree had told me. As for horrors, what could be worse than my own hands in the mush of my father's dead body?

Often on the moors I and other children had caught frogs and cut them up. Then suddenly we grew too big for it, and it seemed horrible and inexplicable. I always pretended that it was not me who had done it but another person. What would I think when those five-foot-high bulkheads held back living people? Were blacks real people? Did they feel like us? Did frogs? Frogs twitched when their stretched bellies were cut, but they never screamed. Perhaps neither they nor blacks felt pain. I did not know.

I was sure that the division on the ship was between those who had seen Africa before and those who had not. Those who had not were told wild anecdotes to test them. We were watched with grins but cold eyes. For all I knew, my qualms might be laughable. More than once, because he often stared at me, I had an impulse to confide them to Mr. Dingwall, but he did not speak much to anyone except Uncle William and I did not know how to speak to him. Whenever I tried I felt stupid, so I resolved to watch and wait and keep my feelings to myself. I knew that if they became unbearable I could trust Uncle William.

In the meantime, the preparation of the ship went on. Since there was as yet not enough room in the hold to erect the bulkhead that would mark the stern end of the women's room, and behind which they would be given a place to wash, Matt True set to work upon the boats. Uncle William had always taken the small punt over the side to test the currents, but the longboat and the yawl had been lashed down since we left Liverpool. The yawl had three oars a side and a set of sails, and would be used for the day-to-day ferrying of people and provisions. The longboat was much bigger. She sailed under a fore-and-aft rig, and True built seats astern and some forward decking to give overnight cover. He would wait until he was ashore to caulk her.

While True hammered away, Davy Morgan made cartridges and ran out his carriage-guns, and the watch took turns to go in the punt and scrub the ship's sides; already there were weeds a foot long growing beneath the waterline. One day the punt crew rowed away from the ship and caught a shark, whose meat proved very oily.

We were now in the second week of the month of October. There were changes in the colour of the water, and we felt the nearness of the land. We felt the dull heat of it, and men joked and jostled each other in an irritated as well as an excited fashion. One day Uncle William's soundings brought up red sand and many broken shells, and after that he sounded every two hours and tried to work out from his reckonings and the chart where he was in the maze of off-shore sandbanks. Sometimes he brought up white sand and sometimes at greater depths struck rock, but when he found red sand again he knew he must be near, and indeed he was, for at daybreak on the twenty-third day of October we saw a smudge of land on our port quarter.

In the early light it looked to me like unbroken grey-brown cliffs, but Mr. Bruce said that we were much nearer than we seemed because the coast was flat. What we saw were not cliffs but mangrove swamps and jungle, and the force of the breakers was exhausted several miles from shore on well-established sandbanks. Uncle William took soundings every hour. Our progress was slow, but the officers who knew the coast were confident that what we could see were the swamps at the mouths of the Saloum River, north of our destination, the Gambia, and when the sun was taken at noon, this proved to be the case.

Uncle William received congratulations with the disclaimer that "If there's one thing I hate it's these blasted off-shore currents."

Mr. McBride took a long pull at his flask and said, "Well, gentlemen, welcome once again to the inferno!"

Peter Case poked me in the ribs and said, "Hey! Did I tell you? There are plagues of flying ants!"

Mr. Partridge ignored the restless excitement. He insisted that the men work normally and behave as though our deep impulse to stare at the new, approaching shore did not exist; but it did, and Mr. Dingwall was possessed by it.

On watch or off, he stood all day at the foreshrouds and stared as though at images of his past life. No one went near him until dusk, when the western sky was grey with a shade of lavender, and Uncle William stood next to him and they spoke easily, as old friends can. In the state-room that night we ate another stew-cum-soup of shark's meat. Mr. Dingwall was gentle but remote, and his wit that always held us off was bizarre: it ran everywhere like cracks in ice.

Next morning we sailed along a tawny and more open shore, and my heart raced when I was shown through the telescope the mouth of the great Gambia River itself.

Our approach took us miles south of the river to the end of a big sandbank called Turn in Time Point, where we tacked north to find the channel inside the bank. It was hard work, close to the wind and against the outflow. The tidefall was some eight feet at the mouth, and we took continual soundings. All morning we beat into the sun, and then suddenly we were over the bar and the water was smoother.

On the starboard side it was a gentle grey, and I saw floating leaves, brown, yellow, and deep crimson. The horizon was mangroves and a fuzz of palm trees. Ahead, the river was so wide that it faded into haze, and there were fleets of canoes like black slivers. To port, between the ship and the northern bank, to which we had kept close, the water glittered. Barra Point was clearly defined. We could see the outlines of mud huts and the peculiar clump of trees known as the King of Barra's Pavilion.

"There it is," said Uncle William, and shouted at the bosun. The yards were backed, and the sails flapped as the wind left them, and then our best bower anchor rattled down from the cathead and Uncle William said, "Thank you, Mr. Morgan!" and Davy Morgan, standing stockily back, applied a match to one of his cannon and a shot roared out in salute and the smoke drifted away in the light breeze. Our officers stared at the shore, for if ships did not salute the King and pay his customs duty, he sent out his war canoes to attack them. After a few minutes the people on shore lit an answering bonfire, and Uncle William called for the yawl to be lowered overboard and gifts stowed in her. Then he put on his best frock-coat and went to pay his respects to royalty.

Part Two

Africa

I verily believe, that the far greater
part of the wars, in Africa, would cease,
if the Europeans would cease to tempt
them, by offering goods for slaves.
—JOHN NEWTON,
Thoughts upon the
African Slave
Trade

Chapter 8

The King of Barra

Uncle William took with him six seamen, Mr. McBride, Mr. Dingwall, and me. It was strange to look back at the *Margaret* and see how small she was on that vast river, twelve miles wide. The southern bank was so low and far away that in the glare it was a grey disappearing outline: a wisp of straw laid flat on the horizon. The yawl creamed the water as the men rowed to help her against the wind. The officers did not say much. They had their swords and hats and looked keenly at everything, as though they might read in the hot hazy sky or the bubbles of water the probabilities of trade that season. Ahead of us the foam was milky where the waves broke on a beach that rose to raggedy-grassed sandy bluffs. Clumps of palms leaned gracefully to the water. There were canoes drawn up but no people. The yawl grounded in shallow water, and we jumped into the warm surf to drag her clear. Then I ran up the beach, and for a moment I was dizzy; after the motion of the ship, the land's stability seemed alien. I lay down. Parts of the beach seemed to move. I gasped and pointed. Uncle William laughed. "Crabs," he said, and they were, crabs the colour of sand except that they were grey in the colour-draining light. At a footstep they disappeared down little bolt-holes.

Half a mile away, smoke still rose from the signal fire, and when we climbed the bluffs and halted under the trees, we entered a dry landscape of straggly, spiky thorns and beyond them thickening trees and greener cultivated land. Some of the trees were like shapes in a fantastic dream: huge, naked, and leafless, massive at the base and all spidery twigs at the top. Their fruit dangled from thin strands. "Baobabs," said Mr. McBride, seeing my astonishment. He took a swig from his flask and jerked his head. "And those are banana palms." The palms rattled and peeled, and there were other trees that looked like English ashes, but were spikier and more fierce. High in the sky, great birds of prey were wheeling. After the river breeze the dry heat burned and exhausted. I gasped and sweated, and then the hairs on my scalp tingled at what I heard and saw.

A fantastic procession approached us. It shimmered in the haze. It loomed back and forth in clouds of dust as white-robed horsemen turned their mounts this way and that. There was drumming and the flash and crackle of muskets fired into the air and the clapping of many hands and the high chanting of women. Then the procession opened and spread out in front of us, and we saw the goats and bullocks being dragged on ropes, and the mounted lancers and bowmen, and the arrogant pride of the people. They were tall and straight-backed and very black-skinned. They wore white cotton caftans and breeches, and the more important the man the baggier his breeches were, so that when the King dismounted from his white Arab charger and walked to meet Uncle William, his breeches hung like a sack in front and at the back reached to the ground and waggled in the dust like a tail. Uncle William, Mr. Dingwall, and Mr. McBride doffed their hats and bowed, and the King surveyed them with a slow smile and contempt in his slanted eyes.

Uncle William gestured to our men, and they came up with kegs of rum and brandy and some tobacco, a pair of pistols, and a few rolls of cloth. The King nodded and waved the gifts away. He was a powerfully-built man with fine facial planes, grey hair, and a mournful, doubting expression. His smile of recognition at Uncle William and Mr. Dingwall seemed only to deepen his disdain for them.

The King's servants brought mats and stools and broached a keg of brandy. We sat in the dappled shade, I with my back to a tree trunk, and the King's drummers and musicians surrounded us and the praise-singer, or griot, sang what Mr. McBride guessed to be a poem in the King's honour. The King had a holy-man in a red cotton cap who seemed to be his secretary, for he could read and write and took notes in ink of what was agreed. He wrote backwards in a script that looked like tracing and not letters. A big man with his sword in a red bandolier stood behind the King. Mr. McBride said that he was the Master of Horse. It was he who, whenever we tried to commence our negotiations, called suppliants from the crowd. Some were in rags and poured dust over their heads. Others knelt low and clapped their hands. Mr. McBride said that the hand-clappers were Muslims and the others pagans. To preserve their local powers the river kings had long ago accepted Islam and become the vassals of Muslim emperors inland, but many of the common people still worshipped the spirits.

The King seemed to grant many wishes without properly listening to them, and the musicians twanged their bowstrings for applause. The display achieved its purpose. We were impressed by the power of the King and his personal army, and we waited most obediently. We all gasped in the breeze that seemed to be cool and yet was not. Sometimes the palm fronds were blown inside-out, like a woman's long hair, and they were full of finches that twittered and whistled.

Uncle William and Mr. McBride muttered observant asides to each other. The sailors were impatient and shouted lewd comments about the dust-throwing petitioners. Uncle William shut them up. Mr. Dingwall took a mug of brandy for politeness but never so much as looked at it. His hands trembled. They held the mug so tightly that I thought it would be crushed.

When the King did allow our business to commence, he said that he had come not to negotiate for himself but to help us to negotiate with his sons. There was no issue in the negotiation with himself, he said. The comey, or customs duty, on a ship of our size was sixteen bars and was as immutable as the law of God. "The law of their God forbids alcohol," said Mr. McBride, "but they're still as pissed as black farts in a pickle-barrel."

Uncle William laughed and lit his pipe and spat into the dirt. He settled himself on his stool, hands on his thighs, elbows out, a sweating, untidy, and compelling figure. He smiled genially at the King's sons, one of them a thin-faced youth, the other a taller, older, more impatient man, who fluttered and snapped his fingers. The King looked languidly away while the older son made speeches at Mr. Dingwall, whose command of their language, Mandingo, was broken but adequate.

There was no mistaking why Uncle William relied on Mr. Dingwall and had made the Smallshaws take him. Mr. Dingwall's dignity matched that of the King, his politeness was more natural, his wits were quicker, and for all his tension he was the only one of us who moved in that heat with something of the grace and slowness of the Africans. I began to notice in the bright light all the things that were wrong with our white faces: their stubble and blotches and spots; the creases where sweat had made the skin rub red; the dankness of our hair. By comparison the blacks looked true men; they did not seem to belong to the same race as the creature I had seen in the Liverpool coffee-house. Here we looked absurd, and yet I knew that we were stronger and better because everyone on the moors and ship had told me so.

As I watched and listened and received an increasingly fuddled commentary from Mr. McBride, I began to understand the game that was being played. The King knew well that Uncle William had been ordered to the Gambia River as a consequence of events there the previous season, when another ship owned by Smallshaw and Hill had suffered a voyage of disease and misadventure. Her Captain and half her crew had died before their cargo of slaves was completed. The First Mate had decided that if he bought more slaves he would not have enough white men to contain them, and so he had deposited some thousands of bars' worth of goods on account with the mulatto slave merchants up-river, an account that would hopefully be rendered a year later to such vessel as Smallshaw and Hill thought fit to send.

They sent the *Margaret* and Uncle William. Like most Liverpool captains, Uncle William hated the Gambia, and he had protested on the grounds that because he had not been there for a couple of seasons he did not have the rise and fall of people and prices at his fingertips, as he did in the Sierra Leone, and so it would be easier to cheat him. But old Mr. Smallshaw thought this less important than the fact that because of the actions of the French in the Gambia it would take a strong man to recover even part of the credits. I had heard this discussed many times in the *Margaret*'s state-room, as well as the pros and cons of the original decision to leave the goods with the mulatto merchants. They were generally agreed to be the biggest rogues and liars in the world, bigger even than the French, whose reckless treachery and determination to master the world had forced up prices and ruined the trade.

For a hundred years we and the French had maintained forts on the river and competed for the bigger share of its trade. On the land itself we could barely impinge, because the African kingdoms were too strong. Mr. McBride told me that no European had travelled farther inland than the distance that could be covered in a week's time, and that the mighty Emperor to whom the King of Barra owed allegiance could put tens of thousands of horsemen into the field. The most that white men could show was when during European wars we and the French sent warships to the river to destroy each other's forts and shipping, although for the last thirty-odd years the French had concentrated their efforts in Senegal, and the Gambia had been an English waterway.

Officially it was the preserve of the Royal African Company, but Liverpool merchants in particular had ignored the Company's monopoly to such an extent that the Government abolished it, and said that although the English fort on James Island was in disrepair, the Royal Navy would not rebuild it until the old Company was wound up. In the meantime the Company's Governor still lived there with little or no authority, a situation of which the French took full advantage. Their ships reappeared on the river. They re-established their post at Albreda, and rebuilt their fort at Juffure. They attempted to drive us out, not by force but by paying high prices, and so far as most Liverpool ships were concerned they had succeeded.

"Why should we lose our profits?" argued Uncle William in the *Margaret*'s state-room, but he knew well as he sweated under the trees at Barra that he could not expect anything like last year's value from Smallshaw's deposited goods. He was fresh from England after eight weeks at sea. He did not know our strength in relation to that of the French. He did not even know the value of a bar here, let alone the number of bars that it was reasonable to pay. He must deduce what he wanted from the King's demands and comments.

Mr. McBride said that the King's arrival with so large a retinue was a sign of friendship, and probably indicated that he wished to treat the English and French impartially. On the other hand, the sixteen bars asked for the comey was six more than when Uncle William had last entered the river. This was pointed out to the King's son, who ascribed it to the omnipresence of the French. The King toyed with his beads. He had said that the comey was settled, and did not even listen as Mr. Dingwall discussed how much we would pay the two sons for the right to cut wood and refill our water butts, and what other presents we would give if any of the business came to actual slave-trading.

Uncle William's response was to interrupt the chatter between the King and the Master of Horse with demands for definite information. How many ships had come up the river so far? Had the French substantially rebuilt Albreda? How was the Governor of James Island? Did he still own the talking parrot? Had Senhor Voss taken any more wives? "If he has," slurred Mr. McBride, "he'll show no interest in us at all," for the Portuguese mulatto Senhor Antonio Voss was Smallshaw's principal debtor. The King said that Senhor Voss had indeed taken a new wife, a Fula woman of such startling beauty that when Senhor Voss went up-river with the canoe fleet, men with poisoned arrows guarded the lady. "From the other wives," added the Master of Horse, grinning.

Uncle William rumbled his belly laugh and asked about the King's own prowess. Mr. Dingwall translated with bravura. The King disclaimed the praises heaped upon him. A lion he may have been in his youth, but now . . . He gestured at his sons, who scowled. "He's got a prick like an elephant," said Uncle William. Mr. Dingwall made the compliment sound like one of the griot's epic poems. The King threw up his hands in mock denial. The musicians twanged their bowstrings. There was huge laughter. "I'll pay twelve for the comey," said Uncle William, and Mr. Dingwall slipped it in like a knife.

The King's laughter was diplomatically even huger, and then for a second it stopped and his eyes looked at Uncle William with an old, scornful, self-despising irony. "Sixteen," he repeated, showing the number with his fingers.

Uncle William said, "How much in a bar?" and the serious horse-trade began.

For the first time they spoke the pidgin as well as Mr. Dingwall's Mandingo, and everyone shouted at once. My head ached. I joined our seamen, but they, too, were haggling. One of the King's bodyguard had a Spanish silver dollar round his neck, and our men wanted to barter it for their own sweatrags and knives. But the soldier knew its value, even though to him it was not money but an ornament, and he laughed in their faces.

Then a great commotion saluted an agreement between the King and Uncle William. The King snapped his fingers at the Master of Horse, who snapped his at the soldier with the Spanish dollar. The soldier dragged from the crowd a fine man slave, who was about twenty years old and tall and quiet, and wore a long cotton shirt.

Mr. Dingwall translated the Master of Horse's description of the slave. Look at him. He is no ordinary specimen. He was born into a noble household, and in normal circumstances could never be sold except as a punishment for serious crimes. He could be sold now because he had been captured in war, or, rather, when he invaded Barra as one of a raiding party from the adjoining kingdom of Baddibu.

"Nonsense," said Mr. McBride. "I'll not believe 'em. They take men off their own streets if they've no others."

Then Mr. McBride spluttered because he realized that everyone was waiting for him to inspect the slave. He cleared his throat and walked none too soberly forward. The soldier nudged the slave, who took off his shirt and stood naked. The soldier grabbed his shirt and like everyone else stared at the man's long black penis.

Mr. McBride bared the man's gums to look at his teeth, and bent down to inspect the penis. He actually pulled back the foreskin. Then he walked round behind the man, and peered up into his ears, and tapped his back. He lifted up one of his feet like a farrier shoeing a horse. He felt the man's muscles, looked at his hands to see if he was used to hard work, and slapped him genially on the back. He nodded.

"Ninety," said Uncle William. The King agreed. It was his policy to sell one good slave to each ship, irrespective of nationality. The musicians played and the women sang. Uncle William invited the King to visit the *Margaret*, and the King accepted. They embarked in the yawl, and I in a dugout canoe with the Master of Horse.

In the high blue afternoon the river ran cloudy, and where the breeze and the falling tide met the salt sea there were little waves. The westerly sun made them glint like a thousand leaping fish; it shone through the spray at the bow and the drops from the rowers' paddles.

At the ship there was a lot of shouting in pidgin and private trading between our men and the canoe crews. In our absence Mr. Partridge had put up the awning, and the cook had erected his cauldron in the open with bricks to make a fireplace, so the maindeck was another world of filtered light and smoke.

The elaborateness of the King's breeches meant that he had to be lifted in and out of the yawl by three soldiers, and that he seemed to fill the state-room. He rummaged everywhere and inspected everything. For the slave he took six muskets, six small kegs of gunpowder, some rolls of cloth, four kettles, a pint of good brandy, two iron bars and some knives, beads, nails, and trinkets. This gave us a basic value of ten bars for a musket, and upon that calculation Uncle William agreed to pay sixteen bars for the comey, and fixed a price for the wood and water.

The King's sons, who had wrinkled their noses at the faint stink from Uncle William's commode, were invited to use it but declined. The Master of Horse obliged, however, wiping his backside with his left hand, and then calling for a soldier to wash the hand with brandy and throw a fatly majestic turd out of the stern window. The King laughed patronizingly, as though we had been done an inconceivable favour, and Mr. Dingwall said afterwards that the King's sons had talked in their own language about what savages we were.

The King was then lowered into the yawl and under the command of Mr. Bruce escorted ashore. We fired another gun in salute and the retinue on shore shrilled and shot off their muskets.

Throughout the haggle in the state-room the slave sat on deck with some of the King's soldiers. When the King emerged with smiles, and the soldiers saw that a contract had been agreed, they handed over the slave to our bosun. The slave began to howl and struggle. The bosun hit him in the stomach to wind him so that there would be no unseemly noises during the King's farewells. When the man recovered his breath he struggled and bellowed again. This time the bosun kicked him in the stomach. As the man fell to his knees, four sailors spreadeagled him. The bosun took an iron out of the fire, blew on it, and branded the man on the chest. There was a hiss and a brief acrid smell. The man heaved and threshed. His winded howls were cracked and horrible.

The sailors put irons on his wrists and took him below, where they attached his irons by another, longer chain to a ringbolt. The slave sat on the floor in the almost-dark, making noises like an animal. I went to stare at him. He urinated over himself without seeming to notice. I was confused and excited. I felt ashamed, and then angry, because I was so interested by everything and what had happened to the man was not my fault. I felt superior to him. He was scarcely a human being, and did not respond when the bosun gave him a piece of cloth that would be his covering. Then the bosun reported to Uncle William, who entered it in his books: the issue of the cloth and the man's number, description, and cost. By then the sun had disappeared into the hot, dirty-yellow haze of evening. We heard drumming from the shore, and on deck the cook was boiling fresh rice in the cauldron.

Chapter 9

Fort James

We weighed at first light, and although we sailed all day, the river was still so wide that its southern bank disappeared into haze and glare, as did the arm of land astern that we knew blocked our sight of the ocean. The haze was a grey and faded shimmer in which the blurred tops of trees seemed sometimes to float above the water. The river was a world, silent, peaceful, and majestic. Its water was warm and grey-yellow, but became more blue as the sun climbed higher. In the afternoon the blue deepened and we saw James Island ahead, a grey bulk suspended like a mirage above sparkling water, and near it a ship that we assumed to be a big Frenchman described by the King. By the time we anchored it was dusk, and the water swirling round us was the dirty-yellow outflow from the creeks on the far bank. I could just make out Albreda on the north bank, a big clearing by the water. Pinpoints of light appeared there, and then the beacon flared over Fort James. I understood why these two places were so important, for in a day's sail along the northern shore I had seen only one other break in the mangroves, a small golden beach twenty paces across. But there were thick palm trees and bushes behind it, so for all practical purposes Albreda and James Island were the first and best landing places.

That night the men were restless and the fiddler, O'Sullivan, played wild jigs, and then slow, haunting, broken tunes of the rain-swept north. The men went quiet, and in the hush the slave cried out for loss. "Shut up!" they jeered back at him and laughed as they had done at the cats, but since he was the first slave of the season they looked upon him as something of a man. They called him Howler, after his cries of anguish. In time this became, almost affectionately, Old Howler, and they would show him slapdash kindness if they recognized him.

I was on Mr. Partridge's watch from eight to midnight, and our three seamen were the Welshman Parry, Wilf Sadler, and Butterworth, a stocky little man from Royton, on the edge of the Pennine moors. They laughed at their comrades in the fo'c'sle, and once Parry went to the hatchway and threatened Howler, but Mr. Partridge's quiet voice checked him with, "Are you drunk, sailor?"

"Indeed I am not, sir," said Parry, but I think he was, for their chatter grew wilder.

They began, as sailors will, by boasting about their Captain's skill at navigation, and ended with complaints that so far they had not got ashore. They discussed what old Jack Mossop had promised himself when he did, and how they all wanted to see it. When the watch was changed, Parry slumped down where he was and went to sleep curled up against one of the guns. Next day as we worked up towards James Island, he told me that he had woken up covered in dew. Certainly his face was badly blotched by insect bites, and some days later he was the first man to go down with fever.

We anchored to the south of the island, with the fort between ourselves and the French three-master. "Sloppy buggers," said the bosun, and indeed the ship did look less well scrubbed than ours. Washing hung out of the state-room windows, and her sails were untidily reefed. Mr. Dingwall, once again having a smattering of the lingo, was sent to pay our respects to her captain. The longboat under Mr. Partridge's command would then proceed with our empty water casks to Albreda, where the King of Barra's headman would have them filled. The yawl set off with Matt True, James Lees, four deckhands, and orders to cut wood. Mr. Bruce was left in command of the ship and Uncle William took me in the punt to the fort. We were rowed by Mossop, Taylor the Manxman, and a cross-eyed rogue called Morton, one of the two drunk men that the slop-shop owner had tipped on board before we sailed.

The little fort covered almost the entire island, which was perhaps a hundred yards long, and consisted of a battlemented keep with projecting bastions, and various outlying buildings such as a barracks, a cooper's shed, and slave quarters. There were some small trees and bushes, and in one of them I saw a big white heron. The masonry was of local sandstone, and its dilapidation showed here and there the rubble filling, and bits of the oyster-shells from which the mortar had been made. Smoke drifted up from a few fires. Mossop started to laugh because he could actually see white women, and Uncle William told him to behave himself until he was let ashore at Albreda that evening. There were a few small boats and dugouts at the downstream landing place, and a bit of muddy foreshore. The water was cloudy, and our oars stirred up the earth and leaves in it. We grated ashore, and some of the Company's blacks helped us pull in the punt.

There were white soldiers in very faded uniforms, and Governor Bayliss himself, a tall, delicate, stooping man much racked by fever, had recognized Uncle William through his spyglass and come out to meet us. His famous long-tailed parrot flop-walloped after him.

"Welcome!" said the Governor, and took both Uncle William's hands in his. He had shaved his head and wore a broad-brimmed straw hat.

"God bless my soul!" said the parrot, who was very green and shiny.

"I expect you jolly boys can take a drink," said the Governor, and sent our seamen to the cook-house. The parrot squawked and bounced. "I'll thank you not to smirk at my guests," said the Governor.

"Jolly boys!" replied the parrot. "Jolly boys!"

Bad health had slowed the Governor's walk, and it was an effort for him to climb from the courtyard to his apartment in the little tower. Not that he complained. He had full, wryly-smiling lips and was ironical about the affairs of the Company and deprecating about himself. He poured Uncle William a glass of Madeira and listened attentively, grunting and nodding to acknowledge a point. His room was whitewashed over the rough finish and contained a four-poster bed, a thing that I had never seen before, a desk and chairs brought from England, piles of well-worn books, red local pots and the Governor's own glass and china, and a litter of nut-shells, half-pecked fruits, and parrot droppings.

Wooden steps led to the roof-top battery and lookout, and while Uncle William and the Governor talked, I climbed up there and felt once again the completeness of the river world: grey-green horizons broken at each end, the enormous sky, the flood itself, wide, slow, and generous. A swift dipped over the water for insects. I felt safe and calm. Even the *chink-chink* of the smithy hammer making chains seemed gentle and far away. I went down again, and the parrot looked up at me from the bottom step and said, "Chamber pot's frozen, John. Best wear your comforter."

Governor Bayliss threw the parrot a nut. There was a black in the room now, a thinnish, irascible man who talked rapid pidgin and shrugged his shoulders and then stood and sulked. He wore a European waistcoat and native breeches. The Governor spoke quietly, and sometimes his mind seemed far away. Then he looked up and there was a cruel determination in his eyes, but the black refused to look at them. His smile was mournfully impudent.

Uncle William laughed and said, "Just now you go tomorrow I pay one bar." The black nodded and struck hands on it and went, shouting loudly for a crew. He was one of the overseers for Senhor Voss, and spent his time between Fort James and Albreda, dispatching canoes whenever they were needed. One would go now to Senhor Voss to say that we would visit him tomorrow.

"Where's the Bishop?" said the parrot. "Where's the Bishop?"

"Bishop?" said Uncle William.

"My late wife's brother," said the Governor.

"Is that a fact?" said Uncle William, impressed.

The Governor's wrist flicked the subject away. He glanced at a book and put it down again. He had waited all through the wet season for the sight of an English ship, and now that one had arrived he was bored with us. "I occupy my time with Latin verses," he said, indicating his manuscript.

"Is that a fact?" said Uncle William, and shook his head and stabbed at his pipe bowl so energetically that it snapped to pieces. "God bless us!" he said, and threw the entire smouldering handful out of the window.

"Why not consider me for once?" said the parrot. "Why not consider me?"

The Governor smiled and stood up. The effort made him tremble. "What can we do for you?" said Uncle William.

The Governor said that we could ask our surgeon to visit him. His own surgeon, his chaplain, and two other officers had died during the wet season. "We need a new water system," he said.

Uncle William waggled a finger at the parrot. "Jolly boys!" he said. "Jolly boys!"

But the parrot ignored him, and the Governor begged our pardon because he was too fatigued to accompany us to the landing place.

Uncle William took advantage of this to send me for the punt crew while he peered into the slave quarters to see what the merchandise was like. I found Mossop, Taylor, and Morton in the shade of the barracks wall. Sometimes the common sailors made edgy jokes about my being Uncle William's nephew, and when I saw the gleam in their eyes, and heard Taylor's little feminine giggles, I expected them to do so now to show off in front of the soldiers and their wives.

But although they laughed they insisted on introducing me, especially to Mrs. Patterson, a thin-faced, flashing-eyed Scots girl, and to Sergeant Wood, a fat, grizzled man with bad teeth. I sensed a destructive excitement. The barracks were too dark and smelly to sit in, and the sun too burning. I suddenly experienced the island for what it was, a prison, and I was glad to be back in the punt, where Uncle William looked sharply at the men, as though he, too, felt some suppressed danger in them; but he had his plans on his mind and dismissed the notion.

Mr. Dingwall had been sent back in one of the Frenchman's boats, and when Mr. Partridge returned, Mr. Bruce took command of the watering, and the senior officers held a conference in the state-room. The Frenchman had paid as much as a hundred and twenty bars for a sound young male, and had made it clear to Mr. Dingwall that he would offer more if necessary. Mr. Partridge said that the French had ten or twelve good males and some women and children in the handling-station on shore. All he had been shown by the King's headman was two long-breasted women.

"Aye," said Uncle William. "That's about all Governor Bayliss has got."

"Will it come to a fight with the French?" asked Mr. McBride.

"Not yet," said Mr. Dingwall.

"Thanks be to God," said Mr. McBride, "for my wife's brother holds a commission in the army of the French King. I'd have no quiet with my dinner at all."

"Where does that leave us Protestants?" said Mr. Partridge.

It was agreed that where it left us was in a situation in which, whereas Governor Bayliss would do all he could to keep the Union flag flying until the Admiralty sent engineers and marines, he would not spend any of the Company's money to help Liverpool interlopers. "What he hopes," said Uncle William, "is that folk like us can bribe the local kings and him take the credit." But we would not spend a penny more than we had to, and as soon as we met an ivory or timber ship returning to England, we would send a full report to the owners.

As this was heartily approved, a commotion on deck announced the arrival of one of the French officers on a courtesy visit. He was a dark, dapper man, more vainly attired than our officers, and his breath smelt of garlic. He brought us some red wine and toasted us all. Then he admired the items in our shop, and said that since our manufacturers were so much better than the French, what a pity it was that our commerce and plantations were not more efficient. He was smiling and gaily ironic. I liked him.

Mr. McBride described his brother-in-law's military career at some length. "Ah!" said the Frenchman, on learning that gentleman's regiment, "he ees a Gascon, no?"

"He is not," said Mr. McBride, "he's a Donegal man," and went to pay his professional call upon the Governor. The same punt crew volunteered very eagerly to take him.

Then the yawl arrived, piled with the wood that Matt and his party had cut in the brush between Albreda and Juffure. They were stained with sweat and yellow dust, and Peter Case and Mark Baker, who had gone with them, were wildly excited. Davy Morgan, the gunner, had cadged a trip in the yawl and found a black woman in the grog-shop in Albreda.

"He stood her up against this hut," said Peter.

"Shafted her there and then," said Mark. "You should have seen it. He went into her so hard the hut started to fall to pieces."

Soon after, as the silhouettes of the bank darkened and the water assumed a glassy sheen, the longboat itself returned, deeply laden with full casks. Davy Morgan had a blatant smirk, and two of the

73

other men were merry with drink. Mr. Bruce blushed and stammered his commands.

We worked hard and well, with a lot of excited laughter, to get in the wood and water. From somewhere on shore there came the dry rattle of drums, and in Albreda the cooking fires were lit. But it was still not dark when there was a flurry of signal flags on the fort and we saw Mr. McBride come towards us in a dugout canoe. There were four black rowers and two soldiers. One of them was the fat Sergeant Wood, who stood up and started to bellow at us. The canoe swayed. Mr. McBride tried to pull the Sergeant down. The Sergeant resisted. Mr. McBride's arms described a huge shrug. The Sergeant shouted and blubbered. It was impossible to tell what he was saying even when the canoe came alongside. Then he sat down with his head in his hands and refused to budge at all, and Mr. McBride explained what had happened.

Mossop, Taylor, and Morton had rowed the punt to the island and said that they would wait for the surgeon in the barracks. They had then sent word to the Scots girl, Mrs. Patterson, and stolen off with her in the punt to Albreda. In the confusion of our work, and because of the number of canoes in the river, we had not noticed them. Sergeant Wood was in disarray because Mrs. Patterson was his common-law wife.

Some of our men leaned over the side and laughed at the sight of him: an overweight, ugly, sweaty mess of a man whose tears streamed down his cheeks, and who now repeated to anyone who would hear, "She was my jewel, she was, I've not never seen nothing like her. She was my bleeding jewel. . . ." When he recognized me he said, "Well, you saw her. You tell 'em. You tell 'em. . . ." I remembered her wild eyes, her thin cheeks and ratty hair, and could not look at him.

"You!" shouted Uncle William. "Don't behave like a two-year old!"

"Eh?" said the Sergeant, but he stopped blubbering, and as he did so, he realized how stupid he looked and was ashamed.

His shame communicated itself to our crew, except for one, Butterworth, who laughed aloud. Uncle William slapped his face. He ordered the Sergeant to return to the fort and set off himself for Albreda. He took Mr. Bruce, the bosun, six men, and me and Peter Case. Our task was to find the punt, for the problem was not simply one of discipline; there was the probability that while the three sailors got drunk the natives would steal the punt, and we should either not see it again or have to pay for its return.

Behind the ship the sky was orange and yellow, but it was grey over Albreda and dusk when the yawl grounded and we jumped into the shallows. Beyond the foreshore, hard, sandy soil sloped gently inland. The French handling-station was an arcaded building at right angles to the water, under towering trees. It looked arrogant in that fading light, defying the climate and the land, not hiding modestly within wattle fences like the store-houses and the village at the edge of the bush. Here and there fires burned in the open and palm-oil lights cast a golden glow. Peter soon found the punt among the dugouts drawn up on the mud, and when we had checked the oars and fittings he stayed where he was and I went to guard the yawl.

Uncle William had led the others towards the grog-shops that were half-way between the shore and the village, and after a few moments we heard men shouting and a woman scream, followed by the ironic cheers and laughter of bystanders. Then Uncle William appeared out of the gloom. Two sailors dragged the seemingly unconscious Mossop by his arms and Taylor and Morton walked meekly behind. Our other sailors, Mr. Bruce, and the bosun brought up the rear. A few Frenchmen and natives followed, and Mrs. Patterson, her dress open at the front and yellow dust all over her back and skirts, walked alongside. She yelled abuse, not at Uncle William but at Taylor and Morton, and from time to time picked up handfuls of dust and tried to throw it in their eyes.

When Uncle William reached the foreshore he motioned two men and Mr. Bruce to the punt and had Mossop flung into the yawl. The rest of us climbed aboard except for two men to shove off. As they did so, Mrs. Patterson grabbed one of them. He pushed her aside. She lunged again and missed, and then as the yawl floated clear she ran after it, but in the water her skirts impeded her and she half fell. She was muddy and sopping. She started to shout at us. Uncle William took the tiller and did not look back. Mrs. Patterson realized that our punt was also on shore and ran towards it, but they, too, had pushed off. She shouted obscenely. Some of the watching Africans laughed and cavorted. The Frenchmen threatened them and cuffed the children away, and one of them went and held Mrs. Patterson tightly, as if he were a strait-jacket, until her shouting and her struggling ceased.

By then all that we could see was the shine of a Frenchman's white shirt in the gloom. I realized for the first time that Morton's nose was bleeding. Mossop groaned. Nobody spoke. When we reached the ship I saw that Mossop was battered about the face. Uncle William had a bucket of water thrown over him and put him in irons, the irons being chained like Howler's to a ringbolt in the deck; yet, unlike Howler, Mossop knew that eventually he would be released.

Then Uncle William had the entire ship's company drawn up on the maindeck while the bosun gave Morton and Taylor twelve strokes apiece with a rope's end. They were tied by their wrists to the shrouds. Morton held his head to one side and hunched his shoulders, and Taylor, whose skin was as white as a girl's, trembled like a girl. The first strokes made red marks and lumps. Morton and Taylor shuddered. The crew grinned and gaped. On the latter strokes, pieces of skin stuck to the rope and were torn off.

I turned away and looked at the moon on the water. The sound of the rope was like that of a cook slapping meat on to a board. I looked again when Taylor screamed; it was because Mr. McBride had inspected the men and thrown salt on their backs. There were dribbles of blood and raw patches. Taylor's knees were weak. I disliked him and I knew that he had done wrong, but I felt sorry for him. I wondered if I would ever have the blind confidence to be an officer and order punishments. I did not think I would. Then I realized that from where he stood in the shadows Mr. Dingwall was watching me. I felt his understanding and wanted to respond, but he looked away.

Curiously, doubts about myself made me more proud of Uncle William, who, now that he had emphasized his authority, called for the cook to dish up dinner, and a pannikin of spirits for every man. There were cheers and laughs at this, a snort from Mr. McBride, and a thin smile from Mr. Partridge, who knew a bluff and ruthless master of men when he saw one.

Chapter 10

Senhor Voss

Next day Mr. Partridge, with orders to trade and to cut what wood we needed, was left in command of the *Margaret,* and ten of us sailed up-river in the longboat to find and negotiate with Senhor Voss and, hopefully, to bring back our slaves. We were Uncle William, Mr. McBride, Mr. Dingwall, five men, and Peter Case and myself. We had a swivel-gun mounted in our bows, and would need to sail and row hard for three and a half days, anchoring at night in the middle of the stream so as to foil the worst of the insects. At first the river was still very wide, but then it turned north and narrowed.

We marvelled at hippopotamuses and crocodiles, and when the river bent eastwards again, it wriggled in a leisurely fashion between green, densely foliaged banks, so that to this day when I see branches that trail into slow, swollen water I hear Uncle William's voice and smell his tobacco, and feel the greasy heat as he explained to me our situation on the great Gambia River.

The Portuguese had been the first Europeans to sail on it, and Portuguese mulatto traders founded villages all along the northern bank, but Senhor Voss was at the moment established in none of them. He was living at Kaur, in the territory of the Bur of Saloum, which, given the rivalry between England and France, was a choice that showed determined political ambition. The other kings on the northern bank, the kings of Barra, of Baddibu and Niani, were Mandinkas, and had for centuries owed their allegiance and paid their taxes to the south of the great river, to the Mansa of Cabon and thence to the great Emperor, the Mansa of Mali, in the western interior.

The Bur of Saloum and his people were Wolofs, a tribe whose allegiance was owed northwards to age-old empires in the grasslands and the desert. European firearms from the Gambia River trade, to which Saloum had access at Kaur, had made the Bur strong enough to disown his ties of obligation, and refuse to pay taxes, to an overlord too far away to take them. Saloum was a sturdy kingdom that stood apart from its neighbours and fought its own battles. It was farther up-river than Senhor Voss's usual quarters, and by living there at this time he had declared his independence and his determination to become the most powerful dealer on the river; for as Uncle William argued, another practical reason for Senhor Voss to be in Kaur was that from there he could more easily secure his contracts with the up-river kings and with the Portuguese mulattoes inland.

Uncle William's plan was to behave as though none of these ambitions existed and the only thing that mattered was Smallshaw's credit. He reckoned that if he made a nuisance of himself, Senhor Voss would pay him off as quickly as possible in order to concentrate upon his own vast designs.

By the last day the country behind the river had become more undulating, and along much of the northern bank there was tangled waterside and then palm trees at the foot of red sandstone bluffs. There were surprisingly few clearings and landing places, and hardly any settlements on the river itself. Almost every village stood back, hidden from our sight, although sometimes we saw smoke rising and there was frequent canoe traffic. Above the reach of the tide the water had a green smoothness.

Kaur announced itself with a worn, dusty, grassy clearing and a score of posts sticking out of the water and foreshore at which dugouts could moor. We tied up at one of them and sloshed ashore through lukewarm water. There were two of Senhor Voss's river cutters nearby, swift, brightly-painted little vessels with a raking fore-and-aft rig. There were store-houses and groups of porters and canoe crews; some of them were almost naked, and Mr. McBride said that this was customary among the low-caste Wolofs.

We left two men with the longboat, Parry and another Welshman, named Owen Williams, and set off to walk to Senhor Voss's compound, which lay a few minutes away between the river and the town. Uncle William hired a team of porters to carry our gifts. At either side of the dirt road were fields from which the ground-nut crop had just been gathered; the bushes drooped over grey-black earth. There were tall, dry, crackling grasses, thorn bushes with dead brown leaves, and patches of burned-off land. Many of the trees were leafless, and I had to remind myself that despite the stifling heat this was the African winter.

Suddenly there appeared before us in the grassland a bizarre avenue of trees that in the European fashion lined the side track to the compound. The surrounding grass had been cleared to allow better watering, and the trees stuck up from the bare earth in an assortment of bright green, outlandish shapes: guavas with knobbly stems and droopy leaves, paw-paws in thick green bulging clusters, banana palms, limes, and oranges. These were the fruits that the Portuguese had brought to Africa from Brazil, and beyond the avenue they had been arranged into an ornamental garden, with walks marked out by baulks of earth as in the African village fields, and benches in shady places, and a wattle fence at the limits.

There were round mud store-houses and servants' huts and slave quarters, and women cooking at fireplaces scooped out of the earth. Wattle enclosures contained mountains of ground-nuts, and there were many hens and goats. There were tall African trees, and two or three vultures wheeled overhead. But the house was not round and windowless. It was as strangely half-European as the avenue, for although it was built mostly of mud, it had small square windows and stood on piles two or three feet above the ground, and there was a thatched wooden verandah at the front, from which Senhor Voss, surrounded by wives, children, and numerous domestic slaves, held out his arms to greet us.

He was a huge fat black man with the face of a fleshy, gone-to-seed hawk. His eyes rolled and his lower lip was full. He wore a red velvet frock-coat, a white ruffled shirt, and white breeches with no stockings. His feet were in beaded Moorish slippers. His hands were ringed. He filled the compound with sheer vulgar violent strength and the brashness of the self-made, and yet he was very warm and gentle.

He clucked his tongue and said "Oooh!" and "Aaah!" and shook his head at our exertions and called for washing-water, and when I was introduced as Uncle William's nephew, his brute nail-bitten fingers fluttered, and his touch on my shoulder was gossamer-light. The water when it came was deliciously cool, and Senhor Voss and the ladies grunted their approval as we splashed it over our faces. Then refreshments arrived and Senhor Voss chuckled with delight at the comic fuss as we arranged ourselves on the verandah.

The wives were called Senhoras. They were spectacularly dressed in layers of long flouncy petticoats and muslin jackets, and all sorts of gold beads and bangles. Their head-dresses consisted of as many as a dozen coloured handkerchiefs tied in a pyramid, and each wife had a little slave girl who was similarly dressed and wore the additional jewellery that would have weighed her mistress down. So what with the little girls clattering about because of their huge gold anklets, and Senhor Voss being so massive that he overflowed any stool he sat on, and the ladies having to sit in an order of seniority, and Mr. Dingwall's sword getting hooked in their skirts, and Uncle William himself colliding with people and shaking each of the little slave girls by the hand, and Mr. McBride offering his snuffbox and making everyone giggle and sneeze, it was a scene of grotesque politeness, not least because it was conducted in a mixture of languages. It was also the first time in my life that I got drunk.

Palm wine seemed so refreshing that I did not notice how much I had taken until I felt so dizzy that I held on to the verandah rails. My head pounded. It's a fever, I thought.

Mr. McBride stared at me. "Are you not yourself?" he said.

"It's a fever," I said. "I won't die, will I?" He crowed with laughter.

Then I felt a cold sweat and nausea and was sick over the rails. My vomit spattered heavily into the dust. The yellow dogs sniffed at it. "You daft bugger," said Peter Case under his breath. I felt that my growing-up had once again vanished in an instant.

They put me in one of the little rooms off the house's central passage. It had a mixture of mats and European chairs. I lay on a mat and went to sleep, and when I awoke, it was dark. I could hear the conversation still in progress. I felt empty and very hungry. Then Peter came in with a firepot. A palm-oil light glowed through the holes in the pot and cast a soft illumination.

"How are you?" said Peter.

"I'm hungry," I said.

"Look what I've won," he said.

It was a gold collar, and he wore it under his ragged shirt. He'd found the sons of the household playing some gambling game with sticks thrown in the air, and after a calculation of the odds he challenged them and won.

"You can have it in my will," he said, and then his mind raced to another topic. "Hey," he said, "you should see the youngest wife. She didn't come out till it was dark." He lowered his head confidentially. "I think the women live on the other side of the corridor," he said, "and old Vossie picks the one he wants and she crosses over. Know what I mean?" I stood up. "You won't spew again, will you?" said Peter, suddenly alarmed.

"No," I said, "but I'm very hungry."

We went to the verandah, and whatever shame I might have felt was soon wiped away by Senhor Voss, who chuckled and cooed at me like a big, throbbing, understanding dove and every so often during the long night's talk would turn from the men to smile at me; he did the same for each of his women and children, whether they took part in the conversation or not.

The darkness was deep and the stars sharp, and in the glow from the firepots the Senhoras' headgear was here silhouetted and there threw fantastic shadows. The new Fula wife sat quietly on a mat at Senhor Voss's feet. She still wore her plain black tribal robes. She had the most fine, pale, even features and a dreaming smile. Cooking fires flickered in the compound and we could hear the thick laughter of our sailors round one of them. Food arrived in pleasant profusion: the Wolof rice with tomato sauce and vegetables, fish wrapped in green leaves and cooked in palm oil, rich stews of chicken and beef served with little balls of millet flour, an oddly sweet porridge, and all the fruits of the tropical garden. The slaves burned sweet-smelling gums to perfume the air, and sometimes the women sang and clapped.

Mr. Dingwall became highly excited. He seemed intoxicated by our natural human goodwill and the extent to which we were all so pleasantly at ease. He left the verandah and paced the compound. His fists were clenched at his side. His lips moved in an amazed conversation with himself. Once or twice he laughed out loud—an explosion of energy, a child's laugh when it is near to tears. Then he declaimed in Latin the same phrase but with different inflexions to make himself laugh again. He stood outside the verandah and looked up at us. Senhor Voss leaned over and placed his hand on Mr. Dingwall's brow as if to draw out the fears that knotted it. Mr. Dingwall smiled wryly and sat on the steps. He had been gently and respectfully calmed, and when the slaves forgot until we were eating fruit to bring the mashed cassava that should have been eaten with the fish, Senhor Voss similarly forgave them with "Him slowslow domas likeman," which in English meant "Too late but human."

As people do who can speak to each other only in fragments of languages, we went back and forth across the same jokes and topics. The reason for our visit was never mentioned, or how long we intended to stay. Uncle William and Senhor Voss were old hands at the game of who would lose patience first, and played it with relish. They also liked and amused each other because they shared a similar balefully comic interest in life. Senhor Voss had travelled widely; in his youth he had sailed to Lisbon, and he had seen the Cape Verde Islands and the Canaries, and crossed West Africa from the edge of the great desert to the rain forest, and he used grand rhetoric to describe it all, especially the different varieties of women.

His own he treated with expansive delicacy, embracing each Senhora as she retired to bed. When they had all gone he turned to Uncle William and the officers and invited them to take their pick of the female domestics. Our seamen, to judge from the giggles and gasps in the dark, had already made themselves free, but Uncle William declined. Some temptations an officer should always refuse, and some debts he must never incur.

In our own room we had a muttered dissection of the day's events. Mr. Dingwall said that our refusal to have women would puzzle and offend Senhor Voss. In African eyes, a strong man should act strongly and take the spoils. Senhor Voss could be expected now to regard us as indecisive and to act aggressively. "Good," said Uncle William, "for we'll know where we are, and I'll not change my principles for any black villain alive." Mr. McBride chuckled, as he always did at scruples and confusion.

Next morning the domestic slaves gently wakened us and brought us bowls of goat's milk. We arose stiff and aching from the mats, and washed in the water that kept so miraculously cool in the tall, narrow pots. Senhor Voss was already ensconced on the verandah. He wore a fine sprigged cotton dressing-gown and turban, and his fingers and face were slippery from guzzling paw-paws. He rolled his eyes at his own stickiness and invited us to join him. We had hardly done so when a black came up the dirt road from the river with a message from the sailor Williams. Parry was delirious with fever. "At least they stayed with the yawl," said Uncle William, and sent down Mr. McBride.

Senhor Voss saw that we were worried. "No make tieface," he said. Don't frown. He knew an obeah woman who could make a very powerful spell. Then in the same consolatory tone he said, "Domani me andar andar make palaver for King of Wali him house."

Uncle William and Mr. Dingwall stared at each other. We had not even opened our business, but Senhor Voss intended to go up-river to meet the King of Wali. No make tieface, however. We could live in the compound until our sick man was better. "You want stay stay?" This was indeed the challenge and display of sly contempt that Mr. Dingwall had predicted, and Uncle William stoutly rebuffed it.

"Me want make palaver for Smallshaw him credits," he said, giving almost as good as he got. "Me absolutely no stay stay. Just now me go go."

Senhor Voss laughed. He poured water for us to wash our hands. Good. Let palaver commence. He called for his overseer. His voice was loud, to show that business was being done and power exercised, but he still spoke politely. He produced a list of the goods deposited last year, and Uncle William compared it with one from Mr. Smallshaw. In a few quick sentences they agreed that three thousand bars last season was worth some two thousand two hundred and fifty this season. The overseer then brought out six slaves: three men, a boy, and two young women, all in excellent condition. Uncle William agreed to ninety-six bars for the biggest man and eighty for the boy, and after some haggling settled on a grand total of five hundred and fifty bars for the six, subject to Mr. McBride's medical approval.

That done, he made a great show of subtracting five hundred and fifty bars from the total deposit. "Seventeen hundred, isn't it?" he said, turning to me and Peter. "You lads have younger brains than me. It is seventeen hundred, isn't it?" I did the sum in the dirt with a stick. Senhor Voss added that seventeen hundred bars would buy some eighteen to twenty more slaves, depending on age and condition.

"How soon can you supply them?" said Uncle William.

Senhor Voss shook his head, and touched Uncle William's arm most consolingly. We were his dear friends, but we clearly did not understand the state into which the trade had fallen. It could take weeks to assemble twenty strong adults, and even then the price might be ruinous. It was the fault of the kings, of course. "If the truth was known they're the bloody dealers' puppets!" muttered Uncle William, but Senhor Voss was launched by now into a piteous lament for the greed of the river kings, their craving for firearms, and the fact that without the breaking of taboos, and more cynical warfare, the supply of slaves would dry up altogether.

"How few have you got left?" bellowed Uncle William.

Five, complained Senhor Voss, where two years ago he would have had fifty. He had two in his compound at Gillyfree and three here. We went to inspect them. As Senhor Voss said, the men were too old, and the woman too long-breasted, for a client like Smallshaw and Hill.

Uncle William pushed my stick into one of the cooking fires and lit his pipe from the glowing end. "Oh, yes," he said, in his absurd mixture of pidgin and West Riding. "Oh, yes, sweetmouth aside and so on and so forth, me savvy too much your problems. Times are badbad. Plenty man no get slaves. It must be very awkward."

"Frenchman get slaves," said Senhor Voss, and Mr. Dingwall looked warningly at Uncle William. Senhor Voss sighed and shook his turbaned head at the sight of the gold collar around Peter's thin, sun-reddened neck. On the other hand, he conceded, if we took these three slaves he would sell us the two magnificent young women at Gillyfree.

"How much for these three?" said Uncle William.

"Ninety," said Senhor Voss. The old woman slave muttered and dribbled. Senhor Voss proposed that the two young women should be ninety each, which left fourteen hundred and thirty bars outstanding. Uncle William agreed, subject to an inspection of the young women, and asked about the balance.

Senhor Voss looked tragically downcast. He pouted like a giant child. He could not hope to obtain more slaves before he sailed up-river, and he would be gone for weeks. Months, even. What a desolation.

"Not at all," said Uncle William. "Tell him we'll take what's owed in goods."

Mr. Dingwall told him. Senhor Voss unhooded his eyes. He was beaked and cruel. He spat in the dust. "Goods?" he said. "What goods?" His men gripped their muskets. The overseer stared as though we were trapped men. I felt afraid and naked. There were very few of us, and more than twenty of them. Uncle William seemed not to have noticed. He coughed over his pipe and looked about him as though the compound were his own quarterdeck.

At the sight of such composure Senhor Voss shouted, "Hah!" like a man who sees a vision. He hit himself on the head and knocked his turban skew-whiff. He laughed deeply and clasped Uncle William in his arms. How could he have been so foolish? He cuffed the overseer. Imbecile. Why didn't you remind me? Porky Ben. That was it. Porky Ben!

"Porky Ben?" said Uncle William, affecting bewilderment, when he knew perfectly well that Porky Ben was a down-river slave dealer.

"Him good too much," said Senhor Voss, and explained that by one of those coincidences of the good spirits, fourteen hundred and thirty bars happened to be almost exactly the credit that Senhor Voss himself had given to Porky Ben. And by another happy coincidence Porky Ben had gone up-country to meet one of the caravans that at the end of the rainy season set out from the banks of the great inland river to trade across the grasslands to the forests or the sea. Porky Ben's intention was to buy slaves and to travel back with the caravan. Senhor Voss's messengers said that he was not many days away, and on the south bank of the Gambia River. The caravan would go as far as the Bintang Creek to exchange its goods for salt and dried fish. Senhor Voss drew a map in the dust. We were here. There was Bintang. We could sail down-river, meet Porky Ben, and take possession of the slaves.

How did Senhor Voss know that Porky Ben had slaves? "Drum-talk," said Senhor Voss. Uncle William nodded. What proof was there that Senhor Voss was Porky Ben's creditor? Senhor Voss smiled, and announced in a loud voice that he would of course give us a note of hand that Porky Ben had given him. Excellent. But could Porky Ben be sure that the note had been freely transferred, and that we were his new creditors? Not only would Senhor Voss give us Porky Ben's note, he would send messengers to meet and advise him before we did. A glance flickered between Uncle William and Mr.

Dingwall. "Goodgood," said Uncle William, "we'll go with the messengers."

Senhor Voss's eye gleamed appreciatively. It was what he would have done himself, no doubt. Mr. McBride returned and said that the plan was too dangerous. Uncle William said that Senhor Voss had trapped us and we had no choice. Our only hope was to ensure that Porky Ben met his obligations, even if we had to take less than value for our credit. If we waited for him to come to us, we would be deceived or endlessly delayed.

Senhor Voss said that since we had already wasted the cool early morning we should not leave now until past noon. This was good sense; it gave the smiths time to chain up the slaves, and Senhor Voss himself the excuse for more toasts and conversation, during which he pointed out that, as we had no doubt realized ourselves, he owed us slaves to the value of fourteen hundred and thirty bars but was giving us credit with Porky Ben to the value of fifteen hundred. The seventy bars' difference he would take as his commission, to be paid at Bintang or Albreda when the transaction was completed. It was, after all, a further guarantee that we would be fairly treated, and that the word of Senhor Voss was law.

"I am bigman," he said, and the Senhoras fluttered at the power of him. His laugh rumbled in his belly, and he brushed his women's praises aside.

"You're a black scoundrel and that's the truth," muttered Mr. McBride, but when we set off for the river and Senhor Voss waved us farewell, he did so like an emperor who watches soldiers go forth upon his purposes.

Chapter II

Caravan

Uncle William put Mr. McBride in command of the longboat and the slaves, and sent with him Peter Case and the seamen, of whom Parry was very sick; his eyes were filmy and he sweated profusely, his mouth was open and dry and white-caked, his breath rasped, and he was only half-conscious. It was agreed that the *Margaret* would anchor off the mouth of the Bintang Creek, and when our message was received, dispatch the longboat to collect us. Uncle William wrote orders to this effect for Mr. Partridge and gave them to Mr. McBride, who took the tiller with one arm and in the crook of the other held a blunderbuss. Peter sat in the bow with a slow match in his hand and the swivel-gun turned round upon the slaves.

Then the longboat shoved off, and we followed it downstream in a river cutter. The courier from Senhor Voss to Porky Ben wore European breeches and cocked hat, and a blue Wolof caftan. He had a bodyguard of three men with muskets, and laughed delightedly when our leaner craft overtook the yawl, and at the birds we disturbed, and the monkeys who peered at us from the banks. Once again there were few landing places, and in these higher reaches the swamps were not of mangroves but of trees choked by creepers and overtangling, trailing flowers.

After an hour or two our helmsman took us across to where on the south bank little sandy cliffs interrupted the vegetation. We saw the dugouts and the mooring-posts and the waiting donkeys, and knew that we had come to the landing place for the village of Jappani, which lay two or three miles inland, and where we hoped to intercept Porky Ben and the caravan. In the last grey light of evening, when the sun had gone but the darkness had not yet fallen, we approached the village, which was scattered over a flat plain from which grew many enormous baobab and silk cotton trees. There were people still at work in the fields, but they ran away because the sight of white men in the company of Senhor Voss's heavily-armed servants was not a reassuring one. We heard shouts and even some screams before a group of men came out to meet us.

There were a few elders, a dozen warriors with spears, and in the middle the tall, frail headman in an ankle-length white caftan. He greeted us politely and inquired after our business. We said that it was the caravan. The headman regretted that the caravan had spent the previous night in the village and moved out westwards that morning. The courier laughed at him and gestured contemptuously. This angered the warriors, who shouted and waved their spears, but the headman bowed his head.

"What's happening?" said Uncle William.

"They want us to go," said Mr. Dingwall, "but it's nightfall. By custom they should offer us shelter."

The courier shouted at the old headman, who smiled sadly but did not speak.

"We'll make camp in the open," decided Uncle William, and the headman agreed, but insisted that we pass through the village and sleep on the far side, away from the river.

The compounds were higgledly-piggledly and the streets ankle-deep in sand, and the buildings, four or five to each compound, were of sand-coloured mud, roofed in wattle. Wattle fences divided the courtyards, which were built around thick green trees all full of trilling birds. Smoke drifted from cooking fires and there was the smell of the oil. In one compound I saw an old white-bearded man weaving on a knee-frame. His donkey had pushed its watching head through a joint in the palm-frond fence.

Then we came to the plain again, and the warriors escorting us pointed excitedly to a bundle of bark and feathers that hung from a tree. It looked like a weird dead bird but it was obviously man-made. "Mumbo Jumbo!" laughed Senhor Voss's courier. "Mumbo Jumbo!"

"What's Mumbo Jumbo?" I said.

"It's one of their disgusting heathen habits," said Uncle William. "It comes alive in the night to punish adulterous women."

I did not see how that could be, but there was no time to press my point because near some scattered houses and store-places we saw a well, and beyond that a group of large trees in which there was a colony of marabou storks: large, cruel, scrawny birds that could catch snakes in their beaks and slam them to death—the ground below the nests was littered with ripped and spat-out skins. We made camp a little way off, amid dried grass as tall as a man. Uncle William joked as we hobbled our donkeys, but it was to keep our spirits up, for the meeting with the headman and the hostility of the villagers had unsettled us, and away from the artifacts of our own world, the wood and tackle and metal cannon, and the chairs and tables and other engines of superiority, we all three felt vulnerable.

Mr. Dingwall clutched his pistol for security and then withdrew his hand as though the grip were scalding. I noticed that Uncle William watched him as carefully as we watched Senhor Voss's men, and I think that we all felt the immensity of the land mass. We were engulfed by tall, rattly grass, and our clothes and our knowledge and our white skins and instincts seemed of no avail on such dry and dusty earth.

I was stiff from the donkey ride and from having slept on a mat the night before, and I wanted to rest. When the Africans rested they squatted easily on their haunches, or lay on their sides upon the earth, wriggling their hips to find a convenient hollow. But without a chair or a bed or a hammock I was lost. I wanted to lie upon the bosom of the earth, but it rejected me. I was exposed to the elements and at war with them. I could not start a fire without a steel and flint; the Africans made one in a few moments with a stick and a dead branch. From the village came the twitter of birds roosting, the thud of women pounding corn, voices both near and far, goat bleats, and the scuff of a dog's chasing feet. They were the sounds of human settlement, but we were not delighted, because we strained to detect among them the one that would mean danger.

Our fire flared in the dusk. The earth was tawny. The trees were black. Each one seemed to have stood on its spot for ever. Then abruptly there was darkness and we cooked salt fish in the fire and ate ship's biscuits. Uncle William rested awkwardly against a tree trunk. The robes that had shaded the Africans from the sun now wrapped them against the night, but our clothes constricted us. They were stiff with dried sweat and our blankets were rough. As I tried to sleep I heard the tiny buzzing of mosquitoes close by. Occasionally a dog howled. I felt oppressed. Because the heat of the sun was dry I did not sweat in the day unless I exerted myself, but at night it would suddenly burst out. I slept without sleeping. I drifted into wakefulness. My sunburn stung and ached and rubbed raw against the blanket. I thought that I heard strange noises in a dream, but then I awoke and they were real. There were howls and groans all round us, and I saw Uncle William scramble up with his pistol, and people run wildly through the flame-lit dark.

There were screams and rattles and drummings, and the courier shouted, "Mumbo Jumbo!" and capered with glee. Lights bobbed in the tall grass.

Mr. Dingwall, too, shouted, "Mumbo Jumbo!" and set off towards them.

"Come back!" shouted Uncle William, but Mr. Dingwall did not, so we set off ourselves.

We crashed and stumbled through the dry stems towards the shouting and the lights, and suddenly, at the edge of the village, confronted a shaking, whirling, howling creature that was neither man nor any beast that I had seen or imagined. I cried out for fear. Uncle William grabbed me. "It's the nonsense from the tree," he said, and so it was, the bark and feathers come alive with a man inside them, and whirling, whirling between houses to the dusty square where the drums hammered, and the people were as confused and half-awake as I was.

Yet women danced and sang in a shrill frenzy, until the thing in bark and feathers spun through their ranks and seized one of them, and flung her down in the dust, where men stripped her as she screamed. She rolled black and naked in the torchlight, and the thing in bark and feathers danced round her and beat her with a wooden rod. The women dancers screamed for joy. The headman watched with a grave sorrow. Then as suddenly as it had begun, the drumming stopped, the bark and feathers vanished, and the people dispersed.

As they did so, they chattered happily. The naked woman was smeared with dust that had stuck to her frightened sweat, and there were welts all over her. She snivelled and shook, and could not get up until a group of both men and women, smiling with welcome and forgiveness, wrapped clothes around her and gently lifted and caressed her. We walked confusedly to our fire.

Mr. Dingwall was there already. "Mumbo Jumbo!" laughed the courier, but Mr. Dingwall shook and tore at himself, as though to rip something out of his heart. Uncle William held him in his arms. They talked earnestly and wandered into the dark. By then I thought that I could not sleep because of the smell of the ashes, but in fact it was morning, and I was awake.

The new day was cool and miraculous. I was refreshed, yet with the memory of no refreshment. I had the memory of unchanging heat, and I longed for the sun not to rise, or for an English rain shower. I longed to know that today might be different from yesterday, but it was not, and because we had to overtake the caravan we did not stop but urged the donkeys across the grasslands in pounding heat and haze. Once when the view was open we saw vultures and marabous at a kill, a grey, heaving, dusty mass, and the sky full of great birds wheeling down, but mostly the horizon was shut in. Tall grass was all around us, and we drove onwards, despite the protests of our escort, with a European conviction that life and the landscape can change.

We did not speak. Mr. Dingwall wore his superior smile and ignored his torn shirt. My temples ached and my shoulders burned. I had stomach cramps and my bowels were loose. Every hour or so I would have to take my breeches down, waiting if I could for one of the bigger trees to loom up, for under them there were circles of shade around which a breeze really did seem to stir. So I squatted in my misery and our escorts laughed at me. "Him shit pass me too much!" Uncle William nodded encouragingly, but I could see in his eyes the question: Did I have the running flux, or would I right myself in a day or two?

Often the landscape seemed about to open out, but it always closed again, and I rode with my head down, so that all I saw were my own hands in the donkey's mane. I heard the crackle of his hooves on dead leaves and grass, and sometimes I almost swooned. I thought that I had done so when in silence I felt myself fall, but it was only because the donkey had halted and almost thrown me. I looked up and saw an expanse of mud and water and brown marsh grass, and beyond, a horizon of thick green luscious trees. I could hardly believe it. Our escorts were delighted by their own navigation, and turned along the bank of the marsh, which brought us eventually through green leaves to a narrow, muddy-brown creek. There were dugouts to take travellers across, and on the other side, under the trees of a small village, the caravan.

There were about seventy-five merchants and half again as many donkeys. It was in the last heat of the afternoon rest, and many of the merchants were still asleep on their mats, not having bothered to display their wares in so small a place. But their donkeys were unloaded, and spancelled by their forelegs, and in the dark shade other men played a gambling game, laughing as they moved their twigs and stabbed them into the dust.

Elsewhere, merchants in long robes and embroidered caps sat easily on the roots of trees with their goods spread out before them: woven cloths, ivory, beeswax, hides, gold, gums for incense in small bags, vegetable butters, and iron bars. There were civet cats, for their musky perfume, and green parrots and long-tailed monkeys, and the bundles of European goods that the caravan would take back up-country: Manchester cottons and Yorkshire woollens, beads, brass basins, rum, brandy, tobacco, writing-paper, pistols, gunpowder, and flints. Smoke drifted through the shafts of sunlight. Local people stared in wonder. The donkeys stamped their hooves and lashed their tails at the flies, and in the middle of it all, in the place from which escape would be most difficult, were Porky Ben's slaves. They rested against the bundles they carried, and lay at unnatural angles because their necks were linked together by leather thongs.

Porky Ben was asleep ten yards away. His men did not want to wake him, but our courier gestured at Uncle William and insisted. Porky Ben's people were still timid, and so the courier did the deed himself. Porky Ben sat up with an angry splutter. He was a fat, coarse man who, unusually for an African, had very large buck teeth. He must have been self-conscious about them because he immediately clamped his mouth shut and scowled. He swung his arms and barked orders at the courier. The courier laughed, as though Porky Ben were the best joke he'd seen since leaving Senhor Voss.

Porky Ben squealed with rage and slapped the courier in the face.

The courier swung back at him, but Porky Ben blocked the blow, whereupon the courier walked away in a sulk. Porky Ben sighed and frowned and beckoned for us to join him. He sat down on a tree root with his legs splayed open, and so did we. He grinned a vast, protruding grin and touched us all in a reassuring way.

The courier turned back from his sulk and shouted, "Mumbo Jumbo! Mumbo Jumbo!" into Porky Ben's ear as loudly as he could, so that the merchants looked up and began to smile and take notice. Porky Ben tried to ignore the courier and to continue his conversation with Uncle William, whom he invited to inspect the healthiest, best-proportioned, and most hard-working slaves we would ever see in our lives. The courier would not be put off, however, and continued to shout and point at Porky Ben.

Porky Ben's reply was to grab a stick, hold it in front of himself like an erect penis, and make blatant motions in the direction of the courier. That brought bellows of laughter and applause, and the courier became involved in individual arguments as to why Porky Ben was or was not ridiculous. The noise drew the attention of a tall, sombre man in white robes and a many-coloured woven cap, who pushed through the people and by his very presence brought the laughter to silence. He nodded at Uncle William and introduced himself as the leader of the caravan.

The leader spoke quietly to Porky Ben, who answered in a manner which implied that whereas he and the leader may have been equals, the courier was merely an inferior nuisance, a buzzing dung-fly to be brushed away. The leader agreed to the extent that he asked the courier to stand back. The courier shrugged and obeyed. Uncle William hissed at Mr. Dingwall to explain, and Mr. Dingwall said that, so far as he could tell, the courier had made a joke of something that had happened when the caravan halted at Jappani: Porky Ben had seduced a woman there, and unfortunately she was not a domestic slave, which would have been permissible, but the respectable third wife of an important member of the headman's own family. It was she whom we had seen publicly chastised by the Mumbo Jumbo.

As the leader of the caravan grasped the story he became angry, and men who had laughed now seemed to take it more seriously because the success of a caravan largely depended upon the goodwill between its leader and the headmen of the villages on the route.

A headman was chosen by the local king from the richest and most important family in a village, and the council of elders consisted of the headman's relatives and equals. Porky Ben had thus not only endangered the relations between Jappani and this particular group of travelling merchants, he had humiliated the headman and insulted his family and his hospitality.

There were shouts and accusing gestures, but Porky Ben was brazen; when someone mimicked his ridiculously protruding grin of defiance, he rushed to the man's goods and rummaged through them, and with yelps and roars produced muskets and Birmingham basins, and some cheap tin mugs with handles. He threw them in the dirt and stamped his foot and shouted the same words over and over: "That's what you want. That's what you want. How do you get them?"

He dragged one of his slaves to her feet and shoved her down again with a snort, as if to say: I buy them with this cheap animal. You may think you barter beeswax for muskets, but I bought the muskets with one of these animals. So don't tell me how to behave. Then he banged his chest and snuffled like a boar and glared round. The other men were overawed, and for all his dignity the leader did not know what to say. His face was like that of the headman in the torchlight, proud but bewildered, authoritarian but sad.

Porky Ben turned his back on them. He giggled and showed his buck teeth. "This man's a rascal," said Uncle William. Porky Ben coughed and threw himself once again into the posture of the fearsome but worldly negotiator. He asked us to explain the exact nature of our business and snapped his fingers for the courier to confirm the details. Then he leaned against a tree in an attitude of deep thought.

Mr. Dingwall raised his eyebrows at Uncle William, who signalled patience and said, "What's really ridiculous is that the headman at Jappani's a Muslim." I stared at him. "So Mumbo Jumbo be buggered," he said.

"I'm sorry, Uncle William," I said, "I don't understand."

Uncle William took out his pipe. "Tom," he said, keeping a weather-eye on Porky Ben, "silly women might believe that a spirit inhabits the costume of the Mumbo Jumbo, but a Muslim or a Christian doesn't believe in spirits, does he?"

I didn't know what Muslims believed. I thought they were heathen sinners, and I had been surprised to find them so calm and serious.

"Take it from me," said Uncle William, "the headman always

knows it's a fraud and so does everybody else. If they weren't savages they'd not put up with it, would they?"

"I don't know," I said, for it had been very obvious to me that there was a man inside the bark and feathers. I had even noticed a scar on one of his legs. How could the women have failed to do the same? If they knew it was a man, why did they accept the idea of a spirit? I looked at the black faces around me. I felt afraid. I did not understand any of them.

Then I remembered the end of the ritual, when the woman's friends had lifted her up, and clothed and embraced her. There had been no peace in the face of Mrs. Patterson when we left her to howl on the shore at Albreda, and only mockery in the voices of our crew when Morton and Taylor were released after their flogging. I opened my mouth because I had a spate of questions, but Uncle William checked me.

"Look out," he said, and Porky Ben turned, and with an enormous sigh and shrug announced that the good name of Smallshaw and Hill was safe with him, and that he would be overjoyed to honour Senhor Voss's debt to us. So with a shaking of heads and a good deal of haggling over the price of individual slaves, it was agreed. We dismissed Senhor Voss's men with a gift of cheap spirits, and for two days travelled in the caravan to Bintang Creek.

Chapter 12

Ambush

It was a journey of immemorial pace. It began each dawn, when there was a lightness in the sky more like the moon than the sun. Then the lightness spread, and the land was grey-brown and the trees dark silhouettes, and men and donkeys would stir, and by the time the small clouds were pink the merchants would have said their prayers and with clinks and clatters and hee-haws but not much conversation the caravan would be on the move. From first light to the appearance of the sun's pale disc was about an hour. There was no early breeze. The creeks were flat and gave perfect dark reflections. The eastern sky was yellowish, and until the sun became too bright to look at, there was another hour of miraculous freshness and stillness, of grey and brown and delicate shadows, of untired peace, of warmth left by the centuries past that was a hopeful warmth, not jaded and exhausted.

Egrets rose in whirring flocks from the mangroves. They thrilled me, even though I did feel sick and miserable. On the grasslands damp early mist hung low. It trailed like scarves through the palm trees. Often I could not tell which was mist and which the smoke of early-morning fires of grass and thorn. The orange flames had a marvellous brightness. Cattle were in overnight rings, each roped to a central stake. Women were at the wells. Ant hills made a contrasting statuary with the trees.

After another hour or so the caravan would halt. The slaves, who as well as being roped together had to carry bundles on their heads, would lie gratefully down. The merchants would eat, and then unroll their mats and rest during the worst heat. If the halting place was a village where they intended to spend the night, they would unpack their wares and make a market under the trees, but if it was not, they would in the late afternoon set off again and travel almost until dark. Throughout the journey the red dust covered their ankles and seeped up their calves and got inside the collars of our European shirts, so at the final resting place came the ritual of washing before prayer, and then the making of fires and the evening meal.

The leader knew the country well. The routes had been handed down from father to son, so that as the heat became unbearable a place of shade would beckon, and in the evening there would be water and fuel. It was with the caravan that I first heard lions roar in the darkness beyond the fires, and the sound made my already aching stomach quiver.

Once, during the day, the whole procession made a detour of respect around an extraordinary sight. There was an enormous hollow baobab tree and in front of it the half-eaten, half-dried-up corpse of a man in a mess of torn wrappings and feathers. The griots, or praise-singers, of the Mandinkas had always resisted the Muslim religion, and always had a reputation for loose living. It was said that if they were buried in the earth the crops would fail, and if they were thrown in the sea the fish would rot, so when a griot died his body was put in a hollow tree, and this one had been dragged out by hyenas.

"The anger of a poet," cried Mr. Dingwall. "May his song live on!" He peered more closely at the remains than any of us. "Did you see where his brains were?" he said. "I think a vulture ate them."

By then I was very weak, and Uncle William walked beside me and held me on the donkey's bare back. On his advice I ate nothing during the journey, and drank only sips of brandy. More than once I sobbed as the donkey jogged me, and I was so lightheaded that when we made camp on the second night I had no notion of our surroundings.

Happily, when I awoke the next morning I knew that the spasm had left me. I was tired and empty, and my limbs ached, but I no longer had a piercing headache or the pain in my stomach. I smiled at Uncle William and he nodded. "You've a stocky build," he said. "I thought you'd be right." Porky Ben displayed his grin and applauded. Several of the other merchants greeted me, and one of them offered me a bowl of pure clean boiled rice, which Uncle William said I should eat. I took a few mouthfuls.

We were camped at a crossroads village near Bintang Creek. Beyond the crossroads were rice fields and palm trees, and then the creek itself. There was a landing place at a break in the mangroves, with the usual dugouts and river cutters, and that was where Porky Ben had a small compound. He explained that the creek was the boundary between two kingdoms: Kiang, where we were now, and on the far bank, Fogni. Fogni had been for centuries a territory contested by the Mandinkas and a fiercely independent people called the Jolas, with whom the Mandinka King of Fogni was usually in dispute, not least because if the Jolas dealt with Mandinkas at all, they looked not to the King but to his overlord, the Mansa of Cabon.

Like the other important dealers Porky Ben lived on the north bank of the Gambia River, but he had been born in Fogni, of a Portuguese mulatto trader and a local woman, and he regarded it as his area of personal influence. He liked to shake his head over the King's peccadilloes, and to recount the advice he had given him, a line of reminiscence in which Uncle William, head cocked and pipe smoking like a chimney, was not slow to prompt him, and to chuckle afterwards.

When the caravan itself turned north to Bintang town, we sold our donkeys to pay our taxes to the leader, and installed ourselves in Porky Ben's compound, where there were always some of his men and we could more easily guard the slaves. Porky Ben sent a cutter to find the *Margaret*, and word came back in the person of Mr. Bruce himself, who insisted on wearing his sea-boots on land, which made him clump along like a very disgruntled giraffe. But our spirits rose at the sight of him, and we were eager for his news.

The *Margaret* was indeed anchored off the mouth of the creek, and so were two Frenchmen, our old friend and another.

Mr. Partridge had done some useful trading, and the carpenter's work on the ship was well advanced. The longboat had returned to the ship and been sent away again to cut the last timber, but would come for us as soon as possible, with the bosun in command. The seaman Parry had died of his fever, and so had one slave. Three slaves were ill. Mossop had been released from his irons on the promise of good behaviour. The ordinary seaman Donovan had met with an accident on shore and broken his arm. The she-cat was palpably pregnant. Mr. McBride had paid another professional call on Governor Bayliss of James Island, and the Governor had sent word that he expected more English ships, but so far only one had arrived, from Bristol, and she had not stayed long. The extraordinary news Mr. Bruce saved until that quiet hour on the verandah when we had eaten our rice and sat by the light of firepots over brandy and tobacco. It concerned Mrs. Patterson and Sergeant Wood.

Governor Bayliss, like Uncle William, had considered that the best punishment for Mrs. Patterson was a night in Albreda. He reckoned that the French officers would lock her up in the handling-station sooner than risk trouble over a white woman, and this had proved to be what happened. Mrs. Patterson was set free at first light and waited on the foreshore. The English sent a boat for her. She was bedraggled, quiet, and crushed. She apologized to the Governor, and when invited to explain herself, shrugged and asked after Mossop. She was told that he was in irons. "I'm awful sorry," she said. "Can that be passed on?" The Governor said that boats from the *Margaret* would be calling at the fort and she should pass it on herself, which she did, a bit haltingly, to Mr. Bruce. Mr. Bruce advised her to brazen out the jeers of our boat crews and look lively.

He was none the less curious about her, and learned from the Governor that she came to be on James Island because she had married her husband, Patterson, to escape the drudgery of service in a Scottish farmhouse. When Patterson was discharged from the Regular Army he enlisted with the Royal African Company and she sailed to Africa with him. After eighteen months he died, and so did their child. Mrs. Patterson took up with Wood, who was promoted Sergeant in Patterson's place.

On the *Margaret* Mr. Bruce heard rumours that he knew to be false about Mrs. Patterson's night in Albreda. One said that she had given two or three Frenchmen her favours, another that she had refused them all but had danced naked, a third that she had spent the night in the open with an African rower. When after a few days he saw her again, she had cleaned herself up and put a ribbon in her hair, but she looked haggard and older. She could be seen to work hard for

Wood, washing his shirt, mending, cooking for him and his men. She kept her mouth shut no matter how cruelly she was taunted, and she was obedient when Wood shouted at her. She nodded respectfully at Mr. Bruce when he bade her good day as he shoved off in the punt.

That afternoon, in the high blue haze, and with a school of dolphins leaping in the river, Wood went to the little foreshore behind the slave quarters and stabbed himself with his bayonet. He shoved it into his sloppy belly and tried to rip himself apart, but the pain was too great and he lost his nerve.

He drew the blade out, and some of his guts came glistening with it. He tried to stuff them back and then fell on his knees.

He was carried to the barracks, where although he was numbed by the shock of what he had done to himself, he was able to explain that the day before he had heard one soldier repeat to another the story about Mrs. Patterson and the African rower. He had not faced Mrs. Patterson herself, he could not check with the French because they had already sailed down-river, and he was too proud to challenge the soldiers. For twenty-four hours he went about his duties in the stifling heat of the courtyard, until his thoughts became intolerable and he stabbed himself.

Mrs. Patterson was abruptly her wild self again. She stood at the door of the barracks and called Wood every foul name under the sun. But he was too confused and in too much pain to understand, so she sat on a chair outside until at nightfall he died. Mrs. Patterson spat on the white mess of his body.

Then she went to the Governor. He said that he would send her back to London. She shrugged but did not speak. She rummaged among his clothes for a black neckcloth, and tied it in her hair for mourning. He did not stop her, and still she did not speak, not to him or to any other man.

She spoke to other women and did chores for them. She fed the women slaves, but never the men, and not even the boy children. She had a thin smile, and there was grey in her hair that had not been there before. No one had the courage to jeer at her, and very few to meet her eye. Yet everyone talked about her.

It was not their fault that she hated men. It was her own fault. What did she expect to happen if she opened her legs to the likes of Mossop? As for Wood's death, any man could be driven by jealousy and the sun, even a stupid, fat . . . But by then, for all my fascination in what Uncle William and Mr. Bruce said, and my realization that Mr. Dingwall had said nothing, their voices were a lullaby and I slept.

Next morning, after my breakfast of rice and a mouthful of brandy, I walked along the creek. I thought again about Mrs. Patterson's fierce distress, and about Sergeant Wood, and Parry, and my father and mother. It seemed strange that people I had known were dead while I was alive. I wondered what it was like to be dead, for I was still sure that it was a state, and not oblivion. My own senses were very awake.

It was low water and the mangrove roots were exposed. Their reflections gave a curious three-dimensional effect, as though there were a black hole between the bank and the smooth, greasy, silent, sliding surface of the creek. There were many dead leaves upon it. I saw a kingfisher and heard the calling of doves. Faintly I heard sounds at the landing place, and beyond them, because I was so open to impressions, I detected the longboat before it came into view. I heard a banging of wood and an English pitch of voice, and then the boat appeared, gliding under still sails, breaking the grey-green surface.

There were Peter Case and the bosun's solid bulk, and there were Uncle William and Mr. Dingwall and Mr. Bruce squelching on to the foreshore. After some cheery orders our men neatly backed the sails and cast a line around one of the mooring-poles. "Hey up! Hey up!" the bosun shouted. The day was clear, as everything is those few hours before the heat haze, but there were none of Porky Ben's people to be seen. I wondered why not. I saw Uncle William stop at the edge of the mud as Peter Case and the bosun jumped down to join him. Peter held another mooring-rope. Then I saw Uncle William turn in an agony of slowness and dismay, and I knew that he was looking for me.

I was fifty yards away, squatting on the gunwale of a dugout where the foreshore was engulfed by mangroves. Before I could stand or wave there was a volley of musket shots. Mr. Bruce sat down and the bosun began to shout.

There were more shots and then Porky Ben's people ran out of the compound with muskets and the six-foot-long reed spears. I saw a spearhead sticking out of Peter Case's back. The bosun was behind him, and he put one hand on Peter's shoulder and with the other pulled the rest of the shaft through and then lifted Peter up into the boat. Blood ran down his arms. He gripped the gunwale to haul himself up but fell backwards. He must have been shot. I saw two crocodiles splash into the far side of the water.

One of the seamen in the longboat fired a pistol. Someone cut the mooring-rope and the longboat began to drift away.

Uncle William had seen me, and he and Mr. Dingwall ran towards me. The bosun had scrambled ashore dripping wet, but Porky Ben's people surrounded him. One fired a musket and missed. A second man fired and the bosun was hit. Then three or four men stabbed at him with spears.

I started to shove out the canoe. When Mr. Dingwall reached me I saw blood on his sleeve. Uncle William still had not fired his pistol. Then he remembered it, turned, and aimed very carefully at his pursuers. They checked. Uncle William fired. One man went down and the others backed off. We floated out in the canoe.

There was one paddle, and Uncle William worked it furiously. Then he stopped because he was out of breath. My heart pounded and all three of us gasped and retched for air. The canoe sat heavily in the water. I wanted to laugh. I felt wildly happy and excited. I tried to pick up the pistol but my grip trembled and wouldn't close.

On the foreshore a man ran into the water to fire at us. I knew he would miss and he did. The whole ambush had lasted about half a minute.

Porky Ben's people were as dazed as we were, and they walked up and down the foreshore and picked up their hurt comrade, and stared at the corpses of the bosun and Mr. Bruce. Then one of them realized that the longboat was yawing in midstream because there were not enough fit men to work it. They started to shout and run for their dugouts, and Mr. Dingwall laughed like a wheezy bellows when he saw that they were arguing about which to go after first, us or the longboat.

This brought Uncle William back into action. He paddled as hard as he could towards the tangled Fogni bank. Mr. Dingwall was still laughing and then he gasped, "They're after us."

"How many rowers?" said Uncle William. They had four. We had the start but must inevitably be overtaken.

The one chance in our favour was that we were just about to take a bend and for a few minutes the pursuit would lose sight of us. Uncle

William awaited the moment, and when Mr. Dingwall shouted, "Now!" he drove the dugout at the barricade of mangroves. As we crashed into them a shock of birds flew up into the air.

The minutes that followed were desperate: now scrambling, now climbing, now crashing through leaves, now tripping, now sinking to the knees in foul mud, now observing, without feeling the pain of them, cuts and bruises and rents in our clothes. We heard the pursuit behind us. They fired a shot and the ball whacked and pattered through the branches. I sobbed out loud with fear.

Yet for me, being smaller, it was easier to scramble through, and miraculously there was higher, harder ground and daylight a few yards away. The pursuit fired again. I forced myself to concentrate on the deliberate, thoughtful extrication of each limb. We had to travel about ten yards, but it seemed like ten miles.

Mr. Dingwall was the first to get through the branches and scrabble on all fours up the hard earth of the true bank. I followed him and lay on my face. The soil was hard, dusty, and ridged. The grass was crackly and strewn with dead and bleached palm fronds.

"God bless us!" I heard Uncle William say. I could see his head and shoulders still in the mangroves. He was holding his pistol well up and trying to reload with calmness. There was another shot from the pursuing dugout. Uncle William checked his movements. I thought that he had been hit, but it was done to compose himself. He clicked back the hammer.

"Your flint's soaking wet," gasped Mr. Dingwall.

"How much do you bet I misfire?" said Uncle William.

"Fifty thousand guineas," said Mr. Dingwall.

"Done," said Uncle William, and fired. I heard a cry and then a clatter and splash, and Uncle William lunged up at the bank. "Run!" he said, and set off.

I have never in my life known such agony. At first the heat of the burgeoning sun upon my wet clothes was pleasant, but then it was torture. They chafed. My head pounded. My tongue swelled. I vomited up my rice breakfast and it went all over me. I fell down. I pleaded to be allowed to stop. I was picked up and thrown forward. I was blinded by sweat. I stumbled over the earth baulks of dry rice fields and felt tall grass whip and stab me. Power drained from my legs. I could not feel the ground. I reeled. I felt myself lifted and thrown down again, and I lay on my side with the taste of vomit in my mouth. I spewed again, but all I brought up was misery and frothy liquid. I was on my hands and knees like an animal.

I turned my head and saw that Mr. Dingwall was unconscious. He had thrown away his coat, and his shirt was soaked in blood. I looked for Uncle William. He was on his haunches, sobbing for air. We were in the shade of dense foliage at the edge of a rice field, and all round us were tall, grim, naked warriors, their faces cicatriced, their chests and arms festooned with amulets.

Chapter 13

A Pistol and Palm Wine

My next distinct memory is that I awoke after dark in the glow of a firepot. I lay on a mat in a round, mud-walled hut. The roof thatch was in shadow. A girl was watching me. The oil light gleamed on her skin. She had little sharp naked breasts, and when she saw that I was awake, she darted out.

I felt very calm. I lifted my head to look around the hut. Mr. Dingwall lay near me. He was asleep and his breath was ragged. His arm was bandaged with a piece of torn shirt, and like me he was naked except for a piece of cloth thrown over him.

After a moment or two Uncle William appeared. He was wearing brass-buckled shoes, a piece of cotton wrapped round him like a skirt, and his tricorn hat. He was smoking his clay pipe. "How are you?" he said very earnestly. He was bent double because of the low doorway. I burst out laughing.

"What's so comical?" he said, and sat down. His fleshy, hairy stomach bulged over the top of his skirt.

"Why are you wearing your hat?" I said.

"It keeps off the insects," he said, "and what's more, the blacks call it very smart." He tipped it forward and chuckled, which made him cough. "Blasted pipe," he said, and waved his hand to disperse the suffocating fumes. He peered at Mr. Dingwall. "Poor old Henry," he said. "Poor old Henry lad." He sighed and cleared his throat and spat through the door opening.

"Where are we?" I said.

"Among the Jolas," he said, and proceeded to describe our situation.

We had run for our lives with one pistol, six bullets, a powder flask, and the clothes we stood up in. They were now torn and useless, and the Jolas had confiscated the pistol but to show their goodwill had left us the powder and shot. We had to assume that the longboat was captured. We did not know why Porky Ben's people had attacked us or what else they had done. Porky might even have sent his cutters to attack the *Margaret* herself, or he might have acted as he did because he had learned that there was open warfare between Britain and France. We did not know. All we knew for certain was that we had outrun our pursuers, that a bullet had furrowed Mr. Dingwall's arm and caused him to lose a lot of blood, and that the Jolas would now put us to ransom.

"How d'you mean?" I said.

"Ransom," said Uncle William. "It's always done with officers. They've sent messengers to Mr. Partridge."

"What happens in the meantime?" I said.

Uncle William did not answer.

"You mean we're prisoners?" I said.

Uncle William watched me through clouds of tobacco smoke.

"Will they kill us?" I said.

"Not yet," said Uncle William. "If we're dead we're not worth the ransom, are we?"

He puffed at his pipe. There was a warm trust between us. We were naked and in a mud village on low-lying, fever-ridden ground. We had lost touch with our companions, and our own country seemed a lifetime away, and yet during the days that followed, as we waited for the Jola messengers to return, we were strangely—and in the case of Mr. Dingwall, fatally—content.

From the fields the village was like a fortress that showed the hostile world a blank, mud-walled face. Inside, its compounds were arranged round trees to give shade. There were circular wooden cages for goats, and chicken-houses on stilts. There were tall frames with dry thorns piled on top. Wattle fences shut out animals and protected vegetable patches, and made little private areas behind the houses. Old men could gossip in the village meeting place in the middle of the street and still hear indoor laughter and the rustling of chickens and goats, or they could rest in seclusion and still hear children and the *thud-thud* of women pounding corn.

Posts stuck in the earth dissuaded wandering animals from entering our own compound, which consisted of four or five buildings, vegetable patches, clumps of vivid green guavas and paw-paws, and a big wattle-fenced area at the back for cattle.

Our host and jailer was an old man whose hands were stiff with rheumatism. His eyes would slowly shut and then open again with difficulty. His jaw and features must have been very fine before he lost his teeth and his cheeks collapsed. He spoke quietly but the young men respected him. He did not often leave the compound, and would send us small gifts of food and drink by one of the youths who were always there to ensure that we did not escape; not that we were restless to do so, because Mr. Dingwall was weak and I was as happy as a sand-boy in the company of our girl nurse, whom Mr. Dingwall called Fourfarthings, after the music of her actual name.

On the moors I had often imagined a sister, a tomboy who ran with me across the peat, and fished for sticklebacks, and did not displease my father. I talked to her even though she did not exist, and sometimes I was jealous of her, although I was sure that I was superior because one day I would be a man.

She teased me for that, and darted from hassock to hassock so nimbly that when I tried to catch her I stumbled into the black slime between. She was slight and pale like my mother, with curly auburn hair and peals of laughter, yet when the clouds shifted and sunlight raced across the moor she took my hand and we both gazed in wonder.

That was my dream, which in the Jola village came outlandishly true in the person of Fourfarthings and the bond between us. From her first giggle at the sight of Uncle William's tricorn and cloth skirt she was the sister of my imagination. My face was white and sun-sore and hers was black and ritually-scarred, and neither of us spoke a word of the other's language. Yet we shared perfect days.

When we awoke, the thorn and dung fires smelled sharp. The women went to the wells and the older men and boys drove the cattle to the open grassland. Smoke drifted like mist through the palm trees.

When the young men and women who did the heavy labour went to the fields, Fourfarthings and I walked with them, and clapped our hands and swayed our shoulders to the rise and fall of their mouth-music.

Later, in fiercer sun, we sought the shade around the washing-pools, where the unmarried girls chattered as they worked, and in the heat of the day we sprawled asleep like two puppies. When we awoke we were delighted again by the simple colours of the compound: green leaves, blue sky, the sand and ochre of the earth and houses, the patterns of different kinds of straw fencing. When the heat lessened, the noises of domestic work and children were all round us.

Then Fourfarthings bathed Mr. Dingwall's wound, and the old women, whose rule within the compound was absolute, came to inspect us. They grunted with satisfaction at our improved condition, and nodded at Fourfarthings. Uncle William doffed his hat to them. Fourfarthings giggled. Uncle William made a mock bluster, at which the old women cackled with laughter. We all joined in, even Mr. Dingwall, because of the joy Fourfarthings made us feel.

Then the women went away and Fourfarthings sat with us, and in the slanting light of evening the cattle came home through a haze of red dust. Chickens strutted. The yellow dogs reappeared, and so did a man with one foot at a right-angle to his leg; because he could not do heavy work he supervised the fermentation of the palm sap into wine.

Once Fourfarthings took me and a Jola boy whom Uncle William called Nipper to watch a colony of green monkeys as they came out for their sport, and afterwards we went to a creek pool and splashed in the lukewarm water with much laughter and ducking of each other, and no thought for the differences between our skins and bodies; but mostly we were happy to sit with Uncle William and Mr. Dingwall, and to accept the beauty of the ending day.

I felt a kinship with everything, with the dainty white egrets, and the motes of dust that the sun illumined. My limbs tingled. I was sure that the light itself had feelings, as I did, and I knew that Fourfarthings shared them; I knew it from the smile that passed between us, and even Uncle William was inspired one evening to some of his most comically-heartfelt rhetoric. His theme was the fact that our escape from death, and the simple kindness of the Jolas, had made him aware yet again of how little was needed to make sense of life.

"A helping hand," he said. "That's all we need in this world, a helping hand; black or white, what's the difference?" He slapped and scratched at the insect bites on his stomach. "I suppose that another name for it would be human love," he said. "In imitation of Jesus Christ."

Mr. Dingwall stared in silence. There were long shadows and the leaves had golden haloes.

"What is happiness?" said Uncle William. "What does make men superior to the beasts? It's when we entrust our own weaknesses to those of somebody else. That's what it is. It's nothing to do with being top dog."

He cleared his throat and shook his jowls, as though awestruck by the vastness of his own imagination.

"It's very easily forgotten, is all that," he said. "Although not by women. Women always remember, don't they, damn their eyes. Even this girl Fourfarthings. Look at her. Look at that Mrs. Patterson. She knew the simple truth. I suppose the reason's childbirth and so on and so forth."

I looked from one to the other. Fourfarthings grinned. Mr. Dingwall was silent and would not catch my eye. Uncle William jabbed the air with a powerful forefinger.

"But then we all resist the truth, don't we?" he said. "We all know that we should treat other men as brothers, but we don't, do we? We betray them and they betray us. But that," he went on, with a breathtaking twist in the argument, "is just the very reason why a Christian is superior to a black. A Christian knows where the fault is. A Christian knows that every man must wrestle with his own original sin. That's the very truth, Henry, to which I've sought to bring you."

The man with the bent foot hobbled past, very gravely. I thought of the slave Howler, chained like living evil in the darkness of the *Margaret*'s hold. Mr. Dingwall looked tired. He had a ghost of a smile. Uncle William persisted.

"Of course these Jolas are very happy," he said. "Of course they are. But what else have they known? They've never been tempted, have they? They've never known despair."

By now the magic had gone. The light was flat and grey, and from somewhere in the village we heard drumming: a hard, dry, rattling rhythm, fading and then intensifying. There seemed to be an answering bustle of people. There were occasional whoops and shouts.

Uncle William looked sharply at Mr. Dingwall, but Mr. Dingwall had closed his eyes. Uncle William went to shake him but decided against it. The drums stopped. Uncle William puffed at his pipe.

The women at the cooking fires stared at us and whispered. Four-farthings nodded her head. She smiled and pointed and jabbered excitedly. "I think the messengers have come back," said Uncle William, and so they had, and as the light thickened and the flowers that had glowed very brightly in the first dusk drooped and faded, and the fruit-bats flickered overhead, we were summoned to the council meeting.

There was a planked frame in the middle of the main street. The oldest men sat on the frame and the rest on the earth nearby. There was a fire burning. The trees were a washed-out green and then in a few moments black, so it was in firelight that our old host introduced us to the meeting, and stood at our side throughout. A libation was poured, and amulets clutched and shaken. Uncle William raised his hat and said, "Amen!" The two messengers stood beside the fire. One had a musket, and the other a javelin and shield.

There were twenty or thirty members of the council, and all were elderly. Other people watched and reacted, both men and women, but they did not take part, except for one man whom Uncle William later identified as the spokesman for the heavy-labour gang. There did not seem to be a particular headman, and since they were all naked it was impossible to tell at once if one was more important than another. Three or four of them talked at once, and then after a silence our host intimated in pidgin that Uncle William might question the messengers himself.

Uncle William raised his hat again; he turned to salute the people behind him as well as those in front, and said, "What Partridge him been speak yesterday?"

The messengers shook their heads. Partridge him no been speak. Partridge him been go.

"Go?" said Uncle William.

"Him sabby just now you dieman. Him been go for Company him house."

"God bless us!" said Uncle William. "He's been told we're dead, and sailed to Fort James."

Mr. Dingwall giggled.

"Shrewdly done, though," said Uncle William, "to use the cover of the battery."

"Why didn't they go after him?" I said.

Uncle William pressed the point. The messengers said that as they travelled along the Bintang Creek they were intercepted by Porky Ben's people, who showed them the captured longboat, and the clothes that had been torn from Mr. Bruce, Peter Case, and the others before their bodies were mutilated and thrown into the creek. They had been forced to watch a palaver at which our slaves were sold to the French, and then had been harangued by Porky Ben himself. He had advised the Jolas to hand us over to him so that he could get the ransom both for us and for the longboat. In return, although he could not give the Jolas a share of the ransom, he would speak on their behalf to the King of Fogni, who on Porky's advice had concluded a treaty with the French. The implication was that unless the Jolas met Porky's demands they would be raided for slaves.

"Fat bastard!" roared Uncle William, and threw his hat into the dust. "I'd snap his teeth off! That's what I'd do! Snap 'em!"

He glared at Mr. Dingwall, who winced. Uncle William retrieved his hat.

"Porky's done all this on his own, you know, Henry. There's no war. The French have been manoeuvred as much as we have. Porky's greedy. He wants power. He's killed men just to thumb his nose at Voss and get a few more bars for those slaves."

He slammed his hat on. Sand fell out of it and made him blink. Mr. Dingwall giggled again.

"Eh?" said Uncle William. Mr. Dingwall flicked his eyebrows at the Jolas.

"Ah!" said Uncle William, and peered at them. They stared back, wide-eyed, in a stricken silence. The fire crackled and sparks whirled up. There were deep shadows.

"Henry," said Uncle William, "I think that if Porky does get hold of us we can wave Smallshaw's credits farewell."

He flung out his arms and spoke very cheerfully, as though the solution were one that a child could understand. If the Jolas valued their independence, which they did, and if they wanted the firearms that would protect it, they should resist Porky Ben. They should consult their other villages and send an ambassador with beeswax and honey to the Mansa of Cabon, to ask him to influence in their favour his Mandinka vassal, the King of Fogni. Above all, they should ask Ben Riley to negotiate our ransom; he was the only English mulatto dealer on the Bintang Creek, and Uncle William sang his praises.

There was another long silence.

"Actually," said Uncle William, "I'd feel safer if I had the pistol as well as the ammunition."

"Where is it?" said Mr. Dingwall.

"In his hut," said William, indicating our host.

Then, without warning, the council broke up. The old men drifted silently away; because we did not know what had been decided we were uneasy, until at first light we realized from the excitement in the compound and the way in which Fourfarthings drew our attention to it that the arguments were being restated for the benefit of wives and relatives. It was the ordinary person's chance to speak, and the village buzzed with discussions.

Uncle William was convinced that his good humour could influence them in our favour, and that if he followed the flow of debate it would lead him to the men of power, the ones whom Ben Riley must bribe when the moment arrived.

That there was no power in the sense that he or Governor Bayliss or Senhor Voss or the King of Fogni understood the term never occurred to him, and with a guard and Fourfarthings at his elbow, he made sure that his bare-torsoed, tricorned figure attracted warmth and attention wherever it appeared: under the shade of a tree in a wattle-fenced field, or with a child in its arms at the angle of some compound.

But he was none the wiser, until late in the afternoon our old host poured an offering of milk over the stone that none of us was allowed to sit on because it was the abode of the household spirits, and very painfully, supported by two younger men, walked to one of the shrines that hid among wet and muddy groves at the heads of tributary creeks. "He's gone to consult his ancestors," said Mr. Dingwall, "because his ancestors speak to the spirits." Uncle William set off at once, and so did the guard and Fourfarthings and I, but Mr. Dingwall declined.

At the edge of the grove Uncle William, who had run out of tobacco and puffed at foul-smelling grasses, would have shoved through the tangled thorn and creepers, but the guard jabbered and Fourfarthings took our wrists and gently turned us away.

"She's a good lass, is this," said Uncle William as we ambled back to the village. "I think what they've got there is masks hanging from the trees. It made my flesh creep, actually."

When our host returned from his devotions there was a meeting of the council to which we were not invited. It decided to resist Porky and to send messengers to Ben Riley. They set off next morning, loping through the veils of mist—much to Uncle William's delight, because he was sure now that our own host and his ancestors were the bribable power in the village.

"No matter what anyone says, Henry, no matter what whoever you care to name pretends, every government in the world from St. James's to this flaming village is the same. A handful of people make decisions and the rest accept them."

It was our morning stroll through the village. The sand of the streets flooded our shoes, and we stopped to empty them and watch a woman drawing water from the well. She faced it and with big, free, upright motions of her arms swept the fibre rope first above one shoulder and then the other. Her breasts bounced up and down. Uncle William stared at them. Mr. Dingwall lifted his face to the breeze.

"What it is with these countries here," continued Uncle William, "is that they're too small. There must be a dozen on the Gambia River. Well, that's ridiculous. It's like having five different kings between Liverpool and Manchester. No wonder they're so backward. All we need to do is find the two or three men who have to be bribed and we can take what we want."

He looked at Mr. Dingwall. Mr. Dingwall hung his head. He had been listless ever since we had found ourselves in the village. Uncle William had discussed it with me, and put it down to the effects of the wound. He said that like all recovered drinkers Mr. Dingwall had lost the spark in his personality. That was why he was able to cope with normal life and why on his return from the voyage, having regained respect for himself, he should seek a suitable post in Liverpool.

As though these thoughts were in both their minds, Uncle William smiled affectionately and touched Mr. Dingwall's unwounded arm. Mr. Dingwall looked up. There were tears in his eyes but he blinked them away. "What really disturbs me," said Uncle William with comic resignation, "is that you still owe me that fifty thousand guineas." Later Mr. Dingwall sat for hours in the shade of a tree, and that afternoon, while we slept in the heat, he disappeared.

At first Uncle William did not question it, and the Jolas were unconcerned. They said that Mr. Dingwall had gone for a stroll with his young guards. Even when the first of the cattle had come home but Mr. Dingwall had not, Uncle William joked around the cooking fires, tasting the stew and asking questions in a mixture of pidgin and mime.

Fourfarthings was decorating a firepot she had cast, and our friend Nipper and I sparred, as we often did, at the wrestling. He would rush at me to gain a quick throw, as was the Jola style, and I would teach him some of Crabtree's entangling holds. Now as we leaned and heaved, his sweat smeared into mine, and we did not at first notice the commotion at the entrance to the compound.

When we did, it was to see the man with the twisted foot helpless on the ground, our old host standing above him, young men rushing in and out of the huts and peering into storage jars and wood-piles, and Uncle William suddenly among them, very agitated and demanding to know what had happened. By the time I arrived he had kicked the man, who retched in the dust, had been held back by young warriors, and had abused them all most foully in English.

"What is it?" I cried.

"What is it?" said Uncle William. "I'll tell you what it is!"

He jostled loose, picked up the firepot, and hurled it against a tree. "Dingwall's got drunk again, that's what it is!"

Uncle William shouted. He demanded to join a search-party but was refused, and so he paced the compound, and when he was tired of that he sat and fidgeted. Fourfarthings held his hand, and our host produced a keg of French brandy. Uncle William drank deeply. He groaned aloud and said how much he blamed himself, and then in the light of the fires he paced again, up and down, as Fourfarthings and the other Jolas watched with huge eyes.

What had happened was that Mr. Dingwall had stolen our pistol from the old man's hut and taken his guards for a stroll. They awoke the palm-wine man and asked him to explain the fermentation process. The man agreed. After a while Mr. Dingwall asked for some jars of wine in exchange for the pistol, and again the man agreed. Two hours later the man awoke from a drunken sleep to find himself sick and ashamed, with no pistol, one guard drunk in the hut, and no sign at all of the other guard and Mr. Dingwall: they had disappeared into the grasslands. As one wag put it when long after dark the search-parties returned empty-handed, by now they'd probably got the lions drunk.

"Tom," said Uncle William, "always remember. Do your duty and obey your conscience."

We had obeyed, both of us, according to our lights at the time, and I stared at Uncle William because his behaviour was new to me. I had been with him in many dangerous and difficult situations, and he had always known what to do. Now for the first time I saw him afraid and confused; it troubled me, and my sleep was broken.

More than once his groans awoke me, as he prayed for the safety of the ship and the honourable discharge of his duties as an officer and a friend, and must they of necessity be exclusive? Surely to God, I heard him say, a man must rise above his instincts. He must not waste his life, because there is such a thing as damnation. Later I heard him cry, "God! God! Where are you?" But there was no answer, and eventually, in that lifting darkness before dawn, when a breath of air vaguely stirs and the owls squeak and rustle as they return to their roosts, we were all awakened by dismayed shouting and drumming. The first search-party of the day had discovered Mr. Dingwall. He was not asleep, but in his ranting glory, where he had set the grasslands on fire.

Chapter 14

Burning Ground

We ran through crackling grass towards the bulk of trees around a creek. Beyond them there was a blur of smoke in the new grey sky, but it was impossible to tell how far away it was. We skirted dry paddy fields. A heron stood on one of the earth baulks. Uncle William gripped my wrist and forced me to my knees. His eyes were screwed shut.

"Pray that he's dead, Tom," he said. "Pray that he's dead and safe with Jesus."

That would no doubt have been the tidiest outcome—for Mr. Dingwall to have incinerated himself and his problem, for the dirty smudge of him to have risen above the trees and vanished like everything else on that continent into the grey, hazy heat. But it was not to be.

We crossed two rivulets, and in a thicket of straight-trunked trees and whispering leaves met the edge of the fire. A line of small flames crackled in the grass, and there were illogical, unconnected bursts of bright orange among the leaves. There was a lazy mist of smoke, and we were able to move in and through the fire, which left large patches unburned and advanced at a much slower pace than we could walk.

On the other side of the thicket there were stretches of earth that smouldered and stank, but the fire was dead.

Mr. Dingwall was waiting for us. He looked grimy but thoroughly at ease. He wore his strip of cotton across one shoulder and held it at the waist with his leather belt. His Jola companion was grey with tiredness. They seemed to have drunk all their wine and thrown the pot away. Yet there was no tension in Mr. Dingwall's stance. His fists were not clenched, his shoulders not defensively hunched. He was more at ease than I had ever seen him. "Good morning," he said, as though he were welcoming us to his family estates.

" 'Morning, Henry," said Uncle William. "What's all this?"

"All what?" said Mr. Dingwall, and looked round with a mock alarm that made Uncle William angry. Mr. Dingwall smiled. "We lit a fire to scare off the bushbeef," he said. "Bushbeef" was pidgin for large wild animals, and what could be more prudent than for a man caught on the grasslands at night to keep himself safe from them?

Uncle William flushed and blustered, but he had lost his advantage. Mr. Dingwall ignored him and nodded gravely at me, as though he were sure that I would understand him. I saw what it must have been like when Uncle William first met Mr. Dingwall: the dangerous, rough man, and the person who was effortlessly superior.

The Jolas approached Mr. Dingwall with their arms outstretched, not to calm him but to be themselves calmed by him. His poise was too powerful, too divine, too full of inspiration to be shaken. When he set off along the line of the fire, they surrounded him. They waved their amulets and held them out for Mr. Dingwall to touch. When Uncle William tried to break through to argue, they stopped him. He had to stumble along at the edge of the group, and in the centre of it Mr. Dingwall preached as to disciples, except that most of what he said was gentle nonsense.

Sometimes he capered like a scarecrow, and the Jolas imitated him. He spoke gibberish, which they delightedly tried to repeat. He walked round in circles, and once he sat down and preached a dreamy sermon about the number of embroidered stitches on a fashionable Englishman's waistcoat. By then the first sun was on our backs and we were dizzy and sick of the smell of ashes. Uncle William had run again and again at the Jolas like a clumsy bull. Now he threw handfuls of soil and bellowed.

Everyone looked at him. His eyes glared into those of Mr. Ding-wall. He shouted—not words but long-drawn-out, jeering, envious noises. Mr. Dingwall's lip curled. He strode to where a tree still idly burned and wrenched off a thin branch whose leaves were on fire. He whirled the branch round his head until the flames roared, and then he flung it into the tall, rattly grass, where a dry gust blew the flames into an explosion, and within seconds there was thick smoke and the air shimmered. Then the breeze veered and the fire leaped towards us.

In the swirl of smoke we could not see which way to run. The Jolas shouted and howled. I stumbled and fell into thick dry stalks. When I looked up, their tops were ablaze. Ash whirled. There were clouds of escaping insects, and small birds the colours of jewels swooped through the flames to catch them.

Then, as suddenly as it had flared up, the fire subsided. We were spluttering, and scratched by the dry grass. Mr. Dingwall had not run. He had let the fire swirl round him. He watched us for a moment and then looked slowly about.

For all the patches of black earth and charcoaled branches, the horizon was as shut in and hazy as before. Mr. Dingwall stamped his foot. The dry, cracked, yellow earth refused an imprint. Mr. Ding-wall set off towards the village. The Jolas walked quietly with him. When he had walked twenty yards or so, he stopped and looked back. We followed his gaze. There was still a faint grey smoke-haze, but we could not see the exact line of the fire nor where precisely it had burned around us. Mr. Dingwall's smile was ironic and resigned.

Uncle William shouted at him, "Not true, Henry! Never! Our lives do not go unnoticed! We are not feeble! Who makes these fires in the dry season? Your savages do, to clear and enrich the land! Poor beasts! Our Liverpool trade will enrich the universe!" Then suddenly he was red-faced and exhausted.

Mr. Dingwall put his arm round Uncle William's shoulder, and as they walked easily along, I was happy because I thought that every-thing might after all be resolved.

It was a false hope, but one that Mr. Dingwall could always bring momentarily and painfully to life, for on his best days he was serene and marvellous. His mind soared and his whimsy was incorrigible. It spun word-webs out of the sounds around us. It made pattering nonsense-rhymes fit the haste of the drums, and laughed at the pidgin that said "womanfowl" for "hen" and "bigeye" for "greedy."

The Jolas sat round him merely to hear his chuckle, and little green-and-red finches came out of the trees to eat from his hand. He talked for hours about his boyhood and did not seem to have a care in the world. He seemed to be not drunk, as Mr. McBride would get drunk, but utterly assured and reasonable. It was Uncle William who looked blotchy and spoke with a slur, whose temper was violent, and who greedily gulped down whatever spirits our host offered him.

Once Mr. Dingwall had depended upon Uncle William. Now Uncle William could not even approach Mr. Dingwall. He withdrew into silences from which Mr. Dingwall tried very gently to draw him into another life. Love one another. Feed my lambs. What need have we of money or clothes except to cover nakedness? But in my heart I knew that Uncle William's confusion was not yet entire. I knew by sameness of blood the stubbornness that had driven my father to so much wasted misery. It made me determined to know the truth about myself, and in Uncle William it was a will to survive.

Uncle William did not intend to go mad over the question of whether or not Africans were human beings and our trade in them a blasphemy. His stubbornness fought against it. If Mr. Dingwall had been burned and gone to Jesus, Uncle William would have coped with the remorse. It would have enriched his spirit. As things were, I knew that he followed an instinct, and that what he sought was to restore his own force and dismiss that of Mr. Dingwall. His talisman was the pistol. Mr. Dingwall had flung it into the bush fire, where its wood had been burned and the metal distorted. A warrior had found and returned to Uncle William the useless remains, and he clutched them, and talked silently to himself, and awaited his opportunity.

It came when Mr. Dingwall ran out of liquor and his behaviour changed. Late one night he was restless and the next morning his face was twisted with hate. He swore and jeered and accused us of having made a mockery of his life and of wanting to sell him into slavery. He suddenly hit Fourfarthings, not in panic but viciously, with a mean pleasure. When her eyes reproached him he blustered at the Jola men and rolled in the ashes of a fire. He shouted at Uncle William and tried to crawl into the fowl and goat cages. Uncle William ignored him until he threw himself at the trunk of a tree, whereupon Uncle William stood up and said, "Henry! Come here!"

Mr. Dingwall sulkily came, and Uncle William went to one of the wooden scaffolds in the compound and from the middle of the pile of thorns on it pulled out the gourd in which he had hidden the drawstring bag that held our pistol balls.

Mr. Dingwall took the bag and disappeared, and when we next saw him he talked wonderfully about a theatrical performance that he had seen when he was on shore leave in Naples. He had bought more liquor with the bag of bullets, and he was able to resume for a moment his dream life, in which he cat-napped at noon and roamed out at night because he drank alone and did not want us to find his hoards of palm wine and cheap English spirits.

But we always saw him at the time of day he loved best: that hour of evening magic when the light was slanted and the shadows long, when the dust raised by the cattle became a golden haze, and the motes that danced in it were insects. Mr. Dingwall would gesture at the scene as though he had created it, but on what proved to be our last evening in the compound he did not share it with us. He needed drink again and in the heat of the day had awakened Uncle William and, shivering and blinking, implored him to surrender our powder flask, which Uncle William did.

That evening Uncle William and Fourfarthings and I stared in silence at the mellow haze. Men walked with bundles of dried grass on their heads, and lashed together conical wooden roof-frames. Women pounded corn or leaned over the cooking smoke. Their mothers gossiped and played with the children on a dusty doorstep. Slowly and deliberately a young girl squatted to chop the branches of a sapling for firewood. They were all most beautiful. Their sores were obscured, their deformities transfigured, their filmy eyes in shadow. They were gold-fuzzed and perfect, and abruptly one of them was unfamiliar and cackled with laughter as he ambled from silhouette to fully-revealed elderly cynic.

He was Ben Riley, the Mandinka dealer from the other side of the Bintang Creek, and he had grey, crinkly hair, a thin build, and a slack belly. He wore a frock-coat and native cotton breeches. He wagged a slow finger at us and announced in a lazy, head-shaking, tut-tutting, chuckling way that he was very pleased with himself for having inspired Uncle William's confidence, which he proposed to justify to the utmost.

"To the utmost you can get out of us," said Uncle William.

Ben Riley cackled again, and said that if he helped us as much as we deserved, it would be no help at all. We'd all marry Jola women and our daughters would inherit their mothers' property, and our sons would need more help than we did now. Look at us. White officers dressed like nomad cattle-drovers.

The old man who administered the compound came up to greet Ben Riley, and Fourfarthings offered Ben a bowl of cocoanut milk, which he sipped very loudly. He made amiably suggestive jokes about her young body, and told his servant to hand out gifts of bangles and metal basins. He shook many hands, and amid comic admonitions and smiles exchanged quick, serious sentences with the old man and some of the others. "But who has he bribed?" said Uncle William. "Who has he talked to before this?"

When bowls of rice appeared, Ben Riley elaborately declined them. He had ridden from the creek on a donkey and must get back there to cross over before dark.

"God bless us!" spluttered Uncle William at the delays. There was no sign of Mr. Dingwall. Fourfarthings watched us earnestly, her eyes flicking from Uncle William's face to mine.

After two or three belches, some head-shaking, and a powerful fart that was acknowledged by laughter and applause, Ben Riley settled himself on his shrunken haunches and in three or four minutes said what he had come to say. He had parleyed with Porky Ben and arranged a price for the return of the longboat. There were accepted rates for all such transactions, and Porky Ben had been firm but not greedy. He had even offered to pay Ben Riley a special commission on the deal.

"He did what?" snapped Uncle William, who suspected that this signified Porky Ben's ambition to make himself the most powerful dealer on the south bank of the Gambia River, and to keep the English off it if he could. To Uncle William this was an outrage, but Ben Riley was an old man. He was happy to accept a subservient role, if that would make his life peaceful. Uncle William swore. Riley shrugged. He had seen Fort James pass from English to French and back again. He called it ripples on the surface of the water. "What about Smallshaw's credits?" boomed Uncle William.

Ben Riley held up his finger, rolled his eyes, took a deep breath, and seemed about to make an almost religious pronouncement. Then he belched, and shook his finger warningly, and with a sigh went from the embarrassment of the credits to the matter of our ransom from the Jolas. They expected political assistance against the King of Fogni as well as the usual number of bars, on which Ben Riley would take commission from both parties. "God bless us!" said Uncle William.

"Me want God you save too much," said Ben Riley, who despite the fact that he wore a cluster of charms round his neck had already confided, "Me big Godman pass daddy"—he was a better Christian than his English father.

"Your lot wouldn't sell Jesus Christ for thirty bars," said Uncle William. "It'd be ninety-six at least."

"Jesus Christ him very big Godman," said Ben Riley, as though describing a person of whom we had not heard before.

"What about Smallshaw's credits?" persisted Uncle William, and Ben Riley came to the point. Porky Ben would not trade with us. He would not even return the longboat unless we agreed to go back to Senhor Voss and ask him for Smallshaw's credits. Uncle William picked up a stick and hurled it at the wattle fence. His anger startled the goats, and they stamped and jostled in their cage. "Baaa!" said Uncle William, and everyone laughed at him.

His eyes gleamed dangerously, but he breathed deeply to stifle his feelings. Without the longboat he could not trade properly, and without the help of Governor Bayliss and Senhor Voss he could not influence the King of Fogni, who would hardly change his policy to please one ship that did not want to match French prices. He was outsmarted. At least he had recovered half the credits. He took a deep breath and nodded. He and Ben Riley smiled at each other, like cardplayers who are beaten but still pleased because they counted correctly.

"Agreed," said Uncle William. "Tell Porky Ben I agree; and these people here. Wonderful people. I agree to what they want."

Ben Riley laughed happily and shuffled towards his donkeys. He waved at the Jolas and assured them in their own language that everything was settled and secure. They were delighted. Some of them clapped, and others touched Uncle William, as if to share his energy. Uncle William reassured them. "Don't worry," he said. "It's all ship-shape. Don't worry."

Ben Riley's parting words were that he was in communication with Mr. Partridge, and we would be on board the *Margaret* before

the next sundown. He rode off into grey light. The trees looked dry
and shrivelled. Negotiating with old Ben had livened up Uncle William, but now we both seemed, like the day itself, to be exhausted by
the heat.

Mr. Dingwall returned soon after dark. His mood was a nervous
one, and for the first time he had brought a jug of spirits with him,
and drank it as we sprawled in the hut. When Uncle William explained Ben Riley's settlement Mr. Dingwall ignored him. He
brushed at the dust that caked his bare feet and legs. Sometimes he
spoke at the same time as Uncle William but about different things.
He gulped at his jug and stared restlessly about him. The firepot
threw a warm light. Our shadows were soft blotches. Fourfarthings
sat with us, and when Uncle William and Mr. Dingwall spoke at
once, she reached out and held their wrists. She kissed her amulets
and muttered imploringly. Mr. Dingwall smiled and touched her
forehead.

"Look at the moon," he said. "Look at the moon, Fourfarthings. I
knew an English duke once, and his teeth were rotten."

We were all silent. When Mr. Dingwall got up and left us, Uncle
William hardly seemed to notice. He had been bested and he'd sail
away, but he would return for what Smallshaw's was owed. He'd not
be beaten by a few treacherous black buggers. His anger wearied
him, and I was amazed that he had not released it against Mr. Dingwall. His face was tired and pouchy. The whites of his eyes were a
queasy yellow. He drank deeply from a bowl of spirits that our host
sent him. His voice was low and his language foul. He insisted that
he was a good man and that the rest of the world was rotten. He
sniffled. Liquor dribbled down his chin.

He was bloated and self-pitying, and he was frightened because he
knew that tomorrow was the day of reckoning for Mr. Dingwall. Had
the drinking bout exhausted itself? If it had not, how would Mr.
Dingwall buy more liquor now that the pistol, the bullets, and the
powder flask were gone? Where would he turn, and to what humiliations would he agree?

Uncle William had to wait for his answers until the stifling glare
of midday. Mr. Dingwall returned very slowly but very upright. He
held his left hand down with his right to stop its jerking. To him his
head may have seemed proudly and disdainfully high, but to us it was
stiff and awkward. He looked old. He moved his mouth as though it

were cracked and dry. His voice was harsh. He asked very politely for a glass of sweet dessert wine from the cooler. Uncle William laughed at him.

Mr. Dingwall smiled. He walked. He turned his head from side to side. He complained about the insolence of the grooms and stableboys. Once our host limped up to him but Mr. Dingwall ducked away. He was soaked in sweat. He smiled at me and said, "Poor Tom."

"Poor you," said Uncle William.

"Give me a drink, William," said Mr. Dingwall.

Uncle William said, "No. I can't pay for it."

Mr. Dingwall looked at him closely and shouted, "Vulture!" He turned and tripped over the root of a tree. He floundered in the dust. He held his hands over his ears. He looked for an escape. There was none. He cracked at last. He rolled and shouted in terror. He screamed hoarsely.

Uncle William's rage burst out. He got up and flung Mr. Dingwall against the wattle fence. "Stay here! Stay here! Spend your life on drink in this compound!"

Uncle William swung heavily away. There were tears in his eyes but he was himself again. He would save our lives. He would reassume command of the ship and discharge his duty to the owners. He would do what God wanted. He tried to speak, but his mouth would not form the words. He held my shoulder. He was trembling. He breathed deeply to calm himself and called out to our host.

He said that he would like to address a meeting of the village council because Mr. Dingwall admired the Jolas and wished to spend the rest of his life with them. Uncle William wanted to know how many bars this would cost.

It was a crude and biting stroke that Mr. Dingwall could not parry. For an instant his face was radiant, and then, almost as soon as the Jolas began to chatter among themselves, it became desolated; and what made it so was not our contempt but that of the Jolas.

He had seen their surprise and their realization that sooner or later they would have come to despise him: in the wet season, when he slumped on his haunches and rain and vomit mingled down his chest; when he slurred and jumbled the pidgin; when his red nakedness had nothing left to trade for liquor. Would they have sold him? Would a Ben Riley have taken pity and given him clothes and the run of a compound? What would Mr. Dingwall have had to do for his liquor? Chop wood? Collect great bundles of thorn? Where would he have slept? With the dogs? Would memories of the past have tortured him? Did they do so now, as he sobbed loudly and pitifully, and Uncle William knelt by him and held him in his arms and rocked him like a child? "We're your own people," I heard him say. "You can't leave your own people."

Even then, I think, the Jolas might have given him a home in return for a few bars, for I am sure that some of them felt that it was his destiny. But the moment passed. Mr. Dingwall himself had seen it and set it aside. They would have had to wrest him from Uncle William now, and that was impossible because there was a mystery here, a terrible confusion of the heart.

Yet they were drawn to the two men, and so was I. I had tears in my eyes. I sat in the dust in front of Uncle William and Mr. Dingwall, and they each put out their hands to touch me. On an impulse Fourfarthings joined us. We were a circle of ruined energy, and around us stood the naked, mutely watching blacks. Then our old host brought a bowl of palm wine, and Mr. Dingwall drank it and was calm again; but Fourfarthings sobbed because she knew that it was time for us to part.

I embraced her, and we clung to each other, and then, as children are, we were embarrassed by our own feelings. Fourfarthings pushed me away, almost with a giggle, and we nodded and smiled at each other. The Jolas murmured appreciatively. I'll not see her again, I thought, and never run home with her across the darkening moor.

Then I ached for loss and saw that she did, too. I wanted to embrace her again but knew that I must be brave. So did she, and we were grateful for Uncle William's interruption. He pointed to where Fourfarthings's body oil had stained my rags.

"God bless us!" he said. "I forgot to ask Ben Riley to bring us fresh clothes!" And even Mr. Dingwall smiled, with the sweet wryness that seemed to give him such understanding.

Uncle William put his hand on Fourfarthings's head like a blessing, and then we mounted our donkeys and did not look back, but rode half-naked to the creek, where Ben Riley's men had already unloaded piles of goods for the Jolas.

It was good after the unchanging hotness of the grasslands to see water again, and the black and red crabs that scuttled over the sandy mud of the landing place. We boarded Ben Riley's cutter and he took the tiller himself. In the shallow water I saw a long thin silver flicker of a fish with an eye the size of a sixpence. We glided past Porky Ben's compound, where his people jeered at us, and Bintang village, and the banks of jungle and mangrove. The leaves were very bright and yellowy in the late sun.

Then the water quickened round us, and there was the river, suddenly vast and open and noble, a blue and hazy world with sparkling spray, and a breeze that sang in our dusty lungs and made the cutter dip. Ahead were two reassuring silhouettes, those of Fort James and the *Margaret*, and as we approached the ship Mr. Partridge came most sternly but calmly to the quarterdeck rail and the men rushed to look at us.

Our bodies were dirty with sweat-streaked dust. Our skirts were ludicrous and so were Uncle William's tricorn and my roughly-tied turban. Yet no one laughed, for they saw the change in us, just as we saw the change in the ship. The carpenter had done his work. The barricado of new planks rose twelve feet high, and jutted out over the sides to block off the quarterdeck from the rest of the ship. Under the maindeck awning swirled the steam of a great cauldron. Swivel-guns poked through the barricado, and the deck guard had muskets. There was a stench of sick humanity. The *Margaret* looked what she was: a prison and uneasy fortress under sail.

Chapter 15

Windward Coast

Uncle William's first action upon reboarding the *Margaret* was to greet each man by name and shake his hand, staring deeply into his eyes as he did so; he confirmed Mr. Partridge's decision to make the seaman Thompson our new bosun and went on a tour of inspection of the ship. Only then did he souse the dust off himself, put on a clean shirt and breeches, and visit Governor Bayliss on James Island, to say that he was determined to return for what was owed at the end of the season, by which time he hoped that the Governor would have informed the Board of Trade and Plantations in London of Porky Ben's insult to English pride and interests. He returned to the *Margaret* so that we might catch the dawn ebb, and by the next nightfall we had left the Gambia River and were once again upon the ocean.

Our destination was the Windward, or Grain, Coast, five hundred miles south of the Gambia, and the part of Africa most frequented by Liverpool slave ships. It was the coast not of hot and tawny grasslands but of the rain forest, and the air was humidly oppressive even at sea. When we arrived there, our routine was one of ceaseless din and cruelty.

Our boats might be gone for a week or more, often in one direction while the *Margaret* went the other, passing and repassing the same ships, soaked sometimes by unexpected storms, but sweltering more often in a glare that made the deck seams ooze and bubble. Wherever we anchored, the dugouts would come out from the shore, and our decks and cabins would be crowded, and our ears tired of the continual arguments of dealers and men with goats and fowls.

There were the entreaties of dealers who wanted us to hire their cousins and nephews as seamen for the dugouts that brought water and vegetables. There were the complaints of merchants who had been given short measure; a constant movement of goods and a heaving-aboard of great planks of camwood; the sulks of blacks who wanted more gifts; the drunken silliness of everyone; and the terrified screams of slaves who as soon as they were landed on deck saw the iron cooking pot and thought that they were going to be cut up and eaten. It took the jeering blows of the crew and a branding with the *DD* mark of Liverpool to convince them otherwise.

Uncle William drove himself hard, and his domination of Mr. Dingwall seemed complete; the death of Mr. Bruce had left us an officer short, but Mr. Dingwall was given less to do, not more. Mr. McBride took Mr. Bruce's watch and other duties, and when Mr. Dingwall took his own watch the gunner, Davy Morgan, was always there to see that he behaved reliably.

The only tasks that Mr. Dingwall supervised alone were menial ones, such as taking the boats ashore for wood and water, or shifting goods from the hold. He was rarely asked to translate or to meet important men, and seemed not to care.

Most of the time he was drunk, but no longer in an exultant way. He was downcast and unkempt, and since he did not hold liquor well, he was often sick; if he tried not to drink, he shivered with fear and distress. Once he had talked like a prophet, but now he mumbled to himself in the squalor of his cabin.

Yet I knew that he wanted to communicate with me, because on Sunday mornings when Uncle William conducted ship's prayers Mr. Dingwall made it a point to stand behind me. Davy Morgan and Matt True led the hymns, Morgan with a blunderbuss under his arm as he looked down through the grating into the women's room; and when Uncle William spoke of Christ's love for us, and indeed for the heathen blacks in our charge who did not understand the Word, Mr. Dingwall put a hot, reminding hand upon my shoulder. But afterwards, if I turned to look at him, he would duck away and avoid me.

He avoided everyone when he could. He did not even pretend to be a self-possessed officer like Mr. Partridge, and he seemed content for Uncle William to ignore him, and the rest of the crew to behave as though the agony were not happening at all. They smirked and leered. They pitied him. They believed that when they called him "Sir" they saved at least some of the dignity that he could not save himself.

What was Mr. Dingwall, after all? He was a gentleman, and he was drunk because he was feverish, or because he was crazed by the sun. It was Africa. It was the heat. That was it. The heat and the vapours of the swamps. It was not guilt and horror. It could not be. They did not exist.

But I knew that they did exist. The question was: How would I adjust to them? Uncle William did not ask. He did not even speak to me much, because he was busy, but he always seemed to know where I was and he told me to work once again with Matthew True.

At first, because as the number of slaves increased the iron cauldron became too small, we put down sheet lead and built a brick-and-plaster furnace and oven between the mainmast and the barricado.

That was pleasant work. It was when we went down into the hold to complete the women's room that I knew I had been put to the test, and that Uncle William had decided to rub my nose in the daily agony of the blacks.

The men slaves were in near-darkness and stacked on top of one another on shelves that ran down each side of the room with a gangway in the middle. Two rows of men lay on the floor of the hold, and two on the shelves; each layer had a two-and-a-half-foot clearance.

The shelves were of broken staves, and the upright stanchions and supports of locally-cut wood, so that some parts were smooth and others as knobbled as when they came from the tree. The structure had to be strong enough to support a system of chains and ringbolts as well as people, and it was inspected every two or three days because the men constantly tried to loosen the upright stanchions in the hope that they might use them as weapons.

The men slaves were sullen and disobedient, and had to be shoved and struck before they would do what they were told. They were chained in pairs, the right hand and foot of one to the left hand and foot of the other.

At night the chains were run together through ringbolts, so that no man could move without in some way disturbing others, and limbs and chains and cloth coverings were foully entangled.

There was a space set aside for the sick, but it did not stop men waking up to find that their chains had huddled them around a corpse, or that the flux from sick bowels splashed through gaps in the shelf upon arms and faces beneath.

The women were more docile, and would sit for hours in the light from the grating. They were chained only when the mood of the men seemed dangerous. There were still trade goods piled in their room, but Matt had built half the shelving and we heaved the goods on deck to make space for the remainder.

Behind the aft bulkhead there was a place for the women to wash, and it was here that our sailors would interfere with them, clutching and slapping their breasts, and sometimes holding a woman against the bulkhead and fornicating while another sailor or Mark Baker kept a lookout, for our officers punished such behaviour with a bread-and-water diet and irons.

Sometimes other women kept watch, but it did not make them any more trustworthy than the men. Only one or two days after we started work in the hold, the seaman Butterworth made a woman sob for joy as he took her on one side of the bulkhead while we worked on the other. The woman and her friend who kept watch grinned when they returned to the half-built shelving.

A few moments later Mr. McBride made his daily inspection of the sick, and as he did so, one of the men unexpectedly sat up and slashed at him with a knife. Mr. McBride's shirt was torn and he fell backwards. Matt True and I ran in, and as True seized the knife I hit the man in the face with my hammer. He cried out, but I was angry and hit him again because it was his stupidity that forced me to be brutal.

This incident led to the only occasion on which Uncle William allowed our sailors to fondle and excite the women—in full view of the men slaves when the rooms were searched for more weapons. None was found, but the man who had tried to kill Mr. McBride was flogged and put in an iron collar with spikes, so that he could not lie down properly or turn his head. Butterworth had to admit that the offending knife was his and had been stolen by one woman while he embraced the other. He was put in irons for a day, and the women were punished with thumbscrews.

After that I carried a pistol that I would jab into the belly or groin of any black who obstructed me or refused to do what I ordered. Some of them, women and children as well as men, would jostle and spit and had murder in their eyes; I understood why, but I had not been born when this strange trade in flesh began and I did not know how white men and Africans had become entangled in it. The most that a white man could do, it seemed, was to avoid deliberate cruelty and preserve his own life.

Even this last might not be possible, as it certainly was not for the blacks, many of whom were broken from the start. They were the ones who would most often gag on their food, and develop fevers and fluxes and stoppages of urine overnight.

They would go to the buckets to make water and find themselves unable to do so, the women pushing down as they squealed in panic, the men bucking with the strain. Their limbs would be drawn up by the pain. They would grimace. Their teeth and glazed eyes would plead in the dark.

When they died their bellies would be swollen, their skin grey and shrunken, and their limbs so thin that it seemed the chains might slip off of their own accord. But we kept them on so that the bodies would sink as we flung them overboard.

Mr. McBride worked shrewdly among the sick, our own as well as the blacks, not indeed for love but with a certain rough geniality for profit. Once a week he had the men slaves on deck to wash and exercise, and he tried to find out what they were used to eating and to vary their diet accordingly.

As we worked south, the numbers of slaves increased. They spoke several languages and could often converse with each other only in pidgin, which they had to pick up from our sailors in the first place. But by this time we had been two months on the Windward Coast and I had long since passed Uncle William's test.

He assumed that I had adjusted to the trade in an acceptable way; because I did my work well and kept my thoughts to myself there was no reason for him to think otherwise. So I was released for other duties, which since I could read and write were usually those of a tally clerk to check the goods that went ashore.

In the Sierra Leone and Sherbro rivers there were swamps and jungle islands and calm anchorages. Some of the dealers were white men out from England, but the richest were mulattoes such as Mr.

Tucker of Shebar and the Cumberbatch brothers. The slaves were big and solid, more useful for field labour than the fine-boned people of the Gambia.

Farther south there were no white dealers. The ships anchored outside the sandbanks and sent their boats through the surf to trade, sometimes with local kings but mostly with mulatto dealers who lived at the mouths of the many small rivers or in villages on the bluffs above the beach: such men as William Purcell of Liverpool Town, Peter Freeman of St. Paul's Town, and Yellow Will of Bassa.

We were at Cape Palmas, farther south even than Bassa, four months and a thousand miles from the Gambia, when despite all that Mr. McBride could do, sickness suddenly rampaged. In three days we buried ten slaves of the flux, and Uncle William decided that it was time to clean out the rooms.

The slaves were brought on deck, under the awning and the in-ward-pointing guns. Those of us not actually manning a gun went below and with the help of some of the women scraped the filth from the bulkheads and shelving. The stench was fetid.

We sweated and panted in the half-dark, and most of us retched as we did so. Then we lit braziers of tar, tobacco, and brimstone and went on deck.

The slaves were huddled. Matches burned at every cannon. I watched one slave wash himself. He rubbed his hands ritualistically. Then he held them for an instant under water poured by his chain-mate. He massaged his head and then rinsed it, movements so natural, efficient, and graceful that I thought with pain of the Jola village.

Smoke poured from the hold. It stank of brimstone, and in that hell-world under the awning, the slaves coughed and wept.

For two hours Uncle William kept the braziers burning, and then we went below again and swabbed everything down with vinegar. After that the sickness was not so rampant, and Mr. McBride was more severe in his medical examinations ashore or when slaves were first brought aboard the ship; but the true case of their ailing he could not cure, because many of them were so broken that they did not have the strength to live.

Beyond Cape Palmas were the Ivory Coast and the Gold Coast and the Slave Coast, and then the steamy, hot islands at the mouths of the Niger, and then the Congo and Angola—another thousand miles of coast along which ships fired a gun as the universal signal of their eagerness to trade and waited for the answering bonfire on shore. But we turned north again because the change in wind and weather would soon bring the season to an end.

As we did so, we encountered a new problem. The cats we had brought from England had long since died, and so had their kittens, which meant that rats were everywhere. They terrified the slaves at night and found their way around the barricado into our cabins and the state-room. One day we opened our sail lockers to air what we would need for our Atlantic crossing, and discovered that rats had gnawed through entire folds of canvas.

Uncle William decided that this was a danger to the ship, and one afternoon, when we were anchored off Little Bassa, north of the Seven Trees, he sent me ashore in the yawl to buy some new cats from the slave dealer Will Adams.

It was, as he put it, with a solemn exhalation of tobacco smoke, my first command, and despite everything, I warmed to him again. "Poor Henry's ashore already," he said, "for the water and vegetables." He sucked at his pipe and said, "Does he speak much to you?"

I looked at him. His eyes stared frankly into mine. "No," I said. "I wish he did."

Uncle William nodded and patted my shoulder. "Off you go," he said. "Steer a good course."

The force of the sea was checked far out by reefs and sandbanks, inside which the surf was broken but not fierce. The yawl bucked excitedly and the soaking refreshed me. Our punt went by with a full water butt. I could not see Mr. Dingwall. Perhaps he was in one of the dugouts. The sun beat through a haze of spray and glare on to a beach several miles long. There was black-streaked sand and lines of smashed shells, some yellow and plum, others with great multi-ridged backs, or broken halves of elaborate whorls and bells.

Then the sand became soft and the ground rose to palm-topped bluffs. There were many dugouts, and fishing nets stretched on poles to dry. There were boats from the other European ships, French, Dutch, and Prussian, that were grey shapes on the horizon, and rickety grog-stalls, and women traders who shouted and tried to grab me and the cooper, James Lees, as we walked up to the village.

There were clusters of huts, fences of palm leaves and creeper, a patchwork of fields beyond the worst of the windblown salt, and then the forest. Will Adams had the only house with a verandah, and a mud-walled yard with outbuildings. There were several armed guards.

Adams himself was absent, but the guards called his wife and two sons. The sons were slender young men in European clothes. Mrs. Adams was a massive, strong-faced woman in an elaborate head-dress and gold ear-rings. When I said that we wanted to buy cats she threw back her head and laughed. She offered us spirits. James Lees accepted and I asked for cocoanut milk.

"I knew you were dangerous," said Lees, "I knew it. Cocoanut milk today, and then one night you'll say your prayers and leave these blacks out altogether." He was a trundling little man who blinked a lot.

Mrs. Adams denied all knowledge of cats. "All finished," she said. "All dead."

"How much are they?" I said.

She looked at the lengths of cloth I had brought, and sent the elder son into the house. The other one laughed. After the sea the land seemed punishingly hot. The elder son reappeared with a small ginger cat in his arms.

"Have you any more?" I said.

"No," said Mrs. Adams.

Lees nudged me. A big black tom was sunning himself on the far side of the yard.

I gave Mrs. Adams the brightest length of cloth. She and the sons spoke in their own language.

"You give me more cloth," she said.

I gave her another length. She disappeared into the outhouses. The younger son smiled. He observed our interest in the black tom and waved his hand, as though to imply that it did not exist. It was a mirage cat. The elder son poured Lees a stiff drink.

Mrs. Adams returned with a greyish cat that struggled fiercely. She yelled, and the servants brought a strip of cheap cloth. She bundled up the two cats and tied a knot in the bundle and put the bundle into a basket and handed the basket to me. I gave her my other two lengths of cloth.

"You very lucky," she said. "All finished. Give me something to buy tobacco."

I had some beads around my neck because I knew that such a gift would be expected. I took them off. Mrs. Adams nodded. I held out my hand. She gripped it like a man, laughing, and pulled me to her. Her energy was immense. Her skin was like thick velvet, her body massive, earthlike, and strong. Her sons grinned. The black tom yawned and licked himself. Then Mrs. Adams released me, and our purchases growled and threshed as I carried them back to the beach.

A high breeze had got up and there were streaky clouds. Everything was blowing. There was a glare on the jumbled surf. Crabs scuttled. Soapy foam ran up the sand. I saw Mr. Dingwall with his bare feet in the water. I waved. He smiled and shrugged as though to say that he could not react adequately to the bright, spray-hazed beauty of the scene.

"Give me them cats," said Lees, and walked back to the yawl.

Mr. Dingwall and I stared out to sea. We had to squint. A fish eagle flapped heavily along a trough in the waves. Its claws trailed and there was a thin, silver gleam of prey in them. Mr. Dingwall seemed very peaceful. I could not tell whether he was drunk or not. A dugout approached to take him back to the ship.

He did not speak until the last moment, when the rowers worked their paddles furiously to hold the dugout in shallow water off the beach, and he said, "You do understand, don't you, Tom, that it's not William who shows me the truth? I show him. That's why I sailed with him."

For a moment his eyes had a piercing strength. Then he moved so that he was shadowed and I was blinded by the sun. He splashed long-leggedly to the dugout and swung aboard. The rowers turned away. Mr. Dingwall looked back at me, and I thought he nodded. As I walked to the yawl, the foam rolled a dead, hollowed-out, gaping-eyed fish at my feet.

Uncle William was delighted with the cats and said I had done well.

"I met Mr. Dingwall," I said.

"Aye," he said.

Perhaps he already knew that behind Mr. Dingwall's despair there was an awesome serenity. I could not tell. I wanted to talk to Uncle William, but I did not know how. I began to feel between us some of the restraints that had spoiled my love for my father.

At the same time, if the question was how I should spend my future, I knew that I should not discuss it until the end of the voyage, when I would be more sure of myself and my opinion.

Next morning Will Adams sent word that he had reserved for us a prime man slave, but when Uncle William went ashore he found himself in a courtyard auction with three other captains—the same message had been sent to every European ship off Little Bassa. Uncle William came back angry and empty-handed, but at least he had heard from a Dutch Captain that the British sloop H.M.S. *Badger* was anchored off Peter Tucker's town at Kittam.

We sailed north at once because this was good news that might ease one of our worries. We now had a hundred slaves aboard and a depleted crew to guard them. To make matters worse, some of our trustiest men were sick and some of the healthiest unreliable.

Their flogging had subdued Taylor and Morton, but Mossop was still difficult and had found a new ally in Butterworth. They were always after the women slaves and had several times made drunken trouble on shore. Now Uncle William saw his chance to be rid of them. Naval ships, having a closer discipline, would take bad seamen off merchantmen, and this Captain Hale of the *Badger* readily agreed to do.

One evening, with the surf running high and the sky white and purple after a storm, Mr. Partridge put Mossop and Butterworth in irons and took them in the punt to the sloop. They swore and shouted as they went, but Uncle William looked stern and expounded the text "Except the Lord keepeth the city the watchman waketh in vain." Captain Hale returned in the punt to dine with us and brought two new seamen, who seemed to bear no ill will at having been ordered to join us. They were slow-thinking countrymen named Tuffrey and Willis, and very different from our sharp Liverpool sorts.

Mr. Dingwall took the watch so as not to have to sit with Captain Hale, but the rest of us learned more of the season's gossip: who had traded well, what others besides ourselves had been ambushed, how prices had varied, which captains had sickened and died, and, most important, that Captain Hale had carried letters to Governor Bayliss from the Board of Trade and Plantations, and left him a consignment of firearms that were intended as bribes for the local kings. The Admiralty had indicated that a surveyor and engineers would be sent to Fort James as soon as possible, perhaps even next season.

This was good luck, and Uncle William made the best of it. He calculated that what was left of our trade goods would buy some twenty-five slaves; however, if he paid Mr. Tucker more than the true rate, he would get twenty slaves in half the time, and this is what he decided to do.

We were in the month of May 1752, and the wet season was about to break over us. There were sudden winds and heavy rain. There were unexpected fogs and heavy seas that kept the boats in danger.

One night at dusk we watched the yawl battle to our anchor buoy and tie up to ride out the night there, soaked and pitched about; next morning the sea was still full, and the yawl tipped over as we hauled it aboard. The seats were stove in and the supplies swept away.

In such weather the slaves would be seasick, and in night storms they shrieked aloud; the breakers showed violet in sudden lightning, and we prayed that our anchor would hold. Then the mornings would be calm, with smashed palm fronds all over the beach, and the canoes would swarm out again.

On our last day at Kittam, Mr. Tucker came aboard in a gold-threaded coat, and to everyone's amazement a slave whom we had brought up to wash put his hand on Mr. Tucker's shoulder and used it as a lever to jump overboard. He fell into the water not two yards from Mr. Tucker's boats and was fished on board again to huge laughter. Then Mr. Tucker toasted us in brandy and we weighed north for the Gambia.

Our season was nearly over and we took stock. Although we had continued to bury slaves we had kept up the numbers, and we had in the hold seventy-nine men, thirty-four women, and seven children, a total of one hundred and twenty that we hoped, with the credits still owed us in the Gambia, to raise to one hundred and forty. To contain them we had seventeen men and two boys, seven fewer than when we set out from Liverpool.

Chapter 16

The King of Fogni Him Make Palaver

The palaver from which Uncle William extracted the last farthing of what Smallshaw's was owed took place not at Fort James but at a creek village in the territory of the King of Fogni. We had fired our salute and paid our comey to the King of Barra, and anchored in the main channel of the Gambia River, away from the insect-teeming foreshores, and sent canoes to Governor Bayliss and Senhor Voss. For two days we waited in rain that hissed into the swollen flood. The banks were lost in mist. Rubbish swirled in the currents. We took down our awning and set casks on deck to catch the water. Our bodies steamed in the heat, and humidity made the hold a torment.

Then, although the sky was still grey, the mist lifted and we could see the smoking banks, and Governor Bayliss and Senhor Voss came with two cutters and a fleet of canoes to take us to the palaver. We were soaked in our own sweat, and the heat was wearisome and tight in our chests, but we began nevertheless with hospitality aboard the *Margaret*.

Senhor Voss came over the side with a flourishing bow. We might have been royalty. He asked after us with concern. He deeply regretted the death of Peter Case. He gave us gifts of fruit from the Senhoras, and said that we were the first to know that his Fula wife was with child; if it was a boy he would send him to Fort James to learn proper English.

He seemed to know all about Mr. Dingwall's troubles, for he clasped him to his massive chest and after that did not waste one more glance upon him. He peered through the ports of the barricado and clucked his approval. He slapped our seamen on the back and sighed because, as he said, he was so happy to see his dear friends again. Then he bowed low and insisted that Governor Bayliss take precedence in entering the state-room.

Governor Bayliss was accompanied by three Company soldiers, two blacks who carried him where he could not walk, and the parrot, which fluttered up to the stern windows and blinked out at the water.

Since our goods were all gone except for a few trinkets that Uncle William proposed to take to the palaver, True had dismantled the shelving, and the state-room was back to its proper appearance. Governor Bayliss sat in the commode chair. He looked frail, and Mr. McBride produced his medicine chest. The Governor was in his faded coat and straw hat. He sipped his brandy and described in a dry way what would happen at the palaver; he implied that in his day he had seen far more important events.

Then when he was ready, but before the others had drunk up, he announced that we should go. We lowered him over the side in a bosun's chair. The parrot sat on his shoulder and said, "Jolly boys! Jolly boys!"

We sailed with Senhor Voss and left our own boats behind. His canoes would bring back the slaves. Uncle William took Mr. McBride, the new bosun, me, and two men. At the last moment he jerked his head for Mr. Dingwall to join us. They sat next to each other in the cutter but did not speak. Uncle William smoked his pipe, and in the damp its smell was acrid.

We reached the south bank in an hour or so. The flood poured sluggishly through the mangroves. Most of the small islands were awash, and when we turned into the Brefet Creek the water was on a level with the leaves.

At Brefet village the dun-black sandbanks were half submerged, which made the landing treacherous. The King of Fogni's people stepped into the muddy swirl and carried us on their backs to the land, where instead of the exhausted, burned-out grass of the dry season there were green sprouts everywhere, and a glory of flowers

—some had huge, sodden, glowing, sagging heads whose richness mingled with the smell of the creek and the damp whiff of our clothes.

Governor Bayliss then produced from a hamper his best braided coat, full white wig, and tricorn hat, all of which he put on before he formed us into a procession and led us to meet the King. Muskets were shot off in our honour. Bowstrings twanged and women whooped.

A straw roof had been built out in front of one of the huts, and under it was a semi-circle of stools and European chairs. The King sat in the middle in the biggest chair, and Porky Ben on a stool at the end. They rose at our arrival, the King with condescending dignity, and Porky Ben with a snort and an awkward head-jerk, like that of a naughty boy made to own up. Old Ben Riley shuffled about in the wet, because if he sat still for too long, his legs went stiff.

Senhor Voss rivalled the praise-singers with the extravagance of his introductions and compliments, and when we took our places we were given brandy and tobacco. The famous parrot was gleefully applauded, at which it squawked in dismay and hid under the Governor's chair. Small gifts were exchanged. A bullock was sacrificed, its blood not much darker than the wet sand. Then it was taken away and roasted for the night's feasting.

Governor Bayliss spoke pidgin without any attempt to inflect it as the blacks did, and Uncle William sat heavily in his chair, hands on thighs and elbows out. He puffed at his pipe and hardly spoke, but there was grim satisfaction in his face.

Day after day he had traded speeches and false compliments, and drunk toasts when his head ached and his mouth was foul, and palaver blurred into palaver, and month into month. He had haggled, and smiled whenever he was angry, and ignored petty thefts from the crowded state-room, and allowed dealers' wives to sleep in his own hammock, and wheedled favours, and by sheer force of personality disciplined rough men; and here for the first time in more than six months on the coast, he could watch the farce of compliments and display, and know that it was a farce, and that his interest would prevail.

Mr. Dingwall knew it, too, but if he smiled it was ruefully. He gradually edged his stool back, so that he was behind the line of the other dignitaries and could be anonymous; but Uncle William had an eye on him. Porky Ben also knew that the palaver was an ironic charade; he would be the loser by it and could not hide his chagrin.

The King was a short, powerful man with a contemptuous mouth. He wore a white caftan and voluminous breeches. His gestures were peremptory. He was bad tempered, as though he did not want to be soothed by Senhor Voss yet could not help himself. Senhor Voss chuckled and his emotion went far beyond the needs of the occasion. We are all brothers, he said. Life is short. Surely we can make it pleasant for one another?

I thought that Porky Ben would squeal and stamp with rage, but one of the King's chopping gestures warned him to be silent. Governor Bayliss seized the moment to suggest to Senhor Voss that the gifts be brought up, and Senhor Voss clapped his hands, and his porters laid in front of the King the boxes of guns and ammunition. There were some two hundred muskets in all, a substantial bribe even by African standards.

The King had one box brought nearer. He looked at it with his mouth turned down. Senhor Voss invited the King to choose a musket, and gave it to one of his men whom he knew to be a crack shot. The man took aim at a pot set on a mark fifty paces away.

Mr. McBride nudged me and indicated Ben Riley, who had fallen asleep. The marksman fired. The pot was demolished. Ben Riley nearly fell off his chair. He hobbled about and stamped his legs and rubbed them, and shook his head at the frustrations of old age.

Senhor Voss himself reloaded the musket, and invited the King to try the mark. It seemed to me that under the cover of Ben Riley's ailments and Senhor Voss's rhetoric the mark had been moved in at least fifteen paces, and from Mr. McBride's comic throat-clearing I was sure of it, but Uncle William kept a straight face and so did the Governor. The King took aim and fired. The pot shattered.

"Bravo!" said the Governor. "Bravo!"

There was tumultuous applause and bow-twanging. The King shrugged as though no less were to be expected. There was a momentary burst of rain, after which the sun burned through the haze and the leaves and thatches steamed as though the village were on fire.

Governor Bayliss, whose wig was the object of much pointing and comment, now called out, "Sergeant!" and a grey-haired soldier who had taken the place of the hapless Wood came forward with a small, flat, brass-bound case. Governor Bayliss produced a key, to which he had tied a strip of yellow ribbon, and handed it to the King. The King grunted.

"I shall now invite His Majesty the King of Fogni," said Governor Bayliss in English, "to accept on behalf of the Board of Trade and Plantations and the merchants of the former Royal African Company this set of duelling pistols."

The King opened the case. The pistols lay in their velvet beds. They were superb. The King snapped down the lid and waved the case away; it would be examined later. He looked sharply about him, as though more gifts were his due.

Senhor Voss breathed deeply; the air was fresher after the rainburst, and there was the promise of a breeze. Uncle William drained his mug. A servant refilled it. Ben Riley sighed. The King drummed impatiently upon his knee. The Governor waited. Senhor Voss looked at him and raised his eyebrows, and the Governor gave a little bow.

He was about to speak when the parrot, thinking that silence meant safety, peered out from under the chair. There were one or two hoots of laughter. The parrot scampered sideways. It picked at the matting that had been laid upon the sand. Governor Bayliss waved at the Sergeant, who felt in his bandolier for some nuts and threw them at the parrot.

"Why not think of me for a change?" said the parrot. "Why not think of me?"

"Oh, for God's sake, show some dignity," said Governor Bayliss irritably, but he knew that the parrot had given him everybody's attention, and he was not one to waste it.

"For his part," he now said in a louder voice, "the King agrees to trade with English ships only, as was the custom of his ancestors."

Senhor Voss translated into Mandingo. There was applause, as though the King had won a concession and his ancestors had never played fast and loose between English and Portuguese.

"As for our good friend Senhor Alonso Vasco de Alvares," continued the Governor, and Uncle William looked wildly confused, which had been the Governor's intention. His tired eyes glinted for the first time that day. "Known to most subjects of His Britannic Majesty as Porky Ben," he said, and looked to Mr. Dingwall for the answering gleam of another educated man's irony.

There was none. Mr. Dingwall stared at his feet. The Governor's eyes narrowed, and I saw again the coldness in him; but he put it aside.

"Our good friend Porky Ben," he said, "has agreed to pay in full the credits owed by him to Messrs. Smallshaw and Hill Company Limited, of Liverpool, England."

There was more applause. What it truly meant was that the King had been paid an enormous bribe to ignore the French, and to persuade Porky Ben to do the same.

Senhor Voss translated the agreement into Mandingo. Porky Ben grimaced. Ben Riley began to chuckle, but when Porky glared at him he somehow translated the laugh into an old man's ruinous cough.

I could see that the King was bored. He turned round and smiled at his women. To him the agreement was no more than a way to obtain two hundred muskets. He did not care which white men he dealt with, so long as there was a flow of trade. Next season, if it suited him, he would try to get more muskets and a new agreement, but that was not uppermost in his mind. The white men kept mostly to their ships. They were neither a danger nor a preoccupation. They were simply there to be used: a source of goods and muskets that would make the King strong and enable him to defy his overlord.

"He has no notion," said Mr. McBride, his lips wet with brandy, "that the English and French might decide among themselves what lands to trade with. Look at him," he said, swilling the drink in his mug, "and see how he despises us."

He did, and perhaps rightly; yet to us he was a puffed-up joke, because we measured superiority in quite different ways.

His advisers had counting-frames and sticks in the dust. We had double-entry book-keeping. The villagers who crowded round to watch the palaver had been born into occupations that they could never leave: smiths, fishermen, canoe crews, household slaves. We were each one of us free to be as rich or poor as we were able.

Not that I felt superior. I did not. I felt the first stirring of those subtle sorrows that are born of knowledge, and a mixture of envy and pity for the black faces around us.

"Can the slaves be produced?" said Governor Bayliss.

Senhor Voss and Porky Ben flared into an argument over what exactly was or was not owed. Uncle William rapped out the figures. Senhor Voss had in any case the original note of hand and a list of his own repayments. Uncle William said that these were correct.

Porky Ben snuffled but had to agree. He was about to shout angrily at his overseer for the slaves to be produced when Uncle William held up his hand.

"Just a minute," he said. "Just one minute."

Everybody stared at him. He raised his hat to the King. The King blinked.

"I savvy too much there's been a great deal of inconvenience here," said Uncle William. "Because Porky Ben him bigeye five Smallshaw him men been shoot."

Porky Ben's buck teeth jutted as he began to bluster, but Uncle William's outburst was well calculated. First he shook with justified anger and then he begged our pardon and controlled his feelings. He repeated that Porky Ben's men had killed an officer, three men, and a boy, and he demanded compensation.

Porky Ben was outraged, as the Governor had predicted he would be. Such killings were regarded on the coast as hazards of the trade. What about the two or three men that Porky Ben and Senhor Voss lost every year in brawls with white sailors?

Compensation? Compensation was a joke.

Not for an officer, argued Uncle William, and even the King took an interest. It was indeed the custom to ransom officers, not kill them, and Porky Ben's people had known well enough who Mr. Bruce was.

"No!" said Porky Ben. "I no pay!"

Senhor Voss spoke soothingly in Mandingo. Porky Ben grumbled. Senhor Voss shrugged expansively. They looked at each other like men who faced the same problems and were somehow above the rest of us.

Porky Ben knew when he was beaten. He muttered that he would pay a hundred bars for the officer, and Senhor Voss moved swiftly to have the slaves brought out, but again Uncle William held up his hand.

Behind me Mr. Dingwall laughed in an amazed, drunken way.

"The boy who was killed had a gold collar," said Uncle William. "Where is it?"

Porky Ben shot up from his stool and almost ran across the semi-circle to stand in front of Uncle William. He bawled at him in Mandingo. Uncle William blew tobacco smoke. Porky Ben spluttered

Everyone started to argue among themselves. Porky Ben bellowed for silence.

He had three or four gold chains round his neck, and now he took them off, flung them on to the matting in front of Uncle William, and stamped on them.

Ben Riley laughed.

Porky Ben went up to him and held up his hand in the sign of the evil eye. There was consternation.

The King stood up, and his authority took command. The dealers bowed. Governor Bayliss gestured at Uncle William, who stood up and took off his hat. Everyone was mollified. The King called for the slaves to be brought out.

Uncle William picked up the gold chains and threw them at me. "There you are," he said. "Didn't Peter Case say he'd make his will in your favour?"

I put the chains round my neck. They were unexpectedly heavy. There was a buzz of interest, and Senhor Voss grimaced in mock horror. I was hot and embarrassed, and I bent my head to examine the workmanship of the chains.

Then I heard a cry from Mr. Dingwall. I turned round. Mr. McBride had dumped him into his seat. I looked to see what had moved Mr. Dingwall, and there, held together by neck thongs, was a line of slaves.

They were wet and naked, and most of them had tribal scars and amulets. I could not understand why Porky Ben was laughing. Then I did, because the slaves were people we had lived with in the Jola village.

Uncle William seemed not to have noticed. "Thank you, Mr. McBride," he said, and Mr. McBride got up to make his examinations. I wanted to scream and shout, but I knew that I must not.

One of the slaves bellowed because he had recognized us. It was the leader of the village field gang. A guard banged him in the stomach with a musket butt.

"Take care of that man!" snapped Uncle William. "He's in prime condition!"

I had been friends with half the people in the line. I had wrestled with Nipper and laughed with the others. Now they were damned but I did not care, because my dream sister Fourfarthings was not among them.

I felt myself smile and I stood up for elation, and then blood rushed to my head and I did not know what to do because Fourfarthings was there, and her huge eyes stared into mine.

I was dizzy, and I saw her silent scream and her shock at my smile, and I wanted to yell out why I had smiled. I smiled for your safety. I tried to move my lips but no words came.

I was stupid, but Uncle William must always have known that if we took slaves from Fogni they would be Jolas, and that his promises of protection had been worthless.

Senhor Voss and the Governor chatted about the parrot. Ben Riley lolled in his chair and watched the slaves with old-lizard eyes; once I had seen him flattered by the hospitality of the very same people, and heard him fart for their amusement.

The King offered me brandy. I took it. I still had a grin like a rictus and a cold sweat of shame and misery. I wanted to look away but could not.

Senhor Voss said that of course Porky Ben had suggested a raid upon the village that had befriended us, but that in his own opinion it was not the action of a true bigman. The Governor agreed. He was sure that Senhor Voss himself would have shown more tact. Senhor Voss gobbled up the compliment, and said that the palaver was nevertheless a triumph. It was best to have only one white power on the river. Conflict between the whites meant uncertain trading, and that was badbad for everyone.

Mr. McBride was peering into mouths, and inspecting vaginas for any signs of discharge. He held Fourfarthings by the jaw and shoved her head this way and that. Her eyes still burned into mine. Porky Ben called for a big handsome youth to meet the hundred bars owed for the dead officer. He said that when he actually came to pay a debt he was his father's son and would pay it properly.

"What do you take me for?" he asked. "A white man?"

Uncle William laughed and spat, and they struck hands. Uncle William sent our bosun and two sailors to go in Senhor Voss's dugouts with the slaves. Fourfarthings watched me. I ducked away and then glanced back. She still watched me.

As she was marched away she twisted herself round in the leather collar as far as she could. It made her stumble, and the slave behind cuffed her, but she still watched me until the file was hustled out of sight.

The King dallied with one of his wives. His red-capped secretary wrote furiously on a scroll. The domestic slaves brought meat and rice laid out on palm leaves. As the drums rattled and throbbed, dancers came out.

Governor Bayliss looked exhausted. The parrot was under his chair again; it did not like the drums. I looked at Mr. Dingwall. He pretended that he had not seen me, and drank deeply.

Uncle William, Mr. McBride, and the mulatto merchants stood in a group, their hands clasped behind their backs, chuckling with a great respect for one another's cunning; now and then they glanced keenly around. They exuded satisfaction, and reminded me of the cattle-drovers at Low Crags after they had sold a beast.

"Well, young man," said Governor Bayliss. "What do you think of it all?"

"Very satisfactory," I heard myself say. I thought of Fourfarthings. She would be branded. Her flesh would sizzle. I touched myself on the chest, in the place where it would happen. I tried to imagine the pain, but I could not; I could only think how tight the scabs must feel.

The King's dancers wore masks of leaves and creepers. One of them stuck his staff in the sand and whirled himself round it with his feet in mid-air.

When more food came I realized that I was hungry, and ate.

Eventually, with torches in the bow of Senhor Voss's cutter, we slipped out of the creek and steered towards the *Margaret*'s feeble lanterns. The breeze was against us, and the stench of her cargo carried across the moon-bright water.

Chapter 17

The Middle Passage

I once heard Uncle William argue that we could see God's hand in the slave trade because in the dry season the trade winds blew ships on to the coast of Africa, and in the wet season they blew them away and across the Atlantic. Be that as it may, after we had weighed for the West Indies it took us days of tacking and sounding to get clear of the coast and the shoals, because the *Margaret* was so foul with weeds that she needed the stronger ocean breezes to drive her along. Then the days turned cold and blustery, and we had to keep the slaves below and lay tarpaulins over the grating. Eventually the weather cleared and we were able to assume a proper routine.

Twice a day the slaves were brought up on deck in groups of thirty or more to exercise and eat raw yams and horse beans, varied sometimes with rice and salt fish, and to drink half a pint of water. When Mr. Partridge was satisfied that the chains were properly run together through ringbolts, he would say, "Thank you, Mr. Bosun. Let's see them jump."

The bosun ordered the slaves to jump up and down. If they were very stiff or sullen he would leap up and down himself and shout gibberish. Then he would flick the slaves with his rope's-end until they unwillingly jumped themselves, their chains clanking, their limbs bending and jerking in a mockery of high spirits.

While this took place on deck, Mr. McBride would oversee the scrubbing-down of one section after another of the hold.

The women and children and more docile men brought up the buckets of excrement and emptied them overboard. There were often spillings of one sort or another and sometimes shrill arguments in which the filthy slops would be thrown at someone and the culprit given the thumbscrews.

But punishment was a delicate matter. A physically damaged slave was worth much less than a sound one. It might often be better to kill outright than to maim, even though killing was an escape that could not be too lightly offered, and a dead slave was worth nothing at all.

Once a week the men slaves were washed under the pumps, and occasionally they were shaved. This task, performed with relish by such as True and Davy Morgan and James Lees, who were craftsmen and liked to exercise their hands, took an entire day. The slaves came up in pairs and sat back to back upon two stools.

The women were brought up in the afternoons and could sometimes be made to dance and sing. But if their hearts were not in it, at least they were not so openly hostile as the men, who often refused to exercise as an act of defiance. Mr. Partridge and Uncle William walked among them and hit them, Uncle William with a lot of earnest and regretful conversation that they could not understand, and Mr. Partridge silently, with his straight back and his dark, watchful eyes.

Another trick of protest was to refuse to eat, and that is why they were fed on deck—they could be watched. If they threw their food overboard, they could be given more. If they had a genuine sickness, its warning signs might show at this time, and the sufferer could be put in the sick-bay and given a special diet.

Each slave's cloth had his or her number stamped on it and the men were chained together in the order of purchase, so their progress could be checked in Uncle William's ledger and their identities kept track of as some died and others were linked to new partners.

Despite this close observation I often saw slaves on deck pretend to chew and swallow, and then when they returned to the hold, spit the mess from their mouths into the buckets or try to hide it in the recesses of the shelving. Sometimes a man would be ignored in the hope that hunger would defeat him. Another would be dragged out and made to chew and swallow. It depended on Uncle William's estimation of his character.

But many must have made this silent protest undetected, and its effect upon their health did not concern them. They dwindled into sickness and death with a resignation that infuriated us. They lay with their own flux seeping round them, the flow that a man cannot stop and runs from him even while he walks or crawls or tries to eat. First it is yellow, and then, when there is nothing more to pass except the very moisture of his body, it is glassy and of no particular colour, and sometimes blood and pus are in it like flecks or tendrils, and sometimes it is just a steady, wet, run down the legs, like water down a rock face. I saw men in that extremity kicked and beaten, and I knew why: they had allowed themselves to become disgusting and bewildered animals, and yet they still had reproach in their eyes.

At first I tried to convey to the Jolas that I had had no part in their capture. It was neither my fault nor my wish that they had been enslaved. But if they allowed me to catch their eyes all I saw there was hatred, and if I went near them the men tried to strike me.

Fourfarthings refused to look at me. She averted her head so persistently that in the third week I lost my temper. I grabbed her jaw and tried to force it round. She did not resist, but went limp and fell on the deck, and still refused to look at me. Her body had filled out since the time we lived in the hut. I hit her as she lay there. Our sailors jeered and Uncle William told me not to go near her. But there was still a desperation between her and me.

Many slaves responded to the ship with blank obedience. They did not live off hatred; they did not live off anything, because they no longer had any idea what they should do or think or feel. They sat for half the day and rocked themselves. When told to jump for exercise, they jumped up and down like mad puppets and had to be made to stop. Then they chattered happily, as though this were a dream from which they would soon awake and find themselves in their huts in the stillness of the morning.

A few others tried to get what advantage they could for themselves, as though the routine of a slave ship were a natural way to live, and they could improve themselves or even be set free by compliance.

Some of these, men and boys as well as women, gave their bodies to the sailors, and others made a great show of eating up their food, or of exercising, or of helping Mr. McBride on his medical rounds.

When we were four weeks out in warm and sunny weather, Uncle William had our men put the boats in order after the wear and tear of the season. He wanted us alert and occupied on deck because he was afraid. He thought that the slaves were too quiet and too well behaved.

With the mixture of languages, and the groans and stench of the sick, the increasing filthiness of all their bits of cloth and coverings, and the litter of broken pots and human mess, the hold was a confused scene at best, and yet Uncle William was convinced that there was a common and mutinous mood among the slaves.

He held two unexpected night searches for arms, but all they produced were bad temper and blows in the lantern shadows. He made True and James Lees inspect the stanchions every day. He abruptly changed the positions of everyone, moving some men from the shelf to the deck on the opposite side. He checked our own weapons daily, and spoke severely to our men, because he had known one mutiny started with a pistol that a woman had wheedled from her sailor lover.

He hoped by this vigilance to make our own men aware and to dissuade the slaves; it was obvious that they knew what we were doing from the way in which some of them grinned and chattered during our weapons searches, or when Matt True checked the stanchions and ringbolts.

Uncle William then sent Mr. Dingwall to overhear the Mandingo speakers, but Mr. Dingwall was drunk, and laughed as though we were pissing into the wind. In any case some of the slaves had heard him speak Mandingo on shore, and they shouted a warning to the others.

This made us more nervous. If we swung in our hammocks at night and heard an unaccustomed creak or patter, we started up as though it were a naked foot coming to kill us. We all at one time or another saw black men with stanchions in their hands, and were about to scream out when clouds uncovered the moon and the shadows changed. Our tempers frayed. The blacks gave us many slow and arrogant glances in reply.

To Uncle William these glances proved that he was right. He had sniffed murder. He would not be satisfied until he had rooted it out. Yet it puzzled him. There was a strange odour, something that he could not explain.

He had made me take up my lessons again, but because of his irritability I could do little right. The space between us widened; yet in measuring it we knew that we still had great love for each other.

One day I was on watch at dawn, when the misery and wet cold of being on the ocean is turned to magic by the spread of light. Mr. Partridge, who at that hour always wore a tarpaulin hat and a woollen scarf, called me to the rail and pointed. There were large bundles of gulfweed in the water. It seemed strange that they could live like that, floating plants hundreds of miles from any coast.

Uncle William noted our sighting in the log and told a few blood-curdling stories of the Sargasso Sea, where the weed grew so thickly that it held ships fast; and there they stayed, sails rotted, crew a heap of bones, for ever. Then he laughed, the first time that I had heard him do so for days, and I was sure that the weed had been the omen of a change in our situation, and I was right, because that evening we discovered the plot.

We did so not by cunning or precautions but in the simplest way, by treachery. Our informant was Nipper. He was a sturdy youth now, and we kept him chained. Presumably he hoped to be better treated and to pay off some score against his elders.

What he did, when he saw Mr. McBride in the hold, was to clutch at his stomach and howl. Mr. McBride had him removed to the sick-bay for examination. Nipper knew a few words of pidgin and whispered that the water was poisoned.

"Nonsense," said Mr. McBride. "You've an internal cramp."

Then he understood that Nipper was not describing his complaint but giving a warning. He sent for Uncle William. Nipper repeated his whisper.

"When?" said Uncle William.

"Been do," said Nipper.

"When?"

Nipper held up one finger.

"Yesterday, by God," said Uncle William. He put his finger under Nipper's chin, lifted it up, and looked at him sternly. He pointed at the great water butts in the hold. Nipper shook his head. Uncle William pointed upwards. Nipper nodded.

They had poisoned the casks on deck, those we left open or loosely covered for daily use and to catch the rainwater.

Uncle William grunted. "How?" he said.

"Obeah," said Nipper, his eyes rolling in fear.

"Obeah!" said Uncle William. "I should have known it!"

He squeezed Nipper's shoulder and beamed at him as though he were his own son. He left Mr. McBride to the pretend examination and nodded at me to follow.

On deck it was almost dusk. "Bosun!" shouted Uncle William, as he marched to the water casks. "Tuffrey!" The seaman Tuffrey ambled up. To me Uncle William said, "Take off your shirt," and explained that I should hold my nose, and with the bosun holding one leg and Tuffrey the other, be lowered into each water cask. With my free hand I would search the bottom of the cask for an object that I would certainly find there. I gave Uncle William my shirt and gold chains to hold.

I cannot say, what with the shock of being upside down and the surprising coldness of the water, and remembering to hold my nose with my left hand rather than my right, that I performed very efficiently or without a lot of ridiculous spluttering, and a moment of panic when Tuffrey accidentally let go; but I did find an object at the bottom of each cask.

They were the little wooden charms that Jolas wore around their arms and necks. To make them sink, their strings had been wrapped around nails prised from the shelves and bulkheads.

The Jolas believed that by saying certain spells over them they could draw from these charms the power to kill. Somehow they had been dropped into the casks during the exercise period, and the Jolas now believed that the water was poisoned.

Uncle William shook his head. He sighed. He was always touched by what he called childish ignorance.

"Poor devils," he said, "whatever in the world can become of them?"

He untied the thongs and put the nails in his pocket. Then he replaced the charms, made sure that they floated, and balanced the lids on the casks again.

Next morning he had the Jola men and whomever they happened to be chained to brought up first. They were uneasy. Mr. Partridge was expressionless. Some of the women came up. Uncle William told them to dance. Fourfarthings was with them. Her branding scab was almost off. There was yellow under one bit of it.

"I like a sing-song," said Uncle William, and incited the Jola women to make their mouth-music. "Where's Mr. Dingwall? He likes a sing-song, too, doesn't he? Doesn't he like operas? Eh? Where is he?"

Mr. Dingwall was called from his cabin. He was unshaven and shirt-sleeved, and there was mess all down the front of him.

" 'Morning, Henry," said Uncle William, and strolled through the jumping blacks to the water casks. He had a pannikin in his hand. He took the lids off the casks. The blacks stared at him.

Uncle William dipped the pannikin into each cask in turn. He drank deeply. He smacked his lips.

Then, as though remembering a message that he should have passed on to an old friend in the coffee-house, he said, "Ah!" He fumbled in his pocket and flung down the nails among the men slaves. They stopped jumping. Their eyes stared.

"What have we here?" said Uncle William, and fished out the charms. He held them up and flung them overboard angrily, one by one. The slaves watched them with pain and shock in their eyes.

"Perhaps they'll poison the ocean," said Uncle William. "What do you think, Henry? Can a bit of the old obeah poison the Atlantic?"

Mr. Dingwall hung his head. The gunner, Davy Morgan, laughed.

"Silence!" snapped Mr. Partridge.

Uncle William smiled. "Mr. Partridge," he said, "you're the best officer I've known." He pulled his pistol from his belt and walked up to the Jola who had brought the messages to the village council. He hit the Jola across the face with the butt. There was a crack as the man's teeth broke. Uncle William hit him again.

"Fool!" he said. "Ignorant heathen fool!"

He ordered the man to be flogged, although there was no evidence that he had inspired the plot, and indeed Uncle William did not seek any. He did not care to. He cared about riding roughshod, and after that the atmosphere on the ship changed.

The blacks were downcast and confused, and our men cocky and aggressive; they had no doubt now that they were superior.

Nipper was given the freedom of the deck. He capered about, very pleased with himself. He wanted me to wrestle with him, but I did not have the heart. When he was left on deck at night, he sulked, and after two days he went back to the hold and sat among the women.

At first he scowled and snatched at other people's food. When they pushed him back he pouted and argued, but after a while he said very little. He cuddled all day against Fourfarthings and sucked his thumb.

We had already seen tropic birds and boobies, and now, unexpectedly and excitingly, there was a flock of small birds that meant the land was not far away. We were all of us, even Uncle William, so cheered by this that we did not notice until it was too late the change that the discovery of the poison plot had wrought in Mr. Dingwall.

It was a warm evening. Mr. McBride was on watch, and Uncle William, Mr. Partridge, Mark Baker, and I sat at dinner round the state-room table. The cook, Joseph Fielding, a sallow, flat-footed, dark-haired little man, grumbled as usual about his wife in Liverpool. Mark helped him carry in the dinner.

Since the discovery of the plot Mr. Dingwall had hardly been seen. He tacked some old canvas across his cabin doorway so that we could not watch his shame, although we had heard him retch often enough, and been disturbed by his efforts to clean up when he thought that we were asleep. Fielding did not even set him a place at mealtimes, but left him to take what he wanted from the galley—which was not much, because when he was drinking he did not bother to eat.

So the last thing we expected was that he would enter the state-room, apologize for his lateness, and with one flicked glance inform Fielding that he expected a place laid, and food. Uncle William stared and said, "Are you sober?"

"Perfectly," said Mr. Dingwall, and he was. His hair was half-white, and where his skin did not pucker into folds it shone with a strange inner light. He was round-shouldered, and if he did not concentrate upon his walk he shuffled. His mouth seemed to have fallen in without his having lost any teeth. He looked fifteen years older, and yet his eyes were bright, and his mind sparkled.

He asked Fielding to bring him wine and sipped it lightly. He talked about the vineyards of the Burgundy escarpment that once when he was a young man he had visited, rolling along in a private coach with his brother and a tutor. He described their subsequent journey over the Alps. There were summer snow-patches and cattle bells in the mist, and then the descent to the sudden blue warmth of the Mediterranean, the ivied ruins, and the laughter at night on narrow Venetian canals.

He smiled at me, as though to say: Here is a world that you must try to enter. When Mr. McBride appeared for a moment to take a nip of brandy, Mr. Dingwall reminded him that the poets of the Irish west extemporized to the harp like the Mandinka griots. Mr. McBride's glance was vulnerable, and I realized for the first time that his cynical talk was a defence. He was a person who felt himself excluded. In his heart he liked the English no more than the blacks did.

Mr. Dingwall put mean and puffy Mark Baker in his place without ever shaming him, and Uncle William he entranced and at the same time deflated his personality. For an hour or two he was utterly and effortlessly the master, and Uncle William's crude dominion disappeared.

Then when he had fascinated and charmed us, when he had persuaded us that we were in some ancient palazzo and not the low, ill-lit, swaying, stinking state-room of a slave ship, he brought the talk from Rome and the autumn sun upon its ruins to what each man in the world must do to meet his conscience and respect himself.

I felt Uncle William stir and want to respond, but he did not. Mr. Dingwall's voice was husky and his glance straight. It was like that morning on the burning grasslands, except that now Mr. Dingwall was calm. He was sane and wonderful. When he said that the worst thing in the world was for a man not to have the courage to act upon what he believed, we all agreed with him. We all knew that it was true, and we were silent.

The ship creaked and groaned. The run of the water bubbled outside the stern windows. My heart thumped.

"But if I did what I believed," said Mr. Dingwall, with a wry laugh in his throat, "I would free the slaves and cut off every white head on this ship."

Uncle William stared at him. Mr. Dingwall opened his clenched fist. There was a key in it. He smiled. He stood up and bowed, and left the state-room.

In the silence Mr. Partridge said, "That was the key to the shackles."

Uncle William said, "If he did cut our throats, the blacks would cut his last."

Mr. Partridge repeated what he had said about the key.

"Aye," said Uncle William, and loaded his pistol. We went on deck.

"Where's Henry?" said Uncle William, and Mr. McBride pointed. Mr. Dingwall had scrambled around the barricado to reach the main-deck. We did the same. The sentry at the grating looked agitated.

"He's took the fo'c'sle lantern and gone down there," he said.

We could hear whispers and a surprised rustle through the dark hold.

Mr. Dingwall had unlocked and moved the grating. The ladder down was shadowy, but Uncle William did not hesitate.

Mr. Partridge followed. I scrambled last.

Black shapes stirred all round me. My skin prickled. Uncle William went to the gap in the bulkhead and said, "Henry! Give me that key!"

The lantern cast lurid shadows. Mr. Dingwall unchained the slaves. They seemed surprised. They rubbed their chafed wrists. Mr. Dingwall spoke in Mandingo and gave one of the men his pistol. The man held it as though it were red hot.

"Very well, Henry," said Uncle William. Mr. Dingwall did not look at him. Uncle William fired. Mr. Dingwall banged backwards against the shelving.

Uncle William walked briskly to the slave with the pistol and took it from him. There was the sound of our crew's startled feet on deck.

"Drag him out," said Uncle William, gesturing, and the slaves were so surprised that they obeyed. They dragged Mr. Dingwall to the foot of the ladder. His breath made a bubbling sound. Uncle William ripped the key from his hand and gave it to Mr. Partridge. Mr. Partridge and two men locked the slaves up again.

Uncle William and the bosun heaved Mr. Dingwall up on deck. His shirt was soaked in blood and there was a massive exit wound in his back. Uncle William shook him and said, "Henry! Henry!" Mr. Dingwall did not reply, because he was dead.

Uncle William had him wrapped in canvas and weighted, and there and then, in patchy moonlight, said the burial service, and the bosun and the fiddler, O'Sullivan, tipped the body overboard.

I could not believe it. I thought about the black with the pistol and why he had not used it. It must have been because he did not trust a white man.

Part Three

Hawksbill

The profits of a sugar plantation in any of our West Indian Colonies are generally much greater than those of any other cultivation that is known in either Europe or America.
—ADAM SMITH

Chapter 18

Leslie's Scramble

Three days later, and six weeks after we had weighed from the Gambia, the *Margaret*'s best bower anchor plunged into the clear water of our West Indian destination: the land-locked harbour of St. Johns, Antigua, the capital of the Leeward Islands. The bay was a mile wide, the sky was blue and the breeze refreshing. There were two yellow freestone forts, scallop-shaped bays, and scrubby hills, and the little town sparkled white amid lush green; to welcome us a shallop brought out Smallshaw and Hill's agent in Antigua, Mr. Leslie, a dark man, thinnish, stooping and sallow, with long arms and a long face and nose. He wore his own hair but it was lank and receding. There were shadows round his eyes and a boil on his cheek. He was about thirty years old and a Scotsman; over the years so many of the merchants in Antigua had been Scotsmen that the dusty street behind one of the lines of waterfront yards was called Scotch Row.

Mr. Leslie greeted Uncle William warmly, with a grin, and handed him a packet of letters that had come from Liverpool. Nearly two years ago he had passed on the letter from Mr. Sayer that announced my wish to go to sea, and now Uncle William introduced me. Mr. Leslie shook my hand and said how good it was when a widower like himself saw a family united. Then before anyone else could speak he reeled off a list of figures about the price of everything—slaves, corn, tobacco from Virginia, draught oxen, and sugar itself—and said that because there were two other Liverpool ships off Parham Harbour we must sell our slaves first if we wanted the highest price.

Happily he had already contracted to sell fifty sight unseen to Cochrane's Plantation. The average agreed price was fifty pounds and these slaves should be the best and the strongest; we should get them ashore at once to be collected by Cochrane's overseer. Mr. Leslie talked so excitedly that he seemed about to stutter, but never did.

He thought that another twenty slaves could be sold by a similar private treaty to the Five Islands Plantation. This left us—ten having died on the voyage—with sixty slaves to account for. Uncle William and Mr. McBride reckoned that forty of those were sound and could be sold by scramble. The rest would have to be prepared for auction.

Mr. Leslie went into the hold to look over the merchandise. He was pleased. He said that he would wash and shave the slaves for Cochrane's and rub them with palm oil, so that when they were taken away their appearance would impress the onlookers and attract more people to the scramble.

In the state-room Uncle William brought out the slave book and the check-lists that he had prepared for Mr. Leslie. Mr. Leslie suggested prices for the scramble, which Uncle William accepted, and they marked on their lists which slaves would go to Cochrane's, which to Five Islands, and which to the scramble and auction.

Uncle William had a full mug of brandy. He spilt ink on the ledger and had to be reminded by Mr. McBride of which slaves were which. Yet if Mr. Leslie thought him drunk he gave no sign. Mr. Leslie would not take a drink himself until the immediate business had been settled, and when it was, his excitement stopped and he had nothing more to say.

He was embarrassed and graceless. He crossed and uncrossed his legs and tried not to touch his boil. He asked me questions, but when I answered he did not listen to what I said. He was withdrawn. He was very shrewd, and yet he had no idea that his mannerisms unsettled other people. He put the tips of his fingers together and waited. Silence. Mr. McBride excused himself and so did I. I joined Mr. Partridge at the maindeck rail and watched the boats get the first lot of slaves away.

Some of the other small craft that criss-crossed the harbour were rowboats almost awash under a full hogshead of sugar; one black in the bows steadied the hogshead and another sat in the stern and rowed. Our own cargo for England would be delivered in the same precarious fashion, said Mr. Partridge; and of the other vessels in the bay he advised me to study one in particular, a lean, raking thing like an enormous Gambia River cutter. It was a Virginia schooner, from our colony in North America, and none other than the *John and James*, the command of the notorious Captain Fogg.

"What's notorious about him?" I asked, but before Mr. Partridge could reply, Mr. Leslie came on deck with Uncle William. Uncle William had to report to the Customs House, and sent me ashore with Mr. Leslie for more papers and receipts.

We crowded into the shallop with ten slaves. I stared at the shore. Behind the waterfront the whitewashed houses climbed the hill for four or five streets. They had balconies and green jalousies over their windows. There was one much more imposing building; it was the Court House, said Mr. Leslie. Above the houses was the church, three-quarters of the way up the hill. It looked strangely English among the palms and creepers.

Mr. Leslie's yard was one of several that lined the sandy banks of the foreshore. One of his sheds had big doors that opened on to a jetty and a crane. There were open timber sheds and long, low, window-less slave quarters, the floor of which was strewn with crackling leaves and vegetation that Mr. Leslie said was the trash cut off sugar canes. Streaks of sunlight came through cracks in the planking. The door was open, but guarded by a white overseer with a whip and a gang of blacks in bits and pieces of European clothing. They carried cutlasses and spoke what sounded like a fuller and more fluent ver-sion of the pidgin.

On the ship, when our men laughed and cheered at the first sight-ing of Antigua, the slaves had been excited. Now they sat in the trash and looked bewildered, even ones whom I knew to have been rebel-lious.

I looked for Nipper and Fourfarthings. Nipper was crouched against the wall. He was sucking his thumb. Fourfarthings I could not see. I looked at my check-list. Nipper was to go tomorrow to Cochrane's, and my heart pounded as I saw against the Number 131 a quickly scrawled letter *S*; it meant that Fourfarthings was put down for the scramble.

On the street side of the yard, three or four black women gossiped around an outdoor kitchen whose smoke drifted in the sunshine, and yellow dogs slumbered on the steps of Mr. Leslie's house. It was half-stone and half-wood. One end of it was a shed in which Mr. Leslie stored his imported trade goods, from crockery in straw to candles, tobacco, and glue. In the middle was the counting-house, and then the living-rooms. A verandah ran along the front. Palm fronds whispered, and red flowers trailed against the jalousies.

We entered the counting-house. There were high shelves, desks, and a mahogany wardrobe. The rooms beyond opened directly one into another; they were dim because their jalousies were closed, but in one a bar of sunlight cut the gloom. In the counting-house an old white man and a young one sat on tall stools, and a black man sat on the floor with his back to the wall.

The old man hopped off his stool to be introduced. He was a scrap of a fellow with a withered leg that made him dip as he walked, but his eyes blinked ferociously.

"Lomas," he said. "See that ledger? I've got it all in my head, and more besides."

The black man groaned and chuckled. Lomas brandished his skinny arm at him. The black pretended to flinch.

"Caesar," said Lomas, "keep your place."

He flicked his quill pen, and ink spattered across Caesar's face. Caesar smeared it dry with his forearm.

The young clerk looked round and winked. He had a round face, and his dark hair had been shaved off and had just started to grow again.

I was sweating. I leaned against the threshold of the verandah.

Mr. Leslie took off his coat and shirt and threw them on the floor. Nobody picked them up. There were more boils in the middle of his back. They were livid on the pasty skin. He grimaced. I turned my face to the breeze.

"That's your trade winds, is that," said Lomas. "It makes these islands paradise."

The slave Caesar got up on his haunches and peered at Mr. Leslie's back. He muttered to himself. It seemed to me that the room next to the counting-house was Mr. Leslie's bedroom. I could see chamber pots and old candle ends.

I stepped out on to the verandah. I thought about Mr. Dingwall.

I felt peaceful because I knew what I must do. There were palms and spiky bushes and yellow butterflies among the dumped stores and oxcarts. There was another yard opposite, and mean little shops eight feet square.

Behind me Mr. Leslie sighed. I turned. He had put back his shirt but not tied the strings. Caesar and the kitchen women proposed to treat the back boils with a poultice wrapped in leaves. It was an effort for Mr. Leslie to speak but he did so.

"Your uncle talked about the voyage," he said. "He described your misfortunes. I told him not to reproach himself. A good profit seems assured."

I stared at him. I wondered why I had not noticed before how grubby and food-stained his clothes were; because of their sombre colours, I decided.

Mr. Leslie fidgeted. He pointed down the street and said that it led to the Parade, where the merchants strolled in the cool of evening to discuss business. Then he fell silent, until with a quick glance at me before he spoke he said, "There's one question I've always wanted answered, Tom, ever since I've known your uncle. I wonder if you can do it for me."

I was surprised. I mumbled that if I could answer the question I would.

"Was—er—I wonder if you do know—was Henry Dingwall, late of your ship, blood kin to the Dingwalls of Alcaig?"

I stared. My mind was blank. Outside the verandah the sunshine was brilliant.

"Alcaig," said Mr. Leslie, "was of course the title bestowed by courtesy upon the eldest son of the Earl of Orrin."

"No," I said. "I mean—I don't know."

Mr. Leslie nodded. He moved his back to ease the pain of the boils.

"I only asked that question, Tom, because my dead wife's family were the Dingwalls of Strathaven, who were, in centuries past, a cadet branch of the Alcaig line."

I nodded. A white man went past on horseback. He saluted us with his whip.

"Today there is no Earl of Orrin. The title is vacant," said Mr. Leslie. He smiled ruefully. He drummed on the rail with his fingers. I thought that he would speak again, but he turned and walked past me into the counting-house.

I was alone in the scented shade. When I turned myself, it was to see Mr. Leslie pick up his coat and throw it into the bedroom.

"How big is Antigua?" I said. It was the first thing that came into my head.

"Twelve miles across," he said. I noticed in the gloom of the bedroom a stack of dining-chairs.

"How many whites are there?" I said.

"Three thousand," said Mr. Leslie, "but you'll understand that not all of them are in society."

The young clerk snickered. His name was Jerry Hoskins.

How many blacks? Thirty-two thousand.

Lomas limped into the bedroom and pissed into one of the chamber pots. He did not kneel because it was too difficult for him, and his first and last spurts went on the floor.

"He's a lazy bugger is that Caesar," he said, and climbed back on his stool.

How many of the blacks were free? A surprising number. Several hundred, in fact. They included most of the women street traders, and nearly all the prostitutes.

Uncle William was very drunk when I gave him the receipts. He sat in the state-room with his Bible on his lap. He took the receipts, shut the Bible, and flung it across the room. When I moved to pick it up, he snarled. Then he repented and grasped my wrist. There were tears in his eyes. He held me to him. He smelled of sweat and stale drink.

Should I talk to him? I wondered. Should I open my heart and tell him what I planned to do? I wanted to, but he was stupidly drunk and my earnest stare annoyed him. "You look like bloody John," he said. Who? His brother John. My father. He shouted for the punt and went ashore. He did not return until the following afternoon, when he took a bottle of brandy to his hammock and was asleep before dark. By then we had landed all the slaves and the ship was strangely silent. She reeked of old sorrows.

Next morning Mr. Leslie hoisted a flag above his yard, the customary signal that a sale was to take place. I was rowed over with my check-list in time for the start at six o'clock. Uncle William was still asleep.

The slaves had been herded into one of the open timber sheds, and the yard and counting-house were full of buyers. Important planters dealt by private treaty and were too proud to attend a scramble, but there were some Army officers, a weather-beaten elderly woman with a parasol, many hard-faced overseers, and owners of small farms and plantations, who were callused and sunburned from working in the fields themselves. There were men who looked like officers from other ships in the bay, and others of all sorts who had come to watch and gossip. There were bullock carts and horses, and numerous ragged blacks who lay in the dust and chewed pieces of sugar cane and argued with the women traders who had set out their wares to catch the crowd. I went into the counting-house.

There was a lot of loud talk and tobacco smoke. The most flamboyantly dressed man was a mulatto. He wore a red satin coat, grubby white breeches, and riding-boots, and carried a straw hat and a silver-knobbed cane. He had a big, square, grizzled, European-looking head, and laughed very conceitedly at his own jokes. He seemed to me to be tipsy on the pepper-punch that Caesar replenished and young Jerry ladled out from a china bowl. Mr. Leslie was careful to call him "Mr. Hanson," but when he did so, the other men sneered.

Mr. Leslie was in his near-stuttering, excitable state. His boil looked bigger, and he dabbed at his sweat with a large crimson handkerchief. I suddenly panicked and went into the bedroom. It was shuttered and Caesar still had not emptied the chamber pots. As well as a truckle bed and clothes strewn everywhere, there was a folded-up dining-table. Then there was a pantry used as a spice-store, and what seemed to have been the drawing-room. It was here that the jalousie was broken, and the shaft of sun illuminated dust and spiders. Next to that was what must have been the bedroom before Mr. Leslie's wife died of fever, for it contained a four-poster, and a child's cot, and a pierglass, and several travelling trunks. Lastly there was a maid's room that had a hammock and a man's clothes everywhere, and smelt of tobacco and empty rum bottles. I knew because Mr. Partridge had told me that this was where Jerry slept. Old Lomas had his own quarters in the town.

Outside were the bright light and brilliant colours, and inside it was dirty and uncared-for after the death of the woman and child.

Mr. Partridge had told me that Mr. Leslie was the younger son of a village schoolmaster on the Ayrshire coast. His wife was the daughter of a draper, and a little above him; it was her uncle who had been a plantation overseer, and found the young couple a place in Antigua.

By his own efforts Mr. Leslie had risen in twelve years from being a clerk like Jerry to the important merchant that he was today, yet in these dismal rooms it hardly seemed worth it.

Outside, leaves scraped the jalousie and insects whirred. Mr. Hanson's laughter seemed far away. I was very aware of myself. Nobody knew I was here. I was free and secret. I could do what I pleased. I remembered High Top, where no one could see me because the moors were empty. Then I turned my back on childhood, and went to old Lomas at the open ledger.

"How much for a girl?" I said.

"Eh?" he said.

"I want to buy a girl in the scramble."

He looked at me in amazement.

"Buy one?" he said. "Buy one? You can fuck one for nothing round the corner."

He meant it. I suddenly poured sweat. I thought: All these men are staring at me. They weren't, but Mr. Leslie was. He asked me what I wanted. I told him. I said that I would pay with my gold chains.

"I've told him he can fuck one round the corner," said Lomas.

Mr. Leslie seemed about to expand this argument, but advised me instead to think what Uncle William might say. I said that the chains were mine. Whether Mr. Leslie misunderstood me or took refuge as he always did in business, I could not tell.

"It's how I began, Lomas," he said. "I bought and sold on my own account, did I not?"

He called for a balance, and talking briskly about the price of gold, he weighed my chains, nodded, and walked away. I expected him to take the chains with him, but Lomas made me pick them up again. "We settle up at the end, sonny; in case you're unlucky." I felt foolish for not knowing, and went outside.

I was trembling. I took deep breaths. Then I pushed through the people until I saw Fourfarthings on the other side of the shed. Before I could work my way round, young Jerry rang a handbell for attention. Mr. Leslie came out of the house and stood on a chair to repeat the rules of the scramble.

There was one price for men slaves, one for women, and one for children. At the drop of the crimson handkerchief we could enter the timber shed and scramble for the slaves we wanted. A slave would belong to the first person who grasped his or her right wrist. A handkerchief tied round the wrist would be accepted as proof of ownership. In the event of a dispute Mr. Leslie's decision was final. Understood?

There were murmurs of "Aye!" Some men had fistfuls of handkerchiefs. Mr. Leslie raised his arm. The boils made him wince.

"Go!" he shouted, and brought down the handkerchief.

There was a roar and I was knocked over. I got up and banged into a man, and ran desperately towards Fourfarthings.

The slaves screamed and started to run themselves. They thought that the crowd was rushing to attack them. People collided and fell over. Mr. Hanson made a noise like a hunting-horn and waved his arms up and down. I stumbled over a pile of wood and saw Fourfarthings twist and turn. The weather-beaten woman with the parasol was running towards her.

I clawed at the woman's skirts and pulled her back. She slipped, and I rushed past her and grabbed Fourfarthings by the wrist. Fourfarthings screamed and then stopped in surprise when she saw that it was me. She cowered. I dragged her out of the shed and into the yard.

I suddenly realized that there was calm. There were coughs and splutters, and some abuse. I was out of breath but elated. I wanted to jump and shout.

Lomas and Jerry handed out bills of sale. I received, as well, an I.O.U. for three guineas. The overseers and small farmers marched off with their new slaves. The weather-beaten woman snorted at me and shook her parasol.

Fourfarthings wore her cloth from the ship wrapped round her and tucked in above her breasts. She had a thin, alert face. Her short hair was ragged. I let go of her wrist and stood back. She did not realize that I had made her free. The men stared at me. I held out my hand. Fourfarthings did not move. I walked away from her.

I heard my own feet scuff the sandy grass, but not hers. I was determined not to turn round. I slowed my pace and saw from the corner of my eye her shadow following mine.

At the punt she jibbed, but the bosun, Thompson, grabbed her round the waist, dumped her aboard, and shoved off. She was terrified again at the ship, but calmed down when she saw that Matt True was dismantling the barricado. I took her not to my cabin but to Mr. Dingwall's. She sat on the floor against the bulkhead.

Uncle William was still asleep and Mr. McBride ashore. Mr. Partridge had heard the men's catcalls, and stalked along the alleyway. His eyes flicked from Fourfarthings to me.

"How did you pay?" he said.

I told him. He nodded.

"Have you got a bill of sale?"

"Yes," I said.

He looked at me, but seemed to be remembering Mr. Dingwall.

"Then you're within your rights," he said, and went.

He knew, as I did, that many blacks had been taken to Liverpool. He did not need to add that I would require Uncle William's permission to take one myself.

Chapter 19

Why Hast Thou Forsaken Me?

My happiness made everything seem beautiful, even the flecks and stains on the cabin wall that I knew to be Mr. Dingwall's vomit. The sun through the port was beautiful, the sounds of leisurely work on deck were beautiful, and the plans in my head were perfection. I explained them in a rush of English. Fourfarthings stared. I laughed. She did not know much pidgin, so I touched all the objects in the cabin and gave them their English names. I touched her arm and said, "Sister," and then I was confused because how did I explain that an arm was an arm and she herself was the sister? If she had to be baptized, I said, she should be named Dingwall plus a given name of her own choosing. Maria Dingwall. Henrietta Dingwall. She would have to wear a big worsted cloak because the moors where we would live were rawly cold.

Crabtree, I said. Can you say Crabtree? Sayer. Mr. Sayer. High Top. Top Vale. I had already admired her nimble fingers when they wove mats and baskets in the village; in England they would help us earn our living at the loom. We would live with the Crabtrees, and Uncle William would visit us when he was home from the sea. When at last he gave it up, the three of us would live together. He had described to me once a cottage he envied, white and isolated, that overlooked the sad, grey sands of Dee. That would be a fine place to be quiet with one another, and know that we each remembered the haze over the surf beaches and the rattle of drums at evening.

Fourfarthings could not understand what I said. She was upset. I touched her. She shied away. I pleaded with her. I want to save you. Believe me. I made a sign for food. She did not respond, so I fetched some from the galley. Fresh fruit had come aboard, and she ate it as though she had forgotten the taste. Her little tongue thrust into it. Her lips slipped and slithered. Her teeth were quick and her nails sharp. She smiled and grunted. I brought more fruit and then water to wash. I found her a comb and a string of trade beads. She giggled and splashed water at me. I splashed some at her. I was entranced.

I touched her with the back of my hand. There was so much I wanted to say. She stared at me. She seemed to expect something, but I did not know what it was. We held our breath. I heard my own heartbeats. Then she sobbed and angrily hit the bulkhead. She was exhausted. I should have foreseen it. How would I feel, I thought, if I had just been released from captivity? I made the sign for sleep— my hands together like a pillow and my cheek upon them. She complained in her own language. I smiled protectively.

She sniffed and blinked and sighed like a little old woman. Then her eyelids drooped and her limbs sprawled out. She turned her back on me and lay on the deck, hip bone in the air, in that elegant African way. In a breath or two she was asleep. For a while I watched her, and then I slipped out and drew Mr. Dingwall's canvas across the doorway.

From the alleyway I could see land through the stern windows, green sunlit slopes and vividly yellow beaches. Uncle William snored. His face was pressed against the side of the hammock. He looked like a big, unshaven child. I smiled. I loved and felt pity for him. Then he snuffled and woke up, and when he saw me, turmoil and suspicion returned to his face, which in sleep had been defenceless.

He swung out of the hammock. He swayed for a moment in his shirt-tails and then banged open the commode and pissed into it. I stepped across the alleyway into my own cabin. I heard the heavy slap of Uncle William's feet as he blundered past. He shouted for a bucket. I heard one pitched over the side and then the splatter as he threw water over himself.

I stared out of my port. Vegetable boats had come alongside, and a black in a straw hat held up bunches of bananas. Our men laughed.

Uncle William returned. In the alleyway he stopped, and there was a scuff as he drew aside the canvas over Mr. Dingwall's door. He grunted, and from the way he did so, I knew that someone on deck had warned him about Fourfarthings. Then he walked on. I turned and saw his wet footprints in the alleyway.

I went to my cabin doorway. Uncle William was in the state-room. He was naked. His body was white and powerful. He rubbed himself dry with the shirt he had slept in, and without looking at me said, "Fetch me some salt, will you, Tom?"

I brought a handful from the galley. He had put on a clean shirt and a pair of loose cotton trousers like those worn by planters and overseers. He took half the salt in his mouth, rinsed it round in his own saliva, and spat it out. He took the rest and with his finger rubbed it over his teeth and gums. He spat that out and opened all the ports and windows. The breeze began to clear the staleness.

Uncle William stowed his hammock, smacking his lips as he did so at the tartness of the salt. He rinsed his mouth with water and spat out into the commode and emptied the commode out of the window. He replaced the bowl, put the lid and his cushion on top of it, and padded to the bottle to pour himself a peg of brandy.

Only then did he look me in the eye, coldly, as though I were a grown male and a threat. Then he squinted, because he had a head-ache. He grinned and toasted me.

"Well," he said. "Since you're a man, perhaps you'll join me in a brandy."

I smiled and shook my head. He threw his tot straight down. He gasped but it pulled him together. He breathed deeply in the breeze and sat down. On the table there were dirty mugs, pipe-ash, fruit-skins, and bottle rings. He looked at them with distaste. Then he took another drink and smacked his lips again.

"By God," he said, "but I'll tell you what. I could eat one of my mother's oatcakes."

I could not stop myself. "Oh, don't laugh and pretend. You know she's on board. Say keep her or not."

Uncle William seemed mystified. Laugh at me? He loved me like a father.

"You know she's on board!"

"What I know," he said, suddenly sharp and jabbing a finger at me, "is that when you bought her it was an act of private trading; and private trading is a privilege exercised at my discretion."

It was true. I mumbled excuses: I know it's a privilege. I wanted to tell you. You were drunk. If you hadn't been drunk—in any case I only thought of it at the last minute.

"What you thought was act first and tell me afterwards," he said.

I nodded. That was what I had thought.

"Good," he said. "Smartly done. I wondered when you'd come out of your shell."

I stared. Had he misunderstood me? Did he still want to mock me? I watched him, and he seemed embarrassed, as though he did not know how to show that he was proud of me, as though somehow affection were unmanly. He laughed, as much at his own confusion as at mine.

"Nay, nay," he said. "You've bought wisely. You're a quick learner. You'll make a good profit when you sell her in Liverpool— very good if you can teach her English and get her used to proper clothes. Can you afford to buy any?"

I nodded. I felt my sweat break out.

"Good," he said, and downed his brandy. The colour had come back to his face. He looked mischievous and ready for the day.

This was the moment I had feared, and I could not step back from it.

"I don't want to sell her," I said. "I want to set her free."

My voice was far away. Light from the water made wave-shapes on the panelling. On deck someone sawed at the barricado.

"Set her free?" said Uncle William.

"With us," I said. "I mean—to live with us."

"I live at sea," said Uncle William.

I had expected that he would be angry and that I would be calm and logical, but somehow it was the other way round. I almost sobbed. I insisted that he knew what I meant.

He laughed and shook his head. "I don't, Tom. I don't know what you mean."

It had seemed self-evident to me. Now I was so confused that my explanation was no explanation at all. But in my heart the decision was still simple; it was true and right. Why else had Mr. Ding- wall died? Fourfarthings was my sister, and Uncle William should give up the trade. Stay at sea if he must, but not in a slave ship.

"Not that I care," I said, "because whatever you do I bought her. I own her. She's mine. I can do what I please."

I shouted despite myself. Uncle William slammed the table top to stop me. I trembled.

"You mean that after all I've done for you a bit of a black girl's more important?"

No. In my own mind I did not mean that. I did not want us to shout. I wanted us to be calm. So did he. Yet there was spittle at the corner of his mouth.

"Well, is she or isn't she? Is that girl more important than me?"

Why did he twist my ideas? I loved him. What did he fear? I implored him to listen to me.

"Listen? To what you say? Why should I? You're as stupid as Henry Jesus Christ Dingwall!" His laugh was bitter. "My God, my God, why hast Thou forsaken me? Thought about that, have you? Realized that there's no God there at all? Eh? Henry Dingwall? La-di-da! Why did he mutiny? Eh? Because he knew that I'd shoot him!"

Not true. Not true, I shouted out.

"Why did he want me to shoot him? Eh?" Uncle William's face was blotched and twisted. "Because he was mad and done for and feared to shoot himself!"

Feared. That's how people on the moors said it. Uncle William laughed again and held out his hands like a man who freely admits that there are other points of view.

"But you live as you please," he said. "I'll not stop you. You do as you please."

He sat back and smiled. I had hurt and failed him, and he knew why. Oh, yes. Henry Dingwall. I was too young to know better and the madness had burned my brain.

"It's the sun, God blast it! That's what dazzles us. You'll see differently at home."

I felt dizzy. Henry Dingwall was not mad. If he was, there was no sanity. My nails dug into my palms. I stared at the heavy set of Uncle William's neck and shoulders. My own set, and my father's. His skin was red and worn. I felt violent. I wanted to hit him, to pummel him into the shape of the man I loved, and who I knew loved me.

He looked up at me. His eyes pleaded. He was desperate. I stood my ground. He smiled ruefully. Then his pride stiffened him, and in his eyes there was his older man's conviction that not much can be done about the world. He stood up to look for his shoes. I sat down. He made an exaggerated show of putting on his coat and a straw hat that he sometimes wore in the sun.

Our quarrel had run out of energy. We each felt uneasy and wanted to be alone. At least, I thought, he has not told me to get rid of Fourfarthings. He admits that there is wrong on both sides. I was sure that we would talk again, calmly, in the balm of evening. I smiled. He blushed and grunted, and clumsily stuffed a handkerchief into his pocket.

He had an invitation to play cards with the officers of the garrison, and called for the punt to take him ashore. I went on deck with him. The men had heard our shouting and pretended not to look at us. Uncle William made the effort to ask me how the scramble had gone, and to respect my replies. Our voices were off-hand and we did not look at each other. I felt a yearning, and so I am sure did he. Yet when the punt took him away he did not look back.

I turned. The men stared at me. Some of them giggled. Their relief at no longer having the slaves on board was explosive, and our officers indulged it. The king of the grog-shops, Black O'Riley, was allowed to send his punt alongside, and there were black girls in the fo'c'sle all night, and much hard drinking by day. The men made me feel alone and foolish. I went below and sat in the state-room; but I felt a stranger there, and so I slumped uncomfortably against Mr. Dingwall's bulkhead and watched Fourfarthings sleep. On deck the men made filthy jokes about her, and yet in a way they were impressed —not even Peter Case had bought a slave to sell.

When Fourfarthings awoke she had more to eat, and I found her a toilet bucket and showed her how to use the hammock. She laughed at that, but when I offered my hand to help her out she pushed me away. I lost my temper and shouted. She sulked. I tried to explain what I felt, but it was impossible. We snapped at each other in our own languages, and she was by turns sullen and over-excited. The nearness of the land and glimpses of other blacks unsettled her, yet when in sign language I offered to take her ashore she refused. My kindness bewildered her. Why would it not? A few hours before, she had been hit and jostled by armed guards.

So we sweated and argued, and more than once I went on deck and stared at the shore and the white houses and the other ships, but always I felt love and sadness and went back to try to tell her that she was free. She refused to look at me. She sobbed, and hugged her frustrated limbs, until at the end of the afternoon, when the sun had lost its power to burn and the breeze came in stronger, gusty swirls, she fell asleep again. I went on deck. A water boat was about to shove off. I was so restless that on an impulse I scrambled into it and went ashore.

They landed me at Mr. Leslie's. The mulatto Mr. Hanson was still in the yard and laughed drunkenly at the kitchen women. The overseer asked me what I wanted. I had no idea. Then I remembered my I.O.U. and asked for Mr. Leslie. The overseer sent me to the slave quarters, where Mr. Leslie sat in the trash with his back to the planking, more like another captive than the master. He grinned and said, "I'm here to weigh up these people for the auction. What do you want?" To cash my I.O.U., I replied, and buy Fourfarthings some clothes.

"Aye," he said. "Of course you do. You must."

He stood up. Bits of trash stuck to his breeches. I wanted to laugh. Mr. Leslie noticed it and furiously brushed himself.

"Don't you fash yourself," he said. "Don't you worry. I know my own faults. I know every cranny of my nature. I'm so intent upon Smallshaw and Hill's reputation that I forget my own self. After all," he said, jerking his head at the nearest slave, "what concerns has that man got?"

None at all, so far as I could see, except that he was grey and wasted and his bones stuck out. The flux dribbled out of him, and he had tried to drag himself away from it, but without strength, so that he was twisted against the planking, and up to his haunches in the filth-soaked trash.

"It would be awful easy," said Mr. Leslie, "to follow the example set by dishonest auctioneers. We might smear rust and gunpowder over a man's sores, and stuff oakum up his anus to absorb the flux. It's awful easy, and in my opinion both foolish and immoral."

It was at auctions of the sick and unwanted that as a young clerk Mr. Leslie had begun his private dealings, and he knew well that the bidders were not fools. Mostly, in fact, they were surgeons, who bought the slaves for a shilling or two, fed them up, and resold them at a profit. Mr. Leslie had soon learned, and never forgotten, that a man so feeble that the surgeons did not want him was not worth keeping alive. Better for reputation's sake to write him off, as one would write off destroyed or fire-damaged stock.

"Write him off?"

"Starve him," said Mr. Leslie, with a sigh. "Let him die in peace, for Smallshaw's sells prime goods only."

Light glowed through gaps in the planking. A friendly breeze stirred the trash.

"Not that I myself have faith in surgeons," said Mr. Leslie, his boil purple and yellow. "Surgeons killed Mrs. Leslie."

He breathed deeply and blinked back a tear. "My wife's death shattered me," he said, and then, to recover, and to speak of normal things, he forced himself to ask, "What did you say brought you here?"

"My I.O.U.," I said.

"Aye," he said. "Oh, aye. Your siller." He brushed more trash off his breeches.

The sick slave lifted his head and looked at me. I realized without much shock that it was Howler. How his body had gleamed when he was brought out before the King of Barra, and how he had agitated me when I stared at him in the *Margaret*'s hold. Now he bared his gums, but whether to smile or snarl I could not tell.

Outside, Caesar had joined the kitchen women, and the sun was a grey glare. The trees swished and rattled, and the fall of the waves seemed to echo them. Of Mr. Hanson there was no sign.

Mr. Leslie said that I should buy slave clothes at the drapery; he himself had run out, and was awaiting a delivery from Liverpool. He gestured grandly at the kitchen. Perhaps when I returned I would take dinner with himself and the clerks?

I said that I would like to very much, and smiled. Even if it was by Mr. Leslie, I had never before been invited anywhere on my own account. I knew that Mr. Partridge would protect Fourfarthings, and there was a part of me that was distant and afraid, and did not want to return to the ship. I knew that I would not feel easy there until I was at peace with Uncle William.

At my acceptance Mr. Leslie nodded and twitched, and loped ahead of me into the counting-house, where at the sight of Mr. Hanson lying dead drunk on the floor he swivelled and walked out again, shouting angrily for Caesar. Master and man stood in the yard and argued.

"I can't shift the bugger," said Lomas, "not at my age." I gave him the I.O.U. and he counted out the money. Mr. Hanson lay on his back and snored. Jerry Hoskins grinned. I made my way to the drapery.

There was still warmth in the hard-baked earth of the streets, which had deep runnels where in the rainy months water ran down the hill. The sun burnished the harbour. Birds rushed about before roosting, and there were sudden gusts of cool air. The shops were little more than booths, since the planters bought most goods directly from the merchants who imported them. A barber proclaimed himself with a bunch of human hair tied to a stick, and I saw a grog-shop that sold tin-ware as well as drink.

The drapery was half a butcher's: on one side of the shop, meat hung on hooks and a black youth swilled blood and offal into the street, and on the other there were cloth-laden shelves up to the ceiling. What I wanted were some of the cheap dresses already made up for household slaves. Fourfarthings was a little taller than I, but by having the draper hold the clothes against me I could tell the size. I bought one dress in calico for that climate, and another in a heavier, bleached, jean material for cold days at sea and Liverpool.

When I stepped outside again, the light was even, with no shadows. The sun had disappeared into its familiar dirty-yellow tropical haze. The clouds were large and ragged. The outline of the hills was sharp. There were people on the balconies of their houses, and in the street itself Caesar, abused by huckster women and snapped at by dogs, struggled uphill with the impossibly drunk Mr. Hanson in a wheelbarrow.

Mr. Hanson came to his senses, got out, and fell over. Caesar heaved him back into the barrow. Mr. Hanson shouted very loudly that Caesar was a damned impertinent nigger, and tried once more to stand.

This time they both fell over, with the barrow on top of them. The draper and the other onlookers howled with laughter. I ran to help.

We got Mr. Hanson in the barrow, and I stuffed my bundle of dresses into his hands, which startled and confused him so much that I was able to hold him steady. Caesar wheezed and groaned as he drove the barrow across the downhill ruts and into Corn Alley, one of the streets that ran parallel to the waterfront, and where the going was easier. When the barrow stopped, Hanson realized where he was and shouted, "O'Riley! Save me! O'Riley!"

We were at a grog-shop, and through the door I could see a green courtyard in which white men sat drinking, one of them a massive unshaven fellow with a shock of dark hair and bright blue eyes. Caesar grinned and stepped back from the shafts.

Mr. Hanson floundered. The big man got up, lifted Mr. Hanson, and carried him like a baby through the shop and into the courtyard. I followed because Mr. Hanson still clutched my bundle.

On two sides of the courtyard there were whitewashed wooden sheds with half-doors like stables, except that women and not horses peered over the top of them. I realized that I must be in Black O'Riley's famous brothel—the nanny-house, as our sailors called it—and that the big dark man was O'Riley himself. The third side of the yard had an outdoor kitchen, a few goats and fowls in a pen, and a lean-to for liquor barrels. There were dense trees in which green-and-yellow finches trilled.

O'Riley laid Mr. Hanson down in one of the booths. A woman laughed. When O'Riley turned he said, "Who the hell are you? Are you from Leslie?"

I shook my head. "I want my bundle," I said.

His little screwed-up eyes took in the situation. "But who are you? Are you a ship-boy?"

I nodded. He grunted, took my bundle from Hanson, and carried it into the grog-shop.

Caesar would not drink inside with the white men, but stood on the doorstep while O'Riley quizzed him about the slave auction. O'Riley seemed older than I had thought at first glance. His shoulders sloped, his belly sagged, and there was grey in his hair. His history I knew from our sailors. He was an Irishman who had been transported to the plantation for theft. When his seven years were up he lodged with a free mulatto woman and sold rum from a cask strapped to his back. Other whites despised him for it. He sopped up their spittle with blarney and a heartless obsequiousness; "Ah, and it's the truth you speak, sir, for what is an Irishman but a poor, stupid, English Negro?"

Then, with a bit of money saved, he rented a hovel and installed two half-caste prostitutes, with himself as their protector. After five years he owned three grog-shops and the brothel, and after ten, it was said, he had made a fortune out of smuggling. The Virginian Captain Fogg was called notorious because he, and his sleek, fast ship, were O'Riley's reputed partners.

I thought that O'Riley had dismissed me from his mind, but abruptly he unrolled my bundle, so that the dresses hung down in front of him. He postured and pouted. "Some ship-boy!" he said. Everyone laughed. His smile was slobbery and contemptuous, and I was sure that he knew who I was, and that I had bought Fourfarthings. He refolded my bundle very neatly, thrust it into my hands, and winked at me. I resented him, and at the same time wished I could have made him respect me.

When Caesar and I walked back, the sun had gone and the harbour was a delicious grey and green. Caesar muttered to himself and shook his head forebodingly, and indeed, when we reached the counting-house, Mr. Leslie did shout at him again for having let Mr. Hanson lie untended on the floor for so long.

Then dinner came, and we made space among the scrolls and ledgers for Caesar to dump fish and rice and cold meat. Lomas used a bowl. Jerry grinned and drank a lot. Mr. Leslie was still sulkily annoyed. He ate greedily, often with his fingers. Outside, the women laughed. There was no conversation until I gave way to my curiosity and asked how Mr. Hanson made money, and by implication why so many white men had extended themselves on his behalf, for I already knew that in the islands even free mulattoes were social dirt and savagely encumbered by the law.

Mr. Leslie said that Alexander Hanson lived in a shanty in St. Paul's Parish, and that so far as money was concerned— But he did not finish his sentence. He huffed, and muttered to himself, and shifted about as though his body were a torture to inhabit. He glared at Lomas and said, "You should have called me the moment the manny collapsed!"

Lomas pursed his lips to defend himself, but Mr. Leslie said, "I'll not listen to you. I'll not listen." Then he sighed and gestured at me. "What must my guest think?" he said. "What must he think?"

I thought that I would like to have Mr. Hanson's importance fully explained, but clearly the subject was too raw. Mr. Leslie cleared his throat and said, "Have I divulged to you my interest in genealogy?"

"No," I said, before I had time to work out that by genealogy he meant his relationship through the Dingwalls of Strathaven to the Dingwalls of Alcaig and the Earls of Orrin. So for an hour I had the whole tale again, with much unrolling and spreading across our dirty plates of dog-eared family charts.

Then Jerry Hoskins went, and so did Lomas, and when Mr. Leslie stopped talking the silence was desperate. His teeth were stained and his nails bitten raw, and in the candlelight his boil cast a disfiguring shadow. The heat was sweaty. Moths banged into the jalousies. Eventually he said that his blacks would row me to the ship, and as they did so, I stared at the stars and pitied him.

I went below to Fourfarthings, who was entranced by the dresses. She leaped up from a sultry doze, and put them on, one after the other. She bared her silky body to do so, and pushed her breasts as high as they would go in the bodices. She tripped once or twice when she tried to flounce, but she giggled and then looked very proud and demure.

Soon she was bold enough to show herself to Uncle William, who sat with Mr. McBride and a bottle in the state-room. His eyes narrowed as he watched her. Abruptly she sat on the stool next to his chair, her elbows on the table, her knees splayed, her feet flat on the deck. Uncle William poked her in the ribs. She sniggered, and from the childish earthiness of the way she sat, sprang up and flowed elegantly away. Uncle William nodded at me curtly, and I went to my hammock.

Hours later I woke up because I heard Fourfarthings cry out. I stumbled into her cabin but she was not there. I doubted my senses. I shook her hammock. It was empty. Yet I heard her wild cries.

I went into the alleyway and saw that in the state-room Uncle William was fucking her from behind. She was on her haunches, like a nanny-goat. She shouted and slapped the deck with her hands. Her body gleamed and shuddered.

When she saw me she cried out in triumph to spite me. Uncle William half knelt and half leaned down on her. He banged into her and stared me in the eye. Moonlight flooded the state-room.

I ran into my cabin. Her cries were louder. She made a gurgling laugh and then wild moans again. Uncle William shouted, "Mary!" and again, "Mary! Mary! Mary!"

I ran on deck. Their noise was even louder.

Mr. Partridge and O'Sullivan were on watch. Their faces were shadowed, but I knew that even in the dark they could see my shame and stupidity. I was sobbing. Mr. Partridge took off his coat, and put it round my shoulders, and over my shirt-tails. It was much too big.

There was only one place in the ship where I could not hear Fourfarthings's ecstasy, and that was in the forepart of the hold, where the men slaves had been. The forward bulkhead and part of the room were still there, and I lay on the top shelf in the dark that stank of excrement, and more recently of vinegar and sawdust.

I was soon soaked in sweat, and more than once I cried out because I heard the voices of lost souls, but when I sat up it was rats and the creaking of the ship. My limbs ached and I banged my joints on the planking. I imagined that I was awake all night but I must have slept, because I was suddenly aware of a dim grey light and the outlines of the shelves and bulkhead. Then I remembered what had happened and I did not want to go on deck. I did not want to be seen.

I pissed in a corner of the hold and skulked about for another hour, but the shelves were uncomfortable and I felt foolish in my shirt-tails and Mr. Partridge's coat. I decided that it would be better to go on deck now, before the morning bustle had properly started, than later.

The light was pale grey, and there was that curious tropical effect of the sun's rising pink reflected in the west. The island breeze was still, and the water flat. There were echoes as someone on shore chopped wood. My bare feet padded.

Mr. Partridge was still on watch. He nodded at me, and I returned his coat. From the way O'Sullivan stared at me I realized that my eyes must be red and swollen.

In the alleyway everything was still. Mr. McBride snored. Had he slept through it all? I wondered. Mark Baker was soundly asleep in the cabin that had formerly been Mr. Bruce's. I glanced at the stateroom. Uncle William and Fourfarthings were in the hammock together.

I dressed as quickly as I could. Only once did I make a noise, when I dropped one of my shoes. I listened. I did not seem to have wakened anyone.

I had no plan in my mind except to go ashore. What I would do here I did not know. I suppose that I wanted to avoid people, and at the same time make them care about me and wonder where I was. I remember a definite notion that if I were allowed to make the decisions, everything would have a happy solution. I felt a sublime confidence in my own powers, and at the same time my mind was blind to everything except details, of which I was abnormally observant: threads in the weave of my hammock, wrinkles in my own skin, the shapes of branches and bushes ashore, individual bubbles in the waves.

I went on deck in my bare feet. The first local boat to come round the harbour was always that of a free black woman and her sons; they sold goat's milk. I would beg a ride from them. I went to the rail; sure enough they were coming towards us, from a Bristol ship anchored nearby.

I bent down to put my shoes on, and as I did so, Uncle William said, "Where d'you think you're going?"

I turned. He was naked, hands on hips, feet squarely planted. I stared at his penis, smaller now than his thumb, and then at his eyes.

"Ashore," I said. "Where d'you think?"

"Don't you flout me."

"Oh, leave me alone!"

"You stupid boy! Grow up! If you want to be a man, be one! You stupid ignorant boy!"

He turned back into the alleyway. I was blindly angry. I ran after him. Mary was my mother's name, and that was what he had called Fourfarthings in the exaltation of the night.

"You called her Mary!" I shouted. "You called her Mary!"

He turned. "Mary?" he said. "Who's Mary?"

"My mother!"

Beyond him I saw Fourfarthings in the state-room. She was naked and turned away, a woman who would not show herself to a man not her own.

"Oh!" said Uncle William. "Your mother! Well, since I'm your father, I reckon I've a right to call on her!"

He turned but I ran up the alleyway. I kicked and shouted and pummelled. For a moment he hopped grotesquely—the space was too narrow to fend me off. Then he hit me in the stomach. I was half winded and sat down.

I tried to tell myself that his jibe was not true, but I knew it was. It was the only fact that made sense of everything. It explained my mother's stories and her secret smile. It explained my father's bitterness, and his spite towards me. Except that he was not my father but my uncle, and my uncle was not my uncle but— Oh, it was indeed the only fact that made sense of everything, and it made nonsense as well.

When I landed at Barra after my first long spell at sea, the beach had heaved. Now the whole world heaved, and I did not know my place in it. I knew that what William said was true. I knew too late that what I had always wanted to do to Fourfarthings was what I had seen him do to her. I had wild notions that even now I could punish and plead with her. Don't go with him. Come with me. Then in my mind I saw my mother in Fourfarthings's nanny-goat grovel. I heard her gasp and shout for him. I felt sick. I staggered as I got up. William breathed heavily. Fourfarthings had scrambled her dress on. She looked at me boldly, as though I were a fool.

I was. I turned round and walked to the rail.

William's voice was cracked, as though he hated me. "Come here! You! Come here! Mr. Partridge! Stop that man!"

But Mr. Partridge did not, nor did any of the crew. I stumbled over the side into the milk boat. There was a goat with bulging udders tied to a thwart, and several wooden buckets. The black woman laughed at me and shoved off.

The first direct sunlight was just beginning to strike from behind the hills. The entire world seemed very clear and fresh.

William appeared at the *Margaret*'s rail. He shouted at me. I gestured angrily and turned my back. He shouted again and then stopped. I was afraid that he would send the punt after me, but when he did not, I knew that he wanted me to crawl. He wanted me to weep, and to admit that I was mad, as Henry Dingwall had been. My pulse hammered. I thought that it would blow up inside my head. But I did not look back, so that although I did not know it, my glimpse of William's white body at the rail was to be the last I had of him for four years.

Chapter 20

Pot-boy

The milk boat put me ashore at one of the public wharves. I gave the woman a few pence and walked uphill. Huckster women setting out their wares called to me in a sing-song pidgin, but I ignored them. I walked quickly, with my eyes on the worn earth where I would plant my next step. I did not halt until I realized that I had left the town and church behind me, and reached the edge of the tumbled and uneven plateau that formed the centre of the island. A dusty road straggled ahead of me. The trees were very green. There were many windmills on humps. The sky was high and clear. I looked back. I could see glimpses of the harbour but not the *Margaret*. I was shaking and covered in sweat. My eyes prickled and itched. I sat down against a tree trunk. Dozing, I drifted into a dream. I was in the yard at High Top, where there was a boy with his back to me. He was flat-footed and defensive. When I shouted, "Who are you?" he turned and I saw that it was me. I woke up. I was calm, and listed facts and alternatives.

What about the Crabtrees, and James Derker and my grandfather, and my aunt Annie and her husband, Dawson? Did they know that William was my father? I tried to remember their faces at the reading of the will. I saw again the steady gaze that had made me trust Mr. Sayer. He knew. He must know. But had he been told or had he guessed? And who else had looked at me in a similar way? Only Aunt Annie, I decided, and I supposed that she knew because my mother had told her, sister to sister, a secret both shameful and triumphant. I did not believe that the others knew, because if they did, their anger at the mortgage would have made them say so. To them William had gone to sea and his brother married a girl they had all known since childhood. Then my mind raced as I thought about my father—I mean, about John Derker himself. Had he loved my mother? I was sure he had, and hated her. Had he even known about me? If he had not, why was he so bitter? I remembered my mother's delirium in the snow. I was sure that she had been pregnant, and that he had discovered it and married her.

But had he done it for honour, or because it was the only situation in which she would deign to look at him? Had she always loved William? Or was he a dream, and John a reality whose jealousy she could not stop? John's love for both of us was desperate. It must have been. Why else had he expressed it in ways that numbed and dispirited?

Sweat poured down my face. I shut my eyes and tried to see him as we trudged across the moors, or as he watched my mother in the winter firelight. I made myself dizzy. I loved her. She had saved me from him. I hated her. She cared for nothing but William. I saw every explanation clearly, and was sure of them, and then I realized that, throughout my life, my inmost feelings had sprung from facts that I now knew to be false. So how could I believe my feelings? What value could I place upon my hopes and judgements? Where could I go to be sure of who and what I was?

Well—I could stay under the tree. Under the tree, alone and watching, I felt very secure. In the distance there was smoke from burnt-off land. White horsemen went past, and blacks with bundles of goods. Ox wagons carried puncheons of rum. The blacks looked at me with a slow curiosity that revealed nothing. The white men were suspicious. They had whips and pistols. When one of them shouted, "Who are you?" I was so confident that I did not even reply.

But the heat was heavy and humid. My limbs ached, and I was hungry, and although I said out loud that when night came I would stay where I was and let the dew cool me, I knew that it was foolish. I had been told by old Lomas and Jerry Hoskins that no slave was allowed on the night streets without a note of hand from his master, and white men who had no ship or place to sleep were locked up for vagrancy. Nor could a distressed person live rough, as he might do for a spell in England; in Antigua the woods hid runaway slaves, and white men went in at their peril.

I was tired and helpless, and still sought a father to accept me. I wanted to sleep where I would not be woken, to rest where some other strength would protect me. On the entire island I knew only two places: Mr. Leslie's yard, and Black O'Riley's nanny-house. I decided without hesitation to go to O'Riley's. He was a rebel, and he owed nothing at all to Smallshaw and Hill.

As I went downhill I clutched the coins in my pocket. At least I can pay, I muttered to myself. Sweat had made the red dust stain my shirt and breeches. The breeze fluttered. Clouds sailed across the sky. The ships in the harbour were like toys.

I stepped into the shade of the grog-shop and said, "I want a bed for the night."

O'Riley looked up and said, "What? You want what?" in such a mocking tone that my confidence deserted me and I blubbered.

The drinkers in the grog-shop laughed, but O'Riley snarled at them, and when he looked at me again, his face was different. He patted my shoulder. There was something of Signor Voss's calmness in the way he put his arm round me and walked me into the court-yard.

I blurted out my whole story. O'Riley grunted, with his eyes screwed up. He waved for one of the women to bring me some water and watched me wash. He gave me a piece of fruit and winced at my innocence and folly. Yet he listened seriously, and I felt that I had impressed him. He sighed and said, "Do you want them to know where you are?"

I shook my head. He made a face and shrugged.

"They'll find out, of course," he said, "for there's no secret at all that can be kept on this island."

He made me pay him a night's lodging in advance and told me to wrap my money in my neckcloth and keep that tight in my hand. Then he led me to one of the booths, where I was too tired to remove my clothes. I sat on the edge of the shelf-bed and O'Riley pulled the shirt and breeches off me, and said that he would have them washed. I stood up. O'Riley laughed. I realized that I must lie down and sleep.

As I drifted off and O'Riley laid a cloth on me, I thought that he promised me eternal help, and at the same moment I seemed to hear fiddle music from the grog-shop, and women's coaxing voices all round me, and as one of them cried out for love I sat bolt upright, awake and cursing them for having stopped my sleep. Then my thoughts came back to me, but instead of exhaustion I felt clear-headedness, and my limbs were soothed.

I wrapped myself in the cloth and went into the courtyard. A girl at the kitchen waved to me. Overhead there were tattered grey clouds. The trees rustled. A few heavy drops of rain felt very refreshing upon my bare skin.

O'Riley was in the grog-shop and raised his arm in salute. He wore a different shirt, and I realized that I had not been awakened after a few minutes, but that I must have slept the clock round. I felt at a distance from the other people and was glad that they ignored me. I sat on a stool under one of the trees. Blue-and-yellow finches hopped around my feet. The kitchen girl brought me a bowl of beans.

Eventually dusk fell, and tallow lights were lit in the grog-shop, and here and there among the booths. The humidity gave them a vague fuzz. I reasoned to myself that because I had not returned to the *Margaret* William would have to invoke ship's discipline and call me a deserter, and I was not surprised to see Mr. McBride enter the grog-shop and make his way towards me.

He brought a stool from inside and set it down facing mine. He settled himself with his brandy and sighed. His face was half in shadow and half in gentle light, and looked more than ever like a squashed potato. He said that it grieved him to meet me in such circumstances, and that he could not take sides between father and son. He was here as a friend of both and as an officer.

He then made no bones at all of William's intentions. I had signed my indentures and was legally bound to the owners. Absence ashore could be construed as desertion. My situation was untenable.

"No, it isn't," I said. "I can redeem my indentures."

"With what, for God's sake?" said Mr. McBride.

"Cash."

"Cash? Are ye daft, boy? What cash?"

"I own a slave," I said. "I'll give her to Smallshaw's. They can sell her."

Mr. McBride gaped. I was proud of my own sharpness. Mr. McBride whistled between his teeth and took a drink. He wiped his brow. "I was just now with your—with Captain Derker," he said. "The man's drunk and in pain." I stared at him and felt no respect.

"Drunk with you, was he?" I said. "Surely Captain Derker was with his black bitch all day and night?"

Mr. McBride sighed. He seemed to have aged. He looked up. At the kitchen they were cooking a pig on the spit, and reflections of the flames lit both of us.

"Tom," said Mr. McBride, with an attempt at a crack in his voice, "it's not that simple, Tom. The ship's ordered to St. Christopher."

This time I looked up. He talked rapidly. During my absence the monthly inter-island post had arrived, bringing Mr. Leslie a letter from Mr. Guichard, Smallshaw's agent on the nearby island of St. Christopher. Smallshaw's ship *Eagle*, which was engaged in the regular West Indian trade, had lost her fore- and mainmasts in a storm and arrived at St. Christopher in need of repairs. Her cargo was already accumulated in Guichard's sheds, whereas that of the *Margaret* had not left the plantations. William and Mr. Leslie had decided that the *Margaret* should take the cargo already purchased for the *Eagle*. When the *Eagle* was repaired she could sail to Antigua and take on our cargo.

William intended to weigh on the next morning's tide. "So forget all this nonsense," said Mr. McBride, "and come back with me now."

I shook my head and said, "No."

"You'll be left behind."

I nodded. "Good. I want to be."

He tried to persuade me. I shouted at him. It's not nonsense. I won't crawl. I was right. I don't want to see them. I hate them. Smash their faces. Spit at them. Smash that bitch girl's face into the cabin wall. Then people stared at me, so I stopped.

"All that aside," said Mr. McBride, "how will you earn your living?"

"What?"

"There's no work on these islands for white men."

"I know that!" I snapped. I did not, but would not let him realize it.

"Look at O'Riley," he said. "Look at tavern keepers and owners of sloops. They're bound by law to employ white men, to fill the ranks of the Militia. But what do they do? They call it cheaper to pay the fines and use blacks."

"I'm surprised they even have oxen," I said. "Slaves could pull a wagon just as well."

Mr. McBride looked vulnerable. I had the power to humiliate him, and it exhilarated me. "I'm more surprised that William sent you," I said. "What are you, after all, but a pissy-arsed old fool?"

I thought that he would strike me, and was ready to strike back, but he got up and went to O'Riley, and a wry glance passed between them.

Then Mr. McBride swung back and in the flicker-lit courtyard talked quickly and venomously about his youth as a Catholic Irishman: the turf cabin by the arm of the sea, the laws that forbade him to be educated or to hold office under the Crown, the brothers he loved and would never see again because they served in foreign armies, the tramping for work, and forelock-tugging, and the labouring in Liverpool docks and shipyards, until by blarney he became a surgeon's mate. After that he pretended to qualifications he never possessed, but the owners of slave ships cared so little that they always engaged him. So now he lived with his daughter and a maid in a stone cottage of his own. Hey-diddle-diddle. "We were the first nation that England enslaved," he said, "and we'll be the last she sets free."

He and O'Riley stared at me. They were fat and sozzled, and yet they made me feel ashamed. I shifted on my feet.

"I don't care," I said. "I don't care if there's no work for whites."

Mr. McBride laughed and did a little shuffling step of a jig. He toasted me.

"Good boy," he said, "and God bless you. I'll tell the Captain you'll not come."

He drained his mug, put it into O'Riley's fist, and walked out I was alone. I smiled and tried not to tremble.

"If you want the bed for another night," said O'Riley 'I'll take your money now."

I nodded and paid him. He stared at the few coins I had left.

"I don't care," I said. "I can join the Army."

O'Riley nodded. "You could," he said, as his little eyes peered at me, "or the Royal Navy, or any other vessel in the port." He spat, as though all three were distasteful, and left me alone. I felt dazed and frightened. When there were bursts of laughter from the grog-shop, I was sure that O'Riley had evoked them at my expense, and I hid in my booth.

Drunken shouts, and unexpected cries, and the banging of the half-doors kept me awake, but towards dawn I slept, and awoke at midday to be told by O'Riley that the *Margaret* had sailed on the tide and was gone.

I did not know what to say. My heart was like a weight in my chest.

"Do you know any musical instrument at all?" said O'Riley.

"What?" I almost sobbed.

"Pity," said O'Riley. "You could have signed for a drummer boy." I stared at him. I could not understand why he mocked me. "On the other hand," he said, "did I not hear it told that you can read and write?"

"Yes," I said.

O'Riley sighed admiringly. "Now there's a wonder," he said, "and it might help me more than a little, for if I took you as my pot-boy I'd not need to pay the fines, would I?"

I stared. In one of the booths a woman railed in pidgin at a sailor.

"It's time such as yourself worked for me," said O'Riley, "for you're not an idle black ape at all; you'll scrub a tiled floor properly."

I was still silent.

"For God's sake, son," said O'Riley. "Is my offer accepted?"

I laughed self-consciously and nodded.

"Good," said O'Riley, and shouted into the courtyard for the old black woman who had charge of the girls in the nanny-house. "Pegeen! You daft bitch! Pegeen!"

Pegeen screeched back at him. She must have been very fine once, with high cheekbones and flashing eyes, but now she was stooped and toothless. She wore an elaborate scarf head-dress and layers of petticoats. I thought that she liked me, because several times the day before she had chattered to me in a sing-song pidgin I could hardly understand, but when O'Riley introduced me as the new pot-boy she became very agitated and refused to shake my hand.

"You're an old witch!" said O'Riley. "You're a bloody old nuisance, when God knows I've lived my whole life to save you!"

Pegeen shook her fist and shuffled off. O'Riley watched her with a moistening eye.

"Ah, well," he said, "I understand her, for she was my first black whore and I was proud to address her as Mrs. O'Riley. Is that not so, Duffy?"

Duffy was O'Riley's bodyguard, although only about a quarter the size. He was one of those thin, high-cheekboned, big-eared Irishmen, and now he sighed mournfully and said, "That you were, O'Riley, and me to have kissed her black hand."

I thought for a moment that they were both about to snivel, but O'Riley poured two shots of rum, and Duffy said, "Have you met the present Mrs. O'Riley?"

"No," I said. "I haven't."

"Ah!" said Duffy, and he and O'Riley lifted their mugs and drank a toast in the direction of the open stairs and the upper room.

"But she cannot be called down," said O'Riley, "for despite her name she must be gently awakened."

He sighed. They were both silent.

"Er—her name?" I said.

"Trash!" said O'Riley.

"What?"

"Mrs. O'Riley was a house slave," said Duffy, "and her white mistress gave her a bad name and sold her, on account of the fact that she fucked the white master's head off."

"Oh," I said.

"I bought her very cheap," said O'Riley. "Unlike wisdom, which has cost me dear."

Then he shouted for coffee to be made, and gave me my apron, and I took the coffee and two bananas on a tray to the shuttered upstairs room. There was a low bed inside a mosquito net, as well as a desk, and chests that spewed bright dress lengths of cotton. I coughed and said, "Mrs. O'Riley?"

Kitty Trash said, "Uh?" Then she stirred and sat up, and through the netting I saw her pride and her golden breasts and her shock of black hair. "Ah!" she said, and laughed at the length of my apron.

"I'm Tom," I said. "I've brought your coffee."

Kitty yawned. The room had a rank, used smell. Kitty looked round, and then pummelled the bed-clothes. A man sat up.

"Oh!" he said. "Er—is that coffee?"

"No, it is not, sir," said O'Riley's voice behind me, "for what you bought was her body, not her breakfast."

"Oh," said the man, and scrambled out of the netting. He was flabby and absurd, but when he started to dress, his clothes were very sober and respectable. I handed the tray to Kitty Trash.

"There'll be coffee for you downstairs, Mr. Kennedy, sir," said O'Riley, "and maybe a hair of the dog that bit you."

Kennedy half laughed. He looked bleary.

"If you take my advice, sir," said O'Riley, "you'll shave before you return to your counting-house."

"Ah!" said Kennedy. O'Riley gave him a razor. Kitty laughed and threw a banana skin at him. Kennedy ducked past O'Riley and went.

"That man," said O'Riley, "is a merchant with a loving family; God knows what excuses he gives them."

He stared at Kitty. She picked at her nose and stretched. O'Riley licked his lips. "Now you go downstairs, son," he said, "for I must pay my conjugal respects to Mrs. O'Riley."

I went downstairs and served Mr. Kennedy his coffee. As soon as he was shaved and had his coat on, he snapped his fingers and behaved with more self-importance. He was warmly greeted by another well-dressed gentleman, whom Duffy introduced to me as Mr. Waller, the surgeon, come to make his fortnightly inspection of the women in the nanny-house. To no one's surprise he diagnosed the pox in two of them while waiting for his own coffee to boil, and I smiled to myself at the thought of how Peter Case would want to know all about it, if only he had still been alive to ask.

Chapter 21

Wet Season

What I learned from my first day's work in the grog-shop was the trick of all pot-boys since the world began: not to look a new customer in the eye until I had served the old, or drink would be spilt, orders confused, and no one satisfied. I realized that I must be cheerful when drunks abused me, and sit down to rest when I could. Not that there were many lulls in the hurly-burly, because as the captains hurried to load the sugar crop before their ships were trapped by the rains and gales of August and September, the sense of departure made their sailors swill down more drink and lust more desperately after women.

At the sight of them my own thoughts surged, and I had not worked in the nanny-house for more than three or four days when I picked on the girl I thought the most attractive, and asked her to take me to her booth. Her name was Leah, and she was the one who had smiled at me from the kitchen when I awoke after my long sleep. Now she laughed in my face, and walked away with her bottom swaying. I still had money and offered it. Leah said, "Huh!" and snatched it from me.

She went into her booth and lay down without bothering to take off her body-cloth; she simply pulled it up over her knees. The half-door was still open, and some of the other women shouted at her. She yelled back and they laughed. I stared at her vagina. Inside its black lips it was pink. I reached behind me to close the half-door. Leah snorted and jerked her head for me to hurry. I took off my breeches.

Leah yawned and looked about the hut. She had a bowl of palm oil, into which she dipped her fingers to rub the inside of her vagina. It made no difference. She was still dry, which hurt, and at the same time stimulated me, so that I ejaculated after a few seconds, which no doubt was her intention. She got me off her with an expert roll. I went outside. My erection still rubbed against the flap of my breeches. Pegeen shouted. She pulled me by the wrist to where O'Riley and Duffy swung in hammocks under the trees, and started to screech and to slap at O'Riley's face.

"Duffy!" he cried. "For God's sake! You're my bodyguard! Save me!"

Duffy tried to get up, but Pegeen snatched his mug and splashed rum in his face.

"What have you done?" said O'Riley. "What gnaws at the old bitch?"

Pegeen told him. O'Riley sent for Leah and cuffed her. "Never give these whores money again!" he said. "These whores aren't worth good money!" He told me to apologize to Pegeen for having flouted her authority over the courtyard. I did so, even though she had sent me on stupid errands, mocked me in front of the women, and set tasks that made me look physically weak beside the black youths who worked for O'Riley.

He had told me that there were white managers in each of his grog-shops, and white captains on his sloop and cutter, but that for years Duffy had been the only white man in the nanny-house, and I imagined that this was why Pegeen resented me.

I saw now that there was more, because she spat at my apology, and screamed that Kitty Trash was an idle badbad she-bitch. Where Pegeen she house? O'Riley no bigman. O'Riley smallsmall. Where Pegeen she house?

She flailed at O'Riley with her skinny old arms, until abruptly he lost his temper and lashed her away. She stumbled down against a tree. Blood trickled from her nose. She glared hatefully and dragged herself away. There were tears in O'Riley's eyes, and as Duffy soothed him I began to grasp the nature of the quarrel.

Pegeen believed that her entire life was threatened by O'Riley's passion for Kitty Trash, because, like Kitty, Pegeen was a slave and owned body and soul by O'Riley. Once his mistress, she had always assumed that there would be a place for her as the nanny-house madam, but now, old and irritable, she suddenly believed that O'Riley wanted to throw her into the gutter and put the beautiful Kitty in her place; and however stupid the notion, she interpreted my arrival as part of his plan.

"But I'll not throw the old bitch out, will I?" said O'Riley. "And when I do, will I not put her under a roof?"

"You will," said Duffy, "for you always have! There's dozens bought their freedom and eight acres!"

In Antigua, he explained for my benefit, free blacks or mulattoes were allowed to own eight acres of land, and those who did not had to choose a white master or mistress who would be responsible for them at law. Some women worked in the nanny-house to protect their family's precious eight acres; others owned nothing and had chosen O'Riley to be their legal master; more were his slaves. The dream that sustained them all was that they would save enough money to buy both land and freedom, but only a handful achieved it.

Most were flung out on to the street, and if O'Riley felt generous towards them, he would find them a place to sleep among the dock-side shanties, because he was still their owner, and liked to think that he had more power and goodwill among the blacks than any other white man on the island.

"Why else does the Governor's secretary seek my advice?" he asked. "Ignores me on the streets by glare of day, but invites me to speak my mind by candlelight!"

"Governor's secretary, by God!" said Duffy. "I'd stuff his candles up his arse!"

Kitty Trash came down from her afternoon sleep and asked what the noise had been about. O'Riley told her. Kitty pouted. Duffy shook his head and whistled through his teeth, and said that things could not go on this way. O'Riley chuckled and said that he did not see why not.

Kitty tickled O'Riley as he wallowed in the hammock, and tossed her head at Pegeen, and at me laughed and waggled her bottom. That evening O'Riley teased Leah about me, and at Kitty's request dressed her up in different-coloured lengths of cloth. The customers stood Leah on a table, and howled, and she stripped it all off till she was naked.

My having paid Leah was turned by Kitty into a joke and a symbol of my youth and harmlessness. Pegeen never liked me, but because outwardly I complied with the joke and laughed at myself, the other women were soon able to accept me.

What I had not understood was how much they needed to do so, because if I was one of the persons who fetched and carried, and was always busy about the grog-shop and courtyard, I had to be beyond sex. I had to see them fuck, and defecate, and dab at their bruises, and complain at the sores when they got the pox. I saw their bloody wraps when they were menstruating, and took them the fruit and sweet cakes that they preferred to any man. I had to enjoy their childish dressing-up, and take sides in their squabbles, which were caused by combs, and beads, and stolen sixpences, but were really about humili-ation, and the way in which they seethed and schemed for places upon a ladder of status that was calculated by shades of colour and precise percentages of black blood.

The less black their skins, the more they esteemed themselves and put on airs and graces, and the more O'Riley chuckled as he played off a black woman with land and a shack against a delicate pale girl with nothing. He was the master of their emotions because he knew that, although they could be cold and cruel, what they craved most was affection. If he hit them for no reason, they snivelled with grati-tude when he put his arm round their shoulders to say he did not mean it.

Above all, they consoled and caressed each other, for hours on end. They lay on the shelf-beds or, when a booth had nothing, in the trash on the earthen floor and sobbed for joy at the gentleness of each other's touch. Sometimes they lay down with me or the black boys, our limbs all together, for the comfort and the lazy mingling of it.

On other days, they dressed me in their clothes, and piled scarves on my head, and fed me tit-bits off a tin spoon. Eventually they caressed me, as if I were another woman, and allowed me to caress them. Leah was the first. One night we had cuddled against each other for a long time, when she took my hand and put it on her breast; from there I ran it over her whole body, and explored between her legs and inside her mouth, and to do so was peaceful and dream-like, but it was not what I wanted.

What I wanted was to knead and bite and hammer into them. I wanted their response to the limit of what I could imagine. I was frustrated because I could not demand that in the nanny-house and was as yet too timid to seek it elsewhere.

After a few weeks of this life the rains descended, and for what seemed like days on end the grog-shop was grey and empty. August was also the month in which the field gangs planted and then had to weed the fields until the new sugar canes were tall enough to protect themselves with their own trash, so that for eight or nine weeks there were few ships in the harbour and very little business done in town. The women who had homes went back there, and the ones who did not sulked in their booths. They stared at the rain and shouted to make themselves heard above its drumming on the roofs and leaves.

On steamy evenings O'Riley and Kitty held court in the grog-shop, with his big paw on her thigh, and other whores arranged round them like ladies in waiting. In the daytime there were rambling, boozy conversations with Duffy and what few of their cronies braved the weather: captains of gale-bound fishing boats or one of the town watchmen.

When they entered, water dripped from their clothes, and they would alternately tease and bawl at Pegeen, who was rumoured to be an obeah woman and certainly told fortunes, until she sent me into the rain to collect hens' feathers and broken twigs, which she gathered into a bundle and threw on to the earthen floor, reading our futures from the mess they made.

One day I was more thoroughly soaked, when I was sent to Scotch Row to take Leah to Mr. McPhee, the merchant for whom Mr. Leslie had been a clerk. He was said to be eighty-six years old, and in the good weather I had seen him in the street, tall and gaunt, his white hair floating behind him, and a black at his side to hold a straw parasol. But he was too arthritic to walk up to the grog-shop, and every so often a message would come for O'Riley to send him a girl to fondle.

On this occasion he took us into his parlour and gave me a glass of Madeira. The furniture gleamed in the shadows, and outside the rain drummed and splattered. Mr. McPhee had the house-boy bring a tall stool from the counting-house, and he sat on it while Leah stood naked in front of him. She giggled. He looked at her body, and touched it here and there. He held his face against her, as if a decrepit child. Then suddenly he pinched her nose and she squealed. He smiled thinly, but she knew that it was all he could manage.

"Call this rain bad, sonny?" he said. "I was born here. I mind the great hurricane."

Leah slipped her dress over her head. She sat on the floor and held his spindly legs and rubbed them. Mr. McPhee stroked her hair.

"Aye," he said. "Oh, aye. There were ships driven inland, sonny, and drowned bodies wedged in trees."

He sighed, and we heard the rain stop, and as it did so, a brighter light shone through the jalousies. Leah and I walked home up streets that were squelchy and strewn with leaves and rubbish. The court-yard steamed and sparkled, and that night the grog-shop was full of common soldiers of the garrison and a fight broke out.

It flared so suddenly that before I could reach the street the door was blocked by soldiers who whirled belts, and I was unable to get out to fetch the Watch or the Provost-Sergeant. O'Riley and Duffy stood back to back and shouted at me to take cover. As I did so, I saw Leslie's clerk, Jerry Hoskins, come out of a booth with no breeches on and jab men back with the legs of a stool.

Then Duffy was felled and I realized that Jerry could not reach O'Riley in time. Soldiers dragged O'Riley down and kicked him. I barged among them, and although I was winded and bloody-nosed, it gave O'Riley time to stand up, smash off a bottle's end, and jab the edges into a soldier's face.

That decided the fight, and it was the most violent act I saw O'Riley commit. He prided himself on his ability to absorb insults, and even when he jostled a customer or slapped one of the women without warning, he would be agitated and tell his cronies that there had been ingratitude and treachery.

Now in the exaltation of victory O'Riley crowed and embraced us all. Duffy shook his head, and whistled more shrilly between his teeth because one of them had been broken. Jerry Hoskins kissed Pegeen's wet gums and swallowed a mouthful of rum straight off with no thought for his breeches. Then he grinned at me, and lifted both our fists above our heads, and that is when our friendship began.

Big and slow, and five years older than I, Jerry was my first attainable hero, who for all his torpor in the counting-house was among the blacks a hectic fornicator, whom I followed unhesitatingly into shanties and slave pens that I would have been afraid to enter alone.

Jerry had a foul mind, and yet nothing he could imagine was as extreme as the law, whose punishments he so much enjoyed to watch. If a black struck a white person he could have his nose slit, or any member cut off, or be put to death, at the discretion of a Justice of the Peace. If a white man killed a runaway slave he was not punished, but if a slave was killed by a public flogging, his owner was compensated by the Treasury.

"Look at that!" I once heard Jerry exclaim at the sight of a slave woman whipped for theft, and what made him cry out was not the shudder of her flesh but the fact that at the first touch of pain her nipples hardened.

There was nothing like that in shanty-town or the nanny-houses. In a courtyard off Long Street I saw Jerry fuck a pig, and many times he took women so old that they were amazed and frightened that he wanted them; but they only went to show that even in his rampaging he was frustrated.

His dream, and that of all obscure whites like us, was to have an overseer's ability to make imaginings come true: to have slaves who could not disobey. In Jerry's situation, this came down to slaves who were newly landed and had not yet been sent to the plantations.

Those in Mr. Leslie's shed were fair game, and so were the house slaves, apart from the fact that the house slaves soon ceased to be strangers. They even became friends, and took any chance they had to order men around. When Jerry was drunk, which he liked to be, they encouraged him to get utterly fuddled and then eluded him. So sexual meetings were always on their terms, which, as Jerry said, was very frisky but no different from having white doxies.

When there were new slaves in one of the other yards, we would bribe its overseer with rum and say which girls we wanted. Jerry liked them young, with little buds of breasts, and I chose them slightly older, so that I could punish their resemblance to Fourfarthings. But mostly they were too bewildered to be of any use, and they were never our property. Once, when our clothes were damp and the rain teemed down, one of them would not suck Jerry's penis, so he punched her and split her cheek. This caused a dispute between Mr. Leslie and the other merchant, and Jerry had to pay compensation.

At O'Riley's it became a famous scandal. Duffy and the grog-shop cronies shook their heads in mock alarm, and O'Riley explained how he had always known that Jerry had the biggest white penis on the island. Jerry was just cunning enough never to heave it out but to leave the matter to the testimony of the girls, whom O'Riley would invite to make comparisons.

So Jerry grinned, even when he was thwarted; Kitty and the others mocked them all; and some men made very extravagant claims. O'Riley sat back and watched them at it. His little tongue flickered over his lips. He caught my eye and winked, and that is how I best remember him, fat and cruel and indolent, with the night rain dripping from every leaf in the courtyard.

Chapter 22

The Muster

At the end of the wet season there was new green, and flowers everywhere. The young canes were secure, and the next cutting-season would not start until February, so from the middle of October there were three and a half months of brilliantly warm weather with nothing much to be done, and the social season commenced. There were balls and levees in St. Johns, and even the slaves had a three-day holiday at Christmas. On many a velvet night Jerry and I made it a great sport to stand outside a house where there was a ball, and watch the rich white women arrive side-saddle or in carriages. Their dresses floated like mist in the soft glow of candles. The trees were black shadows. Moths veered towards the flames. There were flighty black maids, laughter, and wafting music, but when Jerry and I did a mock minuet in the dust, even the black major-domos waved us away, because we were not what Mr. Leslie called society.

In Antigua, society consisted of only a few hundred persons: planters, merchants, professional men, clergy, officers, their wives and families, and visitors of comparable rank. Shopkeepers and apothecaries were not society, nor were the men who held petty office, nor white smallholders, nor the overseers of big plantations. Mr. Leslie himself was society by the slime on his teeth, which is to say that he was invited to a few balls, but not to most.

O'Riley's domain was not even respectable, let alone part of society, and I was soon used to being cut dead in the street by such as Mr. Kennedy, or by Mr. Waller and his wife, when only twenty minutes earlier the surgeon had cracked jokes with me and peered up the crotch of every woman in the courtyard.

At the same time there was one social duty that rich and poor, whoremonger and hypocrite, were forced to perform together, because Militia service was compulsory for all white males between the ages of fourteen and sixty-five, and the November Rendezvous in Boyer's Pasture was the biggest public spectacle of the year.

A crowd of several thousand gathered to watch the companies vie with one another for smartness, and the best marksmen shoot for handsome prizes. The countryside, where the planters and overseers had their own horses, provided mounted carabineers, and the towns the infantry.

Our company of infantry was commanded by Mr. Leslie, with the rank of Lieutenant. His Sergeant was Mr. Kennedy; and O'Riley, whose uniform would not button across his stomach, was Corporal. The ranker on my left was Jerry, and on my right, Duffy. Our surgeon was Mr. Waller.

Despite the heat and the itchiness of my uniform I enjoyed the ritual of the drill, and looked forward to the Rendezvous, when we would be inspected by the Colonel of the Militia, James Hanson of Hawksbill, who was a member of the Governor's Council, and of the General Assembly of the Leeward Islands.

I was especially eager to lay eyes on the Colonel because he was the reason why the mulatto Alexander Hanson, the bane of our life in the nanny-house, would never be harmed. Alexander could pick drunken fights, and cheat at cards, and run up debts, and foully abuse us, but he was inviolate because the Colonel was his half-brother and one of the most powerful men on the island.

Mr. Leslie had the contract to sell the Colonel slaves and to buy his sugar, yet always grumbled about him. He was convinced that the Colonel envied and secretly opposed him. That was why our drill must be perfect. We must be twice as smart as the other companies. Mr. Leslie's promotion to Captain could then no longer be denied him.

On the afternoon of the Rendezvous we met at Leslie's yard and marched to the field, where, as we waited for the last companies to arrive, Mr. Leslie said, "Did I not warn you? The crowd is larger this year because very many persons of all sorts take an interest in my Captaincy." He had a boil on his neck and could not close his collar. Mr. Waller sighed. O'Riley tied up a dog that had snapped at our heels all the way from town.

Then the bugle called the companies together and the display began. Duffy won third prize at the shooting, and I was disappointed when the tall, stooped Colonel Hanson walked through the ranks because the sun was in his eyes and he stared at our feet, but apart from that, everything went like clockwork—until, that is, we came to the final march past.

The band played an air. Mr. Leslie turned us so that we would come into line with the other companies. Then, at the command of the Parade Major, the band struck up a march and we swung away. After ten paces I heard Jerry Hoskins giggle, and somewhere in front of me Mr. Waller said, "Good God, Leslie, you've turned us right instead of left!"

It was true. We were marching in one direction, towards a scrubby hillside, and the rest of the parade was marching in another. There were bellows of laughter from the crowd, and sounds of hooting and imitation cock-crows. "Leslie!" shouted Mr. Waller. "For God's sake, man!" There was no response. Mr. Waller looked at Mr. Kennedy. "You're the Sergeant," he said. "Stir youself!"

Mr. Kennedy opened his mouth, but all that came out was a croak. Eventually, when dense trees were about ten yards away, O'Riley said, "Company, halt! About turn! By the left, quick march!" and we set off in the true direction, but hundreds of yards behind, and with Mr. Leslie at our rear instead of our head. As we passed the saluting box we were cheered to the echo, and known thereafter as Leslie's Loonies, a joke enjoyed by everyone except Mr. Leslie himself.

But that was the wonder of it. Mr. Leslie ignored more than the joke; he ignored the incident. When we broke our ranks he congratulated us on our turnout and shook Sergeant Kennedy's hand. He greeted his fellow officers with a superior smile and said what a pity it was that their companies had not matched his own; the poor men were so flabbergasted that they slunk away, as though it were they and not he who had made asses of themselves.

Jerry and I shared their confusion. Did Mr. Leslie know what had happened or did he not? We discussed it for weeks, until at Christmas we took advantage of the slaves' holiday and went to Morgan's Plantation, where we bribed the overseer with rum and spent two days in the women's huts. That was where Jerry settled the matter, when on the second afternoon he suddenly looked up from a girl's belly and said, "If Leslie didn't know what had happened, why did he about-turn when O'Riley gave the order?"

It was deadly logic, and to celebrate it Jerry had himself rubbed all over with cocoanut milk; Kitty Trash had told him that it increased virility, but so far as I saw, it made no difference.

Chapter 23

Mamma Dog and the Empress

Mr. Leslie's Militia catastrophe may have been the comic highlight of the social season, but for scandalous interest it was surpassed by a series of events that took place in O'Riley's nanny-house, and which for all their bathos and disreputability set tongues wagging and piled drama upon drama until the months of pleasure ended and the ships arrived again from Africa. The origin of these events was the way in which Kitty Trash queened it in the grog-shop and set her personality against that of O'Riley.

O'Riley was fat, lazy, and cruel. He let matters drift because he was bored and thought that confusion might amuse him. In his maudlin cups he said that his life had no purpose, yet he knew well how to divide and rule, and it was to test his contradictory nature, and to force him to make sense of it, that Kitty behaved as she did; or perhaps she uttered a woman's cry for love, or one of anger at O'Riley's lethargy; or perhaps, as some said, she was a sorceress who knew what spells to cast.

Her tantrums certainly enchanted O'Riley. He liked to see life lived to its limits, and he wheezed his appreciation of Kitty's antics even when Duffy protested that they were against all good sense and religion and that nothing had been seen to equal them.

"My one concern from dawn till dark of night! That's what O'Riley is! My one concern! But will you look at him? He slobbers all over the woman. And what's she? She's a whore, yet she'll not take customers to her bed!"

It was true. One day O'Riley had not wanted to take sides in an argument between Kitty and Pegeen, at which Kitty had retired to the upper room and refused to admit men. That night O'Riley was trapped between his lady and his customers, and pretended that it was some kind of challenge to improve business.

The customers laid wagers and advised him to be of good cheer because Mr. Kennedy would be the first to mount both the stairs and the lady. O'Riley smiled and nodded. Mr. Kennedy downed a tot of rum, entered the upper room, and tripped over the slave girl whom Kitty had told to lie across the threshold.

The girl screamed. Kitty woke up and threw a pineapple. It missed Mr. Kennedy but gave O'Riley a black eye. Mr. Kennedy sprained his ankle when he tripped, and had to be carried home.

Next morning O'Riley made a sheepish plea that he and I be allowed into the room to see the accounts. Kitty was eager to know what damage she had done and let him in.

When she saw his bruises she screamed with laughter, but then melted and sent me for water so that she could bathe them herself. O'Riley sat on her bed like a meek hulk, and she said that he could sleep with her if he asked with a flourish but that no one else could. O'Riley consented, and for weeks Kitty gloried in it.

Nothing pleased her, and I ran up and down stairs all day with scents and beads and tit-bits of this and that. She oiled herself, and sent for a drummer so that she could dance alone, and if Pegeen had cooked the dinner she always sent it back untasted.

O'Riley seemed not to care. He became a laughing-stock. Discipline wavered. There was a fight among the girls, during which one of them was hit and cut by an earthenware bowl. Pegeen cast spells, and Duffy expostulated, invariably to the effect that things were never like this during the reign of the Empress McGregor.

The Empress McGregor was a legendary mulatta whore and the last Mrs. O'Riley but one, who had retired two or three years before with enough money to buy her own land and cabin above the sea at Kidnapper's Bay.

Because she was a legend who had won her own freedom the

Empress was endlessly discussed in the nanny-house. Rumour had it that she had lost her savings in a speculation and was tired of staring at the sea all day, yet for all that, it was the amazement of the season when she decided to take advantage of Kitty's withdrawal and to reappear in St. Johns.

She chose to do so on the night of the New Year's Ball given at his official residence by George Thomas, Governor of Antigua and Captain-General of the Leeward Islands. A crowd of drunks, overseers, white clerks, and whores had come out of the grog-shop into Corn Alley to watch a display of coloured rockets go up from the Governor's garden, and as sparks filled the sky the Empress rode up the alley with feathers in her hair, a billowy scarlet train carried by two grinning young bucks, and a pack-donkey led by her maid.

Word of her arrival flared through the little streets like the rockets through the dark, and within an hour the Governor himself felt compelled to satisfy the curiosity of some of his gentlemen guests. A black footman in gold braid, bare feet, and a powdered wig panted into the grog-shop, and amid cheers and Irish jeers said, "His Excellency done ask is what he done been heard about that old Empress true?"

"You damned blind fool of a boy!" said the Empress, and boxed his ears so hard that his wig fell off.

The footman put it on again, crookedly, and kissed her hand.

The Empress plucked one of her feathers and sent it as a gift to the Governor. There was wild applause and an unlikely chorus of "Here's to a health unto His Majesty!"

Duffy beamed, and O'Riley shook his head as though the excitement were too much for him. "Look at her," said Duffy. "She's rampant. Not even a cash offer would have kept her away!"

Then the din stopped, and heads turned, because Kitty Trash stood at the top of the steps that led to the upper room. "O'Riley!" she shouted. "Give that poor nigger woman water before she back go break with them feathers!" The Empress gaped. Kitty smiled sweetly and disappeared. Too late the Empress hurled a pewter mug at where she had been.

After that the grog-shop was packed every night. The battle frequently flared in public, where after Kitty's initial insults the Empress steadily took command. The reason for her return was her need for money. O'Riley knew that, and never asked her for a penny. He was content with the increased trade so long as she kept to the courtyard and made no attempt to oust Kitty from the upstairs room.

For as long as she kept this tacit bargain the Empress was unstoppable, as she proved when after a week she stood convention on its head. Traditionally the Mrs. O'Riley of the moment was the most expensive whore in the house. The Empress made her own price higher than Kitty's had ever been, and watched the arguments blaze like grasslands in a dry season.

Kitty was young and sinuous. The Empress was an enormous forty-year-old who leaned back to carry her massive bosom and thighs, her great wide hips and stomach. Who gave the more exotic service? More dangerously, how could the question be answered if Kitty gave no service at all? It could not, and Kitty's first defeat was that she was forced to readmit men to her bed.

Her second defeat was that when she readmitted them, they reported her to be less satisfactory than the Empress. Kitty, said those who could afford both, was a wildcat, but only for a man she loved, whereas the Empress sucked you dry.

"Bloody hell!" said Jerry Hoskins, who at once began to save to meet her price. When he did so, I peered over the half-door of the booth, and it was the only time that I heard Jerry cry for mercy. "I no do mercy!" gasped the Empress, and Jerry emerged like a wrung-out cloth.

Not many days after this the Empress succumbed to her vanity. She forgot that her motive was to make money, and announced that she intended to expel Kitty Trash and reassume her rightful title of the present Mrs. O'Riley.

"Never!" said O'Riley. "I beg you—for your own sake and because my love's pledged to another!"

But all he did was sting the Empress into invading the grog-shop, where insults flew like arrows, and Duffy and I were sent time and again to soothe Kitty while O'Riley pleaded with the Empress.

"For God's sake, your majesty! You've made your money and you've rung your bells again. Have you no dignity? Will you spare us nothing?"

The Empress would not. It was now she who seemed to have taken leave of her senses, for when she was not boo-hooing like a girl, or smiling fixedly at the sweaty and cunning O'Riley, she took the mad battle on to the streets, where one of O'Riley's oldest friends was the famous Mamma Dog Codrington, a mulatta trader who sold her wares within shouting distance of the grog-shop, on the corner of Corn Alley and High Street.

Most mornings Mamma Dog called first at McPhee's yard with the best fruit from her smallholding, and then took a tot in the grog-shop. McPhee, who had once been her white lover, and remained her legal master, was the father of her daughter, Missy Dog Codrington, the pride of her life and reputedly the prettiest mulatta in St. Johns.

The Empress McGregor would wait for Mamma Dog to leave the grog-shop and set up her stall, and then would yell at her from the grog-shop doorstep. Her subject was lewd descriptions of Kitty disguised as friendly advice to Mamma Dog. "Kitty she bigeye! She black bitch on belly fire! She make Missy Dog O'Riley him trash whore!"

The notion was that Kitty was so jealous of Missy Dog that she had persuaded O'Riley to make her a whore. How its reiteration was supposed to endear the Empress to O'Riley was a mystery, because all he did was shake his head at the straits to which his old love had reduced herself. "She was as slender as Kitty once," he said, "and walked with more pride in the morning."

As for Mamma Dog, she was older than the Empress, and even more massive: she sat very deliberately on a cask, her buttocks overflowing, her thighs majestically apart. She wore a soldier's tricorn hat, very old and battered, and day after day she rebuffed the Empress with impervious ease. She might lean back and direct laughs and poisonous asides at the sky, but, that apart, was not even stung enough to look at the Empress, who became more hoarse and foulmouthed until one morning she did not appear on the doorstep at all, but stayed in the courtyard, where she was irritable and depressed and screamed at Pegeen for having cast her spells wrong.

This was when Kitty gleefully allowed herself to be dragged into the brawl, and sent me into the courtyard with a mug of water to help the poor old woman keep she-self cool. O'Riley was angry and tried to console and reason with the Empress. But she would not listen, and eventually it was he who lost patience and destroyed her. It happened one April morning, when Mamma Dog came to the grog-shop, not for her customary nip of rum but in tears, to tell us that old Mr. McPhee had died in his sleep.

She had gone there as usual with her basket of fruit, and stopped to gossip with the kitchen women while the house-boy took Mr. McPhee his coffee. He pulled aside the netting and there his master lay, peaceful but very cold, his face that of a scrawny old eagle at the last. The boy ran for the surgeon, and Mamma Dog to us, because this was her ambition's moment, when she would give her daughter, Missy Dog, a proper life.

Mamma Dog knew that when McPhee's will was proved it would leave to his child, Missy Dog, the most that a white could give a mulatto: two thousand pounds. At last Missy Dog could leave the market garden and the whitewashed shack and be a lady. Had she not been taught in anticipation how to sew, and wear shoes, and keep kitchen niggers in their place? "She has," said O'Riley. "God bless her, but I know she has!"

In the courtyard the Empress snorted. O'Riley patted Mamma Dog's hand. She blew her nose on her skirts and said that for the sake of their long friendship she wanted O'Riley to help her.

O'Riley waited. The Empress grumbled and scoffed.

Mamma Dog shouted that although she was only a trash black woman her plan was to ask Mr. Leslie to be their new legal master, and at the same time to accept Missy Dog as the mistress of his household. He would be offered a dowry of five hundred pounds provided that he guaranteed Missy another two thousand on his death, or if he married a white woman, and his domestic affairs and servants would be properly regulated.

"What's that to do with me?" said O'Riley.

"Me want white man him speak with Leslie," said Mamma Dog, and O'Riley laughed aloud because she went on to offer him commission to be the broker between herself and Leslie.

No doubt he would have liked to make Missy Dog the jewel of the nanny-house, but he liked secret power more, and the Empress should have known it and not challenged him: "You slave for black mamma? Huh? White man not slave for black mamma!"

"Shut your mouth," said O'Riley, "and pay me your board and lodging."

The Empress gaped, and could not summon a reply, and in that moment her bubble burst. Within a week she was drunk most of the time, and although Kitty acted now like a loving daughter, and O'Riley fussed and tut-tutted, for they both truly believed her to be a legend, she was broken and old and in a month she was back at Kidnapper's Bay. The rockets had gone up, as Duffy said, and the sticks had come down.

O'Riley was morose about it, and talked of his own insecurity at living with a much younger woman, but that did not stop him taking me with him to Leslie's yard, where the three of us strolled past the slave quarters to the little sandy bluffs at the water's edge. O'Riley broached the matter as one that he had invented himself.

"The fact is, your honour, that I happen to know that in the opinion of a certain young mulatta you're the handsomest man in St. Johns!"

Leslie gaped. He giggled. Then he blushed and walked away from us. He turned. He was trembling. He wanted to speak, but his voice was strangulated. He cleared his throat and said, "Mulatta? What mulatta?"

"Missy Dog Codrington," said O'Riley, as though it were obvious. "She's no master. It's your opportunity, sir. She'll come to your bed like a gazelle."

Leslie was sweating and wild-eyed. "In my opinion," he said, "I should have been a Captain of Militia long ago. I have an aptitude for command."

"It's the mother, though," said O'Riley. "She's the one against you."

"It's yon Hanson!" said Mr. Leslie, and paced about. The breeze fluttered our hair. There was pink on the underside of the clouds, and it was reflected on the ships and buildings.

Mr. Leslie halted. He seemed weary. He looked at me and said, "Surely to God I can trust you, son. What's O'Riley's interest in this?"

"Commission," I said, and felt O'Riley glow at my acumen.

Mr. Leslie seemed about to throw himself into the sea. "Commission?" he yelled. "What in God's name have you done to earn commission!"

"I've accomplished this romance," said O'Riley briskly, "and I'm not ashamed to say so."

Mr. Leslie tried to protest, but O'Riley grasped his arm. "You do know the girl?" he said.

"Of course I know her," said Leslie.

"I wish it was me she sighed for," said O'Riley, "and as for a dowry, the mother would expect to pay seven hundred, but if you accept five, I can persuade her to set her objections to one side."

O'Riley winked, and lowered his voice despite being in the open air.

"If you make the girl safe in your will, sir, I can secure the other moneys."

Mr. Leslie gulped. "Other moneys?" he said.

"She's fifteen hundred at least," said O'Riley. "You could have the management of it."

O'Riley jerked his head, and Mr. Leslie followed him along the shore. Once I heard Mr. Leslie shout, "No! I'll not risk her in the same yard as that fornicator Hoskins." But O'Riley calmed him and they struck hands. It was agreed that Leslie would take Mamma Dog and Missy to a magistrate, and that afterwards they would accompany him to the yard to see what changes the house might need before it was fit to receive a mistress.

When that visit occurred I was among the crowd who followed Mamma Dog downhill from the Court House. She waddled with an air of immense gratification, and as the procession passed Corn Alley she bellowed some vile asides about the poor old Empress, but once in the yard she waited almost bashfully as Mr. Leslie stepped forward and cleared his throat and Lomas and Caesar and Jerry came embarrassedly out of the house.

There was silence. One of the kitchen women laughed, and Caesar grinned at her. Mamma Dog called Mr. Leslie "your worship, sir," very deferentially. He blushed and invited her inside. She declined, but said that she would like a chair in the yard. Caesar protested but fetched one. Mamma Dog sat down and smiled at Missy. Missy hesitated. Mamma Dog nodded and waved her forward.

Missy stood meekly at Mr. Leslie's side. "Very good, child," he said. "Very good." She was slim and kept her head down. She was in her finest flounced petticoats and head-dress, and spoke in so low a voice that I could not hear. Lomas said, "Eh?" and Leslie leaned to listen. Missy lifted her head and looked round as though she were trapped. I saw the gold of her skin and the fineness of her bones. She was beautiful.

Mr. Leslie urged her to speak again. She did so, very quietly, but Lomas heard and said, "Bloody hell!" Mr. Leslie snapped his fingers at him. He patted Missy's arm and told Caesar to fetch the kitcnen woman who had laughed at Mamma Dog. The woman dawdled forward.

"You'll be sold tomorrow!" shouted Leslie, and the woman was, and the money and more spent on a lady's maid for Missy. Now Leslie offered Missy his arm, and they went together to inspect the house, but after only a minute or two they reappeared.

Missy seemed to be trying with great dignity to hold back tears. Mr. Leslie earnestly reassured her. He shaped as if to hold her in his arms, but he was too embarrassed to do so in public. Then he shouted at the house slaves. "Scrub these rooms! Clear out these broken chairs!" He shook with rage. Blacks and whites ran about and exhorted each other.

Mamma Dog declined a pepper-punch, and with a satisfied nod set off homeward. Mr. Leslie would escort Missy Dog later. Missy herself asked to see the kitchens, and Lomas and Jerry joked to keep their spirits up. In the last weeks Jerry had caught the clap, and Lomas chaffed him relentlessly. "Come on, lad! Out with it! Let's see that famous fiery foreskin!" He tried to mock him again now, but the joke had no heart, as though each of them realized that a spell had been broken.

Three weeks later Mr. Leslie paid off Jerry's indentures and sent him back to England with a few pounds, a letter of recommendation, and his clap more or less cured by Mr. Waller. Jerry wanted to stay, and was so drunk when he finally went aboard that he sat on the hatch-cover and sobbed.

"Lad," said old Lomas, "you look daft!" And so he did, with his shaven head and portly body, and tears on his puzzled, moon-like face. One of the bonds between us was that he had confided in me about the death of his own mother, and how he hated his father. Poor Jerry. He never did understand that there was no room on the islands for poor and propertyless whites.

Chapter 24

Letters

Not long after that the ships began to arrive again from Africa, and at the sight and stench of them I felt familiar loathings and grievances. I had forgotten how battered and worn the ships looked, how their timbers groaned and leaked excrement, so that the water round them had cloudy yellow stains. I was shocked again by the howls and clankings, the swirl of cauldron smoke, the mad glare in the eyes of the sailors, and the despair of the newly-landed slaves. They shambled and flinched. They had chain-sores and abscesses. Although I stared into many faces, I never found a scarred and decorated Jola. Nor did the *Margaret* crawl into the bay, or William stand in the grog-shop doorway, which pleased me, because I did not know yet how to face him.

I thought one morning that the moment to do so had arrived, when Mr. Leslie sent me a message that said come at once to the yard; but it was only because letters had at last arrived direct from Liverpool.

I had written months earlier both to Smallshaw's, to offer them Fourfarthings in exchange for my indentures, and to Mr. Sayer, to ask him what it would cost me to redeem the mortgage on High Top, and would he kindly inform me of any other prospective purchasers?

"How will you do that," O'Riley had asked, "except by dealing in slaves?"

"I'll do it," I had said, "I swear I'll do it!"

Leslie's house was a turmoil of painters and carpenters, and he himself had a boil on the edge of his lip. He read me first a letter from young Mr. Smallshaw, who curtly advised him that Fourfarthings had been sold for fifty pounds, which more than redeemed my indentures. The balance had been donated to the Seamen's Hospital.

Smallshaw's deplored my conduct but understood that it was due to the effect upon me of the unfortunate Mr. Dingwall, against whom they had warned Captain Derker in the first place. As for the Captain, the profits on the *Margaret*'s voyage had been most gratifying—more than three hundred per cent, in fact, when the sugar was sold in Liverpool—and the Captain had retired to his cottage on the shores of Dee. All in all, concluded Mr. Smallshaw, events had worked themselves out for the best, and we must thank God for having released Captain Derker from so arduous a trade.

Mr. Leslie refolded the letter. Insects buzzed. "Does Smallshaw know William's my father?" I said.

"You're discussed in all the Leeward Islands," said Mr. Leslie. "I imagine the echoes reach Liverpool. Do I treat you in any less of a Christian spirit?"

I shook my head and half smiled. Mr. Leslie always had it in him to surprise me.

"They gave Partridge command of the *Margaret*," he said, "but from what I hear she's gone to Jamaica."

I nodded. I was glad, because I did not want to see any of them.

"This enclosure is for you," said Mr. Leslie, and gave me a letter that Smallshaw's had sent on from Mr. Sayer. Mr. Leslie indicated that I could read it there and then.

Mr. Sayer thanked me for my communication, and begged to inform me of what he thought I might not already know, that he was the owner of High Top, having bought the mortgage from William. It was this money that had made William's investment in the *Margaret*'s voyage so large, and enabled him to retire. The High Top grazing was leased out. The house was unoccupied, although shepherds sometimes slept in the barns. Apart from old Mrs. Crabtree, who had died, my relatives were well. Mr. Sayer understood my interest in the property, and wished me well on my chosen path. He remained my obedient servant.

My chosen path! Surely he knew that William was my father. I felt foolish because I realized that Mr. Sayer and William must even have discussed the sale of High Top in my hearing, in the coffee-house or the state-room of the *Margaret*, when I was too excited to listen or care. I crumpled the letter, but then thought better of it, and smoothed it out and put it in my pocket.

"I expect my new clerk at the end of the month," said Mr. Leslie. "He's Smallshaw's nephew that he wants trained up."

I nodded and thanked him, and as I walked back to the grog-shop I passed some slave pens where Jerry and I had rampaged, and thought that without him such adventures seemed stale and silly.

There was dappled light in the courtyard, and Mr. Waller sat there with his pipe and a drink. He was telling O'Riley how the clerk at Colonel Hanson's Hawksbill Plantation had just died of a fever, and as I listened to him I knew that a phase of my life had ended. O'Riley and I had made full use of each other, and it was time to part.

O'Riley had received letters that he wanted me to read to him, but I made an excuse and walked out of the grog-shop and into the alley, and down Long Street to the Court House, where the usher told me to wait in a cool, tiled corridor among the lawyers. They had removed their wigs for the heat, and laughed at their own sallies in a superior fashion.

Then Colonel Hanson appeared from the Magistrate's Room. He was very tall, with gleaming silver hair, and his eyes were blue. He nodded to some acquaintances and walked towards the door. The usher was nowhere to be seen.

I shouted, "Please, sir! Please, Colonel Hanson, sir!"

He turned and snapped, "Who's that? Who are you? Who is it?"

I told him who I was, and he said, "Hah! I know that name. I know who you are. What d'you want?"

"To be your clerk at Hawksbill," I said.

He was surprised, and so were the onlookers.

"How come you know I need a clerk?" said the Colonel.

"Mr. Waller told me."

"Where did you converse with Mr. Waller?" he said, and realized at once that if I said "In the nanny-house," both he and the surgeon would look ridiculous.

"Sir," I said, "he was engaged on a professional inspection."

Colonel Hanson half laughed and rubbed his chin. "Good answer!" he said. He looked at the lawyers. "Good answer!" he repeated. He seemed uncertain, and dabbed at his sweat with a silk handkerchief. "Will—er—will Mr. O'Riley release you?" he said.

"He will," I said, which O'Riley did, because he knew that my heart was set on it, and to have a crony in the Colonel's employ was to have a possible spy in high places.

Kitty Trash kissed me and snivelled, and Duffy said, "Don't get too grand for us!" as though I were going to Paris or Rome, when in fact they still saw me every day, and for the time being I still lived in the nanny-house, because my first duties for the Colonel were to supervise the loading from Leslie's yard of luggage and house slaves aboard the ship that would take the Colonel and his two daughters to Nevis.

An island some forty miles from Antigua, and adjacent to St. Christopher, Nevis boasted the best medicinal springs in the West Indies, where planters from many islands congregated at the palm-leaved, tropical version of a European spa and pleasure resort; appropriately, the nearest village to the hot springs was called Bath.

Through attendance at the General Assembly of the Leeward Islands the Colonel knew several men of influence who would be in Nevis at the same time as himself. His daughters could mix in a wider society and improve their manners, and as I overheard him say to Mr. Leslie, he was sure that he owed himself the experience for a month or two.

The Colonel was a widower and his party was not large, consisting of only five house slaves: the butler, Castillo; a coachman named Rupert, who was a tall, haughty youth with the curious reddish hair and spotted complexion of some half-castes; a cook; and two seamstresses to be ladies' maids. It still took me the entire morning of departure to get these persons and their bundles safely aboard, and when it was done I sent the postilion to the Governor's residence, where the Colonel was at luncheon, to say that it was time to embark. Then I supervised the storing of the coach in Leslie's yard, to await the travellers' return in two months' time.

When I had finished I was sweaty and untidy and had no time to wash because Colonel Hanson arrived with the Governor and a large farewell party. Mr. Leslie came out and seemed very composed. He apologized because redecorations and repairs made his house unfit to enter, and Caesar, in new clothes but still grumbling to himself, set out chairs in one of the open timber sheds and offered a tray of cold drinks. I glimpsed a figure that I was sure was Missy Dog, watching from the gloom of the counting-house.

I had hoped to make an impression upon the Governor, but after giving me brisk nods everyone ignored me. They were all so coolly and elegantly dressed, and I was so grubby.

The Colonel's elder daughter, Lavinia, had a grave and beautiful face, and I wanted to stare at her, but she stared at me, and I was nervous. She seemed very severe for someone not much older than myself. The younger daughter, Susannah, was about my age. She had a fuller body than Lavinia's, and I could see more of her breasts. She smiled, and seemed more friendly.

As the party strolled down to the boats, she lagged behind and glanced at me. I drew level. "Yes, miss?" I said. She held out her hand. My heart raced. I held out my own hand.

Susannah put into it a piece of fruit, sticky with sling sugar, that she had taken from her drink. I gaped. She giggled and caught up with Lavinia. I threw the fruit away and tried to wipe my hand on my breeches.

When the Colonel reached the water he asked me to steady him as he got into the boat. I put out my hand. He grasped it and felt the stickiness. "What are you doing?" he said. I mumbled. He snorted and sat down in the boat. "I hope to God you keep the books better!" he said.

I stared at Susannah. Her glance was innocent. "What fun!" she said, as she trailed her sugary hand in the water. Lavinia frowned and did not look at me at all.

"God speed!" said the Governor and took his hat off. Leslie's boatmen shoved off and rowed to the ship across grey and glaring afternoon water that gently rippled in the off-shore breeze. I called for the postilion, and we rode the coach-mules five miles to Hawksbill and my new life.

Chapter 25

The Terror

Hawksbill Plantation was built on two headlands, and two or three patches of flat, half-cleared land, between a line of small, steep, thickly-vegetated hills and the sea. On Guard Point was the house, with one spacious storey, stone walls, verandahs, and cedar-shingled roof. The kitchens were at the back and a little uphill, so that the smoke blew out to sea. In front was Oxen Valley, the gap in the hills that led to the cane fields, and to the south the beach and store-houses and Little Guard Point, on which were built the windmill, the boiling-house, and the overseer's cabin. Beyond that were the curving beach of Little Hanson's Bay, the slave huts and their vegetable patches, and then another, smaller beach and the Hawksbill itself, a rock half a mile off-shore that reared up in the shape of a hawksbill turtle.

Inland, clouds raced overhead, and there were views from each plantation of other field gangs, other mills turning, other canes waving, and steam blowing around other boiling-houses; but Hawksbill was a different, shut-in world, where the trade winds blew from the land and the trees leaned towards water that was clear and quiet because of reefs far out. Humming-birds were enveloped by the flowers they sucked, and yellow butterflies fluttered over the sea. Hawksbill was paradise and hell.

In the absence of Colonel Hanson, the plantation was run by the overseer, Mr. Fishlock, a small, dark, neat man who carried his head on one side like a bird. His glance darted everywhere, and he spoke rapidly with a Welsh lilt. He had been a sailor for most of his life, and still walked with a roll. He was about forty, cleanly-dressed but foully-spoken, and hot-temperedly jealous of his power. He did not sleep in the plantation house when the Colonel was away, but insisted that he and I take our meals there even if Mr. Jarvie could not.

Mr. Jarvie was the only other white man among so many blacks. He was the boilerman and distiller, who had been born on Antigua and was now an old man, red-faced, puffy, short of breath, and bad on his feet. He could not walk from one headland to the other, so his meals were brought to the boiling-house, where he had set up his bed and table, despite the fact that twenty yards away we all had two rooms in the overseer's house; like Mr. Fishlock I slept in the back, and had my desk and ledgers at the front, where the rooms opened on to a verandah that overlooked Little Hanson's Bay.

There was a spare set of rooms used for stores, and old Jarvie had filled his with the debris of his thirty years at Hawksbill: sea-shells, driftwood, old bottles, stones, bits of metalwork, saddlery, some of it rotten and ant-eaten, two travelling trunks, broken chairs, old clothes, and a set of hammers. It was dusty and cobwebby, and rustled with lizards and the occasional small snake.

Jarvie had once been tall, with big ears, and he was training two blacks named Broomer and King to take his place. "Them two disgraceful lads," he always called them, although he defended them stoutly when Mr. Fishlock tried to take them from him.

Mr. Fishlock was new to Hawksbill, to which he had been brought by Colonel Hanson; but whereas the Colonel let Jarvie do as he pleased in his last years before giving up work, the overseer was offended by the rubbish-filled rooms, and the fact that outside the boiling-season Broomer and King seemed to be either idle or collecting sea-shells for Mr. Jarvie. In Mr. Fishlock's opinion, they were insolent young bucks who should be put to field work.

There were fifty field Negroes at Hawksbill, divided into the big gang, composed of men and women in their prime who did the heavy work, and the little gang, comprising children, old people, and convalescent sick, who did the lighter, clearing-up tasks around them.

The head of the big gang was Primas, a thick-chested, grey-haired, vociferous Mandinka, who did very much as he pleased. He had a big vegetable patch and a hut of his own that he was allowed to share with two women. His lieutenant was a younger Mandinka named Jimmy, who led the little gang and, like Primas, had a deep laugh, a cowhide whip, and a European hat and coat. Because these two allocated the work tasks, other blacks plied them with gifts and favours; neither Primas nor Jimmy dug his own vegetables, although both frequently took the best of other people's to sell in the streets of St. Johns.

There were two other fully-privileged blacks, Scipio the blacksmith and Buff the carter, while a young man named Yankee, whom Colonel Hanson had bought because he was a good carpenter, had the same argued-over status as Broomer and King.

All these men, and especially Primas and Buff, had to be cajoled and negotiated with if the work was to be done properly, and it was Mr. Fishlock's contention that Colonel Hanson did not push them hard enough. So the overseer was not unhappy when the Colonel wrote by the September post to say that he intended to stay in Nevis until Christmas. Soon we heard from neighbours that the Misses Lavinia and Susannah were the successes of the social season, and we were not surprised when at the end of January the Colonel wrote again, to say that he would not return for several more months; he had been invited to take the young ladies to Montserrat, to enjoy the hospitality of Mr. Masters, a prosperous planter of that island whom they had met in Nevis. When we received this letter the cutting-season had already begun, and I saw what hard driving meant, for not only did the blacks cut the cane all day, but Jarvie kept the boiling-house going all night.

Each morning there was a roll-call before daybreak and then the creak of the carts as the gang moved out. Hawksbill had two hundred acres, a third in cane, a third fallow, and a third in next year's crop. There were blocks of twenty acres, each with several fields in them, some climbing steeply up the sides of the hills, and every one a tangled mass of trash, weeds, arching leaves, and cane shoots three or four feet taller than a man.

As the gangs arrived they spread out along the rutted cart track at the end of the fields. Each cutter faced two rows of canes. There was a silence, almost as of a ritual, in which the men looked up at the sky and the curved, dancing tops of the leaves. Then Primas blew his conch shell, and the men began to sing to set their cutting rhythm.

Each man cut first the row to his right, with four slashing strokes at each cane—one to sever the stem as near the ground as possible, two more to strip off the trash, and one to trim the top. He laid the cut canes across his line of advance and used the left-hand row as a trash lane.

As the voices rose and fell, the vegetation crunched and the blades slashed and sliced. The ox wagons lumbered up the outside trash lanes. There were four men in the wagon to stack, and four in the field to gather. Women and children relaid the cut trash over the line of advance, to protect the ratoons and keep the soil moist; they had baskets full of animal dung, which they carefully pressed down around the cut edges of the ratoons.

At nine the gangs heard the plantation bell and stopped to eat. They stopped again at two, but that apart, toiled through the highest glare of the day half-naked, sweat streaming, the song cracking for want of breath. More than once in the cane I saw a cutter reel and drop dead. Men turned, reached, slashed, bent. They grasped leaves that had edges sharp enough to cut the most callused hand if it grew tired or casual. Light danced on the uncut cane. There was scrub on the hills, trash tangled around bare feet, and on the men's arms blood and sweat. The cutting rhythm became a reflex, so that muscles set free of it twitched and jumped all night.

At sunset the gangs trailed home through Oxen Valley, where the winding dirt road and overhanging branches could have been England but for the spiky thrusts of cactus that made dramatic, tropical silhouettes against the last greyness of sea and sky.

Then the slaves ate: barrelled salt fish from Virginia, rice, and whatever vegetables of their own they were not too weary to prepare. When they looked up they saw the boiling-house, and although the glow and the clouds of steam through the roof slats were hellish, the scent was sweet and sickly, and it was everywhere, in one's hair and clothes and bed-linen, the staleness of sweat and the heavy fragrance of sugar.

The drudgery of the fields was at least one that the blacks understood, and pride drove many of them to prefer it to that of the mill, where the machine was master, and men of little account, even when the wind veered, work halted, and the tailpole had to be unanchored to bring the cap creaking round and the sails in line again.

A huge arch gave access to the machinery, and that was where I stood when I was called out to relieve Mr. Fishlock or Broomer at the feed roller. It was awesome, as I pushed the cane along the wooden tray, to feel the power of the mill; the canes had a sticky, powdery surface, and when they were grabbed by the rollers, sucked away from my hands and left them tacky. The liquid dripped into a tank, and the delivery roller ejected the crushed cane through a smaller arch at the side, where it was taken away to be fed to the cattle.

All day the machinery squeaked and groaned, and insects buzzed for the sweetness. The earth was trampled bare and littered with trimmings, and machetes, and barrows made of hollowed-out logs. Men and women slept where they could in patches of shade, and the air was perfumed.

At night the mill stopped but the boiling went inexorably on. Along one side of the shed there was a line of open cauldrons, heated by a furnace in the middle; and on the other, cooling boxes and perforated pots. The first boiling was at a moderate heat in limewater, and there was a good deal of scum to be removed. This boiling was good if, when the sugar was picked up, it expanded in a sticky mess between finger and thumb. As the heat of the water increased, the substance thickened, and suddenly-congealed pieces of sugar were called "brick."

"Aye, it's good brick, is that, lads," Jarvie would say, in the steamy glare of furnace and lanterns, and King and Broomer would grin and caper about, as though they were pleased but hardly understood what he said; in fact, for all that it demanded care and judgement, they could have run the boiling-house better without him, and only pretended to be stupid because by doing so they pleased Jarvie, kept him in his job, and avoided responsibility.

After the final boiling, the liquid was poured into the cooling boxes, and from there to perforated pots. Twenty-four hours later the hole in the bottom of each pot was unstopped and the molasses drained off. The brown, moist, crystalline sugar was then put into hogsheads, and it was my duty to check the number and tare weight painted on each hogshead, and to enter them in my books.

Hawksbill reckoned to ship about forty hogsheads—say, twenty tons—of sugar and thirty puncheons of rum each year, all taken off the beach in precarious small boats. When that was done, it was time to clear the ground, plant a new crop, and keep it weeded until the trash arched over to protect the stem—another three months of labour that was always likely to be unsettling because it coincided with the arrival of new slaves.

Mr. Fishlock bought ten that season, to replace those who had died or been sold during the year, and even the introduction of so few, out of chains for the first time in months, and given European rags to wear, was most disturbing. One pretty girl was sent to be a house slave, and the rest were divided among different huts and gangs.

After a month, two of them died on the same day, and Mr. Fishlock was so edgy that he went to old Jarvie and demanded that Broomer and King take their places to keep the field gangs up to strength.

"Never!" said Jarvie. "I need them for repairs."

"Where are they?" said Fishlock.

"How do I know?" said Jarvie, who had seen Fishlock and Primas coming and told his two lads to hide.

Mr. Fishlock looked at me. I looked at Primas, who brandished his whip and shouted.

"Don't make that noise!" said Mr. Jarvie. "Can you do without them or not?"

Primas said that he could.

"You just told me that you couldn't," said Mr. Fishlock.

Primas blustered and Mr. Jarvie mumbled on about repairs. Mr. Fishlock swore and spat but had to withdraw. Jarvie was too decrepit to work, he said, and could get us all killed.

That night I saw Primas come up to the boiling-house and collect his bribe of rum from King, who had charge of the stills, and I knew that despite the arguments about them, Broomer and King were in an unassailable position.

So was Primas, because for all the bad food, whippings, and spells of work that literally killed men, the slave gangs never moved at a pace beyond that set by the slaves themselves. The cane cutters were expected to cut two rows each a day, and if they were asked to do more, or unduly abused in the process, all manner of accidents occurred. Wheels fell off carts, loads were uptipped, harness broke, and the genius of Africans made every upset a social occasion; people crowded round with comments, and Primas and Jimmy knew exactly how much confusion to allow before putting on a display of bullying and whip-cracking.

When Mr. Fishlock said that the Colonel did not push his people hard enough, he did not really mean with regard to their rate of work. What Mr. Fishlock meant was that the Colonel did not ram their servitude down their throats. He did not play Primas off against Scipio, and Scipio off against Buff. He did not humiliate the blacks, and the reason, said Mr. Fishlock, was that some of them were his own flesh and blood.

Oh, not just his half-brother, the drunken gambler Alexander Hanson. There were children as well. "Have you seen the coachman, Rupert?" I had. "Who do his long face and jaw remind you of?" I had to say: Of the Colonel himself. "Correct," said Mr. Fishlock. "Have you seen the house-girl, Cassie?" I had. "Look at her again," said Mr. Fishlock. "Look at her."

I had looked, because she was so pale and beautiful and reserved, but next day I looked again, and it was obvious that she was the Colonel's daughter. She had his tall build and his eyes and forehead. Her mother, Old Cassie, was the laundry-woman. "Hanson's first black whore," said Mr. Fishlock. "Rupert's hers, as well as Young Cassie."

"Who's the Colonel's mistress now?" I said.

"I don't know," said Mr. Fishlock, "and old Jarvie's so crazy he's forgotten."

Fishlock himself never took plantation women. He believed that it led to favouritism, which he resented because he was incorruptible. He used the nanny-house, where I knew that he paid girls not to embrace him but to humiliate themselves while he watched. He frightened me, unlike the Colonel, whose confusions were easy to understand, especially at Hawksbill, a place where even a poor white clerk might live like a king.

He might walk at dusk the beguiling beaches, feel the sea-grass crunch under his feet, and see everywhere patchworks of fireflies; he might eat and drink as much as he wished, and afterwards take his pick of six or seven slim brown house-girls; he might feel himself part of the vast and noble British Empire, and see sunset clouds piled high like those of a triumphant battle painting. None of which, as I knew to my cost, was security against blind terror in daylight.

Once, in my counting-house, I was convinced that the cook had poisoned my coffee, and I ran out into the water. I was up to my chest when I remembered that I was fully dressed. I looked down and saw a small, pale fish investigate my shoe. Another time I walked from the plantation house in moonlight and sat all night in the dew because I had heard a rustling in my room and thought that it was black men with machetes; and at the mill once, I caught the eye of a man and snapped. I ran at him and beat him with my fists until I was breathless and had time to realize that I was no longer afraid.

On those nights I took revenge upon the women's bodies; they at least could be made to respond as and when I wanted, and all the more sweetly because at Hawksbill, for the first time, girls came to me unasked. Oh, they wanted favours, to be sure: ribbons from town, shell necklaces, support in arguments with other girls or the assistant cook. But they came to me, pitty-pat on bare night feet when the breeze rattled the palms, the waves lapped, and pearly clouds crossed the moon.

Nor were they heavy field women, but pretty house-girls, delighted with themselves because to be picked for the house was to be regarded as a human being. House slaves had an intelligence and individuality that seemed to die in field slaves. The eyes of field slaves ceased to gleam, and they expressed their defiance by acts of dumb destruction, as I soon saw for myself.

One night I stood up from the body of my most frequent companion, a petulant and provocative Ibo girl named Emily, and went out to the verandah. The breeze was deliciously cool. There was a chorus of cicadas and tree frogs, and the mill was a bulky silhouette. It seemed to me that there could be no more pleasant or loving place in the world.

Then I saw the glow of Mr. Fishlock's cigar, and in his quick sing-song he congratulated me on my prowess, and said, "All the same, there's something wrong, boy. Have you felt it?"

As soon as he asked me, I knew that I had. He blew out smoke and said, "Who's the one you just shafted? Not that Young Cassie, is it?"

He knew that it could not be. Even the other house slaves were wary of Young Cassie, and she slept with her mother in the laundry shed.

"I've got Emily," I said.

Fishlock grunted. "You know what Emily's fear is, don't you, boy?"

"What?"

"Ask me, it's what they all fear—the day they hate us so much they can't do it, the day they go dry between the legs. Then it's back to the field gang, isn't it?"

I did not answer.

"How was Emily?" said Fishlock, and shifted in his chair. "Distant, was she? Restless?"

She had been. She had turned her back and sulked. I had hit her, at which she half sobbed, and half gasped in her throat, and pulled me on to her.

"It's the women," said Fishlock, "not the men. I think one of the women's had a child."

I grunted. There were never many children born in Antigua, because it was cheaper to buy blacks than to breed, and the male and female slaves were always kept in separate cabins. In many cases the shock of the first two years of plantation "seasoning" made women barren. They did not menstruate again, or they continuously miscarried, or they hated men, or they were simply numbed by work. That was why most of the children were mulattoes born to house slaves.

"What will you do?" I said.

"Find out," said Fishlock. "A black infant can't be hidden. It belongs to the slave owner, in this case Colonel Hanson."

Next morning he called me out of bed to go with him to the roll-call, which was conducted by Jimmy as the field gangs lined up to go to work.

Fishlock walked up to the line and told the women to bare themselves. They did so, slowly and clumsily. They were gummy-eyed, only half-awake, in glorious pink touches of the sun's reflected light. Fishlock walked down the line and squeezed each woman's breasts.

One round-shouldered girl began to weep. When Fishlock reached her she shied away and covered herself. Fishlock ordered Jimmy to hold her. When he squeezed her breast she cried out in pain, and there was an oozy blob of milk at the nipple.

Fishlock called for Primas and asked why the girl's pregnancy had been kept secret. Primas blustered. Fishlock asked where the baby was. The girl shrugged. Primas cuffed her. It's in the field, the girl seemed to say. She spoke a language that most of the others did not, and her pidgin was poor.

"Field?" said Fishlock. "What field?"

"In next year's canes," said Primas.

Fishlock sent the gangs to work and called for his horse. He roped the girl's wrist to his saddle, and with Primas and me beside him, jogged slowly to the fields. When we reached the half-grown canes Fishlock said, "Where?" and the girl walked to the edge of the field and pointed. Fishlock dismounted and told her to get the baby out of the trash and lay it in the alley.

The baby was a full-blooded black boy, and the cord and dried-up mess of after-birth had been wrapped round him. The girl had strangled him with a piece of rag, and he was stiff in an attitude of crying. Fishlock prodded the body with his boot and emptied his flask of rum over it. Primas struck his tinder to light some dry trash and set the body on fire.

"Then it's dig it in, she can, isn't it," said Fishlock, "for the manure."

The girl nodded blankly at the flames, as though they were the best possible outcome. Fishlock muttered a prayer in Welsh. He said, "Amen!" and looked at me.

"Amen," I said. The first direct rays of the sun came warmly over the hills.

At the nine-o'clock breakfast break, Fishlock lined the gangs up and had Jimmy beat the girl. She took off her clothes and lay face down on the earth and manure. She screamed loudly at each of ten strokes. Fishlock strutted along the line of slaves as though challenging the father to come out and show his manhood, but no one did. They watched dully, limbs all a-dangle and shoulders slumped. Then they ate and went back to work.

Chapter 26

Young Cassie

A week later Colonel Hanson unexpectedly returned. I was on the beach to check the last hogsheads away when I heard the house slaves shrill and clap. Then the bell rang, which in the afternoon could only be for a great event or the alarm, and I ran up the leafy lane to the house. The weather was sultry, and blobs of sweat fell from my temples on to my arms and legs. The Colonel was on the verandah with his arm round Young Cassie's shoulder. Her mother sat on the bottom step, and there was much rushing about and weeping. I heard the first footman's angry voice somewhere inside, and doors and jalousies banged open in the rooms that had been shut up since the Colonel's departure, and were now unaired and full of insects. The Colonel himself was happy and waved me up to take a drink. Of the young ladies there was no sign.

I looked round, not for Lavinia, who I hoped would like me but was sure did not, but for Susannah, and as I did so, the breath was knocked out of me by the realization that I loved her. I wanted to see her more than anything else in the world.

Black girls were nothing. The one I wanted was white, and I knew that she wanted me. It was obvious that she did, when I recalled the way she had smiled at me in Leslie's yard. I peered this way and that for her, wildly.

Colonel Hanson praised the house-girls for their scarves and earrings, and said that Lavinia and Susannah had been invited to stay a while longer on Montserrat. Little vixens, he called them, laughing, and patted me on the shoulder. They had asked to be remembered to me.

Of course they had. It was Susannah's message of love.

The Colonel asked me about the harvest, and the clearing of land that was now under way. I wiped my sweat with my sleeve. I heard myself say so many hogsheads, and so many this and that. Good boy, said the Colonel. Hogsheads away.

I returned to the beach. The sun glared out of greyness; its dazzle on the water swelled and heaved, a sheet of brightness impossible to look at. I grinned at the notion of Jerry Hoskins and his vacant stare.

"Don't be a prick," he said, "you don't love that Susannah."

"I do," I said.

"She won't look at you."

"She will. Oh, yes, she will, and Lavinia can stick it up her nose!"

Whenever I thought of Jerry I grinned again, until Mr. Jarvie shouted across the boiling-house, "What's this? What is all this!"

"Nothing," I said.

"Nothing?" he said. "Lads your age don't smirk like that for nothing. It's love, isn't it?"

"No," I said.

"I've seen them before," he said, "and kept my mouth shut!" And then, in a whisper because the carpenter Yankee was at work, "Don't you worry. I'll not tell Mrs. Hannah. Nor the other one, neither."

I thanked him, and he winked and nodded. His mind was a sieve, which forgot and jumbled up. Mrs. Hannah, for instance, whom Mr. Jarvie often talked about, was the Colonel's long-dead mother. Who "the other one" was I had no idea.

Slowly but surely, senility was overtaking Mr. Jarvie. He got dressed in the middle of the night because he thought it was day, he tapped empty sugar casks, and he called the Colonel by the names of the plantation's previous owners. He seemed to think that the returned coachman, Rupert, was someone called Jonathan, and that the butler, Castillo, had been newly purchased in St. Johns.

But the Colonel loved to chatter to him, and so did visitors such as Mrs. Maitland, the leather-faced old lady I had shoved aside at Leslie's scramble. She drank pepper-punch like a man, and sat on the Colonel's verandah with her knees splayed and her skirts heaved up above them—as she said, to let the trade winds circulate. Her opinions were always outrageously direct, and the Colonel and I laughed at them, but Mr. Fishlock was grumpy.

He believed that since the Colonel's return his advice had been ignored, particularly with regard to unrest among the blacks. He believed that obeah spells were being cast against the plantation, and that the girl who had killed her baby had done so because of a curse. The Colonel shrugged and said that he did not think it of any more consequence than usual.

"It's found the sticks and stones they've cast the spells with, I have, isn't it?" said Fishlock, but the Colonel dismissed the matter. He smiled sadly, as though there were things in his heart and on the island that we would never understand.

This angered Fishlock; and when, as overseers will, he contrived to manufacture his own evidence, there was a self-righteous flush about him, and a glint in his eye that was more venomous than the situation seemed to warrant.

Our rowboats were being caulked, and one night Mr. Fishlock managed to have one left out on the beach, in the hope that someone would steal or damage it, and so enable him to make a case for greater vigilance. It was a plan that succeeded far better than he had hoped, and at the same time far worse than he could ever have imagined.

In the middle of the night the rowboat was set on fire. Someone in the slave huts raised the alarm, and by the time I awoke, Mr. Fishlock was outside yelling orders. Then he set off for the Colonel, and although I was still half-naked, I followed him.

At the house there was no sign of the watchman, and the palm-oil light in the lobby was out. We stumbled over the blacks who were asleep on the floor. One of them grabbed me, but I shouted, "Wake up!" and we burst through an empty room into that of the Colonel, where in the clouds of netting his body floated over that of a black girl who sighed and stretched and twisted.

Fishlock shouted our news. Dogs barked. The Colonel got up. I saw his still-erect penis and slack belly as he struggled into his breeches. Then the butler Castillo came in with a light, and although the girl turned and hid in the bed-clothes, Fishlock and I both saw her. We saw the sharp purple points of her breasts, and her eyes, and we realized that she was the Colonel's own daughter, Young Cassie.

Chapter 27

Through the Night

Mr. Fishlock's moralizing Welsh heart had divined a flaw in the Colonel, but when he knew what it was, he was shocked. He knew that the situation was more confused than he had dreamed, and he saw, as I did, fragments of previous knowledge fall into place. He understood what Jarvie must have known but had forgotten, what all the blacks knew, what Mrs. Maitland, and Alexander Hanson, and old Antigua hands such as O'Riley knew about the past but rarely uttered to newcomers such as Fishlock and me. Yet we were the ones who had to face the Colonel.

We were used to his long silences during meals, but now they were unbearable. Moths fluttered and our sweat stood out. Castillo padded on bare feet, and women argued in the kitchen, and none of us looked at each other.

The Colonel was the first to break the spell of shame when on the third night we expected him to get up and say goodnight but he did not. He called for more bottles, and said, "You were correct, Mr. Fishlock. There is an obeah woman who hates us here. Her name is Mamma Sophie Hanson, and she was my father's mistress before he ever met my mother."

Mr. Fishlock made as if to rise, but the Colonel said, "Do you love this land?"

"Love it?" said Mr. Fishlock.

"I do," said the Colonel. "I love it as much as I love Cassie, and want it as much."

He had been drinking all day and by now was very flushed.

"Cassie!" he yelled. "Cassie!" And Young Cassie came, very diffidently, in a flame-coloured body-cloth, and with a flower in her hair. The Colonel took her wrist and drew her into the chair next to his own. He sneered at us. "Do you object, Mr. Fishlock? Do you object to my daughter sharing what is mine?"

Fishlock shook his head. Young Cassie did not look at us.

"Dig your hands into the soil," said the Colonel, "the actual soil of Antigua. It's good, thick, juicy clay here, isn't it? Good coastal clay that makes us rich."

He waved his hands towards the little hills.

"Not so inland, is it, Mr. Fishlock? Not so, sir. Most of that soil is dry and hardhearted, and when you break it, when you bend over it with your hoe and your sweat falls into it, when you break that soil, it runs through your fingers like dust.

"Can you imagine that this is an island without water? How can so green a place have no fresh water? We've all been drenched by the rains, haven't we? Why isn't there fresh water? Well, God said, 'No,' and there isn't. That's why other islands prospered quicker. They had water. Jamaica had water, Barbados had water, Montserrat and Nevis and St. Christopher had water. But here white men dug cisterns. English soldiers dug cisterns, and died like flies, poor bastards.

"That's how my father came here. Did you know that? Corporal William Hanson. He was born in your country, Tom, at Barnard Castle. That's your north country moors, isn't it? He always talked about the main street straggling uphill and about how one day it had been full of horses.

"Oliver Cromwell's horses they were, on the way to some battle, and some of the troopers couldn't find room in the houses, so they slept in the street, among the horses' hooves. My father hadn't seen it, of course. It happened years before he was born, but he always talked about it.

"He was a bellows-boy in a smithy, and when a recruiting-party came round he joined the Army. He put ten years in. I still have his discharge certificate, and when he took the King's Shilling he never spent it. He kept that Shilling for more than forty years, until he gave it to my brother, Alexander—which was justice, since Alexander is the eldest."

There was a silence. The Colonel still clutched Young Cassie's hand; then he let it go, to drink deeply, and when he continued it was to describe how, on his discharge, his father accepted, like many soldiers, the Government's offer to settle on Antigua.

"They needed more white men to keep down the blacks and to piss on the French, and so they gave each discharged soldier who would stay ten acres, three pounds in cash, a barrel of beef, and a barrel of flour.

"Well, that was more than fifty years ago, and even by then the best land had been taken up; it had been given away fifty years before that by King Charles the Second, when he came back to the throne after the Civil Wars and had to reward his supporters. That's how this plantation began, and Five Islands and Mosquito Bay.

"Now you know, because you've worked the plantation, how much sugar can be grown on ten bad acres—not enough to keep a man alive. So after a year or two, some of the old soldiers had been killed by hard work or fever, but most of them sold up, and when they did that, they were finished because there was no work.

"You know why, Fishlock. You're a poor rat like I was. The Government still transported white convicts to the islands, and the convicts were cheaper to employ than free men. But some of us were free, Fishlock, and we put our blood into this island, our blood that ran down our pick handles into the soil of this island, and we—"

He banged the table. His passion choked in his throat. He gripped Young Cassie's hand once more. He smiled at her. His eyes devoured her. She stirred as though to provoke him, and then hung her head. Their passion made my sweat burst out again. Fishlock fumbled with the decanter. The Colonel looked at him. Fishlock drank. Then he put the glass down and smiled twitchily.

"My father always knew that ten acres were useless," resumed the Colonel, "and so for two years he worked as a smith to earn money to buy more acres, and when he had them he built a shack called Barnard Castle, and hired convicts if he needed them, and worked himself like a slave.

"His first crop made a profit. He used it to get credit from Mr.

McPhee and plant more sugar, and to buy himself a black slave woman. 'You should have seen her in her prime,' he'd say. She was a strapping, fine creature whom people always called Mamma Sophie.

"He took her to Barnard Castle, and she's lived there ever since, God damn her black heart and her witchcraft, but she loved my father and he loved her, and when she gave him a son he said, 'We'll call him Alexander because he'll conquer this bloody awful land.'

"When he made more profits he extended his credit. He hoped after one more season to buy a small plantation on a mortgage, but it was the season of the first hurricane to strike the island for more than twenty-five years.

"Have you seen what a hurricane does? It smashed everything. His standing canes were destroyed and his ratoons were washed out of the ground. It blew for a day and a night and ruined him. So we can say now, and have always known. But at the time he didn't admit it. He was as good as a hurricane, and better than rich men and officers. He still had Barnard Castle. He was young. So he went out to work again and—"

He was silent. Young Cassie stared at him. He smiled at some picture in his mind we could not see.

"What he was like is Alexander. Alexander is really his child. None of the rest of us are. None of us even look like him, except for Alexander."

He again smiled to himself, and then continued.

"One day my father went to old Mr. Lucas's plantation to repair a cattle-mill. When he'd done, Mr. Lucas, who liked any excuse for a tipple, said, 'You'll take a pepper-punch, Hanson?' And as they sat on the verandah the governess went by with the children.

"She was a female convict named Hannah Gould. My father always said afterwards that the sun shone through her hair and made it spun gold, and she always said that she gasped at the blue of his eyes.

"When he'd finished his drink he thanked Mr. Lucas and went round the back of the house to where he'd guessed she'd wait for him, and they walked up and down—in the smoke from the kitchen, she always said, but at the time they never noticed it.

"What they said to each other was told to me many a time. My father said, 'I reckon you've heard of me,' and she nodded. 'I'm not spent yet,' he said 'I can be better than such as Lucas.' 'With me you might be,' she said, and always believed it.

"That was my mother. Did you think she'd be a convict? Why should you? Her father was a country curate and when he died he left them with nothing. My mother went to London. She thought that she could attract men and make them pay. When they didn't she stole from them. Or so she said. It was all done for her mother and sisters, she said. She was seventeen when they transported her.

"I've often asked myself why she never set her cap at Mr. Lucas. He was a widower with a fine plantation. But she didn't. She wanted romance, I think, and that meant my father, although he had to wait for her because in those days a female convict couldn't marry until her sentence was ended and the Governor approved her good conduct.

"That took twelve months, and then they were married in St. Philip's Parish Church—it rained but cleared up as they came out into the porch—and went to live in a house that belonged to Colonel Martin, for whom my father worked as an overseer.

"At that time Colonel Martin owned this plantation. Did you know that? Mr. Jarvie worked for him. What? Where did Mamma Sophie and Alexander live? At Barnard Castle, where else? Of course my mother knew about them. What matters is what she thought."

He sighed. I realized that his tall figure and his face were like his mother's; and so, perhaps, were his charm and sullen silences. Lavinia was like Mrs. Hanson, and so were Young Cassie and the coachman, Rupert. My Susannah had more the shape of William Hanson and Alexander; her high spirits were her own.

"What my mother thought," said the Colonel, "is that Mamma Sophie and Alexander were in the past. They had been put in the past forever by a ceremony in St. Philip's Church. She was mistaken, of course. Love cannot be put aside. I think you know that, don't you, Tom? Of course you do.

"No love can be put aside. Not my father's for Sophie, nor hers for him, nor his for Alexander, even when I was born. After me came my sister, Hannah, and then two boys who died, and finally my brother Jonas.

"But as far as my mother was concerned, Mamma Sophie was a yard nigger who did washing and looked after the old shanty. Alexander was called Hanson because we owned him, and for no other reason. He was my hero, but my mother always called him 'that boy who works with your father.'

"Even when Mamma Sophie had another son, called Jonathan, my mother pretended that he wasn't our brother. She talked about she-niggers' filthy habits out of marriage, that was all; about how disgusting it was that a woman of Sophie's age should have a child at all.

"He was my father's, of course, and looked even more like him than Alexander did. When he grew older he looked like my father as he was when my mother first met him. That was when her description made sense to me, because I don't remember that father. The father I remember was a fat man who drank and argued, and as soon as he'd made any money, didn't make use of it but spent it on himself.

"Oh, he always said that he'd make a fortune, of course, and even when the sun had burned my mother up and she was as thin and fierce as a yard bitch, she made a great parade of table manners because she said that when we went back to England with money we'd need to know how to behave.

"We laughed at her but believed it. We believed that we were better than other people and that it was a moot point when my mother sent Hannah to live with old Mrs. Martin, the Colonel's widow. My father sneered and said why should a daughter of his be a lady's maid? But my mother said better a maid in comfort than married and a drudge.

"I expected him to challenge that but he didn't. How could he? My mother was a drudge. When he didn't dispute it, and I saw in his face that he knew it to be true, he seemed to get years older in a few seconds.

"Of course, when I look at it now, I know that it wasn't the things that he complained about that kept him poor—it wasn't hurricanes or droughts or bad soil. What kept people like us poor was prosperity.

"What do I mean? I mean that I can remember, when I was very small, that the sugar in Colonel Martin's boiling-houses was so coarse that it never went to England at all. It was shipped straight to Hamburg and such places.

"Barbados was the great producer then, Barbados and the French islands; but when they improved the boiling, that changed. This island wasn't a poor neighbour, it was a leading producer. There were fortunes made in three or four years. The value of land went up and up, and men like my father had no hope of being able to buy.

"Oh, he had more money, all right, but not enough. So he spent

more than ever. When I was your age, Tom, he gave me a black girl
—Old Cassie, who's in the yard now, God bless her soul, and in time
Old Cassie gave me Young Cassie and Rupert."

He paused, as if he expected us to challenge him; but we did not,
so he continued.

"When Jonas was of an age my father gave him a black girl, and
that was Bella, who lived with him all his life. She was a merry little
dumpling, was Bella, and still is, but their daughter was a beauty.
They called her Pretty Hannah, after my mother, and for my sister,
so it's a family name. I've a great deal of respect for Pretty Hannah."

This time he thought again about things unspoken, and then said,
"My two Cassies lived in a shack near the cistern. My mother knew
that I slept there most nights but pretended I did not. I was happy.
I worked with my father and Alexander. I was in the Militia, and
that's where— Well, I must tell you about a particular day.

"My sister had come on a visit from Mrs. Martin's, and she wanted
to put goat's milk on her face because she'd been told in St. Johns that
it makes you beautiful. We laughed and joked about this as we sat on
the verandah, and in the middle of the afternoon Alexander rode into
the yard on a mule and said that there was fighting in the south of
the island between gangs of slaves and the Militia.

"My father and Jonas and me ran for our horses and guns and went
to our own assembly point, and we left Alexander in charge of the
women and old Mrs. Martin's property. We never hesitated. After
all, he was one of us, and the revolt was over before we heard a single
shot fired. The Governor even made concessions. The island was
prosperous. He could afford to. Why shouldn't trusted blacks hire out
their labour and be trained for responsible positions? So we all said,
although it's not the immediate point.

"The point is that our company had mustered at Buckley's Plantation, and that there was a young white woman there, an indentured housekeeper called Mary Kippax. I'd not talked to her before,
but I did then, and the long and short of the tale is that I married
her.

"There was feeling between us, and she was a white woman. I had
some sort of position. I couldn't play bold with a white woman like
I could with a black, and there were too many other men wanted her.
She was strong and sensible. The right sort. What? Why did Jonas not
marry a white woman? Because he was content. Bella laughed him

out of his worst moods and he wanted no more. But my Old Cassie was—she was a black woman, and that's all I felt for her.

"So I married Mary, and I sent my two Cassies and Rupert to another of Mrs. Martin's estates and I went myself to Buckley's and worked as his overseer, and for ten years I never saw my Cassies. I put them aside, and I never touched a black woman while Mary was alive.

"They were good years. Lavinia was born, and Alexander worked with me as second overseer, while Jonas helped my father. Alexander was in the room when Susannah came into the world. I'd ridden out, and Mary was brought very suddenly to her pains. In ten minutes Susannah was born and my Mary had bled to death. She's buried with the others, in St. Philip's Churchyard.

"After that I sent the girls to my sister, Hannah. There was room at Mrs. Martin's for all of them. Hannah seemed content without a husband, but she liked children, and my mother was pleased. 'At least they'll learn manners,' she said.

"I felt a loss, but I was content to be celibate. Alexander shared my house. We discussed everything under the sun and knew everything there was to be known about each other. Believe me, we were the best of brothers.

"Then one day—who doesn't remember it?—in the month of June in the year 1738 there was to be a great reception in St. Johns to celebrate the King's birthday. Not that the likes of me were invited, but we'd all talked of nothing else for weeks.

"I had to ride out in the morning, to inspect repairs to one of the windmills, and as I went I met a neighbour on his way home from St. Johns, who said that at the last moment the Governor's son had fallen ill, and that the reception had been cancelled.

"When I met Alexander at midday, he seemed unusually agitated, and when I told him about the reception he said that he felt unwell, and that he must go to Mamma Sophie.

" 'It's an hour's ride,' I said. 'You'll feel worse when you get there. Lie down with wet cloths on your brow.'

" 'Mamma Sophie knows the old medicines,' he said.

"I argued, but he'd not listen, and in the end I snapped, 'Then do as you please!' and he said, 'I will!' and rode off. They were the first bad words between us in thirty years. When he never returned I thought that he must be as upset as I was.

"Then at midnight I was called out by the Militia. There was fighting in St. Johns and all over the island. There had been a black plot to massacre all the important whites at the Governor's reception, and when the reception was cancelled, one of the blacks panicked and betrayed the plot to the authorities. All that night we stood to in the yard, and next morning there was more news.

"It was obvious from the names of the blacks who had been betrayed that the ringleaders of the plot were some of the most trusted and educated slaves, men who had been allowed what we called some independence. There were the names of some mulattoes, too, and one of them was Jonathan Hanson.

"Our company commander was a planter named Watkins, and when he read Jonathan's name he looked at me and said, 'Where's Alexander?' and I said, 'At Barnard Castle,' and I knew in my heart that he had gone there to warn Jonathan. 'How old's Jonathan now?' said Watkins, and I replied, 'Sixteen,' and neither of us asked the question 'Who was Jonathan meant to kill?' although we both knew the answer.

"Jonathan was meant to kill my father and mother and Jonas, and maybe Alexander was meant to kill me, and that was when my hair went white, Mr. Fishlock—in the months after, when I remembered our childhood together, in shuttered rooms and on verandahs, and in the warm dust.

"Watkins ordered the company to Martin's Stonyhill Plantation, where my father and Jonas were overseers, and when we arrived there, Jonas was in the yard with his Militia coat on, and his carbine. He had heard of the plot and thought it prudent to guard the plantation. My father and mother were on the verandah. She was very upright, and he was old, and worn out, and drunk. Bella and Pretty Hannah were in the shade.

"Watkins asked Jonas if Alexander or Jonathan had been there. 'No,' said Jonas. 'Why?' 'Jonathan Hanson is wanted by the law,' said Watkins. Bella burst into tears. My mother smiled, and explained very slowly how to find Jonathan at Barnard Castle, as though Mr. Watkins had never heard of the place. My father looked bewildered.

"At Barnard Castle they were eating a meal outside. Mamma Sophie and Alexander never moved because twenty men had their carbines aimed at them. Watkins sent others to search the shack and store-houses, and after five minutes Jonathan burst out of his hiding-place and tried to run into the forest. Two horsemen caught him

"He kicked, and screamed my name, and I looked down at my horse's neck—anywhere except at Alexander and Mamma Sophie—until someone clubbed Jonathan with a carbine and he stopped. They had hoped he would be safe, of course, and that although the plot had failed, it would never be discovered.

"Two weeks later he was one of those hanged, but it was poor revenge for my mother, because from the day of Jonathan's arrest my father never left the house. He was terrified that he'd meet Mamma Sophie in the yard, with chicken feathers and black dogwood to put the obeah curse upon the murderers of her child. Do you begin to understand, Mr. Fishlock? My father did. It killed him.

"Or perhaps he couldn't understand, and so his brain burst. He certainly had a seizure on the day of the hanging. Then he lingered in a half-coma. When he could speak at all, it was to ask for Alexander. 'Over my dead body!' said my mother, but I sent Pretty Hannah, whom I knew I could trust, to Barnard Castle.

"So one midnight, when my mother was asleep, Alexander came, and my father gave him his freedom, and the King's Shilling, and eight acres round Barnard Castle. I wrote it down, and my father managed to sign his name. Alexander never spoke, except to say, 'What the old dieman want?' but I left them alone together, and my father gave him money.

"Then Alexander walked out. Our father seemed puzzled, and talked about McPhee's loans. I said, 'They were repaid thirty years ago,' but before I could explain it, he was dead."

The Colonel stopped and was silent. Eventually I prompted him.

"What happened then?" he said. "Oh! The war against France and Spain! We were hard-pressed in the Indies. This island suffered, I can tell you. We could neither get sugar out nor supplies in. Bad years, Mr. Fishlock. Jonas began to drink. He became a negligible person. Perhaps he had to do that to keep Bella. I don't know.

"I do know that we were ashamed. I couldn't think what to say to my mother, nor she to me. I'd lost Alexander. My children were no comfort. I'd no woman because I couldn't bring myself to trust a black.

"We were a family of poor, dried-up whites, Mr. Fishlock, with nothing to hope for. We didn't even own Barnard Castle, because it had been given to Alexander. We'd nothing except false pride, which was always more than the blacks had, and we lived sourly for six years, until one day—" He snapped his fingers. *Click!* "One day we found ourselves rich. Why? Very simple. My sister Hannah—the spinster, if you remember, the old maid—my sister Hannah met, and was wooed by, and accepted, a man of enormous wealth.

"His name was, and is, Nicholas Leonard, of Patmore Hall in Hertfordshire, St. James's Square in London, and Mosquito Bay in Antigua, where he was born, and which he left, like all rich men's sons, to be educated in England; and to which, like all rich men's sons in the last fifty years, he never returned.

"Why should he? He never saw his own blood soaked up by that damned soil. All he saw was money, thousands and thousands of pounds of it, that could be spent in London, and where better?

"Nearly all the plantations in these islands are owned by men who live in London, and they've most of them bought a Patmore Hall, and a town house, and a seat in the House of Commons, where there's enough of them to bring down any government that won't say, 'Protect sugar and be damned to the French!' Oh, and some of them have bought wives and titles, but don't think that I begrudge them. I don't! I never did, even when I was nowhere near one of them.

"Now that I am near them, I know that they have pain like other people. They may dispose of armies and battle-fleets, but they lose their childhood like the rest of us. Mr. Leonard was fifty-two years old and twice a widower when he took a yearning to see his plantations again.

"He said that it was to see how they'd fared during wars, and slave revolts, and hurricanes, but I think that it was more a search for what he'd lost. Whatever it was, he'd been here two days when he met Hannah at old Mrs. Martin's. He fell in love with her at once, and came to Buckley's Plantation to ask me for her hand.

"I was stripped to the waist in the cane field and he rode up with the Governor's escort. He remembered me at once, Tom, because we'd met when we were boys. He's a gentleman. He walked up the rash lane and treated me with courtesy. I was flattered. I admit it. I'd have accepted very little for myself, but Hannah said no.

"Hannah was proved to be worldly-wise, Mr. Fishlock. It was she who made it a condition of her marriage and her residence in London that Mr. Leonard buy this plantation, and settle it upon Lavinia and Susannah, with a life interest to me. Then he lent me the money to replant and restock, and for the first years I was my own overseer. I'd not worked so much of my life on bad soil not to make use of good when I got it. When the war ended we made more money than I'd dreamed of.

"Jonas could have shared it with me. He could have been every bit as important as I am, but he refused. He wanted Bella more. Well, he could have had her. But he was drunk and refused everything.

"He went to Monk's Hill Fort to be an officer's servant. Bella did the washing. Can you imagine it? I'd be invited there to dinner and cards, and my own brother would be waiting on table. Then he got a fever and he'd no resistance. He'd lost the will and he was dead overnight. He lies between father and my Mary in St. Philip's Churchyard.

"My mother, of course, was not at all surprised by Hannah's good fortune. She'd planned for it. What else did we expect? Her health was bad and she was content not to go to England herself, so I never told her that Hannah had insisted she didn't. I made my peace with her, and brought her to live here with me. So as you see, I've paid each debt, slowly but surely.

"I brought Lavinia and Susannah home, and I'm afraid they ran wild over these beaches, but I'd no care for that. There were Scots tutors in St. Johns, and dancing-masters travelled round the islands. Besides, I'd agreed that when my miss minxes were a bit older I'd send them to Hannah in London.

"My mother aged very quickly. She went blind. Grey slime covered her eyes, and her hair was very thin, and she sat all day on the verandah and listened to the sea. She was bad tempered because she had sharp pains in her legs, and then one afternoon she had a stroke.

"We put her to bed, and at dawn, in that one moment of the day when the trade wind never blows, she came to herself. She plucked at the covers, and when I grasped her hand, said, 'Is she there? Is Sophie in the yard?'

"Mamma Sophie was there, although God knows what blacks had got word to her. She rocked in the grey light. I heard her croon and saw spittle at the corners of her mouth. There were feathers and crushed dogwood in the dust. Then the breeze blew again and she looked up. The whites of her eyes stared into mine, and she spat. I shivered and went back, and found my mother dead.

"I called the women to wash her, poured myself a brandy, and went outside to watch the sun come up. Mamma Sophie had gone, and I knew that her next spell would be for me.

"When we'd buried my mother in St. Philip's Churchyard, I had only one debt left to pay. There was Alexander, of course, but to pay that I must do what's impossible: change places with him. My one possible repayment was that I sent for my two Cassies and Rupert, and gave them security in the yard at Hawksbill.

"I put Rupert in his blue-and-gold coachman's coat, and I gave fat Old Cassie the laundry, and I thought that the daughter—'Oh,' I said to myself, 'the daughter can be a housemaid.'

"But when I saw her, and it was the first time for ten years, when I saw her she was not my daughter, not a child, but a stranger, and the stranger of my dreams, whose body makes my life worthwhile.

"Have you dreamed of that person, Tom? Have you, Fishlock? How many men do you know who've found her?

"Well, I have, and I'll not give her up. Lavinia and Susannah can be damned, and never go to England, but I'll not give her up. I went to Nevis to attempt it, but I can't. She's mine. She's my bliss and the end to my heartbreak."

Colonel Hanson stared at us, and then defiantly kissed her. Each mouth struggled for the other. He groaned, and Young Cassie tore away from him and ran out. He looked at our faces, which were as grey as the light that came through the jalousies. The burnt-out candles smelt stale.

"She makes my life an endless joy," said the Colonel, his mouth open, maudlin and yet coldly dangerous. Somewhere on the plantation a dog barked, and Mr. Fishlock and I got up and walked out into the morning.

Chapter 28

Susannah's Return

Lavinia and Susannah Hanson returned to Hawksbill at the end of the wet season, when the cool of the young spring days redeemed the months of mist and muddy clothes that never dried. A message came from Mr. Leslie to say that the young ladies' ship had anchored. The Colonel discussed it over dinner; he gave the facts, as always after his confession, and none of us spoke our true fears and knowledge.

On the pretext that there would be the two slave maids and a great deal of luggage to accommodate in the coach, the Colonel did not go into St. Johns himself, but waited at Hawksbill. In the middle of the afternoon he walked with Young Cassie along the far, small beach where morning glory grew flat across the sand. He held her in his arms and then sent her uncertainly to her mother and the yard.

Then he asked me to join him on the verandah, where we pretended to go over the accounts, until we heard the coach come through Oxen Valley long before we saw it, so that by the time it rattled up the hill, the bell was ringing and all the house slaves had run out to clap and shout.

When the coach stopped we walked to meet it. Lavinia got down

first. She embraced her father and walked past him to look at the sea.
As she did so, she stared hard at me but did not speak. She seemed
older and thinner, and was tired and travel-stained. Susannah was
wildly energetic and shouted at everyone.

"Mind that box, Castillo! Careful! Careful! At Mrs. Masters's we
had three kinds of fish every day! Pappa, Pappa, you've a button
missing! Rupert, don't whine! Shift it! You, Tom Derker! Help him!
It's full of glass! A nigger can't be trusted with glass, even you should
know that!"

My head pounded and I wanted to touch her. She, too, was weary,
but she gleamed. Her skin was golden. I could see the tops of her
breasts. She flounced up the steps to the verandah, and chided the
Colonel for not having tied his neckcloth in the newly-fashionable
way.

I neither spoke nor moved. Rupert struggled alone with the tied-up
box. As he passed Susannah she looked at me, first to question my
unhelpfulness, and then, when she saw how I looked at her, with
awareness and response. She licked her lips and smiled. She undid the
scarf that held her bonnet to her head, and shook out her hair. There
was sweaty road-dust in it.

I realized that Lavinia had turned back from the sea to watch us,
and that all my feelings were true. I did love Susannah, and she did
feel for me, and Lavinia was our enemy. But Susannah herself was
a marvel.

As I watched her at dinner, I was convinced that I had never seen
anyone like her. She turned our gloom into hilarity. I was sure that
I would marry her and become the owner of the plantation. I would
wear wide trousers and a loose, cool coat, and Susannah's arm would
be light upon mine, and people would stop and take their hats off as
we passed.

I was so excited that I did not sleep, and in the morning I was not
tired but exhilarated. I knew that she would come to me and she did.
I saw her walking from the house, and pretended to be at work on
my ledgers.

Then I heard feet on the verandah, and looked up, and there she
was, bathed and cool, with a green ribbon in her hair. I blushed. She
laughed in her throat and said, "Good morning."

I tried to speak. Then I realized that I should stand up, and knocked over some books as I did so. Susannah laughed again. She walked past me and peered into my bedroom. She wrinkled her nose and said, "Pooh!"

"What's wrong with it?" I said.

"Don't the house-girls clean it for you?" she said.

"Yes."

"Which one?"

"Emily," I said.

"So I've heard tell," she said, and looked at me, with her head on one side and a half-smile. I held my breath and heard my own pulse beat.

"You and Emily do other things, don't you?" she said.

"What?" I said.

She tossed her head and stirred, as though even the feel of the breeze on her body were too much. I did not move.

"Wouldn't you like to do those things to me?" she said.

I could not speak. I did not want to do those things to her. I wanted to hold her, yes, but not to hit her. Not to make her utterly a slave, as I made Emily. My scalp prickled with shame.

She made a little downward turn of her mouth, and suddenly looked plain, and I thought that perhaps I did not love her, and never had, but was merely a silly dreamer.

Susannah laughed briskly and said, "Mr. Derker, it seems to me that if you own up that you're not rich enough to be my lover we can be excellent friends."

She stuck out her hand as if a man. I went to shake it, but as I grasped it, she raised it, and turned the knuckle up for me to kiss. I did so. She smelt deliciously of herbs that the girls must have put in her bath water.

"Is it a bargain?" she said.

I nodded. I felt grateful; she had mocked me, but still treated me seriously, and did not seem to resent me.

"Gentlemen drink to bargains, don't they?" she said.

All I had was the harsh plantation rum, but she threw it straight down like a seaman. Then she pulled a face and made horrible comic vomiting noises. I laughed. She could always make me laugh.

"Oh, look," she said. "Now you're my slave, but I don't know what to do with you."

I stopped short, and the breeze that stirred my papers chilled me.

"Can we be friends and children?" she said. "Can we run along the beach like children?"

"Oh, yes," I said, and we did, and talked wildly for days on end, as though we were not half-grown-up at all, and not heavy-hearted before our time.

Chapter 29

Dinner for the Governor

The prime ambition of Lavinia and Susannah was to join their aunt Hannah in London, and to take their father with them, but in the meantime, and after their successes in the great world of Nevis and Montserrat, they were determined to make the most of the Antiguan social season. I was not invited to the balls and dinners in St. Johns, but Susannah described them to me at great length, as well as confiding how she intended to flirt with So-and-So to discover if he was as true to his wife as Lavinia believed, and with Such-and-Such, a disreputable officer, in order to dismay her father and make him take them to England.

She talked to me about men as though I weren't one—about their frog necks, or how they picked their noses, or how they pretended to listen to a girl's conversation but didn't. She knew some of them from her childhood, when she lived in Mrs. Martin's house with her aunt Hannah, and was half a guest and half a skivvy.

Those years she often described. She and Lavinia yearned for their father's visits, and when he arrived he seemed very tall and awkward as he stood in silhouette against the glaring sun. Then they went to live with him at Hawksbill, although they were afraid of their grandmother, and after she died— But when she reached the arrival of the two Cassies, Susannah shied away, and said, "Let's pick armfuls of flowers and lay them down the dining-table, and inside one we'll put a worm for a joke!"

There were always flowers now, and Hawksbill had many guests —invited indiscriminately, it is true, with more enthusiasm than tact, so that husbands met their wives' lovers, and debtors their creditors, and bitter opponents in the General Assembly sat opposite each other.

Sometimes there were too many people, because the Colonel and Lavinia and Susannah had each invited ten or fifteen, and once there was a laden table and no guests at all, because each of the three had relied upon the other two. But, amazingly, no one seemed to care.

The girls' enthusiasm overcame all obstacles of tact and protocol, and they eventually succeeded in their madcap scheme to invite the Governor, George Thomas, and half the members of his Council, to dinner. In fact, because the house at Hawksbill was not very big, and the Governor and his party slept at Five Islands, on the other side of the hills, the comings and goings were tremendous, and the event became a three-day junket that had its climax in a dinner.

So for some mornings before that, when the plantation bell summoned us as usual to a breakfast of coffee, hot cutlets, yams, and different kinds of cold fish stewed in vinegar, limes, pepper, and onions—caveached, as they say in the islands—Mr. Fishlock and I did not know, as we stumped across after two or three hours' work, what new guests or how many there might be, the men in their floppy shirts, and the ladies in light gowns that the breeze blew beguilingly.

When we returned for a pepper-punch and a light lunch, there would be different faces, and then we rested, they in hammocks on the verandah, or in the shuttered rooms, and Fishlock and I in our hot little ovens in the overseer's house.

In the early-evening cool we worked again, and the young ladies and their guests took a stroll, passing as often as not the work-dazed gangs on their way home.

The dinner, when it finally happened, was a hilarious success, at which the Governor complimented Castillo and told many funny stories. Susannah had threatened to use silly girlish questions to lure the Captain of Artillery at Monk's Hill Fort into the monologue on ballistics that made him the most-giggled-at bore on the island, but at the last moment she took pity on him, and her one prank was played upon the Governor's wife, a thin, drained woman who dressed like a desperate girl and was drawn by compliments into describing how she made her own clothes.

But since most of the guests were flattered to receive such a confidence, the comic malice that provoked it was not suspected, except by Colonel Hanson; and when with cheery shouts and laughter, and leaving only two insensibly drunk gentlemen behind, the guests had ridden off into hazy moonlight, he took Susannah to task.

Her response was to give outrageous imitations of every person at the table. She made her voice scratchy, or tucked cushions down her front, or pieces of fruit into her cheeks to fill them out. Lavinia joined in as the imitated person's husband or wife, and their mock conversation took the form of comments upon the Hanson family as the guests rode home.

The Colonel was shocked, and then laughed despite himself. Then Susannah tickled him until he wheezed, and his callused, workman's hands flapped helplessly from his rich-man's lacy wrists. Susannah called him a beast who refused to take his girls to England, and when he protested she and Lavinia whirled off into mock dialogue again.

They all shrieked with laughter, and the dogs barked and leaped about, and the Colonel became the drooling beast and pursued the girls in and out of every room, whereupon they threw cushions at him, and the black maids squealed and ran like rabbits, and Castillo removed his tired dignity to the verandah until the commotion was over, which it soon was, because Susannah banged her shin on the furniture.

Then tears and panting followed the excitement, and the beast who pursued and ate his brood folded them both to his breast. Each had a thumb in her mouth, and Susannah twisted her hair with the other hand.

That was when Fishlock and I slipped away, and passed among the other shadows in the lobby the shadow of Young Cassie waiting for her sisters to retire, because she was Lavinia's handmaid as well as their father's whore.

Lavinia herself was still reserved with me, and difficult to approach, and whenever her grey eyes appraised me I was convinced that she thought me a fool. What I could not fathom was why she had taken Young Cassie as her maid. When I saw them together they seemed so alike, in their willowy shape and their quietness, that I thought that Lavinia did not know about her father's passion and had sincerely tried to celebrate a sisterhood.

Then I would look more closely at Young Cassie herself, at the grace of her, and the boldness that lay behind the modesty with which she slipped out of my way, and think: Of course Lavinia knows about her father. They all know, and pretend in their despair that they do not. Yet I was never truly sure, not even after my quarrel with Susannah.

It happened one dinner-time, when Susannah pressed her father to read them a letter that had arrived that midday from their aunt Hannah in England. The Colonel did not want to read it, but Susannah persisted until he pulled it from his pocket and threw it in front of her. Susannah picked it up and read it aloud.

It told us what in fact we already knew: that although England and France were supposedly at peace, there had for some time been open warfare between them in India and in North America, where the French had come down from Canada and won an important battle. They threatened the entire western frontier of the British Colonies, and another general conflict was sure to break out in Europe and across the oceans.

"Surely," wrote Hannah Leonard, "if our young ladies are to profit from English manners and an introduction to English society, the time for them to do so is now, before all our interests are endangered by war and God knows what hazards must be faced upon the seas. . . ."

When Colonel Hanson heard this, his lips moving silently as he did so, he smiled that knowing smile of his and glanced away to change the subject.

When he was pressed he said, "No. I'm Colonel of Militia. I can't go to England."

Susannah was wildly angry. They exchanged bitter words, in which the Colonel said that they might go if they pleased, but he would not.

"I'll never go without you," she shouted, "because if I do, I'll not see you again!"

"Nonsense!" he said. "Nonsense, girl!"

"Then why won't you?" she said. "Why won't you go? Why not?"

The Colonel walked out. Mr. Fishlock scurried after him. Lavinia was silent. I knew that I must make some kind of test. I looked at Lavinia.

"Do you not think that the Colonel's reason may be honourable?" I said.

Before Lavinia could reply, Susannah shouted, "Honour? What's honour to you? All you care about is your black bitch at night!"

We all stared at each other. We were frightened. None of us knew what to say.

"They're all niggers!" shouted Susannah. "Niggers, niggers, niggers!"

She ran out of the room. I followed. She turned and hit me, and I let her go. Lavinia came into the lobby and looked at me. I shrugged. Lavinia's mouth twitched, and she made a little bob of the head to excuse herself. Somewhere inside, Susannah was crying. Then Lavinia spoke to her, but I could not hear what they said. Young Cassie and Castillo watched me from their customary shadows. I looked hard at them, but they did not lower their eyes.

Chapter 30

A Visit to Town

Next morning we had to ride into town for the annual Militia Rendezvous. I went early to the house to try to apologize to Susannah, but she did not get up to see us depart in the splendour of our uniforms. As we drank coffee on the verandah, Colonel Hanson said, "Poor Susannah's unwell!" with a glance at me, and I went up to Lavinia and said, "What is it?"

"She's displeased," said Lavinia. "She said, if you asked, to tell you she may never speak to you again."

I thought from a flicker in Lavinia's eye that she was amused, but I could not be sure.

Then she said, "What you did was unthinkable. You know how troubled she is."

Before I could reply she turned away, and the Colonel said, "Mount up, gentlemen!" As we rode along, he said, "You quarrelled with her as well, did you?"

"Yes," I said.

"Mr. Fishlock and I walked along the beach," he said, "and then I went back to talk to her. She flung her arms round me. We both wept, Tom. She's a good daughter. I think she'll do what I say."

I looked at him. He was staring ahead, and obviously believed what he said. Fishlock would not look at us. Our saddle leather creaked and the horses snorted for pleasure.

Our company was, of course, one of carabineers, so that we witnessed but did not fully share the day of Mr. Leslie's glory, when he barked his orders with a new-found authority and his foot company finally was the smartest. To crown their triumph, Duffy won the engraved sword for marksmanship, and at the end of the parade the Governor and Captain-General, after due consultation with Colonel Hanson, awarded Mr. Leslie his Captaincy on the spot, to be effective forthwith.

The ranks cheered, and Mamma Dog Codrington, who had set out her stall at the edge of the field, tipped her old tricorn to a prouder angle, and yelled at her pipe-smoking cronies to show more respect and from now on call her daughter Mrs. Captain Missy Dog Leslie.

Only O'Riley was missing. I had been told that he was ill, and we had heard all the rumours about the ownership of the nanny-house, but I was still not prepared for what I saw when I entered the grog-shop that evening.

Kitty Trash and Duffy were surrounded by dozens of drunken Militia men, and it seemed to me to be Kitty who was telling the girls what to do.

"Where's Pegeen?" I said.

"He paid her off," said Duffy. "He gave her a shack and some land near Falmouth Harbour, so there's the end of an old song for you. Will you come up to see him?"

O'Riley was in bed in the upper room, and the place stank like John Derker's body long before. O'Riley's appearance shocked me. He was a slow-moving, pain-wracked shadow of himself. Whatever it was that tore and burned inside his stomach had consumed him. His shoulders were still massive, but they hunched pitifully around nothing, and his face was gaunt. His beard straggled, and the eyes that had always been screwed-up and suspicious were limpid.

In the middle of our talk he clutched himself and screamed with pain. "For God's sake," I said, "have you no laudanum?"

He nodded and showed it to me.

"Then use it!" I said.

He shook his head.

"Why not?"

"There's no French or Spanish ship in port," he said, "so there's no priest. I confess to myself, and for penance it's so many hours without laudanum."

"For God's sake," I said, "you can't turn to religion now."

"Why not?" he gasped. "Am I not an Irishman?"

Kitty had heard him scream, and had come upstairs. Duffy's white skin was blotchy in the heat, and his Adam's apple went agitatedly up and down, as he explained that he did not want to inherit the nanny-house. "It's too big a load altogether," he said, "when all I want is the money to live at peace in Ireland." Kitty laughed loudly, in a handsome and victorious fashion.

"They talk as though it's dead I am already," said O'Riley, and they did. They were impatient for him to go, and bewildered that he must, because none of them had anything like his power and mystery.

That night Colonel Hanson slept at the Governor's residence and I in the nanny-house courtyard, because he wanted me to go next to Mr. Leslie's to inquire about possible passages to England for Lavinia and Susannah. Mr. Fishlock took our horses back on the bridle, and it was arranged that the coach would collect me, a gift of wine from the Governor, and the Colonel after he had spent the day on the Magistrate's Bench.

There were some Liverpool ships in the harbour, and I saw some sailors I knew, but they did not recognize me because I was almost seventeen now and had greatly filled out. So I slipped past them and went to Mr. Leslie's, where I sat stiffly upright in a house transformed.

Where the desks and ledgers had been was now a parlour in which Leslie entertained his guests. Old Lomas had been told to clean himself up, and then put with the new clerks behind partitions at one end of the warehouse. Caesar was a mere wood-chopper, and an imposing new butler called Constantine had been bought from the Governor himself. The maids had caps and aprons. The dining-room had been refurnished, and beyond it I heard the rustle of silk petticoats. The butler bowed, muslin drapes fluttered, and the rooms that had stunk of urine and stale smoke were scented with flowers.

But this was as nothing compared to the change in Mr. Leslie. What I had suspected from afar at the Rendezvous was confirmed by a handshake: he was another man. He had put on weight, and displayed a belly and a hint of jowls. His clothes were light, and cool, and gleaming clean, and so was he; his complexion was smooth and did not have a boil or yellow outburst anywhere. His breath was sweet and his teeth less stained. His nails had been trimmed, and his hair newly washed and tied at the back with a ribbon, and above all he was happy.

Of course, being Mr. Leslie, he did not have it in his nature to deny himself the pleasure of monopolizing a conversation, but he did not talk now about his Militia grievances or the Earls of Orrin; he talked now about the pride of his life, his new, month-old son, Hector Dingwall Leslie, who, when our business was done and the butler had served punch, was called for and appeared in the arms of a black wet-nurse.

Hector had yellow skin, lank black hair, and a squashed-up face. He was very ugly. Mr. Leslie beamed at me. I felt stupid, and said, "Congratulations."

"I knew you'd agree with me," said Leslie, "because he certainly is. He's the finest wee boy in St. Johns."

Leslie made burbling noises, and Hector farted, at which the nurse took him out. The butler coughed and stared at the ceiling. I thought about the white child who had died, the surgeons who had killed Leslie's wife, and the girls in the nanny-house booths. I said, "Will Mrs. Leslie not favour us with her company?"

When Missy Dog came in, we stood up for her. Her beauty had a bloom of achievement. She smiled but did not say much; she was content to watch her man, who swelled out his chest, asked me what Colonel Hanson thought about the latest political news from Europe, and, before I could answer, launched into a speech that gave his own solutions to every single quarrel between Britain and France.

Missy Dog was steely when with one glance she summoned the butler to recharge our glasses, but that apart, her eyes were quietly down. When Leslie looked at her he seemed about to melt. He sighed and made helpless gestures; her effect upon him was beyond even his words to describe.

Missy Dog asked if I had eaten, and I said, "Thank you, at Mr. O'Riley's," which gave me the opportunity to pour out what I felt about our old friend.

Leslie shifted in his chair. "We don't speak about O'Riley," he said. "He was always most disreputable." You paid him commission for this girl, I thought, as he changed the subject.

Soon after, I took my leave, and the sun made me sweat as I walked up the hill to the Court House, where the coach was drawn up but the Colonel had not yet appeared.

But Alexander Hanson had, in a straw hat into which he had stuck a fistful of chicken feathers, his velvet coat soiled but still half-grand; he was drunk, and wore a mocking smile. When he saw me he removed the hat to make sweeping bows and slurred compliments. I tried to pass him. He blocked me.

"You be my page-boy," he said, "when they make me crowned King of Hawksbill!"

I put my hand on his shoulder. He knocked it away, and on the box of the coach Rupert laughed.

"Get out of my way," I said, and kicked Alexander on the shin. He was so drunk that he fell over. His hat went one way and his stick another. He floundered in the dust. "Boy," I said to Rupert, "shut your fool mouth and call me sir."

The Colonel came out of the Court House. As he strolled through the forecourt, he raised his hat to an acquaintance. The postilion opened the door and the Colonel got in. Then he saw Alexander, crawling like a half-genteel crab towards the shaded boardwalk. The Colonel flinched. He did not seem to know what to do.

"Drive on!" I shouted, and the coach juddered as Rupert let the brake off too quickly. The Colonel laughed ruefully, but did not want to look at me. We were both relieved when he gathered himself and found something to say. The court usher had told him that O'Riley had thrown Pegeen out of the nanny-house. Was this true?

It was, I said, and explained. "There's some think she used the obeah to put raging devils in his entrails," I said, and glanced at the Colonel. He looked away, across the plain surrounded by lines of small, steep hills. We both sat rather foolishly, with our feet up, because the floor was taken up with the Governor's gift of wine.

Chapter 31

The Gang in the Woods

We had heard in town many reports of petty violence, burnings, runaways, and theft, which seemed to prove that the blacks were as unsettled as we were by the rumours of war with the French, and a week later trouble came to Hawksbill itself. When it was discovered I was in the boiling-house, because Mr. Jarvie had suffered some kind of stroke, in which he shuddered and sneezed like a horse, and while he lay in bed I helped Broomer and King at the stills.

I wanted to keep an eye on Mr. Jarvie, and so when on the morning in question the breakfast bell rang, I did not go over to the house, but stayed where I was, with a tasting measure in one hand and a slice of paw-paw in the other.

Suddenly the bell rang again and shots were fired, and there was much yelling and consternation. Broomer and King seemed as surprised as I was, so I assumed that it was not an organized revolt. I ran out of the boiling-house. A cart gang bringing wood for the furnace had stopped work to eat breakfast. They stared now towards Guard Point, where I saw Colonel Hanson on the verandah, waving his arms about in a more angry and excited fashion than I had known.

At least he was alive. I grabbed the pistol that was always under my mattress, and when I reached the house it was to discover that the roll-call, which among the house slaves was always held after the breakfast bell, had revealed that the Colonel's son and coachman, Rupert, had run away.

"Him missin'," said Castillo, to soften the blow.

"He's run away!" shouted the Colonel. "He's run away! It's the gang in the woods!"

Jemmy's gang in the woods was a phantasm of the terror. Most slaves ran away to join women, or fellow tribesmen on other plantations, from which they were brought back and whipped in a more or less routine fashion. But some disappeared for ever, and one of them had been Jemmy of Five Islands. It was always believed that he had formed a gang in the woods—in the rain forest that covered the Shakerley Mountains, the hills that formed the island's south wall. Barnard Castle, where Mamma Sophie lived with Alexander, was on the edge of that forest, and inevitably Mamma Sophie was called the gang's mentor, princess, and obeah woman.

There was no proof of it, any more than there was proof that shadowy figures seen running away from fires, or from attacks upon unpopular black foremen, were members of a gang at all, or that a man called Jemmy was their chief; but everyone believed that they were, and that somewhere in the green tangle there were free men with machetes.

That Rupert should join them seemed absurd. He was much more likely to be with a girl, or drunkenly asleep somewhere, or gambling with the money that the Colonel gave him from time to time. Perhaps he had gone to St. Johns to carouse with Alexander; that was a logical step for his bitterness to take.

The postilion, who slept, with Rupert, in the stable, and was expected to know his whereabouts, was slapped across the face by the head footman, and started to boo-hoo and roll about in the dust, until the Colonel picked him up by his woolly hair. The youth gulped with terror and said, "Him been go make piss-piss! Make piss-piss!" Then he sobbed because in his fright he had made it himself and his breeches were sopping. The Colonel dropped him.

"When? When him been make piss-piss?"

The boy waved a wretched hand. In the night.

The Colonel wavered. He seemed helpless. Fishlock stepped out of the circle of onlookers and kicked the boy. The boy grovelled and sobbed. The plump-bellied Castillo turned in protest. Fishlock put his hand on Castillo's shoulder, spun him round, and stared into his face. Castillo hung his head, and Fishlock kicked the boy again. The boy howled and beat the ground.

Colonel Hanson went up to Fishlock to turn him away, and they jostled each other, saying, "Take your hands off! Take them off!" as only old friends could. Fishlock walked away, petulant, and muttered to himself in Welsh.

I looked for the girls. All I could see was the outline of one of them behind the jalousies.

"He's gone to the woods," said the Colonel. "That's why this boy's terrified. Rupert's gone to the woods."

Nobody answered him. The Colonel walked round the side of the house and up to Old Cassie's wash-house in the yard. Fishlock and I followed. The blacks watched but hung back. Smoke drifted among the trees. Old Cassie sat in the dust. She looked grey and shrunken.

I looked for Young Cassie. She was in the side doorway of the house, leaning on the jamb, and beyond her, shadowed, pressed in pain against the wall, I saw Lavinia. Her hair was unpinned and hung down in a sad, fair trail. So Susannah had stayed at the front.

The Colonel was checked by Old Cassie's stare, which was one of utter loss and pleading. The Colonel tried to talk but could not. His secret smile had become a terrible fixed grimace. He looked round him and saw Young Cassie, who bent her head, and then Lavinia, who was herself weeping but could not help. Did he think of the day when Old Cassie bore him Rupert? My son. My daughters. All my loving children.

It was Castillo, hurt but patient, who broke the spell with the suggestion that we should search the plantation and then await events.

"He's gone to the woods!" said the Colonel.

Castillo persisted, and the Colonel agreed to wait and hope, and sat for the rest of the day and the ensuing night on the verandah. Occasionally he talked about Rupert. "Why did he run? He was a good boy. All he needed was love."

Next morning it rained. A fine spray blew into the verandah and speckled the cloak in which the Colonel had wrapped himself. The sea was ruffled by gusts of wind. Rupert had not returned, and there was no word of his having been seen in St. Johns. The Colonel told me to get my pistol and horse and follow him. As we emerged from

Oxen Valley onto the plain, the clouds swept low. The hills were islands in a soft, grey, drifting sea, but by the time we reached them everything had cleared. The canes sparkled. The sky was blue, and white clouds sailed across it.

At the edge of the forest the Colonel took a track that plunged into a valley, where among vivid scalloped leaves and flowers there was a group of shacks and store-houses, more like Africa than a European plantation. "Barnard Castle," said the Colonel. "Cock your pistol." There were mangy dogs and drifting smoke, and a few blacks lay on their sides in the shade.

Alexander Hanson sat in his shirt-sleeves on an improbable chipped-gilt dining-chair. He was fitting a new handle to a hoe. He had great presence and dignity, and when he looked up, bowed his head, as if to welcome us to his estate, and then bent to his work again. The Colonel made no move to dismount. I rested my pistol on the pommel.

White sea-birds wheeled above the land, and as my eyes followed them I saw mangoes, and breadfruit under thick, dark leaves. The trees were huge and creepered, and sprouted parasites like clumps of grass a hundred feet above the ground.

Mamma Sophie came slowly out of her shack. I had expected some-one massive and brooding, but although she was very tall, with square shoulders, she was also thin, with slow, proud eyes, and an air of distinction and endurance that neither her white hair nor the arthritis that made her shuffle could diminish. She stood with her shoulders bent and her wrists twisted by disease and, in a way that reminded me of Signor Voss in his negotiations with William, gestured at the Colonel with her chin.

"Where's Rupert?" said the Colonel.

Alexander laughed. Mamma Sophie hissed at him, and he was silent. She looked at the Colonel with her head on one side.

"Where's Rupert?" he repeated. "Where is he?"

Mamma Sophie shrugged. I was sweating. Grey clouds had piled up again.

In front of me the Colonel's shoulders sagged. His head swayed from side to side. Then he gathered his failing energy and screamed, "You tell me where he is!" in an almost hysterical voice.

Mamma Sophie's lip curled. For the only time she gestured with her bent hands, one of them so dead that it was held inside the other.

"Where's Jonathan?" she said. "Ask your she-mother where's Jonathan they done hang."

The Colonel was so angry that his horse half bolted. Alexander leaped to his feet and two other blacks joined him. I pointed my pistol at them.

"Oh, you go make shoot," said Mamma Sophie. "Go make shoot."

Her eyes mocked and unmanned me. I did not know what to do. Abruptly the Colonel pulled out his own pistol and discharged it into the cooking fire. Ash and embers spurted everywhere. He shouted, "Hell and damn you! Damn you!" He jerked his horse's head and rode away.

I calmed my own horse and stared at the blacks. A handsome woman and child had come out of their shack to see what the noise was. Alexander smiled reassuringly, and I felt foolish, because I had never imagined him with a child of his own. Mamma Sophie gestured at me with her chin, and in the direction of the track. It was my dismissal, and I was glad to obey it.

That evening Susannah came unexpectedly to the overseer's house. I asked her if there was any news of Rupert. She shook her head, and huddled for a long time on my bed, one thumb in her mouth and the other hand twisting her hair. We neither spoke about our quarrel nor properly made it up. Then the light was gone and the house bell rang for dinner, and she flitted ahead of me.

Of Rupert there never was any word. Wherever he was, dead, or drowned, or stowed away, or free in the woods, he had vanished, and we never saw or heard of him again.

For nights afterwards there were no dinner guests, and when the ladies had retired, the Colonel sat morosely with Fishlock and me and talked about Mamma Sophie—not coherently, for his emotions stopped that, but helplessly, as though she were a mother who did not understand him. He was convinced that she had lured Rupert in revenge for the executed Jonathan, but it did not stop his passion for the others.

Indeed, it seemed to increase it, for although his brother's old mistress, Bella, had died, he brought her daughter, Pretty Hannah, to the plantation. She was a free mulatta, but he held her hand and begged her to stay, and made provision for her in his will. She and Lavinia seemed to like each other, so she did stay, and occupied thereafter an undefined position in the household; sometimes she dined at table and sometimes not, and she slept on a truckle bed in the same room as Lavinia.

After a month the postilion was promoted to coachman, and a youth from Primas's gang made postilion, and soon after that, on a steaming day in the wet season, Old Cassie died. She was buried like all of them in an unmarked pit, except that in her case the Colonel, who had avoided her like the plague since the disappearance of their love-child Rupert, read a service for her. Not that she was ever a Christian, or that anyone cared what other gods she had revered.

Fishlock said that Rupert had run away because he could no longer tolerate the fact that his sister Cassie was the Colonel's mistress, and that when he disappeared Cassie had asked to join the field gang, but the Colonel had refused. Fishlock said that Primas and Castillo knew this for a fact. It was certainly true that Cassie no longer served Lavinia as a maid. She took her mother's place in the wash-house, where, according to Fishlock, she slept upon the floor.

Then one day in January, when I took my dirty linen to the wash-house, I found Cassie there with the Colonel. She leaned forward, her hands on the edge of a big wooden trough, her head down as the Colonel's big paw massaged her neck. There were tears on her cheeks but her body responded. She gasped and stiffened. The Colonel grunted. Then he saw me. "Thank you, Tom," he said, and I put my dirty washing down and left.

After that she must have gone back to his bed, because day by day he became more like his old self; he ignored quarrels and crises, he smiled mysteriously, he was proud because his family were gathered round him. Mr. Fishlock wanted decisions about which stretches of land to clear and which to leave fallow, but the Colonel would not make them. Rumours of war quickened, but he refused to leave the island until Rupert had been found, even when at dinner one night Governor George Thomas made it clear that it would not be thought a dereliction of duty if the Colonel resigned from the Militia. "After all," said the Governor, "Captain Leslie's come on famously."

Susannah behaved wildly and provocatively. She still refused to leave Antigua without the Colonel, who sat hunched and embarrassed while she yelled at him, and at Lavinia if she interrupted. Pretty Hannah, older than the girls, graver, quieter, uninterested in her own beauty, could sometimes soothe them by example; but not for long, because Susannah hated her as well.

Susannah deliberately dirtied her clothes and spilled bottles and sauces over the tablecloth to make more laundry work for Cassie, and she constantly sent Pretty Hannah on domestic errands that turned out to be wild-goose chases. If the maids displeased her she lashed them with her cane.

I tried to console her because I knew from experience how bitter and confusing it was to feel betrayed by a father, and to fear that his faults had been passed on to oneself. But our old intimacy was finished. She visited me often enough, but her jokes about Antiguan high society had become venomous. Then she would weep because she was sure that one day the gang in the woods would kill her father. He loved them all, and what had they done in return? I thought of Mamma Sophie's Jonathan, betrayed by old Hannah. He had been Susannah's uncle, and nearer to her in blood than her uncle Nicholas Leonard in London.

She told me again and again, and looked at me in an odd, hard way as she said it, that she would stop at nothing to get herself and Lavinia and the Colonel away from this island for ever, and one fine dusk at the beginning of April 1755, she sent one of the maids to the store-houses, where I was checking my stock-lists, to ask me to come up to the house.

There was noise from the kitchen at the back, but the house itself was quiet. The sun had gone but the jalousies were still shut and the lamps not yet lit, so that the dining-room, where I found Susannah, was unnaturally shadowed. The long table gleamed, and Susannah ran her fingertip along the back of a chair. Then in the tropical silence came the noise that I always expected to be the first heavy drop of rain. I braced myself for more, for the downrush. But none came because the sound was that of palm spikes flicking together.

Susannah's eyes burned into mine. My love rushed back, and my conviction that she could inspire me. Her mouth was open, her wide, bright face uplifted. She breathed as excitedly as I did. I wanted to take her in my arms but did not know how. I was ashamed of what I wanted to do to her.

"I did warn you that I'd do anything, didn't I?" she said. "I did warn you, Tom."

"Yes," I said, not understanding.

"Well, I've done it," she said. "I've been to the woods at night. I found Jemmy. Do you know what he did to me?"

I stared at her. She giggled and made an odd noise in her throat. Then she put her hands down the front of her dress and ripped it open. I saw her stocky little torso and was surprised at the smallness of her nipples. She screamed and banged the chair up and down. I asked her what she was doing. She shouted wordlessly, with her eyes wide open, like an animal.

The Colonel ran in, followed by Lavinia and Pretty Hannah and Mr. Waller the surgeon, who unknown to me had been summoned to attend one of the kitchen blacks. Susannah sobbed and ran into her sister's arms. The Colonel's smile was bewildered. I was so angry that I banged the chair myself and shouted that she was a liar and how could she have seen Jemmy, how could she, until the Colonel snatched up a decanter and hurled it to the floor. It shattered and the noise shocked everyone. Mr. Waller stood aside as I walked out.

I went to my room in the overseer's house, where I sat at my table and drank rum. I was trembling. Wild plans raced through my head. Then darkness fell and Colonel Hanson and Mr. Fishlock appeared on the verandah with a lantern.

"Tom?" said the Colonel. "Where are you? Are you there?" I did not answer.

The Colonel came into my room, but Mr. Fishlock stayed outside, where his eyes were invisible but I could sense his restless annoyance. The Colonel grunted. He put the lantern on a chair, so that our shadows curved across the ceiling. He sat down and smiled at me. It was a shabby smile, shamefaced, as though he were the one with something to confess. He opened his mouth to speak but snatched the bottle instead. He took a long swig and turned away, still gripping the bottle. A moth banged into the lantern.

"For God's sake," said the Colonel. "We know you didn't touch her. We know you didn't. We know she ripped the dress herself." He looked at Fishlock, and back again at me, and said, "That's true, isn't it, Tom? That is the truth?"

If I love her, I thought to myself, I should defend and help her, no matter what she has done to me. I felt drunkenly sad, and hung my head.

He insisted, "That is true, isn't it, Tom?"

"Yes. Now ask me why I ran away." My voice croaked. I waved an arm.

"What?" said the Colonel, and took another swig.

I suddenly wanted to leave. I had seen enough of the place. It was a sickly paradise between the little hills and the sea.

For a moment I thought that he might hit me, but he was slurred and self-pitying. "After you left us she screamed again. She threw herself down and rolled on the floor. We bathed her in cologne and Waller gave her a draught. As she drifted into sleep she told us everything, Tom."

She was in bed, asleep in the netting, when Jemmy called out, and she found him in the brush near Oxen Valley, dark in the dark, and twice as tall as any of us; his plan was to surround the house at the next full moon. Cassie would let them in and they would kill the Colonel with machetes. Lavinia and Susannah would lie on the bloodstained sheets and be fucked by five black men. Then Rupert would whip them and ride them round the room. Susannah had torn open her dress to show me where Jemmy touched her. Her belly, inside her thighs, her breasts, her arms where he held her down. I would be able to see very clearly, because wherever his body touched hers the flesh had turned black, like bruises, except that compresses would not remove the colour. Where Jemmy had touched her would be black forever.

My head spun. I breathed deeply to try to sober up. I tried to remember my last talks with her. There were several dead moths around the lantern.

"Her body wasn't black," I said. "Nobody touched it. She can't have met Jemmy."

Oh, but she did. They went through the brush into the canes and lay upon a bed of trash. They drank an obeah potion. It enabled their souls to leave their bodies and fly to the Hawksbill rock. From there Jemmy's went back to Africa, and Susannah's to her bed, where she woke up inside the netting.

The Colonel talked at me but I did not hear. There were his choked-off, unexpressed emotions. His twisting and turning in the trap. His will to love that was an incoherent, hot, and vibrant presence. And his stubbornness. Cassie. Our land. Ours. We can't leave it. If we leave the land it's theirs.

We were silent. Acid burned in my throat and stomach. Then with a hurried "God bless you, Tom, God bless you," the Colonel went and took the lantern with him, so that I was suddenly in the dark. Fishlock still lounged on the verandah.

"Want to talk, boy?" he said.

"Not much."

"I did warn you against them stuck-up girls," he said.

It was true. He had warned me many times, but I was so sure of myself that I never listened. I sighed and looked round the room for comfort, but there was none, so I turned back to Fishlock; by then he, too, had gone, and where his silhouette had been, a blaze of fireflies rose into the air and vanished.

Chapter 32

A Man with a Pistol

Six weeks later Colonel Hanson and his daughters set sail for England. Susannah still had weeping fits, and it was when Mr. Waller told him that she would go mad if she stayed in the Indies, but that sea air might work a miracle, that the Colonel knew he was beaten. At Hawksbill they were strange weeks, in which no mention was made of Susannah's hysteria, even though she was plainly a convalescent. She stayed in her own room and only towards the end appeared regularly for dinner, or for evening walks along the beach, when Montserrat was a pale grey shadow on the horizon, and the sisters talked about the fine times they had had there.

The cutting-season had started again, and I made it my excuse not to go to the house very often. If I met Susannah in other people's company, we rarely looked at each other.

The house itself was full of boxes, trunks, and confusion, and Mr. Fishlock and I had to attend endless business meetings. Although he retained the courtesy title, Hanson at last resigned his Militia Colonelcy, which went, not entirely unexpectedly, to Mr. Leslie—as did the Colonel's power of attorney, like those of other gentlemen who decided to remove themselves to England for the duration of the expected war.

It was not a bad time to go. Prices of slaves, and of supplies for North America, were high in anticipation of hostilities, but so was the price of sugar, and the last two seasons the plantation had made extraordinary profits that we had no reason to believe the present crop would diminish.

We know now that this optimism was well founded, because when the war did come, the French fleets were shattered and their ports blockaded, so that English merchants even exported sugar to Europe, and made very large profits indeed.

At Hawksbill there was more of the excitement of having money to spend among the house-girls, who would never see it, than there was among the Colonel and his daughters. He himself was resentful, and each act of relinquishment took days. More than once he joined the big gang, not on horseback, with a cane and supercilious commands, but with a machete in the line of cutters, half-stumbling with fatigue, soaked in sweat, slashing at the trash as though it were the tangle of his life.

Lavinia, in so far as she allowed me to approach her, seemed not so much apprehensive as quietly waiting, as though she were the only one of them who had an accurate notion of what England would be like. In every letter from the aunt there was a long separate epistle for Lavinia, to which she invariably replied. "She writes something every day," said the Colonel, "like a blasted diary."

Susannah was fatter than when I first knew her, but Lavinia was more grave and upright. In the evening she wore a fine shawl, which sat handsomely across her shoulders. Sometimes I tried to talk to her, but she had a trick of turning me aside. I wondered, if she did write diary-letters, what was in them, because her days were mostly ones of humdrum domestic organization, and not for a long time had she come wildly out of her dignity to support Susannah's comic sallies.

Not that these were encouraged now, because whenever she essayed them Susannah became glittery, and then suddenly tearful and inconsolable.

It was assumed that Pretty Hannah would go with them to England, and Pretty Hannah quietly agreed. She gave no reasons and none was asked; perhaps between family, which they were, there was no need. But Pretty Hannah was a free woman who owned property in St. Johns, and I was deputed to go with her to the lawyers and witness the X she made on yet another power of attorney for Mr.

Leslie. I liked Pretty Hannah. She was the one who asked the most quietly practical questions about England—what could be obtained there, and what could not—and the one who insisted that they pack for Aunt Hannah Leonard as many pineapples and exotic fruits as they could.

Colonel Hanson asked Castillo if he would like to go, but Castillo said no, he had spent thirty-five years on Antigua and he would like to die there. The Colonel offered to free him, but Castillo said there was no sense in that because he'd no money and nowhere to go. The Colonel left written instructions with Leslie that Castillo must never be sold, but live in peace at Hawksbill, and turned his attention to the first footman, Grandison.

Grandison was wildly eager to go but had always spent most of his time bellowing and hitting out at his inferiors. The Colonel decided that this was uncouth, and made inquiries about buying a manservant. When Grandison heard this, he displayed heroic self-control and geniality, which persuaded the Colonel that he was a young man of whom something might after all be made. So, to his delight, and Castillo's approval, Grandison was fitted out with a serge suit and a cloak for the voyage, and told to wear shoes, so that by the time he reached England he would be used to them.

Cassie knew that there was no hope that she would be taken. She never entered the house after Susannah's hysteria, but stayed in the laundry and sent the clean linen by another girl. Fishlock swore that the Colonel still needed her, and that they met on the beach at night, rolling and gasping into the water itself, desperate, her limbs writhing, his hair even more silver in the moonlight, her body patch-worked where the sweat stuck sand to it, so that when he had done she lay like sea-wrack, until with a trembling grace she glided into the water to clean herself. He lay crucified, they said, even when she had stolen away.

"Who's 'they'?" I said.

"Primas and Buff," said Fishlock.

"Who told them?"

Grandison told them. The Colonel reckoned that Grandison could be trusted because it would ensure his passage to England, and so he took him out at night as a bodyguard. While the Colonel sucked his own daughter's breasts Grandison stood in the palms with a pistol, and all the while the sky was lurid from the boiling-house, and the air heavy with the scent of sugar.

In Fishlock's opinion the white daughters were deceived, but Pretty Hannah knew that the Colonel still rutted with Cassie; knew it with her black instincts and ignored it with her white. I did not care any more. Fishlock was happy at the prospect of running the plantation, but for me it was an odd, unsatisfactory time. I waited but with nothing to wait for.

As the day of sailing approached, Susannah perked up, and when she asked to talk to me I had a moment's silly notion that we might regain our intimacy. I should have known better; if Susannah had wanted to talk deeply, she would have come to me. As it was, I went up to the house a little earlier than was usual for dinner. Lavinia was on the verandah, and the last flurry of the breeze swirled her skirts. She made hard work of reading a news-sheet. Keen letter-writers or not, neither she nor Susannah had received many lessons, and to the ones that bored them they paid scant attention. Susannah's attempts at copper-plate were like a child's, although at mathematics she was deadly, especially when it came to counting cards.

Lavinia nodded at me. "Susannah expects you," she said, and I realized that she sat outside to be tactful.

Susannah was in the morning-room with Pretty Hannah, who when I entered glided through the open double doors to the dining-table, and pretended to add final touches to the place settings—out of earshot but still a chaperone.

I smiled at Susannah. She nodded and popped a sweetmeat into her mouth. I said that she looked very well. She took another sweetmeat and studied her embroidery. I stood in silence. Outside, the kitchen blacks laughed, and there was a clink of bottles from the butler's pantry.

I realized that although Susannah felt that she ought to see me and make her peace, she did not particularly want to; nor, suddenly, did I. I said that in the waters off the islands she would see flying fish. She shrugged. I excused myself and said that I would wait outside until dinner. Susannah grunted because she was still chewing.

I repassed Lavinia and stood in the dust. Then I felt foolish and turned round. Lavinia's grey eyes watched me. I tossed my head. She went inside and I knew that she was angry with me, but not what

I had done to deserve it. Lavinia and I seemed natural irritants to each other, and I wanted the Hansons to leave now, even though I was involved with them in a way not fully unravelled.

But would it ever be? If the Colonel had his way, perhaps yes. At our last meals together he asked me again and again, and each time as if it were a new topic, what I intended to do with my life; and when I said that I did not know, he always said, with one of the convictions that men inherit with property, "Yet you've surely considered it?"

"No."

It was true. I hadn't. There was too much unresolved. The Colonel pressed me. Lavinia's glance was particularly keen. I could have slapped her face. Susannah clattered a knife and tried to talk across the conversation, but the Colonel would not let her. If I wished to return to England, he said, it might be possible for him to secure me a position with Mr. Leonard. That was the point of his interest. I mumbled gratefully in reply.

I realized that this would be a way for my life to go, but I was reluctant to think about it deeply. I knew that the Colonel had introduced the topic so that he would not have to think about other and more painful ones.

On the very day of his departure, and in the last moments of confusion and embarrassed small talk before he left Hawksbill for ever, he repeated his questions.

The young ladies were in the coach, and Grandison had climbed up next to the driver, when the Colonel raked his stick in the dust and pebbles and said, "What will you do with your life, Tom?"

I looked at him and realized that he spoke to me rather than look at Cassie, who stood in the broken shade of the yard, very straight-backed and with a long-shaped face like that of the Colonel himself, and his mother and sister, and his white daughter Lavinia, and his niece Pretty Hannah.

Cassie had come from the wash-house and her dress was wet down the front. I was surprised by her self-control, and guessed that it was his own the Colonel feared for. He asked me more questions, but when I replied, said, "Yes, yes," without listening to me, and suddenly swung up into the coach and said, "Drive on!" so that it swayed very quickly down the dip and out of sight.

I looked at Cassie and realized that she had numbed herself with drink.

Castillo put his arms round her and they sat together on the side steps to the verandah. She wept. Castillo brought her more drink, but she refused it and went slowly to the wash-house.

That night as we walked slowly to dinner, Fishlock said that he had decided to move into the plantation house by the end of the week. As we climbed the verandah steps Castillo said, "Pepper-punch, gentlemen!" and something in his tone made Fishlock look sharply and walk quickly through to the dining-room.

Cassie sat in a laced gown at the head of the table, and although she was drunk she was quicker by far than Fishlock. "Take off your hat!" she said, and when he said, "Bloody hell!" and stepped forward, she said, "Don't you speak badbad to me!"

Fishlock was so shaken that he never challenged her again, and when she jerked her chin for us to sit down, we did so. She pushed down the table the papers in which the Colonel had made her a free woman and given her enough money to live for the rest of her life. Fishlock passed them to me, and in that moment the initiative was lost for ever.

Cassie was the mistress of Hawksbill, and she ruled it not grandly but well, not often sharing our table, but with an absolute right to the Colonel's bedroom, and the complete respect of the house slaves.

If we had white company, which was rarely, she kept out of our way, and yet it was still her house. We were the overseers, accepted on sufferance, and we never moved in there to sleep. This gave Fishlock something to grumble about, which his character required, and he and Cassie were often at loggerheads. She did not resist in principle when the number of house slaves was reduced for economy's sake, but argued for one more maid than Mr. Leslie and Fishlock proposed. They conceded the point because the sale of the coach was a more important one. Cassie assumed that it would be retained for her forays into St. Johns.

When Mr. Leslie disagreed with her she bought her rolls of cloth from one of his rivals. This stung him into temporizing, and I remember one ludicrous evening on the Hawksbill verandah when Fishlock and Mr. Leslie whispered lest Cassie overhear them; yet that very afternoon Mr. Leslie had told me that she would be out of the house before sunset, and Fishlock had ordered Jimmy to whip a new slave who did not want to work.

After a few months Cassie put on weight, and grey came into her

hair. She had dozens of dresses and changed two and three times a
day. Her time was spent in sewing, altering, trying on, and talking
sometimes to Castillo. Her occupation of the house was gossip for a
time, and then not. People on the island were used to extremes. They
simply assumed that Cassie had become Fishlock's mistress, and forgot about her.

Without the Colonel our lives became dull routine. The house was
shabbier and less used, and flowered creepers spread across part of
the verandah. It seemed to me that work in the fields became not
more efficient but slower and more resigned. The overseers and black
foremen had more power, but it was a dull weight; with the owners
thousands of miles away, there seemed less to hope for and less
possibility of dramatic events.

It was warm in the evenings, and the waves whispered, and at very
low tide I saw through clear water the brown weeds waving. I loved
the butterflies, and the humming-birds, and the chorus of insects, and
I had learned to live with the heat and a constant film of sweat. There
was something hypnotic in the slowness of the slaves at work and the
exuberance of their music when they were drunk. In due course we
learned that England and France were officially at war, and in St.
Johns I met at last the Virginian Captain Fogg, a younger man than
I had expected, tall, wearing his own hair that was bleached by the
sun, and much distressed by O'Riley's slow dying.

Alexander Hanson went less to the nanny-house. I saw him once
or twice, and he had a tired air about him, not so much drunk as
bemused. He had outstayed the Colonel, he had even driven him
away; and yet having done it had changed nothing. There was no
satisfaction in it, and it made no difference to the minor thefts and
burnings on the plantations.

In the same way I had reached a dull limit with the black girls.
They still came to me, Emily and a mournful little creature called
Bronwen, but I was much more desultory with them. I had hit both
of them. I had seen them shudder and gasp at my blows, and to go
further I would have to wound them.

That I did not want. I wanted to see the effects of a flogging but
not the actual whips. I wanted the gasps and cries but not the broken
flesh. I did not want to see it come away with the lash, nor when I
embraced Emily to hear her howl at the rawness, and feel her wet and
open wounds.

Yet what I could bear to do to her was no longer interesting. I was numbed and unmoved. I did not think that there was any agreement to be reached with women, and I understood why Fishlock paid them to masturbate with sticks and bottle necks. If I respected them I could not treat them as my maleness wished, and so I did not want to treat with them at all.

I saw many men in the islands reach that limit, and some who went beyond it and transferred their feelings to persistent acts of cruelty against black men; they invented reasons why So-and-So was worse than an animal, and why insolence must be beaten out of him and obedience beaten in.

I always watched the wives of those men, if they had them, and waited for the moments of dumb silence in which they wondered how it was that their lives had slipped away.

As for myself, I worked hard and tried to be easy. I let the breeze conduct me gently through the days, even though I did not know what their accumulation meant. I drowsed. The lizards blinked and scuttled, and like them I waited for a tremor, not least because I knew what it might be.

It was not a slaver but a ship in the regular Liverpool West Indian trade that brought Leslie a letter from Smallshaw's which said that, having gambled away much of his money and failed to persuade any owners to give him a command, William's avowed intention was to sign on as a common seaman.

Whether he had done so or not we did not know, and the next letter weeks later did not enlighten us, because it was all to do with the fact that old Mr. Smallshaw had been smitten by a stroke, and that his son had taken over the entire responsibility for the business.

Subsequent post-scripts said that William had indeed signed on before the mast, in the *Deerhound*, Captain Stainrod, but by then the first Liverpool slavers had arrived from the coast, and we learned from their crews about both William and old Mr. Smallshaw, who could neither speak nor move unaided, but who still sat in his chair at the turn of the stairs, where he could see into the counting-house, and his son come to the doorway and shout explanations at him. I imagined the son's cold smile and the father's vegetable despair.

News of William was more contradictory. He had lost all his money. He had not lost it at all. He was hopelessly drunk. He lived with a black girl whom he had brought back in the *Margaret*. He had quarrelled with the black girl and sold her to a tavern keeper. He attended the slave auctions and made wild bids that everyone knew he could not meet. He swayed into the churches, and if the preacher said that man and the world had been created in God's image, stood up and argued. At midday he brandished a pistol at the slaves chained to the Goree Piazzas and challenged Henry Dingwall to step out from behind them and fight like a man. He was the laughing-stock of Liverpool. Never. He was highly respected. He was First Mate on a coastal brig. Nonsense. He shipped before the mast with Captain Stainrod, and had been seen on the sands at Bassa and Peter Tucker's town, and in a yawl party in the Bight of Benin, which all came back to me: the churned-up surf, the spray haze, the gouge marks in the sand where men tried to cling on as they were hurled into the boats.

Where was the *Deerhound* bound? Some said Jamaica, others that Stainrod's final orders had been changed. We knew roughly when he should have weighed from Africa, and for weeks at the back of my mind there was the vague, doubtful unease of what I would do if the *Deerhound* put into Antigua. But she did not, and as time passed, it seemed inconceivable that she would. Jamaica-bound for sure, said Fishlock, who at the beginning of June decided that since we had shipped almost all our year's produce it was safe for him to spend a few nights in St. Johns, where he could indulge himself in the nanny-house and take time to select a dozen or so new slaves.

During Fishlock's absence poor old Mr. Jarvie hobbled across the dusty grass and we ate together on the verandah of the overseer's house. On the second night we had finished our meal and I was lighting Mr. Jarvie's pipe from our palm-oil lamp, when one of the dogs at the main house began to bark. Then abruptly it yelped and stopped as though it had been hit, and we thought no more about it.

We stared at the moon on the water, and Mr. Jarvie puffed away and rambled on about his beloved sea-shells. Then he drowsed. I blew out the palm light, and decided that when I had drunk my rum I would gently waken Mr. Jarvie and help him to bed. Meanwhile I was entranced by the silver sky, and the shadows of the mill and boiling-house and palms. Then my heart bumped because twenty yards away there stood a man with a pistol.

I downed the rum, which stung, and went for my own pistol, which was under the mattress. My fingers shook but I managed to load it. I kept looking over my shoulder, but the man did not appear. I returned to the front room and slipped into the cover of the wall next to the door. I knew that I must go out, but I was sweaty and afraid. Then I breathed deeply and stepped on to the verandah.

The man still stood where I had seen him, and although his face was shadowed, even when the moon emerged from behind a cloud, I did not need to see more than the stocky bulk of him to know that it was William.

He saw me move and said, "Dingwall? Henry Dingwall?"

"Huh?" said Jarvie, awakening.

I tried to say "Uncle" but it croaked in my throat. Stupid, I thought, when you know that he's your father. I said it out loud to him. "Father."

"You're a mutineer, Dingwall," he replied, and fired. I saw the blue flick of the flint and then the spurt of flame from the barrel, and the bullet whined off the wall behind me.

Mr. Jarvie shouted for Broomer and King. William bent his head and half knelt to reload. I went up to him. He wore seaman's slops. His face was mottled, and his hair streaked with grey.

Again I tried to speak to him. I smelt liquor. He swept me aside and I went sprawling on the dewy grass. I heard the scrape of his ramrod inside the pistol barrel.

I ran. I ran down the side of the little headland, across the cart track, and down on to the stones at the end of Hanson's Beach. There were no lights in the house beyond me, but I knew that the watchman must be somewhere.

Behind me William shouted, "Dingwall! Dingwall!" and behind him I heard Broomer and Mr. Jarvie. I was on the grass now and foolishly looked back, which made me trip over. My pistol went flying across the sand. I scrambled on my hands and knees to reprime it, and when I looked up again, William was only a few yards away.

"I'm your son," I said. "I'm Tom. I'm your son."

"Get up!" he said. He breathed heavily and took aim.

I leapt up and started to run. I splashed into a few inches of water but had forgotten that it was low tide, and as I zig-zagged to make a difficult target, my foot went over the ridge of sand that the waves had built up, and I floundered in water up to my waist.

"Face me, damn you!" shouted William, and I did, to plead with him. He ignored me. He called me Dingwall and said that I'd ruined him. It was my way or his. It was falsehood or truth.

He was in the water himself, one leg bent, and one flung out as he steadied himself against the sloping sand. The pistol was steady and pointed at my heart. William laughed his old magical laugh, and I shouted, "No!" and in a blur pointed my own pistol and fired. The flash startled me and the recoil knocked my arm up.

As the bullet hit William's chest his legs collapsed and he fell face downwards into a few feet of water. There was a whiff of fired powder. I stared in fascination at the spreading stain on his back. His clothes were sodden and the little waves rocked him. His dead body moved unhumanly, like the seaweed I had seen under water.

There was shouting from the slave huts. Lights bobbed through the palms. My back ached. The pistol hung heavy at my side.

Broomer ran towards me and said, "Master Tom? Master Tom, is you—?" and stopped when he saw that William rocked in the shallows, a dark, soft lump, a shadow, a blur of nothing. Beyond him the moonlight showed the scuffed-up sand of our running and desperation.

Then other men arrived with machetes and sticks. I walked out of the water. The palms rattled in the breeze. I looked around the black faces and hated them, yet at the same time knew that I was irrational. My legs were weak, and as his men retrieved William from the water, Primas put his huge arm round me and made clucking noises in that soothing, enfolding, immemorial African way.

Part Four

Hope's Landing

Harper's creek and roaring ribber
Thar, my dear, we'll live forebber
Den we'll go to the Ingin nation
All I want in dis creation
Is a pretty little wife and a big plantation
                    —Virginian Slave Song

Chapter 33

Hope's Landing

Ashford Hope, Esquire, was on that July morning in 1756 thirty-two years old, tall, fair, ruddy-complexioned, blue-eyed with a distant smile, straight-backed and yet angled a little towards me because he was deaf on the left side—as he explained, from diving too deep for oysters when a child. He was most perfectly and ironically self-possessed, and wore cotton breeches and a lined cotton waistcoat, and to cool himself sat in his slippers. It was one of the last days of the wheat harvest, and to encourage his slaves, and some half-dozen white casual labourers, Mr. Hope had risen early and ridden round the plantation kingdom that his grandfather had named Hope's Landing. At noon he had time to hear my story, and to set me at ease showed me on the map where the plantation lay, on the eastern bank of the Upper James River, in that part of the ancient colony and Commonwealth of Virginia that had received the first English settlers in America, and been called by them the Tidewater, from the fact that Chesapeake Bay and four great tidal rivers penetrated and deeply indented the swamps and the flat, humid, shallow-soiled, forested plain.

Far inland, beyond the Tidewater, and above the waterfall lines of the rivers that drained them, were the rolling woods of the Piedmont and the Blue Ridge Mountains, where I knew from Captain Fogg that Mr. Hope owned thirty-five thousand uncleared acres. Beyond the Blue Ridge was the Shenandoah Valley, twenty-five miles wide, where Mr. Hope owned two thousand acres, and then the bigger and more impassably forested Allegheny Mountains. The Alleghenies were the frontier, the line between civilization and the wilderness, and beyond them were as yet neither land grants nor speculative investments, but only rumoured vistas that few white men had seen: rich, unexhausted soils, waist-high clover, woods that teemed with game, and grasslands dotted with deer and elk and buffalo.

In that paradise roamed God knew how many Indians, but in Virginia, where the crop was tobacco and the plantations were worked by black slaves, there were more white people than black because, although England still sent out many convicts and indentured servants, there was always enough land for their smallholdings; the frontier could always be pushed west.

Thirty years ago it had not even been the Blue Ridge, but the fall lines of the rivers, where towns like Richmond and Petersburg had since grown up around the old trading posts. But they were not the glory of the Tidewater, and neither was the shipping off Newport, nor the races at Fredericksburg, nor even the Governor's Palace at Williamsburg, the elegant little capital built between one creek that entered the James River and one that entered the York.

The glory of the Tidewater was its dozens of plantations such as Hope's Landing, and the grandly independent lives of the men who owned them. The plantations had come into being before the towns, because the rivers had enabled ships from London and Liverpool and Bristol and Glasgow to sail a hundred miles inland and trade with the planters themselves, to take off their tobacco and credit them with goods in return. The plantations grew or made almost all of what they needed. They were self-sufficient, shut-in communities; and yet, because ships crossed an ocean to their doors, the planters looked to the wide world as much as to the fall line and the Indians.

They went to England to be educated, and had the leisure to pursue gentlemanly ideals, so that when, a hundred years later, Fogg's schooner, *John and James,* slid for three days through the heat haze of the James River, I saw from her decks that the low blur of swamps or the mighty pine-tree wall of the forest was broken every so often by wharves and slipways, and behind the wharves by parterres and formal gardens, above which rose stately red-brick mansions.

When we came to Hope's Landing the river was more than half a mile wide, and the opposite bank heavily wooded except at the ferry clearing. Fogg struck his sails and let the ship come slowly to the wharf with the tide. The house stood among tall oaks a hundred yards away. It was three storeys high and not so long as some I had seen, but it had an elegant porticoed balcony over the front door. The walls were mellow, and the roof slated and pierced by fine dormer windows on each side. The other buildings were hidden by the trees, but there were sheds near the wharf. The river bank was churned and littered where a shallop and a rowboat were moored, but elsewhere it was pleasantly grassy, with reeds and tiger-lilies.

After the ship was warped in and secured, Fogg ordered the hatch-covers to be removed and went ashore. His trade lay in the sale of beef, grain, and salt fish to the British islands, and the purchase of sugar, not infrequently from the French, who made it better and cheaper. Mr. Hope was a supplier of grain and a buyer of sugar, which he resold on commission to the local smallholders and craftsmen.

In his home ports Fogg was supposed to pay heavy duty on French produce, but he invariably evaded some of it, either by faked British stencils and seals or because there were many Americans who thought, as he did, that to be forced to buy British goods and produce was unjust and unjustifiable; so when the *John and James* met a coastal sloop and transferred some of her cargo, no questions were asked.

How the war might affect the West India trade was the topic of conversation between Fogg and Mr. Hope when, an hour later, a black led me at their summons to Mr. Hope's library, a first-floor room that overlooked foliage and the river. There were books from floor to ceiling, walnut stepladders, globes, atlases, rugs and a carved fireplace, scrolls, ledgers, pipes, tobacco jars, a chessboard, and piles of papers under glass weights. Mr. Hope shook my hand and invited Fogg to pour me a long, cool drink flavoured with mint. They talked, about prices and the movement of British warships, until Fogg excused himself and returned to the wharf.

Mr. Hope said, "Are you comfortable in the window seat, Mr. Derker?" and I said I was, for my elbow was on the outside sill, in the sunshine, where leaves rustled and branches creaked a little, and reminded me of England, whereas inside, the room was so formal that I did not know how to begin. I need not have worried. Mr. Hope was so at ease himself that he made my confession fluent.

I began with the death at High Top of my mother and the man I had believed to be my father. Mr. Hope stretched his long legs and sprawled comfortably in his chair. If I faltered he prompted me in a way that seemed to make it his fault for not having understood me, and not until I came to William's death did he ask direct questions.

I told him how the Coroner's Jury in St. Johns had established that William had deserted his ship in Jamaica and sailed to Antigua as a seaman on the monthly mail boat. He had landed late in the afternoon, discovered where I was by asking in the grog-shops, and set off to walk to Hawksbill. When he arrived, the plantation was asleep. The watchman challenged him. William asked for Dingwall and the overseers, clubbed the man down, and killed the barking dog. He then intruded upon me; he must have kept his pistol with him through the years, because I was able to identify it from the maker's plate as one that he had used aboard the *Margaret*.

Mr. Jarvie's evidence of William's appearance was garbled. He knew that we had been shot at first, but was convinced that there was another man named Dingwall, who had somehow escaped. Broomer, King, Primas, and the bandaged watchman were closely questioned, and gave statements upon which the Coroner publicly congratulated them.

This surprised Mr. Hope. "In Virginia," he said, "the courts do not accept a slave's word as evidence. Pray continue."

I did, and described how I had been called to give evidence, and had mumbled at once that William was my father and that I had shot him. The courtroom was stifling and the lawyer's wigs and gowns seemed grotesque in such bright sunlight. There were several men on the jury whom I knew, and the Coroner had been a dinner guest at Hawksbill. He asked me about the use of the name Dingwall. Who was Dingwall? Was Captain Derker drunk? What was his mental condition? Had I recognized him when I first saw him and went inside for my pistol? I had not. I had imagined an intruder. What kind of intruder? A runaway slave? The gang in the woods? A French invader? Why had I run down to the beach? To find help?

Voices droned on, one of them mine. When the Coroner summed up, he described it as a bizarre and tragic case, and said that I had his sympathy. Then I sat, numbed, in the corridor, and after an hour the jury delivered upon William's body a verdict of death by misadventure, with a rider that I had committed an excusable homicide and should not be prosecuted. The Coroner endorsed their findings. He said that, whatever the personal aspects of the matter, William was an armed, dangerous, and perhaps insane intruder. I was the responsible white person on the plantation, and I had acted bravely, in defence of my own life and my employer's property. What I must do now was trust in God, put my bad memories and distress aside, and make a new life for myself.

I thanked him. He smiled and said that he had done no more than was his duty. A clergyman shook my hand. I thanked him also, and with Fishlock's arm round my shoulder walked out of the Court House. In the street Fishlock stopped and said, "Well, boy, what's it to be?" I already knew that because they were worried that I might be charged with manslaughter, he and Leslie had talked to another book-keeper. "But if you want to stay," said Fishlock, "I'll disabuse him this instant." I laughed despite myself, and said no, for if I did not leave Antigua I'd go mad.

Fishlock walked me to the harbour, where Captain Fogg's schooner had lain for a week. Fogg signed me on as a cook's mate. I spent that night in the nanny-house, and the next day Fogg weighed for Virginia. I was tired. If I had not killed William he would have killed me. He was my father, and I had set myself free; yet ever afterwards his death ached inside me, not every day, but when I least expected it, like an old wound, or arthritis that apprehends the climate.

What I needed was space and a new land. I needed to live where there were no other men, where life had not been infected before it began. I needed a wilderness, in which I could heal myself and discover who I was. Could Virginia show me such a place? It could, said Fogg; where I wanted to go was to that world beyond the frontier, and if Fogg were I, he would seek the advice of Mr. Hope, of Hope's Landing.

I asked him why. Fogg explained that Mr. Hope had great influence in the Virginian Ohio Company, which sent agents and pack-trains into the unknown. More than that; he had been educated in the law, like many Virginia gentlemen who shared in the government of their colony, and had even practised it until forced by his father's death to manage the plantation; he was a parish vestryman and widely expected to be elected before long to the Assembly at Williamsburg, all of which would soon make him one of the most powerful men in the colony; but really, said Fogg, talk to him because he's strong, and you can trust him.

When I finished, there was silence. A bee buzzed into the study and settled on the folded shutter. Mr. Hope got up to pour peach brandy into clean glasses. From the wharf came sounds of unloading.

My story had moved him very much, said Mr. Hope. He respected my sorrow and understood what I wanted to do. Unfortunately he must tell me that I had chosen a very bad time to do it, perhaps the worst for thirty years, because the war had made everything unsure.

He showed me the map again. Beyond the Allegheny Mountains was the great Ohio River, and the French coming down from Canada controlled its upper waters and had built forts at every strategic point of the river's tributary system. These forts controlled the passes through the mountains and thus the eventual westward flow of settlement.

During recent years the Shenandoah Valley had been sparsely settled, mostly by poor Dutch and Germans from Pennsylvania to whom the government of Virginia had offered cheap land so that there would be a buffer against the Indians. Beyond that, the legislatures of Pennsylvania and Maryland, and the Ohio Company of Virginia, had sent traders and scouts into the Ohio Valley, but a common policy was hard to reach. Two years ago attempts to resolve such questions had collapsed, when the Albany Congress rejected Mr Benjamin Franklin's plan for a union of all the colonies, upon which the British had suggested that at least there should be a joint Commander-in-Chief and a Commissioner for Indian Affairs.

That Commander-in-Chief was General Edward Braddock, whose defeat and death at French hands had, as I knew, been a catastrophe. The Shenandoah Valley had been exposed to Indian raids, in which many settlements had been burned or abandoned, and since then the French General the Marquis de Montcalm had arrived in Canada and greatly strengthened his positions on the Upper Ohio.

To woo the Indians from the French side, the Commissioner, Sir William Johnson, argued that there should be no more white settlement beyond the Alleghenies, and although there were many poor

men, and many investment companies, eager to defy him, they dared
not do so until the French and Indian danger had abated. The frontier had been forced back, and a man could be killed at the plough
in the Shenandoah Valley, let alone on a mapping or trading expedi-
tion beyond the mountains.

What Mr. Hope suggested was that, if I showed a little patience,
he might recommend me as a member of the Ohio Company's next
pack-train to its trading posts along the Alleghenies. One always set
off during the fall, before the heavy snows. Could I wait until then?
There was always rough work to be had if I was willing. My response
was so enthusiastic that Mr. Hope leaned back from it, but without
any loss of courtesy.

Then a bell rang, and we heard dogs bark, and children shout as
they were let out of the schoolhouse, and Mr. Hope said that he hoped
I would dine as he had already invited Captain Fogg to do so. We
went down the finely-carved stairs, and he took me outside for a
moment to show me the portico on the landward side of the house
and the two smaller blocks that each stood fifty yards away, so that
together the buildings formed a square of which the fourth side was
a box hedge with ornamental gateposts in the middle. Outside that
was the worn-earth, smoke-drifting, child-yelling confusion of a
dozen rickety slave cabins.

The kitchen was in one of the smaller buildings, and three or four
blacks were already walking across with the food on trays and
chafing-dishes. As they did so, they whistled, which Mr. Hope said
was his patent way of ensuring that they did not pop tit-bits into their
mouths. Their destination was the marble-topped serving-tables in
the entrance hall, where the butler stood with white gloves ready to
escort us to the dining-room. It was light and airy, with panelling
painted buff and grey, so that the sun did not glare. There was a smell
of beeswax and cut flowers, and much merriment at the table. Mr.
Hope carved at one end and his wife ladled soup at the other.

She was a large, young, heavy woman with a big jaw, blue eyes, and
fair hair. Captain Fogg sat on her left, and on her right was a Captain
Cary, a curious, leathery sort of man, very angular and bright-eyed
and dressed in dark clothes despite the summer. He had a rapid way
of speech, bushy eyebrows and frizzy grey hair. He could have been
any age between thirty-five and sixty, and in his explosive, splutter-

ing style made it his business to be civil to everyone; first of all, he asked each child in turn what he or she had learned at school that morning.

There were three little girls, all fair and all heavy-featured like Mrs. Hope. The tutor, Mr. Glashan, was an indentured Scotsman who greeted me most warmly until I told him I was English, at which he frowned and snorted. There were two older boys, who came to school from neighbouring plantations, and the company was completed by the white housekeeper, Lizzie Holt, a brisk, rosy-cheeked woman who ate heartily and said very little.

It was a happy table, with much chaff and banter and talk about the stupidity of niggers, and horsemanship, and the cousins whom Mrs. Hope and Captain Cary had in common. Mr. Hope fed his foxhound bitch tit-bits, and even when the children were noisy or knocked things over he chided them without ugliness or rancour; he was as unwaveringly polite to them as he was to the butler or to Captain Cary. I envied him. His feelings served and informed him— unlike mine, which blew me this way and that. I supposed that his composure was what people meant by the word *breeding*, but about Mrs. Hope I was less sure. She talked to the gentlemen but seemed to ignore me. I thought her amiable but ungainly.

After the meat the cloth was removed to reveal another beneath. The slaves whistled as they returned the leftovers to the kitchen, and we had dessert with a bottle of champagne. I had heard of this wine but never tasted it, and was impressed to see it drunk so matter-of-factly upon an ordinary weekday. The butler opened the bottle with a tremendous *pop*, and the black waiting-maid, Liddy, gleefully clapped her hands.

Mr. Hope looked at her with half-raised eyebrows, but it was obvious that she was a favourite because of the way in which once or twice she was allowed to join in our conversation, usually to laugh, or to agree in her pidgin English with something particularly pungent.

When the champagne was finished, Liddy removed the second cloth, and we took fruit and sweet wine from the bare and shining table itself. By this time Captain Cary had done the round of his civilities, from each child's letters to the events of Fogg's voyage, and come at last to me. "You, sir! What, sir? Hey, sir?" I suddenly felt distant from this family jollity, and did not wish to explain myself.

Mr. Hope calmly intervened, and without revealing any of my story said that I had been a plantation clerk in Antigua and wanted to make a life for myself on the frontier. This ignited a blaze of opinions about the Massachusetts General who had replaced Braddock, the French regulars who had arrived with Montcalm, and the contrast between the noble savagery of the Indians and the shiftlessness of the blacks, until the eldest Hope child said very clearly, "If Mr. Derker can't go to the frontier now, what will he do until he can?"

Everyone stared at me. It was an odd, fixed moment that seemed to last much longer than it really did. Outside, the sun had declined, but there was still a lazy heat in the day, and the foliage was rich. For the first time in that house, I felt self-possessed, and I enjoyed the silence as they waited for my answer.

Then Mrs. Hope's quiet, warm voice said to the child, "Well, Sarah, I guess that Mr. Derker could be Captain Cary's serving-man."

"What?" said the Captain. "Hey? Who says?" Mr. Hope glanced with a surprised and almost cold awareness at his wife, and then composed himself, and they both smiled at Captain Cary. The Captain cleared his throat and rocked back and forth as he explained that his man, Barnaby, was laid up in Petersburg with a broken leg, but that it should be mended in five or six weeks. "Would you-all oblige until then, sir? Hey? Would you?"

I looked at Fogg and Mr. Hope and the tutor. They seemed to encourage me. Mrs. Hope smiled briefly and asked us to excuse her. In one corner of the room there was a basin and a brass tap fed by the pump, and Mrs. Hope now washed her precious china there herself, and replaced it in the cabinet with her own hands, because the blacks could not be trusted to care.

I asked Captain Cary what duties he required. Wake him at eight with coffee, he replied, and do it slow and easy, not jingle-jangle like a nigger's excuses. Shave him. Look to his clothes. Help him to bed. Play cards with him and let him win, God damn it, and clean his boots and sword and watch the horses. Gentleman's valet and travelling man. Hey? What?

I was unsure about the horses, and said so, but felt equal to the rest. The Captain offered me five shillings a week and board and room. I agreed. Mrs. Hope sent the children out to play and the party broke up. Later, when the gangs had come home from the harvest and the sun was an orange ball in the grey, I moved my box from the ship to a room in the schoolhouse, next to that of Mr. Glashan.

Captain Cary had a guest room in the main house, on the opposite side of the first floor to the library, and as I helped him into his nightshirt I saw that his body was wiry and marked with innumerable knobbles and scars. Hunting, sir. Riding. Capsize Cary, that's what they call me. More falls and up again than my father, and he was the bravest rider in the Northern Neck. God, but he knew horses. The stables were more spacious than the house, sir. I was taught the true way.

I asked how long we would remain at Hope's Landing, and if we would go home to the Northern Neck. He said that so far as meals were concerned, I would eat with the overseer and housekeeper when there were other guests, and with the family when there were not. I put my question again.

"No, sir," he snapped, "we will not go home, sir. But a nigger groom will show you how to ride, sir. Good night!" And he drew the bed-curtains.

In the schoolhouse Mr. Glashan and the housekeeper had a flask of rum and invited me to join them. From another room came the voices of the overseer and a black girl—recklessly, said Mr. Glashan, because in Virginia it was a crime for one race to fornicate with the other, and marriage between them was forbidden. There had to be such laws to curb black men's filthy lusts. The housekeeper giggled and said what did I think of Captain Cary? I hedged. They grinned and told me his story.

In his youth the Captain had been dashing and eligible, but his father was a notorious gambler who had been ruined by a fall in tobacco prices, so that when the Captain inherited his estate it was heavily in debt. For some years he struggled along because a distant cousin was rich and he hoped to marry her. But she would not have him, and one day the Captain sold his lands, paid off his debts with something to spare, and had lived ever since upon the hospitality of other people. Each year he and Barnaby made a slow progress from one to another of his friends and relations. His own home was two horses, battered valises, and a pack-mule, and although he had a tiny income from rents, his profession was that of a gentleman: civility and small kindnesses to the people in whose lives he survived. Virginian hospitality was famous, and the Captain repaid it as best he could.

The rum made us laugh at him—in Mr. Glashan s case, with not a little superiority—but afterwards I lay on my corn-shuck mattress and was moved by the generosity of the offer that would keep me at Hope's Landing until it was time to ride to the frontier. As I drifted into sleep I seemed to hear the overseer's slave girl cry out, and then in grey light a young black child awoke me so that I in my turn might rouse my pernickety Captain with coffee and a bowl of hot shaving water.

Chapter 34

Myrtle Grove

What I tasted at Hope's Landing, and for the first time in my life, was the elixir of a leisured existence. I had duties, but they were not arduous, and many of them actually consisted in being a participant in a pleasant social life, in taking a fourth hand at cards or handing down the ladies at a picnic. I had no responsibility for the slaves or the plantation, and in my own time I was free to keep myself to myself, and improve my horsemanship under the eyes of Mr. Hope's black groom and Henry, a twelve-year-old field boy reckoned to be the best race jockey on the James River. I worked hard at that, in the humidity and the hazy sunshine, and it was agreeable to feel distant from the life around me, which I observed and enjoyed but did not feel was mine.

It was certainly less desperate than that in Antigua. The whites here despised their blacks, but because throughout the colony the races were virtually equal in numbers, felt much safer than planters in the Indies; in consequence they made the life of the blacks less hard. Even though this was harvest time, many slaves returned to the quarters in the middle of the afternoon, because there were set tasks for each kind of work, and when a man had split his fixed number of railposts, or laid so many panels of fencing, he was free to work on his own land as he pleased.

Field gangs also had set tasks: so many acres when sowing or hoeing particular crops, so many cubic feet when cutting drains through different kinds of soil. There was always a fire near where the gang was working, and a boy or girl to tend it. Tobacco required fewer hands but more care than sugar, and had bred a greater tradition of skill than had the work in Antigua. There were more annual holidays and fewer punitive laws: thirty-nine was the most number of strokes that was supposed to be given with a cane.

At Hope's Landing there was an infirmary for sick slaves, and a nurse, and Mr. Glashan made occasional efforts to teach those who were interested the rudiments of Christianity; both were resisted by the obeah man, a scrawny fellow in a frock-coat who seemed not to work at all, and whom the overseer thought more important than the carter or gang leaders. Slaves could sell their own produce to crossroads merchants, or they could bank eggs against cash in the plantation kitchen; since they were all known to be thieves and liars, this led Mrs. Hope to take as much care of her fowls as she did of her china. Again, although Virginia was unsuitable for cotton because of the frosts, there were odd plots of it, and both Mrs. Hope and the slave women spun it up to make work clothes.

For all that, the difference between field and house Negroes was wider than in Antigua. The house slaves may have been humiliatingly on call for twenty-four hours a day, but they were most elegant and fashionable, and when the mistress gave them her old dresses, the girls altered them at once according to the last word that had come to the colony from Europe. The field hands were ragged and dirty, and a bizarre sign of vanity among them was that some had recently tried to dye their grey hair; unfortunately the plant mixture was wrong, and there were several men and women with bright green crinkly polls.

Hope's Landing was a less brutal place than Hawksbill, but its extremes of wealth and enslavement were wider, and its production did not seem to me to be any more efficient. The set tasks were deliberately easy to avoid conflict, and yet it was because their tasks were set that the gangs performed them mechanically, with no attempt at initiative, and in a last effort to gather the harvest Mr. Hope and the overseer hired three or four more whites, when there were at least a dozen house blacks unemployed for most of the day.

When the crop was cut, it was threshed by the simple method of being laid on the ground in a huge circle, and trodden over by five or six pairs of horses. The wheat was then bagged up and put in the barn, and the chaff fed to the hogs and cattle.

On Sunday mornings we rode in a party to church, not so much to hear a lengthy sermon—for the minister, Mr. Ashlin, was even blander and more worldly than Mr. Hope—as to gossip afterwards with friends and neighbours, so that the church porch swirled with silk and muslin, and there were horses and grooms, and all manner of coaches and carts, under the surrounding trees. There were poor whites with patched coats, wild men in buckskin and fur-tailed hats, and local characters such as William Pride the storekeeper, and Old Batty the ferryman and his six sons, each one of whom had a chew of tobacco and clean linen for Sunday, except that they never bathed unless they fell in the river, and all stank like polecats.

It was under the church porch, with its exchanges of snuff and laughter blown by the breeze, its smells of honeysuckle and horse droppings, that Mr. Glashan first heard the rumours about Captain Cary that Mr. Hope had known weeks earlier but was too good a host to repeat.

Their burden was that the redoubtable manservant Barnaby had stayed in Petersburg not to mend a broken leg but because he and the Captain had quarrelled. Some said that the leg had been broken as a result of that quarrel, when Barnaby was so upset that twenty years on the road should end in disagreement that he got drunk, and fell downstairs at the home of their host, the merchant Mr. Meakins. Others declared that the leg was no more broken than Old Sally's, whoever she was, and that Barnaby had been seen upon the streets of Petersburg only the day before yesterday.

There would then be a slow rehash of decades of speculation about Barnaby himself. He was sure as hell an Englishman but what breed? That's the squidgeroo, boys! What was he? Disgraced gentleman? Horse doctor? Footman to some grand old duke? Whatever he was, he knew as much about horseflesh as he did about billiards and etiquette, and he had a voice like an echo in a pickle-jar.

Someone like me would ask what was the cause of the quarrel, and receive from everyone the same surprising answer: the cause was that Captain Cary had declared his intention to marry the rich widow Mrs. Ludwell of Petersburg, but that the lady refused to discuss it if Barnaby were still in his service.

At first I found this hard to swallow. The Captain was attentive to women, and they clearly liked him, but he was just as polite to men, because politeness to everyone was a price that he paid for twenty years of hospitality. Another was the fact that whatever he suppressed in public burst out like a geyser in the brief privacy of his room and bed-curtains, where he talked both to himself and to those people, frequently dead, about whom he happened to be thinking at the time. Mrs. Fairfax, why don't you take your disgusting elbows off the table? My elbow is not half worn through my sleeve like yours, Captain Cary. My lace, madam, is not trailing through someone else's soup. Hey? What? Bull's-eye there, madam! What? From which it will be gathered that the Captain spoke his opponent's replies as well as his own, but never so shrewdly as to give himself the worst of the argument.

In between there would be instructions to me about darning and ironing, questions about my horsemanship, and random comments on the night's card games and conversation, and I suppose that the fact that I knew him to be an eccentric old sportsman of a bachelor made me assume that he was a deliberate neutral in the war of the sexes. He was a tangy fifty-year-old fish, dried in an irreversible way by wind and weather and repetition. How could he even begin to fall in love? As it happened, very easily, and with hapless entirety.

I had been at Hope's Landing for less than a fortnight, and the *John and James* was still at the wharf, when Captain Cary interrupted my currying of the horses after a morning's work to say that we must ride out at once or we should never cross the Chickahominy River before nightfall.

I was surprised but packed our valises. Mrs. Hope seemed offended, and she and the Captain walked round the yard in heated conversation. Mr. Hope was as calm as if this departure had always been our intention. He said that he entirely understood that I must travel with the Captain, and that as soon as he had any information about the pack-train he would write to me; our destination was, after all, only Myrtle Grove, the home of the other main branch of the

Hope family. I thanked him and said that I could not leave the Captain servantless. Mr. Hope called him a man of honour, who would release me when the moment came.

As I said good-bye to Mr. Glashan, he muttered that the reason for our haste was a letter that Mrs. Hope had received from her widowed sister-in-law at Myrtle Grove, the post-script of which said that one of their house-guests was a distant relative by marriage, Mrs. Ludwell of Petersburg, who was, as everyone would remember, a widow with a comfortable portion of her own. Well, Mrs. Ludwell had plunged everyone at Myrtle Grove into a whirl of excitement because she had received a proposal of marriage from the clergyman, Mr. Ashlin.

When Captain Cary heard this read aloud at breakfast, he spilt his coffee, and was more agitated than anyone had seen him before. Then he paced up and down the river bank and summoned me. Mrs. Hope tried to dissuade him, but to no avail, and with cold ham and corn bread in our saddlebags, we were on the yellow dirt roads by noon.

I was astonished to see, even in this most civilized part of the colony, how little of the land was cleared, and how little of what was cleared was under cultivation; most of it was a tangle of briers and bushes and rough grass. Most of the people lived not on plantations but on holdings of a few fields that they worked themselves. Their houses were logged or boarded with a brick chimney at one end, and surrounded by slovenly children, swine hounds, and a few hogs and chickens that grubbed in the trampled dirt. Sometimes the green wall of the forest opened to reveal swampy clearings in which the trees were slanted and fallen, their trunks ashen in death, their leaves gone, the reeds that choked them vividly green, the water pale blue and steel. Ivies obscured the bark of living trees, and crimson birds swooped through the shadows.

"Cardinals!" said the Captain, and continued to mutter—half to himself and half, I realized, to me—a history of the Hope family, with many chuckles at how his arrival would throw them into delighted consternation.

So far as I could tell, and make cohere with what I knew already, the Hopes were an old Tidewater family linked by marriage to the Carters, Burwells, and Lees. Mr. Hope's father, Burwell Hope, had married a Carter, who died shortly after the birth of their son, Burwell II, in 1707. Old Burwell became an associate of Governor Spotswood and the powerful William Byrd of Westover in the opening-up of land across the fall lines, and eventually beyond the Blue Ridge itself, developments that in 1722 demanded a new treaty with the Indians. That was the very year in which old Burwell rebuilt Hope's Landing to welcome his new young bride, who was a niece of Colonel McHugh. They had two children, Ashford, whom we had just left, and Charlotte, who was married now to a member of the Lee family and lived on the Potomac.

The second Mrs. Burwell Hope died of a fever when her children were young. Burwell himself, a grumpy but energetic old man, survived until 1745. He had inherited Myrtle Grove Plantation from his first wife, and settled it upon her son, Burwell II, on the understanding that Ashford would get Hope's Landing. Burwell II was well liked, but he was neither as dynamic as his father nor as intelligent as Ashford. He was tall, heavy, and self-indulgent, particularly when he married for love Ann Michieux, the lovely, but vain and silly, daughter of an unsuccessful and impecunious merchant of Alexandria.

Their home, Myrtle Grove, lay on the southern bank of the Rappahannock River, and as its land became exhausted Burwell grew wheat and Indian corn as well as persisting with tobacco, but he loved his wife and sons too much to be obsessed with politics and land development. His situation slowly deteriorated; as it did so, his life was happy because Burwell II was convivial. He liked his friends, and his friends' children, and balls and hunts and good old-fashioned quilting-parties, and cock-fights, and sinking two bottles after dinner. If Ashford thought his half-brother crass he was much too polite to say so, and although they did not see each other very often, there was no bitterness between them, not even when Ashford married Mary Lynch, which was a particularly shrewd alliance.

The Hopes were old money and the Lynches new, for Mary's father had been the first of them to make himself a gentleman. An Irishman and a former officer in the English Army, he had accepted a few acres as a retirement bounty, and when the Piedmont was opened up, borrowed money and risked everything to own a plantation, and won his gamble when the new soils yielded excellent tobacco crops. He left his son and daughter plantations on the Rivanna River, thousands of acres of uncleared land, and a share in the Virginian Ohio Company. Mary's interests passed at her marriage to Mr. Hope, who preferred, like many of his kind, to live in style on the

James River and to put an overseer in charge of the remote but much more profitable plantation on the Rivanna.

Captain Cary salted his tale with comments upon the sporting and equestrian prowess of its characters, so that the death of Burwell II became an epic of foolhardy good nature. One December day Burwell II took a guest duck-shooting and fell chest-deep through the ice of a creek. He refused to go back because to do so would spoil his friend's pleasure. He lit a brushwood fire but his clothes did not dry properly, and so he caught a chill and two days later was dead.

Since then the affairs of the plantation had gone from bad to worse, although by all accounts the younger son, Walkerton Hope, was a sound horseman, a brave gambler, and an enthusiastic owner of fighting-cocks. This may not have been a recipe for economic salvation, but at least it assured Captain Cary that the true Hope breed was not extinct, as it seemed to be in the personalities of Ashford and of Walkerton's brother, Burwell Hope III, or Young Burwell, as he was always called.

This last confidence I received when we stopped for the night at Chiswell's Ordinary, a pleasant, frame-built tavern with benches under a vine trellis, where the Captain drank too much and said that I should look at Aunt Jemima Hope, look at her, as old as sin now, of course, but what a card player in her day! Compare her with Paul Michieux and Young Burwell and then tell me about the true Hope breed and as for— What? Hey? Who's Paul Michieux? Paul Michieux is the brother of the widowed Mrs. Hope, a merchant who succeeded wherever his father failed, but a vulgar person with no resemblance to a gentleman. Neither had I. The Captain wanted to tell me his sorrows, but how could he? He swayed and mumbled and abused me even more when I put him to bed.

Next day he looked seedy and crestfallen, and his temper was not improved by the steamy weather. It had rained in the night, and all morning the sun beat through a mist. We sweated freely, and at every creek and swamp were surrounded by clouds of insects. Patches of water lay in the fields, and where trees reared out of bright green reeds, the undergrowth smouldered. Tortoises had come out on to every soggy track.

The Captain did not speak to me until late afternoon, when after we had crossed the York River in a sailing scow far more substantial than the two flat-boats lashed together that had taken us over the

Chickahominy, we rode through dense and dappled forests to the Rappahannock. Everywhere flowers seemed heavier and brighter for the damp. We passed several fields in which the corn had been battered by rain, and then turned off the track at a place where the forest screen was held open by ornate brick gateposts.

What everyone at Myrtle Grove called "the carriage drive" was a long, rutted, yellow-earth track through bosky, shadowed conifers. The Captain slowed his pace and then stopped. The trees were full of birdsong. My horse snorted.

"Mr. Derker," said the Captain, with a despairing jerk of his arm, "I owe you an apology."

I opened my mouth to demur, but he had braced himself for a confession, and rattled on with it. "All I can say in my defence, sir, is that the pained heart has a cloak, and that the name of that cloak is mystery. What? Hey? I sigh, sir, but within yonder trees there is a woman—a woman for whom I have already sacrificed—" Sometimes words fail even so torrential a speaker as the Captain. He sighed again, and said that he referred not merely to a magnificent figure of womanhood, for Virginia was as full of fine women as Prussia of soldiers, but to a beauty, in whose heart his arrival would be sure to create an impression of manly ardour and sincerity. And not before time. What?

Abruptly he sat up straight and kick-started his horse, so that mine shot off as well, and with the pack-mule jangling and bumping, we emerged like light cavalry from the tunnel of trees, and scattered the chickens and dogs of the slave huts and workshops that stood in a formal oval at the end of the drive. Whooping like a huntsman, the Captain galloped through them and up to the front door of the house itself.

A black major-domo came out to greet us. He was a tall man with a hawk-like face.

"Agricola!" said the Captain. "I must speak at once to Mrs. Ludwell!" He was already off his horse and climbing the steps.

"Captain Cary, sir," said Agricola, "it's mighty good to see you, but if you step on that hall floor in them dirty boots, you'll make me wax him agin afore the ball."

"Ball?" gasped the Captain. "What ball?"

"Ladies is on the terraces, Captain, sir," said Agricola. "If you want 'em you go round the side."

The Captain ignored these blows to his pride, as well he might, because much worse were to come, and gesturing at me to follow, set off at a bony lope round the side of the house, where he came face to face with a dowdy little woman who had just clumped up from where terrace after terrace of formal gardens descended to the hazy river, and whom I took to be the housekeeper. She had a nutcracker nose and chin, bright eyes, and a perceptible moustache, and when she saw the Captain she started as much as he did. But he was the first to recover. He shook his finger at her.

"Mrs. Ludwell," he said. "What's all this tomfoolery about Ashlin?"

Mrs. Ludwell? This? This ill-made little creature was the beauty at whose altar so much had been sacrificed? Indeed she was, and to prove it she glared like a goblin.

"Ashlin?" she cried. "What's Ashlin? Is it some kind of timber?"

"It's a clergyman, madam, with whom you-all entertained notions of matrimony!"

If Mrs. Ludwell had glared before, I thought now that she would boil over, and steam hiss down from her sun hat. For a second she could not speak at all, and then she drew herself up to her full but squat little height and yelled, "Tell me, sir, do you think that there can be any more presumptuous creature in God's universe than a man, unless perhaps it be a youth?"

The Captain's face was mottled. He shook with anger.

"I don't think, madam. I *know* when I am wounded, and I know why. I know the sly smiles between you. What? I may not have a mansion, madam, but I do have my honour!"

"Pish-jerrydoodle!" roared Mrs. Ludwell.

She scooped up a handful of the path's muddy gravel and threw it at the Captain, who in his evasive efforts slipped over and lay on his back, with his spindly legs waving in desperation as he cried out, "All the rogue Ashlin wants is your money, for he's married three widows before you!"

Mrs. Ludwell hurled more gravel, and as she yelled, and the Captain scrabbled to get up, the entire house-party strolled through the ornamental trees, and from his hands and knees the Captain said, "Good day, madam!" to Mrs. Burwell Hope, and old Aunt Jemima, and three or four excited girls; and as he stood up he nodded curtly at Mr. Paul Michieux, a short, sallow man with a big stomach and snuff-marked waistcoat.

"Humph!" said Mrs. Ludwell.

Aunt Jemima laughed and said, "Glad you invited yourself, Capsize!"

Mr. Michieux offered his hand as though he were the master, but then withdrew it.

Mrs. Hope laughed in her throat and gave her hand to be kissed. For all her heavy breasts, lined face, and crinkled skin at her neck, she wore her hair unpowdered and loosely-ribboned like that of a girl, and walked with the half-flaunting, half-embarrassed glide of a woman who believes that the eyes of all men are lustily upon her.

"I slipped," said the Captain. "Slipped over. What? Didn't I, Tom?"

"Yes," I said.

I was sure that they had seen his humiliation, not least from the way in which the young girls giggled and twittered, but it was not mentioned, and when she had given me a dazzling smile, Mrs. Hope slipped her arm through the Captain's and laughed again, delight-edly, and said that he must not worry because the house was more than capable of giving him a bed, and hadn't she known that on this day of all days there would be dozens of old friends who wanted to congratulate her?

The Captain tried to look at Mrs. Ludwell over his shoulder, but everyone went off in different directions, and then there was a confusion about our horses and baggage, which Agricola had seemingly spirited away. When Mrs. Hope asked a footman about them, he sniggered, and was plainly drunk.

The Captain spluttered. Mrs. Hope appealed to her brother, Mr. Michieux, who cuffed the footman and demanded in a squeaky voice to speak to his nephew Young Burwell. I did not await the outcome of this discussion, but went to seek the baggage and my own room in the bachelors' house, which like the kitchens and the plantation's offices stood apart from the main building. I shouted for Agricola, but he did not reply. More horsemen and carriages were arriving as I entered the bachelors' house and went upstairs towards the sound of laughter.

I found Agricola and another black servant drinking rum and

throwing dice with two whites: a groom, and a young man whose clothes were expensive but untidy, whose fresh face and crooked mouth were somehow familiar, and whose signet ring as well as his confidence proclaimed him some sort of gentleman. My valise was on the floor.

Agricola introduced me as the Captain's man, and said that I would have to share this room with the black servant and the groom. I nodded. There was one bed and two corn-shuck mattresses. "I'll throw you for the bed," I said, and immediately lost, but it put me on a good footing.

"I stabled your horses," said Agricola. "The sorrel's prettypretty."

"That she is," I said.

"Trust Capsize to find a flyer," said the young gentleman, and offered me the rum.

I declined. "I reckon your footman's drunk," I said to Agricola.

"Uh-huh!" He nodded, and the others laughed.

I watched them throw. The black servant won the bed. The white groom swore and grumbled. Agricola laughed, a deep rumble. He was a magnificent man, handsome and confident, and his skin was not so much black as deep bronze.

Then he heard his name bellowed outside. He winked at the young gentleman, stood up, and affected to be waiting on the white men while they played their game. Footsteps came up the stairs, and as pompous a young man as I had seen in my life stepped into the whitewashed room.

He had a pouter pigeon's stomach, and thick lips and a pitying smile, and his clothes were too brightly coloured and embroidered for a person his shape. He took a pinch of snuff, very elaborately, and said, "Agricola, I'm the master here! I am the master in this house, Agricola!"

"Of course you is, Mr. Burwell. Your clothes is all laid out nice and crisp on your bed, Mr. Burwell. Yes, sir, Mr. Burwell!" said Agricola, and did a silly shuffling dance that made him seem like a joke nigger.

"For God's sake, Agricola!" said Young Burwell. "That fool boy of a footman is inebriated!"

"On account of him joy at your happiness!" said Agricola.

"Are the fiddlers drunk? Is the tight-rope walker? Will that acrobatic dancer, Cincinnatus, gyrate as instructed, or will he flaunt his private organs at the ladies?"

The young white dice-player laughed infectiously.

"Walkerton," said Young Burwell, "this matter is not risible," at which his sporting brother, Walkerton, threw the dice at the wall and rolled back on the bed. Burwell attempted to sigh disdainfully, but a grain of snuff caught him and he spluttered.

"I don't think," said Agricola in an almost religious tone, "that nigger slaves on this here Myrtle Grove can be whipped for joyousness on your account, Mr. Burwell." He shook his head. "I don't think them can."

"What exactly does that-all mean, Agricola?" said Burwell.

"Sober tonight, sir, and drunk tomorrow."

"What?"

Walkerton bayed like a hound dog. The white groom exploded with laughter. Agricola put his hand on his gold-braided heart.

"I give my word, sir. There's no drop of liquor touched tonight if tomorrow it's lurgle-gurgle."

Burwell cocked his head. His mouth opened and shut like that of a fish. Walkerton laughed and then, dog-like, panted with his tongue out. At this, Burwell managed to speak.

"Walkerton," he said, "have you no more respect for your name than to dice with niggers and horse-servants?"

Walkerton's blue eyes were cold. Burwell could not face them. He grinned and teetered. Agricola grumbled to himself. Burwell mopped his brow with an embroidered handkerchief. His own lips silently moved. No doubt he was calculating the odds. Sober house slaves tonight against the freedom to be drunk tomorrow. There would be enough food already made to tide over, and enough slaves who did not drink.

Burwell snapped his fingers and agreed to Agricola's bargain. Agricola kissed his hand. Walkerton turned his back on them. Burwell threatened floggings if the agreement was broken. Then he nodded, as if to convince himself, and walked out. His feet plonked heavily downstairs.

There was an uneasy silence. The black valet stood up awkwardly, and was suddenly an inferior again. Walkerton swore and left the room; his feet on the stairs were angry, and Agricola's smile was not a pleasant one.

My voice croaked a little as I asked the white groom about the ball. Why should Mr. Burwell be happy? Was there something to celebrate? The groom shrugged. Agricola asked me in the pidgin what I meant, as though he did not speak English at all.

"You answer me true, boy!" I said angrily, with my Antiguan overseer's contempt, and Agricola did his humble dance again, and said that yes, sir, Mr. Burwell sure intended to use the occasion of the ball to announce his engagement to his cousin Miss Elizabeth Michieux. Whom he did not love, added the groom, but who would bring him his uncle's money. God save Myrtle Grove! said Agricola. Yes, sir!

Chapter 35

The Ball

Myrtle Grove was a longer but lower house than Hope's Landing, and the through hall was wide enough to be used for dancing. The stairs were tucked away at one side, with a musicians' gallery on the half-landing. Downstairs, the master bedroom and dressing-room occupied one side of the house; here Mrs. Hope slept, and she shared it now with all the young ladies in the house. On the other side of the hall was a series of smaller rooms, one laid out for cards—and here the gentlemen left their coats—one for the buffet supper, and one for conversation.

Captain Cary shared a bedroom upstairs with two other gentlemen, and when I went to help him dress he was lethargic and deeply despondent. They had brought him a tub bath but he sat and stared at it and let the water go lukewarm. He had not even taken off his travelling clothes. I persuaded him to do so, and as he stepped into the bath I was moved again by the rickety dignity of his body.

The other gentlemen in the room were in high spirits. They whistled and sang and joked about who should sleep in the middle, and was it to be shoes-on or shoes-off? The Captain wanted to talk to me but could do so only in a mutter; for although he behaved as though every single person relished and grinned at his humiliation, none of them truly knew except myself and Mrs. Ludwell.

Even Mrs. Hope did not understand the Captain's agony, because one question about her letter to Hope's Landing revealed that what she had written about Mr. Ashlin was mere gossip, a joke that some-one had made up and Mrs. Hope had repeated as truth, in the way that she repeated all speculations and rumours of an amorous nature, because she believed that their threads entangled us all, and that we were in their enchanted web for ever; there was truth in them even when we denied them, and in an ideal world we would not need to deny them because there would be no jealousy and men would see the wisdom of the ladies' dispositions.

Which may have been true, but did not in a cruder world make her any less silly. Mrs. Ludwell had scarcely met Mr. Ashlin, let alone received a proposal from him. What actually happened was that she received some tipsy advances from the Captain, put them down to one glass too many, and shooed him away. They were both too old for such nonsense, and in any case Mrs. Ludwell valued her freedom too highly.

In a society in which even the most privileged women could be married at fifteen and dead of childbirth at twenty, Mrs. Ludwell had survived. Her son was grown up. She lived to please herself, and would not change if she were asked to be the Queen of England. Pish-pash and think no more of it! Which she did not, until she heard that the Captain and Barnaby had fallen out over her. Barnaby said don't be a damned fool but the Captain was besotted. Mrs. Ludwell decided that it was a good time to vacate Petersburg and visit a few old friends, such as Jemima Hope on the Rappahannock.

Now here the Captain was, and in the panic of a love that the woman who inspired it thought absurd. He had behaved absurdly; he had broken the code of half a lifetime and discarded his self-respect, and there was every likelihood that he would repeat his blunders, again and again, until his passion was satisfied or spent.

As well as his misery and self-pity, he attempted to involve me in elaborate and fantastic schemes by which everything could be put right. If only Mrs. Ludwell would allow him to organize matters, she would be enabled to see clearly. She would understand what her own feelings really were. The way to approach the matter was through old Jemima. I was a smart young fellow. If I explained matters to Jemima, she would convince Mrs. Ludwell that a meeting with the Captain was imperative. It should take place tonight, on the garden terraces, after the minuets had begun.

All this in whispered and mumbled asides, in a room full of other men and servants, and black maids giggling in and out with the bath water, and being groped by one of the gentlemen, and a good deal of drinking, and candles a-flutter, and the sounds of more arrivals, and of the first tunings-up of the slave musicians.

There were two French horns, three fiddles, and a banjo, and when they struck up from the hidden gallery Mrs. Hope sighed and clapped her hands like a girl and said that the music seemed to come from the air itself. Her daughters looked very like her, except that they had the Hopes' fair hair; the niece who would soon become a daughter-in-law, and bind the money of one family to the old name of the other, was darker and more openly sensual. She would be seventeen at her next birthday, and seemed to me not to enjoy her prominence, because she bit her lip, and opened and shut her fan, and neither submitted to her excitement nor hid it behind a dignified mask.

There were some seventy guests of all ages, many with their servants and tutors in attendance. In the card room four tables were busily at play. In the hall Mrs. Hope, partnered by her son Walkeron, danced a livelier cotillion than any of the young people; in the dining-room Agricola supervised the laying-out of the buffet, and the conversation room had already become a citadel of hard-drinking gentlemen, who discussed women and politics, and plied themselves with wines, punches, toddies, ciders, porters, and the estate's own peach and persimmon brandies.

There was a bonfire in the slave quarters, where anyone who cared could watch the tight-rope walker and the acrobatic dancer, but although I looked everywhere I could not find Mrs. Ludwell. I had decided to speak to her directly because it seemed ludicrous to involve old Aunt Jemima. Eventually I asked Agricola and he jabbed his finger towards the ceiling; Mrs. Ludwell was one of the cronies in Aunt Jemima's bedroom, where they could hear the music but not be exhausted by the throng.

The ladies were so interested in their backgammon and gossip that it was easy for me to catch Mrs. Ludwell's eye, and beg her pardon but would she give me a moment of her time on the landing? She grumbled but said she would. Before I could explain myself further she said that she hoped I was as concerned about Captain Cary as I ought to be, because she was, and about herself as well. Young people laughed as they ran past us. I said that I was very concerned. Mrs Ludwell said that she intended to leave Myrtle Grove as soon as possible, and had little commissions from Miss Hope to make her departure plausible. She glanced back at Aunt Jemima, who nodded encouragement like a sergeant-major.

I said that in my opinion the Captain would be more likely to behave well if Mrs. Ludwell consented to meet him. She disagreed. I said that, as she knew, the cotillions would be followed by minuets, and the minuets by supper, and that if she met the Captain on the terraces after the second minuet, he could take her in to supper.

"He'll more likely try to throttle me," she said.

If he does, you'll be Punch and Judy, I said to myself, and grinned.

"What's your smile for?" she said. Her eyebrows bristled. "Huh?" she said, and dug me in the ribs. I gasped. She looked very fierce and then suddenly forlorn. "Tell you the truth, son," she said, "I'm scared."

She blushed like a girl. She put the back of her hand to her cheek, the way girls do when they are frightened of their own beauty and yet marvel at it. I realized what memories the Captain had unwittingly invoked in her, and that they were memories not of wonderment but of pain at being ugly. To be told now that she was beautiful was a cruel joke; she knew that it was ridiculous and yet could not help wanting to believe it.

She sighed and looked away from me and did not seem to know what to say. Neither did I. She was grotesque, and to the sound of fiddles, and hearty laughter from old Jemima, I realized that my convivial Captain was as lonely as any man in the colony; and I knew how hurt Barnaby must have been, when that was made clear to him, and he discovered that his friendship did not count.

A dance ended to applause and whoops. Then there was a ragged fanfare and ooohs and aaahs of recognition as the first minuet struck up. Mrs. Ludwell snorted and rocked on her heels. "You're right," she said. "There's no sense in cowardice at my age."

She snatched up her shawl and we walked downstairs, and through the hall where silks and brocades swished with the dance, and out on to the first terrace. The night was warm, and there was a humid fuzz in the light that came from the house. Leaves flopped. The sky was grey and luminous with a scattering of stars. The ornamental trees were bulky, and the box had a lazy scent. We glimpsed paler, rustling shadows within the shadows, and heard other feet and other whispering voices. The music floated. We sensed the mist on the river, and suddenly the Captain stepped out in front of me like a comic highwayman and said, "Who's there?"

"Tom," I said, and brought Mrs. Ludwell forward. Her hand trembled in mine.

The Captain gasped and made an elaborate bow. "Madam," he said, "I am glad to have this witness to my most deep apologies."

"Lord sakes, Capsize," said Mrs. Ludwell, "we've known each other thirty years!"

"Never," said the Captain.

"What?"

"You must have me confused with some more ancient gentleman."

"You pish-popinjay!"

"Good God, woman—" he began, but Mrs. Ludwell yelled, "Ha!" and stamped her foot. The Captain stamped his. She stamped hers even harder. Through the darkness I felt the Captain's rage. He gave a strangled cry and waved his fists above his head and strode away.

My impulse was to go after him, but Mrs. Ludwell hauled me back. "Hear that?" she said. "The creature called me a liar!"

"Have you known him thirty years?" I said.

"Either that or twenty-five."

I smiled. She bristled like a cat with its fur up. I put my arm round her.

Then the Captain reappeared, a spindly-dog wraith in dancing pumps, and talked very rapidly, as though we were casual acquaintances who just happened to have met between dances. Damn me, if you'll forgive that expression, but is a stroll like this not the best part of a ball? Hey? What? He offered Mrs. Ludwell his arm. She accepted, and they went very gravely into the darkness. I felt drained, as though it were I and not the Captain who had exercised heroic self-control.

I walked uphill towards the lights and music. The darkness was a pleasantly enveloping humidity. There was a stone bench near the top, and I sat down, half facing the house and half not. I was detached. My decisions had been postponed. Moths were drawn to the house windows.

A couple came out of the house. The man laughed, and the girl fanned herself, as people do when they are out of breath from the dance. Then they were screened from the house by boxwood and their manner changed. They clung to each other desperately. The man's mouth sucked at the girl's; her back arched as if she might swoon. Then although I was twenty yards away, the man must have seen a gleam of light from my white cotton shirt and breeches.

They broke apart but then embraced again for an instant, more nobly and defiantly, and he held her at arm's length before she ran away, her dress floating and swishing, her satin feet scuffing, but not back to the house; she ran round the boxwood hedge towards the schoolrooms, and the man strolled casually towards me.

When he was almost upon me he affected to start and said, "Ha! I never saw you, sir!" It was Walkerton Hope. I identified myself, and he seemed relieved and said, "I'll throw you for luck." I agreed, and we shot his dice along the stone bench. We each threw fours.

Walkerton grinned at me intimately, as though I were too experienced to tell tales about a gentleman's involvement with a lady. I grinned back, and he patted me on the sleeve.

"If you want a nigger girl, ask Burwell," he said. "They don't seem to be mine to give away."

His eyes sparkled with drink but he was very polite. He rattled the dice in his fist. He was bursting with boredom and unused energy. The French horns made a great flourish. He jerked his head towards them.

"Where's the elegance in dancing," he said, "when you've torn your foreskin up a washerwoman's arse?"

He breathed heavily from his nose and looked about him. His lips were fleshy and cruel, but always twitched into an infectious smile. Then he wheeled at the scrape of footsteps.

Captain Cary and Mrs. Ludwell approached, still sedately, as though some kind of truce had been arrived at. "Magnificent!" said Walkerton. "Love unquenchable!" And launched into a conversation about racehorses, to which the Captain rose at once, and Mrs. Ludwell added "Humph!" and "Ha!" occasionally. So the three of them strutted in to supper, and I followed at a distance, because it was a valet's business to be invisible, but at hand when needed to run errands.

I was surprised, when I got inside, not by the mountains of food,

the roasts, and pies, and cold turkeys, and hams, and hotbreads, and
the opossum baked in honey, but by the amount that many of the
gentlemen had already drunk, not least among them Young Burwell;
he seemed heavier and more flat-footed than ever, and stood in the
conversation room, with a plate from which sweet corn dribbled on
to the floor, as he led a group of men in a vigorously bellowed song.
His face was flushed and his eyes squinted.

He should be attending to his future bride, I thought, and then saw
in my mind the girl who had kissed Walkerton in the garden, and the
self-dramatizing way she had swooned back for him. How like her
aunt, the widowed Mrs. Hope, I thought, and then put the idea out
of my head. It must have been another girl, who vaguely resembled
Elizabeth Michieux.

There were bursts of laughter all round me. How assured the men
were, how smooth-bellied, soft-cheeked, and gleaming! How confi-
dently they chaffed each other and how suavely their quick flicked
glances insulted Paul Michieux. He wanted to be like them but never
would, and it was not his money or his bitten fingernails or his
ruthlessness that doomed him, but his notions of gentility; because
he did not think it his place to be assertive in another man's house,
he left matters to Young Burwell. So matters drifted, and the man
whose money dominated them refused to impose himself, and was
despised for weakness, and reduced to being civil to a valet like me.

I assured him that I was being well looked after. He smiled, which
revealed his yellow teeth and bad breath. He did not know what else
to ask and had no skill to extricate himself with grace. Then Burwell
went past with a loud, drunken laugh, and Michieux said, "We drink,
and the harvest is ungathered." His contempt was like a rash all over
his face, and he walked away without another glance at me.

I looked round for Walkerton, but he was not to be seen. Burwell
laughed again. I wondered when the engagement would be announced; and how much money was involved; and whether Michieux's daughter, and even Mrs. Hope, who had encouraged his
schemes, would ever accept Michieux as a gentleman. He was a solid
man, though. He reminded me of my second cousin James Derker,
with all his wet-lipped, stubborn ignorance and self-assertion. I understood Michieux. In one sense I was like him, a determined upstart,
and yet I knew him to be my soul's enemy.

Then the Captain called me. He was exhausted and wanted to go to bed. Would it be impolite, I asked, to go before the announcement? "Oh, put him away," said Mrs. Ludwell, "before he falls to pieces!" The Captain snorted but was too tired to argue. He seemed, indeed, to have downed an entire bottle of claret at supper.

So I squeezed hands with Mrs. Ludwell, and as the Captain swayed upstairs, the musicians struck up again with country dances. I tugged off the Captain's stockings and dropped his nightshirt over his head. He said with many winks and nose tappings that at least the lady had accepted his right to woo her, but that if there was any more interference from Ashlin it would end in pistols. Then he lay down and said, "God bless you, Tom, God bless you," and flipped the tassel of his nightcap off his face and on to the pillow.

I said, "Amen!" and shut the bed-curtains, thinking that Mrs. Ludwell had been scared stiff and had evaded every issue by getting him maudlin drunk.

Then I went downstairs and took great swigs of wine myself, and grabbed a turkey leg, and was uncaringly aware that everything became more wild and loose-mannered.

After the country dances they did jigs, the dances that white people had taken from the blacks, the men and women not holding each other but dancing individually and fantastically, making up the steps as they went along; and the music became by the minute less like Europe's stately measures and more an echo of the hot, dry, inhibition-battering drums of Africa.

I felt myself drunk and did not care. I kissed a black maid in a corner, and talked airily to this gentleman and that. At one time I did sense an urgency round me, a sudden panic in Mrs. Hope's swoop through the rooms, and in Michieux's sweaty face, but I ignored it and it seemed to pass. I saw two satin-clad gentlemen vomit into chamber pots under the supper tables, and at the stroke of twelve Agricola stood in front of the grandfather clock and drank deeply from a bottle of rum.

If the slaves stayed sober tonight, they could be drunk tomorrow, I remembered, and this was tomorrow. Yet where were the young lovers? The musicians played on feverishly, and if any gentleman declined to dance he was whooped at and abused and dragged out to a tune called "Hang On Till Morning," which many people seemed inclined to do.

Eventually I went to sleep where the stairs curved round above the musicians' gallery, and when I awoke I was stiff and my head pounded. The house was grey and reeked of burnt candles. In the hall there were empty bottles and plates with slops on them, and the front door gaped open. Michieux sat on a gilt chair, his fists clenched, his ball shoes torn and sodden, and I did not need to ask him to know what had happened.

I knew that the girl who had kissed Walkerton was his brother's supposed bride, Elizabeth. I knew that Walkerton had made her love him, and why there had been no betrothal, and what the panic was: Walkerton and Elizabeth had run off together.

Michieux saw me without seeing. His lips trembled as his plans raced through his mind. So many thousand acres. So many thousand pistoles. So many humiliations. So much to be pieced together.

Burwell's still-drunken voice came from his mother's room. Walkerton always hated me. Oh yes, he did, and what did you-all care? I loved you both. I'll kill him. We don't even know what direction they took. His mother was tearful, and no one could stop her. No one listened to what other people said. There were silences, and then outbursts in which four or five people talked at once.

Outside, as I walked to the bachelors' house, the sky was dark blue and there was a nip in the air that made me shiver. When I awoke again, I had a worse headache, my black room-mate still snored, and the day tasted, like my tongue, of shame and staleness.

The white housekeeper was active and there were still piles of food, but the blacks had taken their bargain literally. Some of the maids were working but the men seemed incapably drunk, and as guests who had stayed the night came downstairs, they realized or were told what Walkerton had done, and went home as soon as they decently could. So celebrations that had been intended to last two or three days ended ignominiously on the first morning, a tale of disaster and romance, and Mrs. Ludwell took advantage of the general dismay to trundle off in her coach before Captain Cary awoke.

It was a grey day that threatened more rain, and the overseer was anxious to get in what wheat he could; unhappily, the field hands were as drunk as the house slaves. The overseer lashed them with his cane, and came up to the house to propose to Burwell that they hire what white day-labourers they could find, but Burwell was still drunk and interested only in abuse and bile. The overseer turned to Michieux, who refused to take responsibility—a refusal in which for the first time there was neither diffidence nor weakness, but contempt and a sulky withholding of power. When his sister pressed him, Michieux snapped and said very well, very well, he'd buy the plantation, and when it was in his own name he would gladly give the orders, as though it were one of his warehouses.

Mrs. Hope appealed to Captain Cary, who was desperate to ride after Mrs. Ludwell but could not because his sorrel horse was missing from the stable; presumably it had been taken by Walkerton as a spare. This struck the Captain as an outrageous thing for one gentleman to do to another, every bit as bad as stealing a woman; so while he waited to borrow a horse at a moment that would not seem like a headlong desertion of friends in distress, he comforted Mrs. Hope, attempted to admonish the now-comatosely-drunk Burwell, and paid his respects to old Jemima, who stayed in her room and laughed her head off, because she hated Michieux's schemes, and was only sorry that Walkerton hadn't stolen the plantation as well.

"Agricola!" she shouted. "Agricola! Bring me some hot milk!" And not until then did anyone realize that Agricola was missing, lost with some others in the drunken shambles.

That was at midday; in the afternoon there came news of the runaways. They had ridden northwards, and crossed the river at Bowler's Wharf. "What about my horse?" said the Captain, but no one remembered it, and there was understandably greater concern about some of the family silver that Walkerton seemed to have stolen.

Mrs. Hope said that Agricola must go after them because he and Walkerton had grown up together. They understood each other. Agricola would bring the truants home.

But Agricola was not to be found, not even when night came, and not even sad and sober the next morning. Then, on that second afternoon, one of the white men whom Mrs. Hope told the overseer to hire said yeah, they done seen that Agricola, riding like black devil-bones for the Chickahominy—on a real pretty sorrel, too.

"Mine, by God!" said the Captain, and it had to be admitted that, under cover of the drunken day that he had most likely brought about for that purpose, Agricola had run off once again to see his erstwhile wife, Liddy, the house-girl at Hope's Landing.

Chapter 36

Fish Feast

By this time the Captain was trapped inside his desire to be the loyal friend and confidant, and could not for honour's sake leave Myrtle Grove until there had been some resolution of the comedy, or time had healed and reconciled—all of which Mrs. Hope was determined should not happen. She enjoyed too well her shawl-trailing, weeping, self-recriminatory outbursts. She wallowed in her daughters' reassurances, and made the evil genius of the story her brother's late wife, an envious schemer, a breeder of sluts. Burwell might blame Walkerton, but Walkerton was Mrs. Hope's favourite and would return to her. He loved her too much. He would write soon. He would confide in his mother because it was a grand passion. It was an amour and magnificent.

Whatever she said was contradictory. She was confused, and yet cruelly accurate and spiteful when she argued against Burwell, because he was and had been utterly weak and unmanly, so much the opposite of Walkerton. She blamed herself bitterly for having failed Myrtle Grove, for not having brought wealth to it; yet that was the very scent of the flower, was it not, because she had married for love and in a frenzy.

Could Burwell understand that? Could her brother? No, but Walkerton could. Walkerton knew how to live headlong, in the moment, with every part of his being. That, after all, was the most difficult thing to do in life. Had she and her husband not accomplished it too well? Had they not drowned in each other, and taken others with them? "My God," she said, of her encounters with herself in tall and watery mirrors, "I've lived so much it's no wonder I look like a ghost, but once, ah, once . . ."

Yet she was rouged and scarved and ruffed at the neck to hide the crepe-like skin there, and then slashed low to show her bosom. She was more confident than she had been at the ball, her voice deeper, her sad laughter more rich, because now she seemed the centre of things, the drama seemed hers, whereas at the ball she had needed to strain for the attention that slipped away to Elizabeth, who refused it. In fact, as the Captain grasped and tried by little hints and demurs to indicate, she was not the centre at all, and neither was Burwell, because his masculinity had been dismayed and his confidence blunted.

Burwell was crass and contemptuous, and proposed in one jeering moment that he should marry another of the Michieux sisters. It was all for the money, anyway, wasn't it? That's what it was about, and why he had agreed to take Elizabeth in the first place.

Indeed it was about the money, and their belief that without it there was no survival. They had weakened the true Hope breed, they had reduced it to indulgence and self-dramatization, and the greatest effect of this was upon Michieux. He no longer felt inferior. If his daughter had allowed herself to be seduced, she was no worse than her seducer. She was a light person, like her aunt, whereas he, Michieux, was a serious person, who did not ask for respect that he had not earned, or for admiration that he did not deserve. He claimed nothing by right. What he owned came from hard work and realistic decisions, and after another day he made his decision, and went home to Alexandria.

Myrtle Grove was financially ailing. Very well. Michieux would assist his nephew in a businesslike fashion. He would give him a mortgage. No daughters or dowries. A mortgage. Burwell blustered, unable to make up his mind. Mrs. Hope was incensed and made it up for him. She refused a mortgage because it was an insult to past feelings and sacrifices, a mockery of family love and loyalty. Michieux did not care. He collected his younger daughters and took

hem away. He had tasted enough. It was as though there were a
masculine principle that in his hurt he instinctively asserted against
a feminine, as though for years he had seen the planters and gentlemen through his sister's eyes, but now he saw them through his own.

His departure made Captain Cary even more like chivalry's hos-
age at Myrtle Grove, but only for three more weeks. Despite the
overseer's efforts the harvest was a disaster. Burwell had entirely
failed to strike between the rain showers, and with so much of the
field ruined, it would be difficult for him to meet the interest pay-
ments on his existing debts. True, the second wheat crop was being
promisingly sown between the lines of Indian corn, but it would not
be harvested until October, and the corn not until November, and
that was too late. Burwell asked for the mortgage, and Michieux
consented, but with stiffer conditions; and all he would give was the
money. Advice and participation he declined.

Mrs. Hope would not speak to him, and made great efforts at
self-reformations. She read hopeful portents in the tea-leaves, and
decided that she would assist Burwell. She would take an interest in
the plantation. Oh, she might look like a china doll, but in the old
days, before there were children, she and her husband (My God, but
he was more handsome than Walkerton!) had ridden the fields together and she had known every entry in the books.

What a character she is, said Burwell and his sisters, what an
extraordinary woman. The daughters believed themselves less beautiful, and praised her to outsiders; then they bit their lips, and made
little frowns, and giggled wildly about men, and never said openly
that they resented her because their own chances of dowries and good
marriages had faded. But resent her they did, and felt guilt for it, and
she was able to twist that guilt and command them, and so they
discussed her many-times-described passions and dramas as though
they were the events of their own lives; but their own lives had no
events beyond uncertainty and adoration for brothers who had failed
them.

Unlike the mistresses of other great plantations, Mrs. Hope had for
years done all too little work herself—not taken care of hens or hogs
or horses, or of the slave hospital. Now she flung herself into it all,
incompetently and messily, and hating to soil her hands. We heard
later that within a month to two she tired of it, and bullied her
daughters into taking her place. One of them had already organized

the hospital for three years, and was coldly angry. But at first thi
new rallying-around vigour distracted Mrs. Hope from Captair
Cary, and enabled us to beat a retreat.

Coping with other people's crises when, old Jemima excepted, they
were unaware of his own was a hard penance for the Captain. Like
all distressed lovers he needed to talk endlessly about his love, and
because he talked to me, his blindness and repetitions made me won
der if I had thought similarly wild things about Fourfarthings and
Susannah Hanson, and I realized that I had, and that I had changed
the course of my life because of them. Yet they had been the bes'
thoughts of my life, and the Captain thought that his fantasies were
the best of his. Mrs. Ludwell was beautiful because she made the
Captain's life seem good and purposeful.

Despite that, I was glad of my detachment, and glad to leave Myrtle
Grove. It was an out-of-control place, unkempt, untended, over-
grown. Its humanity was confused and confusing, and when the
Captain announced that we would return to Hope's Landing because
Agricola might have left the sorrel mare there, I was doubly pleased.
Life would be controlled again, in keeping with my day-to-day desire,
and I would find out about the Ohio Company's pack-train.

Unfortunately, when I did so I was disappointed. Mr. Ashford
Hope said that there would probably not be a pack-train that autumn,
because within the last few weeks the French General Montcalm had
won a series of victories in the north, and captured the three most
important British forts. After the fall of the last of them, Fort William Henry, the garrison and its dependents had been promised safe
conduct and then massacred by the Indians, a raw and bitter event
that Montcalm should have prevented. He was a European nobleman, and had no right to loose his savage allies in that fashion. As for
the savages themselves, they were brave but should be wiped out.
They should be shown no mercy, because they showed none themselves, and civilization must survive. In the meantime the Shenandoah Valley was not safe. Virginians must lie low and wait. When
more forces arrived from England the tide would turn. It struck me
forcibly that although the war was only a few hundred miles away,
there was less hysteria about it here than in Antigua—a sure sign that
in Virginia white civilization felt itself more secure.

What Mr. Hope wanted to know at once from us was when the
runaway house slave, Liddy, and her children had arrived at Myrtle

Grove. But Agricola came here, we said, and he was last seen at the Chickahominy. When Mr. Hope heard this, he knew that Liddy and Agricola had fled together, and that he had lost her, and he put out a wanted notice on which the Captain's sorrel mare figured as prominently as the slaves.

Our descriptions of Walkerton's elopement, and the Captain's evaluation of the family's troubles thereafter, were more carefully weighed. It seemed to me strange that Ashford and Mrs. Hope had not been invited to the ball, but the tutor, Mr. Glashan, said that Mrs. Burwell Hope was jealous of them and always invited them when it was too late for the invitation to be accepted. That had been the purpose of the letter that contained the post-script about Mrs. Ludwell: an invitation that would not be accepted because, as everyone knew, Ashford Hope never left his plantation at harvest time.

Of course, said Glashan, the black groom who brought the letter must also have been Agricola's messenger to Liddy. Glashan chuckled hugely at the thought of the Captain and Mrs. Ludwell. I tried to divert his attention by asking my own questions about Mr. Hope, who seemed to take the news of Michieux's mortgage very blandly, as though Young Burwell and Walkerton did not share his name, and Myrtle Grove had never belonged to his father. Was that the mark of fairmindedness? Of coldness? Or of a tact that would not discuss family affairs with outsiders?

Mr. Glashan did not care. He was more interested in his own problems, his letters home to his wife in Scotland, and the difficulty of getting his teaching money out of farmers and other neighbours. He wanted to hear about Captain Cary because the Captain was a person in a more ridiculous situation than his own. So he shrugged off my questions about Mr. Hope. They bored him. Myrtle Grove was not important, he said, nor the people who lived there. Not important. Not persons of substance at all. Then he sniffed, as though he had substance himself, but I could not possibly understand what it meant.

But at the fish feast a few days later, I did understand, because Mr. Hope's guests were much more impressive than the hard drinkers at Myrtle Grove. In the morning I went out in the plantation rowboat to help gather oysters. The ferryman Old Batty's sons were out, too, and the beds were so dense, and so near the surface, that we leaned over the side and broke the oysters free with wooden tongs. From the bank Mr. Hope supervised his blacks, who waded into the river with a seine net; it soon teemed with fish that writhed and glittered in the sunlight. Then we drifted downstream to a place where fire-pits had already been dug, and rugs and tablecloths spread under the trees, and one or two chairs and stools brought out, and baskets of bread and bottles of wine, and ice from the ice-house, and piles of fresh grapes; and already there were some horses and a carriage or two, and ladies and gentlemen elegantly but simply displayed, as well as poorer neighbours like Old Batty and John Hood, half guests and half catchers of the fish.

Black servants barbecued the fish on a grid of sticks laid across the coals. They served them on big leaves, and we ate with our hands, the oysters and the iced wine first; and a black strummed his banjo, and it was as pleasant and happy an occasion as I ever saw in my life. The guests giggled, and ate with their fingers, and got pleasantly tipsy in the sun, and talked in a lively fashion about each issue of the day, from Montcalm to a new actress in Williamsburg. They were each other's neighbours along the tangled banks of the river, and some of them were among the most important persons in the colony.

There was Robert "King" Carter of Carter's Grove, as stately as an emperor in his shirt-sleeves, his relations Mr. and Mrs. Carter of Shirley Plantation, and his uncle "Pepper" Carter, a ferocious old man who complained that fish feasts were a waste of money, and that life was going from bad to worse. There was Mrs. Byrd of Westover, who had come with her children because her husband was in Williamsburg, and Colonel and Mrs. Bland and their son and unmarried daughter, and the dreaded Mr. Ashlin, and another clergyman named Mr. Dudley, and numerous children and dependents.

"King" Carter made ponderous efforts to draw Captain Cary and Mr. Ashlin into the same conversation, usually to discuss topics such as whether the moral basis of civilization was intuitive or revealed, and I needed a particularly keen glance to detect the twinkle in his eye, but it was there, faraway and gentle, and trading on his power, so that behind his civility and his sweaty jowls he could be wildly mischievous. He was the richest man in the colony, and seemed to have a great fondness for Mr. Hope, the indulgence of an elder statesman who understood when a young man had exceptional qualities. There was dancing to the banjo, and a game of quoits improvised by the ladies. The sunlight was high and slightly overcast, the river an amiable grey. The ladies swatted insects with their fans, and there were long, rambling, lazy conversations, and only one embarrassment, which thankfully was transmuted into gold.

Colonel Bland and his wife disagreed as to whether he had or had not promised to bring along her playing-cards. Mrs. Bland was suddenly angry, and called for the Colonel's black groom. When he stood in front of her she hit him across the face. The Colonel's response was to slap the black maid whom Mrs. Bland had brought to fetch bowls of water when the ladies' hands were sticky from tearing at the fish. Mrs. Bland gasped and hit the groom again. Everyone looked at the Colonel. He was poised to strike the maid again, but she burst very loudly into tears, at which everyone laughed and the Colonel and his wife made up; the groom was given a jug of rum, and Mrs. Bland promised the maid a blue-and-green handkerchief.

Mrs. Byrd of Westover asked jokingly whether the Colonel was not ashamed of himself for having provoked his wife so, and he answered with an unexpected seriousness that he was. His wife shrugged, and the ladies talked about the silliness of house slaves, and how they sulked and stole and broke things until they got what they wanted.

But the Colonel's answer had touched some of the men, and as they sprawled in the shade, and as the last smoke of the barbecue drifted across the river, they talked in the most enlightened philosophical tones about what had occurred.

There could be no doubt about it, said the Colonel, and "King" Carter rumbled his approval: slavery degraded the slave and brutalized the master. "Pepper" Carter snorted that most educated persons had known as much for years, especially the ones with strapping mulatto sons. The others smiled at his intervention, and Mr. Hope said how to end slavery, that was the question: How to end it? He waved his hand, and a black brought him an ember to light his pipe. I was fascinated because a white man who spoke like that in Antigua would have been considered to be deranged, by fever or the heat, whereas here the questions were elegantly debated as though by an assembly of philosopher-kings.

Not only did most Virginians have their tangible wealth in slaves, the argument ran, but frequently the land upon which the slaves worked was mortgaged to Scots or English merchants. Should children be denied their inheritance, and creditors their due? The situation was particularly difficult in the Tidewater, where the soils were exhausted, and most plantations had turned from tobacco to wheat and Indian corn, and even to raising hogs. Suppose the slaves were freed. Could the planters afford to pay them labourers' wages? No, they could not, and there were further problems. Where would all the slaves be housed? Would all one hundred thousand of them find work? If they were set up as smallholders, who would pay for their tools and seed? More worryingly, the black race clearly lacked the capacities of the white. Would freedom bewilder them? Or did most black hearts hide hatred and cunning? Could they ever live peaceably with white men? Should they be returned to Africa, even those born in America?

It was just such questions, said Mr. Hope, as he drew at his pipe, that had occupied so profoundly the finest minds of Greece and Rome, and prompted immortal questions: Where lay the public good and where the private? What must be done to prepare the world for the general emancipation of all mankind?

In the silence a swallowtail butterfly went jaggedly by, and the questions hung in the heat, in the dappled light under the arms of the trees, and the gentlemen in thin, cool summer clothes were still, as if conscious of some magic. The ladies were still, and the slaves, who scarcely spoke English but sensed the stillness in their masters. A fish plopped in the river, and the breeze fluttered silk bonnet ribbons. Old Batty wheezed and shook his head, and "King" Carter's deep voice said that of one thing he was sure: that the answers to the problem would be found in Virginia because Virginia contained men with minds particularly applied to such matters, men whose wealth and public service on the one hand, and plain neighbourliness on the other, uniquely fitted them to see all sides of a question. Colonel Bland nodded, a tear in his eye, deeply moved by a notion of Virginia that made the group under the trees seem more than ever an ideal made manifest.

Then Mr. Hope knocked out his pipe, and drowsily and pleasantly the fish feast broke up. The heat had gone from the day, and the tide turned to reveal black mud, and I was aware of little aches and stiffnesses and of places where my sweat had dried. I was dizzy from the sun, and half-way down the bank to the rowboat I stumbled and looked back, and saw that Mrs. Hope stood at the top.

Her smile was half-sad and her big eyes looked into mine. I could hear horses and carriage wheels in the dirt. I felt that Mrs. Hope had seen something in me, an impatience, a longing for the wilderness, a disbelief—however much I admired them—in the easy manners of slave owners. But I had little as yet to set against them, and nothing of considered substance. I thought that Mrs. Hope pitied this youthfulness in me, and I frowned. For an instant she looked vulnerable, and her awkward body seemed very female. Then she turned away and I got into the rowboat. The river was smooth and the foliage very thick. The grey-yellow sky would soon be pearly pink, and somewhere on the shore a field gang chanted as it tramped home.

Chapter 37

Library

One of Mr. Hope's kindnesses to me was that when he did not wish to use it himself he allowed me the run of his library, and so it is to him more than to anyone else that I owe, among other things, what formal ordering my mind possesses. There were more books on his shelves than I had seen in all the rest of my life put together, and through them I entered a wider world. I had glimpsed it in the visions and best moments of Mr. Dingwall, but not known how to make it mine, and he had been too distraught to tell me. Now, with my own passions in suspension and my mind full of the things that I had seen, I watched Mr. Hope as he referred me to his atlas, and then to one or another book from his shelves, and realized that they were the key.

It was a heady discovery, but one of which at Myrtle Grove I could not take advantage. The books there were mostly romances that the young ladies read over and over, rule books for card games, and old Bibles, but in the Captain's room there were a few dusty histories that had the Latin on one page and a translation on the other, and these I devoured. In an outhouse I found an even more stained and broken little volume that was being used to wedge a window; the run of its letters was like the blown spume of the sea, and the Captain said that it was Greek, the language of gods and heroes.

Later, when I studied engravings in Mr. Hope's books, I realized why so many people believed that, although the Greeks and Romans had lived so long ago, they had never been excelled in their achievements. The porticoes at Hope's Landing were an act of homage to ivied ruins four thousand miles away, and even the poses of the picnickers at the fish feast somehow recalled, and strove to emulate, statues with broken arms and bashed-off noses. The Captain's knowledge was patchy, and I turned to Mr. Hope. He was delighted to answer me. He suggested what books I might read next, and made me see how one topic related to another. When he talked, it seemed as though the whole world and everything in it could be explained and ordered.

Read poetry for its moral examples, he said, and an occasional novel such as *Tristram Shandy* for its shrewdness, but properly speaking, verses and fiction are for women, and treatises, letters, memoirs, histories, topographies, and the law are for educated persons. Through law, men make themselves. There are laws in every order of creation and they will one day be elicited. Where there is no awareness of law there is no civilization. That, he insisted, was the difference between ourselves and savages both red and black, and our true inheritance from the ancient world. We understood law and logic, and savages did not. God was good, and had given us the power of reason.

I was so exhilarated that I ignored my nagging awareness of the flaw in his argument. After all, Greece and Rome had fallen. Barbarians had cast them down. Their enlightenment had not preserved them, any more than reason had controlled most of my behaviour. There was another life, that of feeling and instinct, of passion and things inexplicable. Virginian gentlemen, like Roman senators before them, might claim in their fine speeches that the disorder of the senses must submit to reason, but the senses did not. As I knew well from my days in the slave trade, reason was a name given to any old excuse for what greed and passion had already demanded—a contradiction that I met again in the book-cloistered cool of the library when Mrs. Hope came there to seduce me.

It was in the afternoon, when Mr. Hope had ridden out to the fields in which the gangs were cutting the corn tops and green leaves for fodder. Mrs. Hope came into the room, and when I looked up, she smiled at me. The breeze rattled the branches outside. I sat on a window seat, with a large book open. Mrs. Hope walked over to me and held out her hand. Surprised, I gave her mine. She held it against her breast. My instinct was to snatch my hand away, but she clutched it tighter and said, "What's the matter? Don't you like me?" I said that of course I liked her. My heart thumped. She let my hand go and I stared up at her. She reached down and undid the buttons on the flap of my breeches. I blushed. She held my penis. I tried to back away and she laughed because already I was hot and erect. She flounced up her skirts and half sat, half knelt on top of me, wet and warm although I had not touched her.

I almost slid off the window seat. I still had the book in my hand. I felt stupid and uncomfortable, and the weight of her haunches seemed not to crush me but to suck me up into her, to lift me and bend my back and draw the marrow from me.

She did not hold me, but balanced herself with one hand on each side of the window. I clutched her, and as I did so, I ejaculated and lost all sense of my own power and energy. I gasped aloud, at which she took her right hand from the wall and used it to hold me against her, pityingly, as though I were a child at the breast. Then her face crumpled and I was more a rag-doll as her body shuddered and the muscles inside her rippled. Then she was slack and a stifling weight, but after a moment she released me, and sat down herself on the seat in the next window.

I was on the floor, where my book had fallen. My head was on the boards, and I looked up at the walls of books. Mrs. Hope breathed heavily. Her hair had come down and she sweated. I sat up with my back against the wall and buttoned my breeches. Mrs. Hope came to me, smiling, her big, plain face illuminated, and ruffled my hair. Then she walked out without another word.

I felt drained and disturbed. I had a vision of what the black slave girls had felt when I used them, and, far more unsettling, I knew that there was a sexual power greater than my own. Mrs. Hope's fecundity had lifted me up and sucked my arrogance dry.

I was uncertain of what a man should do or be except a spasm, and in the weeks that followed I lacked the confidence to approach Mrs. Hope myself, and to attack her body as I had attacked black girls. Once, in the schoolhouse, I wrestled with her and exulted in it, but it was she who held me down at the finish, just as it was always she who sought me out, at odd times of the day when she knew that I would be alone: in the schoolroom when Mr. Glashan had taken her children outdoors, by the river bank when I had gone for a walk, and sometimes in the house itself, when she knew that her husband was absent.

She did not talk much. She was big and hot and I clung to her, and sometimes she had to prise me away, but always understandingly, as I let her desire envelop me, to discover its limits and my own endurance. Frequently she hurt me. My penis was sore and my back ached, and afterwards I would see her at the family meals, large and self-conscious, but smiling, and devoting herself mainly to keeping the children quiet while the gentlemen discussed weighty matters.

My vanity at having taken another man's wife had evaporated after an hour or two, in fact as soon as I set eyes again on Mr. Hope, because as I did so, I knew by instinct that he and his wife did not make love any more, and that his urbanity hid confusion and shame. It was obvious when one knew it, and that first night, after I had helped the Captain to bed in his guest room, I confirmed for myself what had never been concealed: that Mr. Hope slept in a small closet room near the library, and Mrs. Hope in the big family room on the ground floor.

Then as I watched him over the days, and as she sought me out as insistently as men seek girls, my instinct told me that there had been not so much a quarrel between them as a slowly nurtured decision on her part; and that he was confused, because a part of him did indeed deeply believe in a spirit of inquiry and equality, and that his honesty compelled him to admit that women were sometimes as badly treated as slaves; and of course he was a gentleman and one did not reveal one's feelings. I was sure that when his awkward, shyly smiling wife, whose brown hair had golden lights in it, discovered that she was not entirely what convention demanded, she could only have done so with his help and encouragement.

I was sure that he knew that I was his wife's lover, and I fancied that I was one of the first, that she had begun with boys to see what would happen. Or perhaps boys were what she wanted, anyway, because like maids or slave girls they were of no account and would not make demands upon the other sides of her life.

It angered me to think that she valued me as I had valued slave girls, but I knew that it served me right, and I did not resist her. I liked my lack of responsibility. I floated. It was a preparation for the wilderness, an encounter with something primal that I did not have the will or confidence to shape. I was a blank. I neither knew nor cared what qualities she craved in me, and when I tried to think about it I became lightheaded and silly.

When Mr. Hope watched me, there was scarcely one shamefaced, beaten glance from him. His self-control was rigorous. He was curious, and would discuss the books I read because that gave him an excuse to study me, but there were no revelations of feeling; there was nothing, for example, like the sharp glance he had given his wife when she first suggested that I work for Captain Cary. What they said to each other in private I could not guess, but in public there was neither tension nor provocation. Mrs. Hope was so modestly busy and quiet that her husband's occasional attempts to coax a reaction from her were like a family joke at her eagerness to mind her own business and not offer an opinion when one was not especially called for. She would join in the laughter herself, and Captain Cary was so busy talking about Mrs. Ludwell that he suspected nothing.

One subject about which Mrs. Hope was asked for an opinion was tobacco. Having spent her childhood in the Piedmont, she knew more about the crop than her husband, who always consulted her about the small amount that he still grew. On a morning on which the threat of autumn hung in the mist, and I realized how faded and old the trees had become, and how many of them had already begun to change colour, Mr. and Mrs. Hope went to the fields to inspect the yellowing tobacco and decided together that it should be cut now and left to wilt in the furrows. Then they waited for a warmer spell, because the hotter the weather the more yellow the leaves when cured, and had the fires lit in the smoking-houses.

Mrs. Hope was exemplary in these matters, as she was exemplary as a hostess, and I realized that there were many areas in which her husband relied on her and she on him. But as she went about her tasks her quiet plainness hid her strength. She seemed unremarkable, when in fact she had drawn to herself the energy of the plantation and the people round her, and in her marriage decided to redefine the areas in which a woman should support a man, and vice versa.

Had she ever, I wondered, stated those intentions in so many words? I doubted it. Mr. Hope was articulate and educated, but she was not. She liked people to read aloud to her, and the Captain often obliged with a novel, but she knew nothing about politics and did not even care much about gossip. Her wide strong hands were inept at the daintier women's pursuits, such as needlework and the harpsichord, but with her hens, and the plantation cats, and the squirrel she kept in a big cage, and the wounded birds that people brought her, and fomentations and splints in the slaves' hospital, and the flowers and vegetables and watermelons that she grew, she was magnificent. She rode well, too, for so solid a woman, and she had the knack of conveying what she thought by her smile and her presence alone, by the way in which she sympathized while clearly in disagreement.

The more I thought about her, the more certain I was that she did not have a coherent plan to unfold. She simply knew what she was at each moment, and had the courage to be it, and I suspected that Mr. Hope had found himself her fellow conspirator and adventurer almost by surprise; one night she had removed his hand from her body, and when he placed it there again in daylight, and she again resisted, he knew from her smile and the awkward angle of her head that he was embarked upon new waters. I thought that perhaps it was he whose conversation had faltered, and he who had moved his bed; and that his pride and curiosity, and sense of irony, had kept him true to her.

I once asked Mr. Glashan if he thought that Mr. Hope had slave mistresses, and Glashan shrugged as though it did not matter; as though, whether Mr. Hope did or not, it was not one of the things that defined his personality and life on his estate. Nor was it. Mr. Hope had all the power in the world to assert himself against his wife, but preferred not to use it. He could physically extort his conjugal rights and the law would support him. In daily life he could invent all manner of insults and inconveniences, but he did not do so. He was a gentleman and would not be seen to be less. He believed in the power of reason to shape chaos, and refused to abjure it. He was curious to discover how far his wife could go, and how I would behave; and somewhere, dimly, deeply, humiliatingly, he was numbed and wanted to know if it was for ever.

Yet he cannot ever have loved his wife with a sweeping physical urge. She was sensible and presentable, and above all she was an heiress—an excellent match, cold-bloodedly made, with, I was sure, no false protestations on his side. Perhaps the situation in which he now found himself was more intriguing than a conventional money-match of companionship that declined into routine; it was more challenging and dangerous, and there was no doubt that Mr. Hope did welcome danger. When oysters were so plentiful that at low water the tide exposed them, there was no need to dive, as he had done, so deeply that his hearing was permanently damaged; and no reason except amusement to take a genuinely more lively and provocative interest in me, after he realized that I was his wife's chosen instrument.

Mr. Hope knew that sooner rather than later Captain Cary would regather his strength and confidence and once again lay siege to Mrs. Ludwell. Letters had passed between them, and one of the few lazily smiling opinions that Mrs. Hope gave me when we were alone was that since Mrs. Ludwell had replied and not discouraged the Captain from writing again, she would accept his companionship provided that it was not offered in such wildly poetic terms. The Captain seemed to have some inkling of this himself, and if he was more irritable with me than formerly, it was from sadness, because it is sad when a man deliberately quenches his passions, and the most exciting things that he has ever thought in his life, in order to achieve their object.

Mr. Hope also knew that when I left the Captain and claimed the redemption of his promise to send me to the wilderness, he could get rid of me in any one of a dozen ways, each of which would bar me from Hope's Landing and still look like unselfish patronage on his part and a heaven-sent opportunity for me. Yet in an odd way I felt that he did not want to see me leave, because there was something in him that loathed to make use of his power. He hoped that Agricola and the house-girl, Liddy, had run so far away that they would never be found and never have to be sold to the West Indies as an example. He did not want to admit that such a sanction existed, or that he may have been callous because he never offered to buy Agricola, or to sell Liddy once she had travelled to Myrtle Grove with Mrs. Hope and got pregnant by Agricola. Yet surely he had made a balanced decision about Agricola; he had judged him to be too restless, too clever, too likely to cause upsets. Such men must be watched and resisted, not encouraged to persuade their masters to buy wives for them.

Mr. Hope was an effective man of business who preferred to pose as a scholar, and so long as I remained at Hope's Landing he could justify his bewilderment and hurt pride with the notion that he was learning about both me and himself, and with the importance of my studies in his library because he believed that it was his duty to open my mind if he could. He truly believed that there was a sacredness of knowledge above foolish personal feelings, and the more he expounded the idea, the more I became cheeky again at the thought that the wife of so rich and admirable a man desired me.

Towards her, my conceit made me more contemptuous. I had never seen her entire body naked. I had sucked her breasts, but when she pushed them into my mouth, not when I demanded them, and I had not touched her at all between the legs. It was always she who pulled me on to her, or ripped down my breeches, and when I tried to assert myself she resisted. Yet I was determined now to be the master, and one evening I made a hollow in my corn-shuck mattress, and as I lay there with my shoes off I heard her get the fowls into their coops. It was that grey-blue hour before candlelight, and she sang quietly to herself as she came up to where I lived above the schoolroom. When she was on top of me I tore at her dress and slapped her, and roughly tweaked her smeared brown nipples. She cuffed me, and our coupling broke off into sulks.

She sat on my bed and I on the floor, and then I got up and tried to apologize and wheedle her, and I put my arm round her as though she were my own age, and a girl worried about false scares. She laughed in my face. I flared up. That made her smile even more. She stood up and tidied her clothes and held out her hand for me to shake. I would not do so. She nodded, and made me feel about five years old. She suddenly looked vulnerable herself, for the first time since I saw her on the river bank, but there was great pride as well as sweetness about her, and when she went downstairs it was with finality, and I knew that she would not come to me again. The room was chilly and there were dark shadows. I felt loss and shame as I had never felt them before, and an even deeper longing to be hidden in a wilderness.

Chapter 38

Williamsburg

It was a hard lesson in the days that followed, and one that I hated, to have to meet Mrs. Hope at mealtimes and see her unchanged poise and affability. When we were lovers our secret had been easy to keep, but after she dismissed me it was a daily agony. Fortunately I did not have to bear it for long, because we had reached the time of year when Mr. Hope, and the Captain himself, invariably attended the Public Time at Williamsburg, when the Assembly met and the courts were in session, and all manner of private, political, and social business was conducted.

Williamsburg was a day's easy ride from Hope's Landing, and the Captain and I lodged, as was his custom, with the saddler Mr. Norton, who was privileged to have us, although really the house was too small and a gentleman and his servant a great nuisance, because Mrs. Norton was too proud to rent them anything but her own bedroom.

For us the room was portentous because Mrs. Ludwell was due to arrive at the house of her attorney, Nathaniel Tilney; and from our window we could peer through branches, some bare, some bronzed or flamed or golden, and see beyond sheds, kitchens, ice-houses, ornamental evergreens cut like peacocks, and a field in which Mr. Tilney grew hay and, now that it was autumn, fed his sheep from troughs, the white-painted back of the privy to which the Tilney family repaired as necessary each day. Beyond that was the brickwork of their house, on which the sun glowed warmly, and the sandy thoroughfare of Duke of Gloucester Street.

Our mornings were bright blue and sunny, but crisply cold, so that everything was clear and the air a bracing pleasure. When I walked to our own privy I heard the pitter-patter scrape upon the bark of the squirrels I had startled, and beyond that, beyond the leaves and branches, the sounds of people's work: the clatter of milk cans, the whoosh of carpet beaters, a quiet voice that calmed a horse.

There were still the last flowers, and smells of digging and manure, and it could have been deeply rural except that on Duke of Gloucester Street there were noble public buildings, and a confusion of horses and carriages, and lawyers in robes, and scarlet soldiers, and crowds who strolled beneath the trees to the races or the theatre. Then turn another way and, behold, there was a garden, a rail fence, and the tall trees of the wilderness. In Williamsburg, that unique capital city, I sat on the doorstep and saw a deer come shyly out of the woods to raid a vegetable plot, and then walked fifty yards to a tavern in which "King" Carter was among the audience at a demonstration of phrenology. At the fairground I paid one and threepence to see a tiger in a wooden cage; in the theatre I saw actors for the first time, and in the creek at the side of our house there was invariably a turtle.

In the summer the skies had been hazy grey and the air scented with flowers. Now the skies were blue, and in the air were smells of woodsmoke and fallen leaves and occasionally, as one passed a backyard smoking-house, of tobacco. The nights were frosty, through which the town lights sparkled, and day and night the wild fowl passed overhead on their way south. Often I lay on my truckle bed at the foot of the Captain's four-poster and heard through the rattle of his snores the throb and whistle of wild ducks, but when I rushed to the window there were only black trees and the stars as bright as diamonds.

That autumn I put on winter clothes for the first time in five years, and it was with a pang of homesickness that I saw hoarfrost again, and spiders' webs like nets of silver wire, and dull grey ice on the ruts and creeks. They were wild-fowling days and wild-fowling weather, and dearly would the Captain have loved to creep down among the frozen reeds with the long-barrelled flintlock that was always most carefully stowed in our luggage. He taught me to clean and oil the gun, and let me shoot at marks, and one of his great boasts was that he was still, at his age and out of practice, as deadly a shot as any young frontier tail-bonnet. But for weeks he did not venture out, because what happened at Williamsburg was that he lost his nerve.

In previous years he had cut a famous social figure. He had slept at the Nortons' but spent most of his days and evenings on the town. He was a member of the dining clubs in two or three taverns, and a diligent playgoer, and altogether knew so many people, and had so much to say to all of them, that it took him three hours to walk half the length of Duke of Gloucester Street, and by then the Assembly had risen for the day and he could choose his company and tavern; the more prosperous and politicking sorts of men went to the taverns in Duke of Gloucester Street itself, and the young up-country lawyers, the gamblers, the actors and fencing-masters to the Warren Street ordinaries, between the Capitol and the red, gold, and evergreen wall of the forest.

This year he had even muttered doubts about going to Williamsburg at all, and I should have been warned by that. But when he heard that Mrs. Ludwell was to be there, at the house of her attorney, Mr. Tilney, he was so brisk in his decisions, and so convinced that he could approach her in a coherent and persuasive way, that I was deceived. I thought that the instabilities of his passion were spent, but I was wrong.

When we arrived at Mr. Norton's pleasant frame-boarded house that had the saddlery at one end and the stabling across the street, the Captain introduced me and then went inside to take tea with Mrs. Norton. I took care of the horses and was immediately joined by Mr. Norton's apprentices, one of them his son and the other a Yankee, with a harder accent than the native Virginians. They already knew about the Captain's amour and were as anxious to ply me with information as questions.

Captain Cary was the talk of the town. Capsized by love, God damn it, as the wits said. Mrs. Ludwell's lawsuit had begun, but she herself had not arrived, and some said she never would, for fear of scandalous exhibitions from her suitor. Barnaby was here, having found employment for the Public Time with a Piedmont planter and his family. He refused to discuss in public his quarrel with the Captain, but in conversations with old cronies had given five or six different versions of it, so everyone was agog, and until something else came along, the affair of Captain Cary and Mrs. Ludwell was the event of the social season. By comparison, Walkerton Hope's elopement was ancient history. The pair had been seen together in Annapolis, from where they had taken a ship to New York. After that, some rumours said, they had gone to Europe, and others that Walkerton had joined the British Army in Canada as a gentleman volunteer.

When I went indoors with the valises, the Captain was in our room. He sat like a little boy with his legs dangling over the end of the bed, and I knew at once that Mrs. Norton, a short, red-cheeked, well-meaning person, had been less than tactful. Her sympathetic inquiries had made the Captain realize for the first time that he was a laughing-stock not merely to himself but also to most of the people he knew, and to many he did not. Mr. Hope's good manners had made it seem that the agony was over, but in fact it had only just begun, and when he realized that, the Captain's nerve deserted him.

He refused to leave our room, let alone the house, for any purpose whatsoever. I brought in trays of food and took out chamber pots, and what made matters most difficult was the fact that since the best bedroom was also the family room, it contained the bureau that held most of Mr. Norton's papers, and the drawers in which Mrs. Norton kept her linen, the pewter plates, and goodness knew what else besides, all of which in other years it had been easy to bustle in and out for, because Captain Cary was rarely in the room and by common consent never locked it during the day.

Now he locked himself in at all times, and since he refused to answer except when I knocked in a code that he changed every other day, I had to be either locked in with him or stationed permanently outside, where I could intercept and mediate. The room stank because he refused to open the windows, on the grounds that he did not want anyone to know that he had arrived in Williamsburg. It was useless to point out that dozens had seen us already, and that there was a steady stream of callers to the house, from Mr. Byrd of Westover himself to numerous lame jockeys, actors, sea captains, second cousins, and young men at the College of William and Mary whose fathers had told them to look up an old sporting companion.

Thus, at the very moment that the Captain's friends rallied to him and proved that they did not care whether he made a fool of himself or not, he refused to believe that they did not jeer at him in every tavern and coffee-house. He swore that he would not go outside to be questioned about Mrs. Ludwell and take her name in vain. He was a gentleman. He would wait until she arrived in town, slip at dusk through the back yards, and in Tilney's garden ask her to marry him. If she refused we would ride out before dawn.

In the meantime, I was the one who peered through the trees for a glimpse of Tilney's privy and brickwork, and hung around the taverns to overhear conversations and report what they said. Then I would find Mrs. Norton in a great fluster because she wanted such-and-such a set of tankards but the Captain had refused to open the door, and how could her husband call himself a man if he tolerated such a state of affairs in his own house, and what did those fool apprentices have to grin at, she'd like to know.

It was a ludicrous situation, and I was delighted when one afternoon the news that Mrs. Ludwell had arrived spread across the back yards, from Tilney's dairy girl to Bracken's black groom to our apprentices. I walked round the corner and into Duke of Gloucester Street, and waited in the cold until Mrs. Ludwell herself called my name and beckoned me to Tilney's porch and said, "Well? Spit it out, now. What's all this pish-foolery about Cary?"

When I told her she said "Humph!" and "Hah!" and was outraged for the benefit of Mrs. Tilney, but when she said good-bye to me, walked out into the street. The ruts were frozen ridges, and she gripped my hand like a little girl. "Tell that Cary to—" she began, and I thought that she would plead and weaken, but she did not. She sniffed and said, "Pah! Pish-jerrydoodle! Tell him what you please!"

As I went back, the trees were flat grey shapes and the houses pale; there was no break between sky and horizon, and the breeze blew flakes of snow that did not settle. I was cold, but the Captain's room was a sour and suffocating oven. "She's here," I said. "I've talked to her. She wants to see you." As soon as I said it I knew that I had been too eager, because the Captain rolled back into bed and pulled the clothes above his head. Mr. and Mrs. Norton came in and we all three shouted at him, but he refused to move. He lay stiff and bony like a corpse, except that a corpse would not have clung so expertly to the sheet and prevented it from being dragged off.

"You're a dirty old man and I don't care if you is a gentleman!" shouted Mrs. Norton, and flung open all the windows, but the wind blew the snow in, and papers from the bureau all over the room, and smoke and soot down the chimney, and Mr. Norton shouted and fussed and slammed down the windows, and his wife slammed them open again, until the Captain sat upright and shouted, "Don't bang, damn you! Don't bang!" which was the first and only time I heard him abuse any woman except Mrs. Ludwell. But he still refused to call upon his love.

"I won't go," he said, "and don't ask me why, because the reason is that if I don't go she can't refuse me!"

If he didn't go, how could he ask her, I said.

"I can communicate by letter!"

"She can reply with a refusal."

"Don't be impertinent, sir! Know your place, Mr. Derker! Know your place!"

Then who should stick his head through the still-open window but Bracken's black groom, who had heard shouts and was concerned for our safety.

"Safe?" yelled the Captain. "Is we-all safe?"

He leaped out of bed to argue with the man and attempt to drag him into the room. Mr. Norton tried to push the man out and slam the window. Soot and smoke whirled everywhere. The black groom hollered and Mrs. Norton wept. Then our apprentices appeared outside and rammed the black groom into the room, and he and the Captain fell on the floor, and Mr. Norton shut the window. The Captain lay on his back and wheezed, and the groom was so distressed that he had to be given money to calm him down.

Afterwards I heard Mr. and Mrs. Norton discuss in whispers whether they should or should not send out for a surgeon to declare the Captain insane, which persuaded me that it was time to take the initiative. Next day a surgeon did visit the Captain. He bled him, and asked seemingly insignificant questions with such heavy-handed casualness that I was sure some plot was afoot; fortunately, so was mine. I knew that although Mrs. Ludwell liked me she would not be persuaded by me alone, and so I had sought out Barnaby.

At first he was lofty and affected not to know who I was, and even when I pleaded with him he continued to address his remarks to a point about six inches above my head. But there was a certain irony in the way he put things, and much commonsense in what he said, and when he finally looked at me it was not without a twinkle, although the untidiness of my neckcloth did make him wince. I said that unless something was done to break the pattern, the Captain was so suspicious of everyone that he might well be called mad and end up barking "Hey? What? Hey?" at a cellarful of chained lunatics.

"Does he speak well of me?" said Barnaby.

"No."

"Does he vilify me?"

"Sometimes."

"Lies?"

Not lies, I said. More like fantasies. Interpretations. Opinions. A lover's permitted distortions. Barnaby's hedge-like eyebrows were raised in disapproval.

"Permitted or not, young man," he said, "does the Captain wish to meet me face to face?"

"No. You remind him of his former self-discipline."

Barnaby grimaced. I saw that he was hurt, and I noticed his clothes, how worn they were but how carefully darned and ironed. Then he pulled himself together and justified all the gossip about him, because in his sonorous voice he said that the time had come to gamble, and proposed as outrageous a plan as I ever heard in my life.

My part in it was simple but vital. Late that afternoon, when the snow patches were hardening in the cold, and the light was thick, and only in the west a glory of orange and purple, I knocked on the Captain's door to ask if I might clear away his dinner tray. He unlocked everything: key, bolt, and chain. The shutters were closed and there was a horrible tobacco fug. I loaded the tray as casually as I could, and tried to ignore the fact that I had left the door wide open so that the Captain would be sure to hear the voices in the hall.

When he did he almost fell through the bed-curtains. "What? What? What?" he cried, pointing a wild and bony finger.

"What?" I echoed, pretending not to understand.

"It's Barnaby!" he said. I looked blank. "Did you-all know he was here?" said the Captain.

"I've come from the kitchen," I said, which was almost true, and as the Captain hissed, "Shut that door, sir!" I gave an imitation of panic, and dropped the tray and its crockery in a place that ensured that the door could not be closed until the debris was removed.

"What's that?" shouted Mrs. Norton, and Barnaby's rumble drew nearer.

"I can't face him!" said the Captain. "He's a devil with wings! He occasioned this misery! What? Hey?"

"Hide in the privy!" I said.

"Privy?"

Before the Captain could argue I opened the shutters and the window and bundled him outside. "It's cold!" he gasped as his bare feet touched the snow, and he tried to scramble in again. I put my hand on his chest and shoved him back. I slammed the window. The Captain flapped at the glass, a nightshirted ghost, and then stared in horror as he saw Barnaby enter the room. He turned, and cavorted across the lawn to the privy. In the gloom I saw the door open and his white-clad body whirl inside.

Barnaby was immobile and so was I. We looked each other in the eye, waiting, and then heard the bang of the door and the Captain's wild cry as he attempted to escape from the privy in which we had hidden Mrs. Ludwell. We peered through the dark at the Captain's struggling form. It seemed to us that Mrs. Ludwell threw him across her hip and dragged him back to the privy. Mrs. Norton howled for her smashed crockery. "Cease, madam!" said Barnaby, and she did. The privy door banged several more times. Then there was silence for a very long time.

By now Mrs. Norton thought that we were all mad, and her bladder gave way. She hopped up and down and said, "Oh! Oh! Oh!" and rocked back and forth to contain herself while we argued with her husband that she should not use the privy. Finally she ran squealing to a chamber pot, and it was not until another hour had passed that Barnaby yielded to Mr. Norton's concern and began to worry about what might or might not be happening inside the privy. Suppose the Captain had been humiliated and was afraid to reappear?

It was decided to send the Yankee apprentice to find out. He walked across the yard with a scarf over his head and called, "Captain, sir! Captain Cary!" There was no reply. We signalled encouragement from the back doorstep. The apprentice tapped on the privy door. Still no reply. He shrugged. Mr. Norton made vigorous pulling gestures. The apprentice opened the door and said, "My God!" because the privy was empty.

The kitchen skivvy snivelled and boo-hooed and said it was them witches done take the pore ole Cap'n away, until Barnaby cleared his throat so menacingly that she stopped. Mrs. Norton envisaged the

Captain in his nightshirt, mad and half-frozen, and so shocked that he wandered in and out of taverns in search of his memory. Either that or Mrs. Ludwell was strangled, and her body dragged down to the creek. It was all our fault, and her husband should fetch a Justice of the Peace. Barnaby said very well, he would seek out Mrs. Ludwell, and was wrapping himself in his cloak when Mrs. Tilney's maid came to the door with a note of hand that she said was for my eyes alone. Everyone stared as I stepped aside to read it.

> Dear Mr. Derker
>   Please bring my cloathes to Mrs. Tilney's at yr best
> expedition and discretion and ask for ye Mrs. Ludwell as my
> being here in nite attire is not observed and oblige yrs truly
> and God's most happy creature
>   Capt'n Cary

I thanked the maid gravely, and she pattered off into the dark. Barnaby took the note, read it, and announced to Mr. and Mrs. Norton that the Captain was safe and well at Mrs. Tilney's, but required a change of clothing. His tone implied that to scramble nightshirted across a sheep field and enter a friend's house undetected was for a gentleman an everyday occurrence. We packed a valise, and only then, when Barnaby winced at the way in which she or her maid had ironed the Captain's shirt, did Mrs. Norton protest again—this time about her crockery. Barnaby waved money at her but did not actually let go of it, and we walked together into Duke of Gloucester Street.

At Tilney's gate we shook hands and Barnaby crossed his fingers and held them up like a blessing. I knocked at the door and asked the maid to hand the valise to Mrs. Ludwell. Barnaby then very solemnly invited me to take supper with him at Wetherburn's Tavern, which was where, he thought, God's happiest creature would repair to show off his good fortune. Which the Captain duly did, with a very radiant goblin Ludwell on his arm, and the gentlemen at cards or round the club tables actually applauded them as they came in, and rushed to congratulate them, until the Captain stood there with his nose red from the cold and tears on his leathery old cheeks.

What had passed in the privy I do not know, and was never told, but the Captain had a painful limp, and when I put him to bed I

344

observed huge bruises on his backside. A few wags had visions of grotesquely vigorous love-making, and others swore that Mrs. Ludwell had crashed the Captain up and down upon the privy seat until she'd knocked some sense in him. The Captain himself said nothing, and so far as I know mentioned the entire episode on only one occasion, when months later I visited him to say good-bye.

He gestured around his cosy sitting-room and said, "I shan't forget, sir, what I owe to you-all and Barnaby. Hey? What?" Then he dug Mrs. Ludwell in the ribs. She giggled and drummed her little heels on the floor, but had no need to say anything because the Captain was already embarked upon the description of a quarter horse on which his father wagered seven hundred guineas forty years ago, or was it thirty-five?

Chapter 39

Black Betty

That is to look ahead, because the eventual harmony of the Captain and Mrs. Ludwell was not secured without a great deal more bluff and tumble; this time, thank heaven, it was conducted between their lawyers. Mr. Tilney represented Mrs. Ludwell, and Mr. Hope consented to speak for the Captain, a decision that sorely tried his patience, but about which he never complained. As for the love-birds, they walked through the December fair and the rest of the Williamsburg season like a stork and a duck arm in arm. They were swooningly happy, and the Captain did crazy young deeds again, such as take off his coat at the agricultural fair and hurl himself into the straw in an attempt to catch the greased pig, which rushed past him, was startled into changing direction, and as the Captain staggered to his feet, ran into him from behind and sent him flying. It was caught by William Buckley, or Grizzly Will, as he was called, a giant of a man who led the Ohio Company's pack-trains to the Alleghenies. He did a belly-flop plumb on top of the pig, and there was a wheezing squeak as the breath was crushed out of its lungs. Then the pig's little feet scrabbled to run again, but too late; Will grabbed them, and held the wretched beast above his wild, bushy, bearded head.

After his pig collision the Captain limped again, but it did not stop

him from wild-fowling the next day, or from subscribing to a harpsichord concert the same evening; although, while he and Mrs. Ludwell held hands as they listened to the music, Mr. Tilney and Mr.
Hope exasperated each other with their clients' impossible conditions to a marriage settlement. Their disputes were not about money,
of which Mrs. Ludwell had plenty and the Captain none, but the
relative status of Barnaby and Mrs. Ludwell's housekeeper, and
whether the Captain should smoke his pipe in the bedroom, and who
should decide what cuts of meat to buy. The Captain was particularly
aggressive on behalf of Barnaby, whom he wished to put in charge
of the entire household.

Mrs. Ludwell waited until the Governor adjourned the Assembly
and the Public Time ended, and with it Barnaby's temporary job. She
then engaged him herself, and said that he would do as he was told,
at which the Captain instructed Mr. Hope to break off negotiations
altogether. He and his happily quacking love-duck then spent the
afternoon inside his bed-curtains, a pastime that scandalized Mrs.
Norton and drove me to long hours in the saddlery. When Mrs.
Ludwell heard about the latest stratagem she withdrew to her home
in Petersburg and took Barnaby with her; but she still sent the Captain a love-note every other day, and he sent her ribbons and comfits
by return, and was utterly lighthearted about their separation. But
Mr. Tilney's forbearance was strained to the utmost, and so was that
of Mr. Hope.

I saw him occasionally, but Mrs. Hope hardly at all—once in Duke
of Gloucester Street, in a snowfall, when she was wrapped in furs,
and once at the New Year, when I sang part-songs in the street and
Mrs. Hope attended a subscription ball at Wetherburn's Tavern, and
her eyes held mine for a moment through a half-steamed window
pane. Then the Yankee apprentice dragged me off with him, and I
felt a jealous rage because both times, in the snow and at the ball, Mrs.
Hope had been with a young man, and I wondered who he was and
what rights she had given him in her body.

Love was grotesque, but I wanted to feel it because it proved I was
alive. It brought out my violence and self-will, and seemed to me to
have brought out Mrs. Hope's as well; wherever there was love there
was selfish cruelty, and if there was an answer I did not know where
to find it except in the wilderness.

My summons to go there came in February, when the Public Time had ended, and instead of a bustling city of six thousand inhabitants Williamsburg was once again a village of fifteen hundred. We had moved from Mrs. Norton's to the Raleigh Tavern, where often we were the only staying guests, and it seemed incredible that a few weeks ago there had been such crowds and gossip and flirtations and heated political discussion.

The actors and dancing-masters had moved on and Mr. Hope long since returned to the plantation, when his letters arrived: one to the Captain to beg my release, and one to me that told me to make my way to Richmond, and the Ohio Company's warehouse at Shockoe.

Not having a horse of my own, I begged passage on a flat-boat that would sail in ballast to Richmond and return with tobacco to be shipped from Newport, and thus I saw head-on the rapids where the grey muddy river ceased to be salt, and between wintry-wooded bluffs met the broken confusion of islands and fawn rocks, and bare bushes that seemed to grow out of the water. The noise of the falls could be heard along the Richmond quays and grog-shop alleys, and in the warehouse, where Grizzly Will greeted me with a wry contempt as he assembled his goods for the pack-train.

It was my duty as clerk to make the inventory: so many Osnaburgs, blankets, muskets, gun flints, saddlers' tacks, screws, nails, tallow candles, kegs of rum and whisky, and cheap trade goods such as hatchets, knives, beads, mirrors, patterned cloths, and cooking pots. No doubt I should have known what experience I was bound for, because if the goods reminded me of anything, it was of the display in the state-room of the *Margaret*, where black kings had come to despise us and to sell their heritage for trinkets. But I was eager. I believed that I was about to find myself at last, and end my confusions, and I was fascinated by the new sights and people.

There were five of us with the pack-train: myself; Grizzly Will; his cousin Bo Skerritt, a tall, sombre, hollow-cheeked hunter in buckskin trousers and an Indian fringed jacket; a half-breed Indian nicknamed Deadeye; and Julius, a black mule-skinner whose business was the animals. We were to be accompanied by Captain Piquet, a slight, forty-year-old teacher of music and the French language, who had been born in Paris, was commissioned in the Virginian forces, and had been assigned by the Governor to our journey so that he might have his own account of the frontier, as well as that of the Indian Commissioner.

For the first two days of our journey, when we slept in the barns and bachelors' houses of plantations, we were joined unexpectedly by Mr. Hope himself, who had determined to visit his plantation on the Rivanna. He insisted, as we rode along, on conversing in French with Captain Piquet; it was not often, he said, that he had the opportunity to rehearse that language. To me this was more proof that educated men shared a commonwealth above nationality and time, but Grizzly Will was not impressed. He called the French our enemies, and could not understand why an oily little dancin' feller called hisself a Virginian at all, God damn it. But he did not push his resentment in front of Mr. Hope, and we wound at a pleasant gait across the rolling wooded hills of the Piedmont.

The skies were blue, and the land had long, shallow troughs and humps, like the swell of the Biscay Sea, except that it was densely wooded. There were snow patches in the hollows, and our horses pattered through mouldering brown leaves. When we looked up, even the creepers were dead and bare and brown, and the evergreens limp and yellowed by the winter. The woods were a grey blur and the river turgid. Mr. Hope and his black grooms left us at the fork of the Rivanna, and after that we came to more broken country, which afforded glimpses through the trees of rearing foothills, and then the steep line of the Blue Ridge itself.

We travelled in file and for the most part in silence. Deadeye and our three running dogs would be up front, and Julius at the rear. Here and there fields had been hacked and burned out of the forest, but the houses in them were little more than hovels. The clapboards were not even painted, but brown and silver in the winter light, and the children ragged. Nor were the plantations so grand as those on the Tidewater. The overseers here took a third share of the profits, and they were rough, driving men, and the field Negroes were slow, muddy-armed and -legged, and so little used to white men that they spoke fragments of their own tongues and not the pidgin.

On most homesteads there were brush and mould fires burning, to make the piles of ash in which the tobacco seedlings would be nurtured, and we smelt the burning leaves, and the mules, and the strange rancidness of the half-breed Deadeye, who still believed in the Indian ways and rubbed himself with bear grease. Grizzly Will was slyly civil to me, but contemptuous now of Captain Piquet. He made him prove everything—prove that he could light a fire and make corn-meal porridge, and hobble a horse correctly, and read the changes in the weather, the high streaky clouds at sunset, or the different colours and flotsam of the river.

When **we** went through the gorge in the first wall of the Blue Ridge, the river was a rich red-yellow from the soil it carried down, and its banks were so steep that bare branches dipped into the water. Then the track, which was stony in some places and sucking mud in others, wound between rolling foothills, and along narrow rivers with dugout ferries at the landings, and then precariously up the dramatic forested slope of the ridge itself, where sometimes there were tumbledown barns and little shanties in the hard-won clearings. Then there were sweeping views and we dropped down into the Shenandoah Valley itself, a loved, lusher, more seductively rolling country even in winter, with the new grass sprouting through the old; there were substantial clearings on the lower ground and thick, brown, brier-tangled woods on the steep little hills and knolls.

At one of the solid-looking farms we passed there was a gathering of fifteen or twenty men, all with their families and muskets, most on horse- or muleback, but one or two in carts. Some of them were people that Grizzly Will and Bo had known all their lives, and we halted to talk to them. Their patriarch was a heavy grizzled German named Beckman, whose English was thick and broken, and whose son was to be married that day. Beckman invited us to the wedding, and Grizzly Will accepted, despite Captain Piquet's obvious disagreement, and so for most of the morning we rode in a slow-moving, chattering caravan, with much passing-around of jugs of liquor.

Then we reached the crest of a hill and saw below us a farmhouse and barn, and smoking-houses, and rough yellow-earth fields, and others half-cleared, a rawness of felled trees, and some stumps burned out and others not, where this year's tobacco would be planted out. There was smoke from the kitchen and from outdoor fires, and more horses and mules hitched out, and old Beckman held up his hand to halt us, because this was the house of the bride. Then when most of our riders were level with him Beckman dropped his hand and yelled, and with whoops and one or two fired-off muskets that startled our pack-mules, the men raced each other down the slope, swiping out with their reins, bumping their shaggy horses into the next man's, a hectic, boisterous competition that ended when Grizzly Will deliberately blocked two of the valley men so that Bo Skerritt could be the first over the farm threshold and win Black Betty, the bottle of liquor that the bride's father was bound to give.

Then Grizzly Will wrestled with the valley men on the hard earth, and when the bride's father came out, lifted him high in the air above his head, by which time the rest of us had arrived with the women and wagons and pack-mules; and the bride's father, a gaunt, roaring-drunk old devil, shouted, "No niggers and Injuns inside, God damn it!" even though he was in mid-air; and Julius and Deadeye sloped off to warm themselves at the open fire, above which a whole bullock was suspended from a tripod. Some of the meat was already burnt to a crisp; fat hissed and sparked in the flames, and there were sweet potatoes in the ashes at their edge.

The house, built of logs on a stone foundation, and with a stone chimney at one end, was substantial for its kind, but it was still only one big room with a rickety ladder to a half loft. It was wooden floored, with a few plain chairs and tables, and the cutlery and valu-ables hung from the walls. Some of the guests were in good worsteds or fur jackets and heavy boots, but some were much wilder and poorer, shivering with fever even in that weather because it had entered their blood, and one or two of them had bare feet like most of the blacks, whom they treated with an amiable contempt, as if they were dogs, except that dogs ran everywhere and the blacks were kept out of the house.

At noon the pastor arrived, and we crowded into the house and around the door to hear him conduct the ceremony. The bride was a striking girl as tall as her old father, and the groom a stolid young man in his best black suit. The pastor stood behind a table, on which there was a pewter jug with sprays of russet leaves and berries, and everyone was hushed, although there were a few burps and tears and cooking noises from outside. When the pastor pronounced the young couple man and wife, there were whoops and cheers and a drumming of feet on the floor, and then the wedding feast, a roistering occasion for which everyone packed into the barn.

The food was served by four young men and four girls, who were each presented with an embroidered white apron, and as well as fetching and carrying had to defend the bride and stop her shoes being stolen. If one was stolen the bride had to pay a forfeit of a bottle of wine and was not allowed to dance until she had done so. This made the wedding an odd event, because the guests were cautious with strangers, slow with each other in serious conversation, and yet wildly boisterous in their practical jokes. Grizzly Will crawled under the table during a serious discussion between older men, some of whom because of the winter snows had not seen each other for months, but instead of taking the bride's shoe he grabbed her married sister's by mistake, and was kicked by the sister's husband, at which he stood up, roaring, and overturned a table as he did so.

There were several almost-fights like that, and one in earnest, when the same married sister danced with a young man who, said Bo Skerritt, had made love to her last summer. The husband watched from the barn door. The young man stopped dancing and joined him outside. He did not want to fight, but he did not want to look a coward, either. In cold afternoon light the two men panted, and others watched in silence. The young man tried to reason. The husband rushed him. The young man easily dodged him. The husband's shoe came off. He was smaller and looked ludicrous. The young man appealed to the other men, and as he did so, the husband hit him across the face with the shoe. The young man's nose broke with a crack, and blood poured on to his clothes and the mud. The husband put on his shoe and walked to his wife, who had pushed through the women who tried to hold her. He slapped her face. She looked away but did not drop her head. Then they danced together.

After dark, half a tree trunk was thrown on the outside fire. Captain Piquet tried to demonstrate the minuet, accompanying himself on a pocket flute, but was ignored in favour of the wild country dances. He was petulantly drunk, and fell asleep on the fodder that was piled along the sides of the barn. No head for liquor, sneered Grizzly Will, because they ain't even shoved the bride and groom in bed yet.

This ceremony began when the four girls took the bride up to the draughty loft, past groups of old men and women around the fire downstairs, stripped her naked, and put her one and only nightdress, and the pride of her trousseau, over her head. They then yelled for the groom and his young men, and the groom whipped off his breeches and got under the covers in his shirt-tail.

The four girls then took it in turn to stand with their backs to the shuck mattress and straw, and throw a rolled-up stocking over one shoulder. The first one to hit the bride was supposed to be the next to be married, but they all missed, including one who was so heavily pregnant that the young men had to heave her up and down the ladder.

Then the young men threw the stocking at the groom, and one of them hit him, which his friends seized upon as an excuse to get even drunker. Some of them had pannikins of milk that they kept laced with spirits. Eventually the bride and groom were left to get on with their love-making, although nobody vacated the house and ribald teasers occasionally scaled the loft ladder.

I was told by the bride's father that it was a love-match, and a damn good thing, too, because him and them Beckmans had quarrelled for fifteen years about the water rights to a certain creek, and the marriage would heal the breach. Mind you, both his daughters had made true love-matches. Fine-looking girls. Had I shook hands with his eldest daughter? I had. Son, you should have been at her wedding. Biggest love-match you ever done seen in your life, he'd roast him an Injun for breakfast if it weren't. And a shoe, I thought, across the face of a husky young man.

By this time there were revellers, and drunk people, and couples fumbling under each other's clothes, all over the house and barn, and in the shadows of the yard. The only unreservedly sober person seemed to me to be Bo Skerritt, who with his musket in his lap watched over our mules and the fire that Julius and Deadeye had made. There were snatches of German, and talk about tobacco seedlings, and animals that wouldn't damn-well mate, and whiffs of manure and woodsmoke, and the merry madness of the fiddles, and it was a scene that I knew well from my childhood at High Top. It was like the hard-wrested, sullen, shy, but angry and slowly sex-burning life of the hill farms; a conviviality of people who might not speak again for days; an ancient routine, a cruel beauty, and always one eye on the weather or wherever in the yard the hens seemed to be skittering off to lay.

These people were more independent than Englishmen, more stubbornly convinced of their own rights, but John Derker would have been at home with them, and so after a fashion was I. They reminded me of my relatives when they had got drunk with each other after Mr. Sayer read the will. They closed ranks against outsiders, and yet they were themselves riven by deep hates and jealousies and secrets. They were also frank, much more so than any of my relatives except poor Crabtree, because the dangers of the frontier had made them help each other. Their enemies were the French, and Injuns, and niggers, and men in fancy coats who ruled Virginia but did not often send soldiers to protect them. They'd make a good life for themselves, never mind them rich men on plantations. They had treated me with reserve, and yet at each stage of the proceedings I had been most carefully invited to take part.

Now, as people found themselves places to unroll their blankets and sleep, both the bride's father and old Beckman shook my hand, and Mrs. Beckman kissed me. I wrapped myself in my cloak and lay with my head on my saddle and stared at the bright stars and the jagged shapes of the pines. Bo Skerritt said had I heard, the young man whose nose was broke shook hands with the man who did it, and then they got drunk together.

"I don't know why you got that musket," said Grizzly Will. "This here's too-all far south for Injun raids."

Bo did not answer. Julius was asleep. Deadeye seemed to be, but at any unexpected noise looked up. Our dogs were roped to the paddock fence. A few revellers still sang maudlin songs, sparks whirled up from the fires, and I knew as I fell asleep that this was not the wilderness.

I stretched out my hand and dug into the earth. It was thick and cold and sticky, richer by far than the Tidewater sand. In a decade this valley would smile and be prosperous. It was farmers' country, with all their patience and repression, and I had been there already in both England and Africa.

Chapter 40

Runaways

Having killed a bullock and so many chickens and hogs, the wedding party had to eat them, and although the bride and groom rode off on a mule next morning, she tall and self-satisfied and he dour and blushing even at her side-saddle arm around his waist, most of the guests stayed on to finish the food and drink. Some of them had thunderous headaches, and not a few young men were sick in the yellow ruts and dead trash of the corn field. Captain Piquet looked as green as the facings on his uniform, and his cocked hat seemed particularly ridiculous, but he was too proud to admit a weakness and ate a hearty breakfast of fried eggs and corn bread, taking a queasy eternity between each mouthful and attempting to distract himself by explaining to me the difference between French and Italian opera.

Julius thought Piquet a great card, but whenever we sat around a fire Deadeye stared at him with a grim face. Piquet thought that this was another of Grizzly Will's tricks to unnerve him, and at this breakfast his headache finally broke his resolution, and he shouted, "Tell zat feelthy Indian not to look!"

This produced crowing laughter from Julius and some slow, tobacco-chewing mock obtuseness from Grizzly Will, until Bo Skerritt tired of the joke and said, "For God's sake, what Deadeye wants is the cocked hat."

Captain Piquet was flattered. He removed the hat and showed it to Deadeye, who put it on over his round woollen cap. Everyone regarded this as the end of a foolish incident, and ignored Piquet's failure to understand why, when we mounted up, Deadeye rode off with the cocked hat still on his head. At our first halt Piquet asked for it back, and Deadeye spat on the ground between them.

Piquet snatched at the hat, and Deadeye shoved him over. The dozen or so wedding guests who were riding home with us whooped and hollered. Piquet grabbed for his sword and Deadeye for his knife, and I think that Grizzly Will might have let them slash away for a while, for the sheer piquancy of the contest, but Bo Skerritt stepped between them. He spoke curtly to Deadeye in his own language, and took Piquet by the elbow and walked him in a slow, dead-leaf-kicking circle while he explained the difference between these here Injun fellers and us.

In truth the Captain knew already; in his first years in America he had paddled down the Ohio with fellow French traders, which was why he had been selected for this mission. It was, he insisted, his hangover and the lack of respect with which he was treated that had made him forget that Indians judged a man by his bravery and generosity. They roamed freely over the earth that belonged not to them but to the Great Spirit; they were but one link in a chain of being, and what a man owned was of no significance, except to display his greatness. The greater the man, the more he should give away—not the scalps he had taken, of course, or his only weapons that might keep him alive, but all other things that were of no value besides honour. Thus the gift of a cocked hat complimented Deadeye, even if he was a lousy half-breed, and displayed Piquet's manliness.

"Be damned to zat," said Piquet, "parce que in ze French trade we wear buckskin and live à l'indienne, but here I am British officer and ze hat belong not to me but to ze Government of Virginia and eventually His Majesty King George, to whom account will have to made through ze office of ze Quartermaster General."

Skerritt's face was deeply burned by the sun even in winter, and now he narrowed his eyes and said, "Uh-huh," and spat out tobacco juice. I liked him and felt him to be reliable. He nodded gravely, as though he understood and sympathized with Piquet's bureaucratic predicament. Then he loped away, and never mentioned the subject again, and although Piquet grumbled and expostulated, there was little he could do except make a joke of it.

But as so often happens, the way in which he took his discomfiture brought him closer to some of those who laughed at him. The farmers, who were both contemptuous and shy of officers, realized that this one had an absurd streak and could be patronized, and they one after the other eased their mounts alongside that of Captain Piquet, and engaged him in conversation to see for themselves what the feller was really like, and to exercise upon him their dry, straightfaced humour.

He met their sallies with a battery of questions about their lives and work and their views on the Indians and settlement beyond the Alleghenies. He showed such a knowledge of their crops and prices, and such an awareness of their problems, that although they still went through the ritual of making him the butt of jokes he could not understand, they gave him quick and truthful answers and listened carefully to what he had to say in return.

Their womenfolk had liked him at once. They were drained and worn and tough as leather. They could saddle up, and catch hogs, and drive a plough with the best of them, and carry a child on their hip; and although there was plenty to eat, they above all had to work for it from dawn till dark. Their eyes had a steady, screwed-up, all-weather gaze that for all its wariness, and its regret when it looked in the mirror, detected and admired the gallantry in Captain Piquet, the consideration and tact that lay beneath his comic vanity.

As the day passed, one after another of the families travelling with us went its own way. One or two had farms in sight of the trail. Others turned off into the wooded foothills, and when we said good-bye to the last of them, the trail itself seemed to peter out, to be engulfed by the tangled pine forest, so that as we urged our mules uphill we had to discover and pace it out afresh, because we had come at last to the mountains and the frontier.

It was wilder than the Blue Ridge. When we saw the horizon, there were snow-streaked peaks, and when we looked down through frost-worn evergreens, the valleys seemed blocked and enclosed. Water-falls thundered, and when we wound down beside them, moss was unexpectedly green and the mules slithered on the spray-wet rocks. In those shadows it was cold at noon, although far above hawks circled in the sun, and just as I thought that this time Grizzly Will had entirely miscalculated, there was a scrambling path out again, a passage through what had seemed an impenetrable wall of rock and dirty snow and woebegone conifers. Then we climbed again and in an hour or so had scaled another ridge and saw in winter sunshine the grey, vast, unending panorama of the wild.

Grizzly Will and Skerritt and Deadeye responded to it by becoming more relaxed and gentle. They were alert to every bird call, broken branch, and patch of trampled mud, but it was an alertness that showed itself in their slowness and care, and the way in which they moved with an almost exaggerated respect for the lie of the land and obstructions to their progress. Deadeye went ahead, walking his horse and with his best dog at his heel. Julius was nervous, and Captain Piquet had a set military sternness, an officer's determination not to show his feelings.

Yet I knew, and so did the others, that Piquet had been a woodsman himself, and that he read the signs as eagerly as they; and from watching him I knew that they were puzzled. They had found traps set in places where animals were unlikely to run, and old camp fires badly hidden. To them, when they eventually discussed it, and without actually seeking the Captain's opinion gave him time to nod agreement, it could only mean one thing: the presence of runaway slaves, who had sought freedom in the wilderness and might kill to keep it.

We halted for the night half-way down a valley wall, by a stream in which Deadeye caught fish for supper, and where we could shelter among the boulders. We had carried animal fodder with us, and took turns on guard. My watch was with Grizzly Will, who did not want to talk but damped down the fire and was continually on the prowl around our small perimeter. The wind got up, and the forest creaked and complained, and when I rested again, I was cold and my ears were numb.

In the morning there were wet-leaf smells, and birds and squirrels came round us without fear, and I loved the noise of the water, and felt safe in the place where last night I had peered into the dark and thought that I saw trees and boulders become black men and jump the stream.

When we struck camp we stayed on foot to coax the mules downhill, and it was so difficult underfoot that we barely noticed when

after about an hour Deadeye gave his warning bird call from somewhere up ahead. Then we all strained to listen, and Julius clucked
softly so that our tension would not carry to the mules and make
them impossible to handle.

Grizzly Will was decisive and his gestures told us what he wanted.
He and Captain Piquet went forward; Skerritt and Julius and I stayed
with the mules and horses. In a second or two Will's bulk floated
silently into the underbrush. The animals strained. It was hard work
to hold them, and as we did so, small things seemed magnified: the
ragged edges of fungus, a worm that slithered among dead oak leaves,
the rattle somewhere of a squirrel's claws upon a branch. The mules
had a stale smell.

Then they started, and our dogs barked, as Deadeye gave his bird
call for all clear. Bo Skerritt ran his mules rapidly downhill to get
them going again, and we soon came to where Grizzly Will and
Deadeye and Piquet were halted, on flatter ground, where a dead tree
had fallen and brought down others to make a clearing.

Two blacks had stepped into the open and begged Deadeye for
food, and he had held them at musket point until the others came up
and satisfied themselves that there was not an ambush. One of the
blacks was a man and the other a boy of about ten. They were thin
and wild and desperate. The child's eyes were huge and his belly
swollen. Yet despite the dirt and exhaustion I would have known the
man's hawk-like profile anywhere; he was Agricola, the runaway
butler from Myrtle Grove, and in his eyes, too, there was both a
glimmer of recognition and a plea. He remembered me, I thought,
but not yet who I was.

The white men watched Agricola with care. They gave him a slug
of rum, which soon made him talkative, and some salt fish to chew
on.

"You a runaway, boy?" said Grizzly Will.

Agricola nodded.

"Why you-all like this?" said Will, nodding at their ragged clothes,
and the cuts and bruises on their legs.

Agricola's story, when put in order, was that he had come from the
Tidewater with his wife and two children. They had a horse and
travelled by night. Then they sold the horse and crossed the Blue
Ridge on foot and tried to get work as labourers in the Shenandoah
Valley. They were given odd days by farmers getting in their to-

bacco, but felt that people were suspicious of them. They were not used to field work; it was obvious that they were runaway house slaves.

Even so, no one reported them to the authorities because their labour was there to be had at a cheap rate, and they would sleep with the animals. Then they met another casual labourer named Cato, a half-black and half-Indian, who claimed fiercely to be a free man, but whom they supposed to be a runaway like themselves.

Cato was more experienced in the free life, and when he learned that they had money that could be spent on tools, he suggested that they all go farther west, into the Alleghenies, where they might find a white farmer who would set them up as sharecroppers. This they did, and in wild, steep country found a Mr. McGreevey, who with his wife and two sons lived in poverty and danger but owned a lot of land. McGreevey understood the blacks' situation at once, and was willing to have them clear his outlying land (did he truly own it, wondered Piquet, or was he an interloper himself?) in return for a pittance share of the crop.

McGreevey acquired tools for them. He fetched supplies and sent his sons to help build a shelter and a hogpen and a chicken shack. And so, in a valley that when they entered it still swam with bees and honeysuckle, they were blissfully happy.

They worked hard, but without an overseer's cane and arbitrary insults and changes of mind. Agricola had a dim memory of a childhood in Africa, and they cut sprays of honeysuckle and laid it out with bowls of water to please the spirits of their ancestors, and Cato hollow-burned a log to make a drum, and when the valley was muffled in snow they danced, even though their hovel with its moss and brushwood roof was so low that they had to stoop to do so.

In the last months of the fall they had cleared an acre or so, and when the snow melted they lit their brush and mould fires for the tobacco, and waited for Mr. McGreevey to come up with the seedlings. Liddy had given up her scarves and flounces. She wore sackclothes and blankets, and her feet were cold and muddy, but her laugh rang warmly because every night she held her man in her arms and she was sweetly pregnant.

Then one day Agricola and the boy went to walk the quarter of a mile to the creek to fetch water. Cato stayed behind to split some new railposts for the hogpen. When he was at the creek Agricola heard shots. He ran back, and at the edge of the cleared field flung himself down, because he was unarmed and six Shawnee warriors had surprised the little settlement. One of them was drunk already on Cato's rum, and amused himself by shooting the hogs and chickens. The hovel was on fire. Liddy and the little girl were tied to a rope and marched down the valley.

Agricola knew that he should run out and challenge the Shawnees, but that if he did so, he and the boy would be killed. He had expected the Indians to be magnificent, but they were as grubby and tired as himself. He watched them for twenty minutes or more, until they were out of sight, and then went cautiously, and weeping, to look for Cato.

He found him in the hogpen, dead and scalped, shot once and run through with spears, his limbs and stomach slashed open and his penis cut off, so that his soul would not go home to the Spirit World.

But to Agricola, Cato's soul had gone home, and weeping and chanting he half buried and half piled earth on him. Their hopes were burned down and their livestock dead. Agricola did not know enough woodcraft to follow the Indians. He was dazed. He walked back over the ridge to Mr. McGreevey's, to say that he would build again, he would plant the tobacco seedlings, he would be free or die in the attempt, but Mr. McGreevey was not there. The cabin was empty and the animals driven away.

"Git out for safety," said Grizzly Will, who had heard of one or two recent instances at the wedding. It was in any case a frontier phenomenon: sudden flights and panics, abandonments, and then a braggart return when it was realized that the war-band consisted of six men only, more likely youths out to prove their manhood than the systematic burnings and seizures of captives of the previous two years. The captives were mostly women, who would be taken almost to the Ohio and put to domestic slavery. Eventually they would be bargaining counters against the white man's westward advance.

Not that Agricola grasped much of that. He had waited three days for McGreevey and then begun to wander. He was not sure for how long, and the child was too frightened to tell, but we reckoned that it must have been for at least a month, and from a place sixty or seventy miles farther north, because that was where Bo and Grizzly Will thought that they knew of a man named Turk McGreevey.

Agricola and the boy had lived rough, with neither firearms nor tools, and not much experience, and that was hopeless in such a hard season. He had spotted us the previous day and skulked in our wake, not sure whether to accost us or not. He had done so for the boy. The boy was too sick to go on. Agricola had failed to save Liddy. How could he kill the boy?

"You could have gone down to the Shenandoah," said Skerritt.

Agricola was silent. He looked from one to the other. In the Shenandoah, people were more likely to hand sick runaways to the authorities. What Agricola hoped was to be able to get the child fit enough to travel south to the Carolina border, where in that lonely country he might have another chance as a sharecropper. This time I knew that he had some distinct memory of who I was, because he hardly dared to look at me; but I never mentioned, then or ever after, that I knew his name and owner, and had seen him in scarlet and gold braid and a powdered wig.

Grizzly Will sighed. His little eyes gleamed at Bo and Captain Piquet. "Well," he said, "I guess it ain't none of the Ohio Company's concern," meaning that he had enough responsibility and did not want any more. He gave Agricola a trade musket and shot, and some food, and we all felt suddenly very righteous, as though we had proved that left to themselves men truly would be noble. Then Will said, "Aw, shit!" and mounted up.

After a while I looked back because I knew that Agricola would expect me to do so; and when he saw me he raised the musket above his head in a tired salute. I thought about Walkerton Hope and the swooning girl in the moonlight, and turned to my front again. Captain Piquet watched me, but if he suspected anything he, too, kept it to himself.

Chapter 41

A Chant for Dead Souls

At midday we rode in pale and pleasant sunshine along the crest of a ridge, and saw below us grey smoke against the greener grey blur of the forest. "Tuscarora Joe's!" said Grizzly Will, and although it seemed so near, down the side of the ridge and across the wooded valley, we did not reach it until early evening, when the distant mountain peaks had turned from blue to black, the western sky was ablaze, and on the valley floor the shadows were cold and the birds squawked and clattered to roost. When we came out of the trees the land was flat, and there were patches of earth already ploughed for corn and squash and tobacco, and beyond them a palisade, because the trading post and the village that had grown up around it stood on the promontory where two streams made a river, and the palisade was their protection on the landward side.

There was a fish trap across the jumbled stones of one stream; there were bark canoes on the shore, and longhouses made of poles and bark and brushwood, with stones to hold down the roofs and mud to fill the cracks. Each house was shared by two or more families, and there seemed to be about thirty or forty adult Indians and no whites. As we rode in they were not so warmly curious as African villagers, but some of the men walked stolidly behind us to the trading post, a substantial log cabin with a stone chimney at one end and a shingled roof and verandah.

Tuscarora Joe came down the rickety steps. He clasped Grizzly Will in his arms and shook Bo and Piquet and me by the hand. He was a half-breed, a tall man with a big belly and heavy thighs. His skin was a pale copper colour and his profile magnificent. He wore a European shirt and breeches and Shawnee leggings and waistcoat, and his streaky grey hair was cut short. He had a black slave, two full-blooded squaws, and numerous children and dogs.

His house was divided into a store at the front and living-quarters at the back; the kitchen was outside, more like an open Indian fire, and there were various outhouses and pens, one of which contained hogs and another a tame deer. Chickens strutted in the dirt, and there were two roped cows, and what looked like fruit trees at the back.

We worked hard to unload our mules and get the trade goods inside before darkness filled the valley and the camp fires flared, and the Indians watched us, soft-footed in their doeskin shoes, wrapped in blankets and fur robes, impassive and methodical. They wore brilliantly-coloured cloth headbands, and most of the men had their ears pierced; the lobes of some had been pulled down into great loops by the weight of silver rings, and others had feathers stuck through them. They wore beads and quill necklaces, and some of them had silver armlets, or gorgets obtained from European officers. They stank of the bear grease that they had rubbed into their hair and bodies, and there was a sullenness about them, as well as an awesome dignity.

In Africa I always felt that the heat created a human abundance as well as fantastical vegetation, but these Indians conveyed a sense of an altogether harsher life. Tuscarora Joe had not seen a pack-train for more than a year, yet his spontaneous embrace of Will was the only sign of joy that he gave. He had innumerable questions to ask, yet grunted and nodded and deferred until Grizzly Will described of his own accord the progress of the war, the state of the fur trade, and the Company's hopes and cautions; then, to prompt Joe, Will mentioned Agricola and the Shawnee war-band.

Joe said that not for a year had raiders come as far south as the post, and that the local Shawnees were reasonably loyal. Of his white trappers who worked beyond the mountains, old Smoky Sam had survived the winter and been and gone, leaving some very fine pelts, and so had McDougall, but Hirschman had not been seen for six months, and some of the Indians said that he had been killed on the Monongahela.

Joe had been told that because Montcalm wanted as many allies as possible in his northern campaign, he had dissuaded the head chief of the Shawnees from sending too many warriors to raid the Alleghenies and the Shenandoah, and the few groups who did so were either over-eager young men or the protectors of some ancient hunting ground; in the case of the attack upon Agricola's hovel, Joe thought that the blacks must have unwittingly settled on traditionally important ground.

Indians had a friendly contempt for blacks, and although they would enslave them, did not often make them a target, and Joe thought that Cato might have been killed and mutilated because he was half-Indian himself, and they deemed him able to know better than build a house where he had.

I said that I did not understand why a head chief had so little authority that young braves disobeyed him, and entire families lived here in seeming loyalty to the British. "That's why they call 'em treacherous varmints!" Grizzly Will said, laughing, but Piquet said that all men were the same. It was, after all, the British Government in London that had proposed an Indian Commissioner, and the Commissioner who had proposed that to win the support of the tribes in the war against France, there should be no more settlement west of the Alleghenies.

But the Governor of Virginia had to prosecute the war with the aid of a Council and House of Burgesses of Virginia gentlemen, many of whom had made, and hoped to increase, huge fortunes by the purchase of Indian lands from the Crown agents. So the Governor had sent Piquet to study the situation first hand, and behind the backs of the commissioners.

Who were the more treacherous, Piquet would like to know, we or a free-roaming family of Indians making up their minds where they would sell their pelts?

After that, Joe, who had clearly thought Piquet ridiculous, and found it much more difficult to understand why a Frenchman was on our side than why the Shawnees favoured both, was much warmer to the little Captain, and less reserved towards us all. He had the generosity of his Indian blood, and thought that with goodwill all men could live together, and the Great Spirit be respected.

Why, he said, the Shawnee families who summered on the trading post had more true freedom than any of our governors and burgesses. They decided for themselves where they would sow their summer crops, and with whom, and in winter they followed their trap lines, and only when the entire tribe was threatened did they come together for a great pow-wow in which each man's voice was equal.

"How many of 'em thought we'd never arrive?" said Will.

Two families, said Joe. They had packed up again and gone to seek the French traders who came from Natchez up the Mississippi and Ohio rivers.

Grizzly Will spat into the fire. Captain Piquet was affronted, as Will intended, and declared that the French were more skillful traders than the British because they were prepared to live like Indians and to adapt Indian ways, but then the incongruity of his situation struck even him; he stopped in mid-sentence and muttered to himself. I giggled. Bo Skerritt watched us all through the sweat-reek and tobacco fug.

Grizzly Will was a man with one personality for the forest and another, much coarser one, for taverns and civilization, but Skerritt was of a piece, and only seemed truly at ease outdoors. He did not intend his silence on other occasions to be a reproach, but it was, even though we all knew that in the wilderness he had killed the Company's enemies without hesitation. Grizzly Will felt the criticism and changed the subject.

"What are this year's pelts like?" he said.

Joe had seen only those from the white trappers and they were excellent. The Shawnees had refused to show theirs until the supply train arrived, even though most of them were in debt to Joe from the previous season, and that is what their pelts would pay off.

Because they had made him wait, Joe procrastinated when we finally rode in. That first night was for conversation. He would see the pelts in daylight, and so did we all, next morning and the one after, the rich, gleaming black and grey and silver and russet-brown and white of them making me gasp when they were unrolled on the counter and the beaten clay floor of the trading post: bear, beaver, wolf, hare, squirrel, muskrat, mink, raccoon, fox, ermine, and then the glorious hides that the women dressed outside the longhouses on fine days, each hide stretched and pegged into the earth as taut as a drumskin.

The bargaining was monosyllabic and gloomy. The men were stolid, and their dowdy, worn women watched and waited. Joe shrugged. He grunted, and as he did so, rummaged among the furs as though they were disappointing old rags.

Finally the goods changed hands, cheap rum and glass beads and ammunition for pelts, and it was then that the Indians' stolidity broke, and within a few hours they were shouting-drunk, wildly and desperately, so that entire longhouse communities would be incapacitated for two or three days, the women as well as the men.

As word of our arrival spread across the mountains more groups came in to trade, and the drunken scenes were repeated. Men with thin, proud, noble faces vomited over their clothes, and crawled through the river-bank mud to lap water like their own yellow dogs. There were fights, and one burning when a man reeled into a cooking fire and his blankets burst into flames. When they were sober the Shawnees could spear a fish through foaming water, and they were so proud that even when they were sick or injured they would not ask for help, but when they were drunk they pulled their clothes off and threw them on Tuscarora Joe's counter in their efforts to buy more liquor.

The Ohio Company's northernmost trading post had been burned in the war, and Grizzly Will did not think it safe for us to make a tour of the Shawnees' summer settlements, even if we could find them. So we stayed at Tuscarora Joe's and, like the Indian men, got used to a lazy way of life. We had Joe's squaws and slave and the complaining Julius to skivvy for us, although it was invigorating to hunt and fish for the pot, and Bo Skerritt preferred his own cooking to other people's. As for the Indians, they hunted for survival in winter and would not even consent to do so for sport in summer. They left all work to their women, whom they treated with indifference, and spent their own sober days in oiling and attiring and parading themselves.

Once or twice they agreed to shooting competitions with Grizzly Will and Bo. The target was a hatchet, stuck by its handle into the earth, and the notion was to split the bullet on the edge of the blade. The Indians always won when they were sober, but then they drank some of the liquor they had won, and Grizzly Will and Bo won it back again.

About a dozen family groups came in to trade, and there were three settled in the longhouses for the summer. Tuscarora Joe said that this probably represented three-quarters of the Shawnees within a hundred miles in any direction, which meant that we had more than likely shaken hands and smoked the ceremonial pipe with the men who had killed Cato and still held Agricola's Liddy. The rest of the Indians who lived on the post were half-breeds and descendants of tribes who had formerly roamed the Piedmont and the Tidewater; two old women said that they were Nottaways, which particularly interested Captain Piquet because he said that there were only fifteen or twenty of that tribe still alive in the whole of Virginia. Tuscarora Joe's own erstwhile tribe, the Tuscaroras, had all but vanished, and many of the remnants at the post had Negro as well as Indian blood.

"Isn't the Nottaway a river?" I said, and Captain Piquet replied that indeed it was, and that many of Virginia's rivers bore the names of vanished tribes: Chickahominy and Mattaponi, Pamunkey and Rappahannock, Meherrin and Acohannock.

Did I realize, said the Captain, that when the English first arrived, there were some fifty different tribes of Indians, roughly ten thousand people, living in what we now called Virginia? I did not realize it. I said that ten thousand seemed so few, in such a wilderness, when we and our slaves numbered almost a quarter of a million. "English make ze land to fruit!" said Piquet, improbably, his gestures making vivid what his grammar left vague. "Indian mens do nothing!"

But where had they gone? I insisted. What had happened to the ten thousand? A few were killed in battle but not many. Most sold their lands by treaty and moved west, and as they did so, took the white man's diseases with them. I sneezed. The Captain gestured. "Comme ça!" he said, and next morning he had a similar sniffle himself. He cursed the loss of his hat to Deadeye, which he claimed to have weakened his resistance, but that was a month ago, and he had since acquired a magnificent beaver bonnet.

Nor was it sleeping out on the trail that had given me my cold, but the outhouse where we bedded down at the post. It was draughty, and the cold of the earthen floor had got into my bones. I had always been a person more likely to catch a chill at the turning times of the year, and I was annoyed but not surprised when as the young green shoots of leaves appeared, and the days grew warmer and hazier, my head streamed and buzzed.

One of the last of the Shawnees to trudge into the post with bundles of pelts on his squaws' backs was an unusually tall and morose man named Black Elk. As well as the squaws he had his own boy child and two young men, whom Tuscarora Joe thought were nephews; but in reply to questions Black Elk merely grunted, and the little group kept itself aloof from white men.

As Joe and Black Elk haggled I entered the particulars of his pelts in my purchase book, and sneezed continually as I did so. Some days later, when Black Elk and the two youths had sobered up after their trade-liquor drunk, Bo Skerritt said that Deadeye had told him that the family could not move out again because the little boy was too ill. Three days after that, he died of a common cold, and the grown men and women in his group were enfeebled by it.

The other Shawnees wrapped the child's body in skins and carried it into the forest to lodge it in a tree so that his soul might the more easily fly up to the Great Spirit. Then at dusk and into the dark, as we stood on the verandah with mugs of rum, and in its pen the tame deer nervously pawed, they beat drums and wailed and did a heavy, shuffling, circle dance.

I was sick at heart because I had killed a person that I did not even know. Nonsense, said the others, and made a joke of it. "It was Piquet!" roared Grizzly Will. "Piquet and his dang-blasted French fever!" At which they all laughed, because French fever was one of their nicknames for syphilis.

Chapter 42

Thomas

Soon after that, we recrossed the Alleghenies, and the blowy wetness of March, the fish that leaped in April up the still-snow-grey mountain waters, the warmer rains of May that hung in droplets on the flowered dogwood, all those enchantments of the spring were, like the bowed, working backs of Shawnee squaws, behind us, and in the sluggish air of summer there were hollyhocks and clouds of speckled butterflies. We saw the slopes sweep down and the valleys lost in mist beyond them. Turkey vultures sailed among the tree tops. Our mules struggled under obscenely puffed, hide-wrapped packs of furs. In the loved and lush green Shenandoah Valley there were sun-bonnetted women in the fields, and the sun frizzled the sweat on our brows. Then we climbed the Blue Ridge and wound down again through meadows blowing with flowers amid the yellow soil and the shiny green of the Indian corn.

People stared at us as we went by, and when we halted were eager to sit up and talk into the mild, smooth nights. Those nights, and those delicious breezes! Those awkward farm-girls, who stared at us because we were the men who had seen the wilderness and adventure! Grizzly Will told enormously exaggerated stories of his marksmanship and physical prowess; Skerritt smiled thinly, but did not contradict him, and Captain Piquet huffed and puffed. Deadeye and Julius said "Yessir!" a lot and stayed in the shadows, and were admired for it. A good Injun and a good nigger, by God! They made the Piedmont farmers feel safe.

I leaned back on their tumbledown verandahs, and was cooled by the sudden breezes even when I heard in my memory the drums and the Shawnee chant for dead souls. I had grown fond of our dogs. There was a bravery about them that took away my own fear when I was out hunting, and in a sense I felt like them. Civilization was the hunt, and I was to run here and there at its whistle. Very well. I would crash through the brambles with some joy for myself.

I was sorry for Will and Piquet and even Bo. They, too, were England's dogs, in slime and swamp water where their master would not go. Their folksy reputations were their solace, and in the case of Captain Piquet, another vatful of the ironic self-awareness in which he was pickled, like an onion in vinegar and spices, so that even the red blotches that appeared on his face when he was excited were a part of his sad wit—the inevitable fate of a man who would be elegant.

When we returned to Richmond he spent two weeks in and about the warehouse while he composed his thoughts and his report. He lodged in a tavern on the bluffs above the alleys. It was surrounded by massive, dark-trunked magnolias, and Captain Piquet sat and wrote at an open window, with the sickly sweet smell wafting round him and, as he said, the immortal melodies of Lully recalled heartbreakingly to mind.

He had been requested, as I knew, to make a copy of his report, so that Mr. Hope and other influential persons in the Ohio Company might read it; as he said, this was entirely improper, but he intended to accede to it and then resign his Captaincy, in the hope that his fame as a patriot and an adventurer would bring him a flood of commissions for musical instruction. So far as I know, this proved to be what happened, until fashions changed and he was too old to change with them; so that he finished his days alone and in the poorhouse but still clutching the beaver bonnet. All of which was to come and was, of course, unknown to him when in Richmond he wore a straw hat for the summer and conducted a decorous flirtation with the lady who owned the tavern. Perhaps he was not a gentleman at all, but the son of a man who dealt with gentlemen, such as a groom, or a wig-maker, or, come to that, a musician, and had left his countrymen because among us he was exotic.

Whatever he was, there was a natural tact about him, and when he had finished his report and informed the Governor, he was summoned to Williamsburg to present it, and bade me a breezy farewell as though he would return in a day or two; but he did not, and we never saw each other again.

I should have realized, as he did, that it would have been impolitic of him to have delivered his conclusions to Mr. Hope personally, and that the task, like the copied report that awaited me on my counting-house desk, would be left to me. I should also have realized that, with his interest in me, Mr. Hope would have suavely timed my movements to suit himself, but I did not, at least not until I arrived at Hope's Landing.

I went down-river on a tobacco boat. The day was sweaty and sullen and thundery, the water sluggish, the trees on its banks barely stirring. When I scrambled ashore at the jetty, it was late afternoon and the plantation seemed very quiet. The foliage of the big oaks hung heavy, and all the doors and windows of the house were open, to encourage some faint, refreshing movement of the air.

I broke into a sweat just by walking to the house. The oars of the tobacco boat creaked as the crew struggled to work her to midstream again, and a black footman who had seen her came out to meet me. I asked for Mr. Hope. "He been gone down the fields," said the groom. "They all gone make them hornworms."

This had always struck me as the most humiliating and absurd of all the tasks on a tobacco plantation: the search for hornworm grubs and the eggs they laid on the underside of the new green leaves. The fields were full of men, women, and children, and they drove with them as many bewildered turkeys as the yard provided, because turkeys ate hornworms. There was the rattle of the turned-back leaves, blobs of sweat on the green gloss, turkeys scampering, the overseer tetchy, and the planter worried. Black fingertips seized the grubs, and pinky-black palms were sticky with crushing them. Squelch, squelch, unless a turkey gobbled them first; if neither got them, the crop could be destroyed in a twinkling.

"Is Mrs. Hope at home?" I said, and the footman smiled cheekily, as though I should have known better than to ask, and said, "Yessir!" and pointed along the passage to the big family room.

The door was ajar. I went up to it and knocked. Someone said, "Who's there?" above a murmur of voices and children's prattle.

"Tom Derker," I said, and went in.

The room was littered and smelt hotly of child's urine and sweetly of milk and bed-clothes and lazy flesh. Some of the clothes chests were open and their contents strewn so that children could rummage and dress up, a female confusion that reminded me of the nanny-house.

There were Mrs. Hope's youngest child and two or three black toddlers, and a black wet-nurse with her bodice open and purple nipples like squashed ripe figs, and two more house-girls, and an open bureau on which Mrs. Hope's accounts and letters lay like piles of leaves; Mrs. Hope herself sat up in bed with the curtains open, on the chance of some air's coming through the windows. She was white and fat and untidy and dazedly happy, because in her arms she held a baby of two or three weeks. When he had belched milk over her naked shoulder she handed him back to the wet-nurse, who put him to the breast. Another of the girls wiped Mrs. Hope. They had cologne in bowls of water, and there was that smell, too, and the piddling noise of a wrung-out cloth, as they stopped talking and stared at me.

I blushed. I did not know what to say. My mind raced to count the months backwards, but really I did not need to do so. When they show you another man's baby, women are defiant, but when they show your own, they are subtly proud and entrapping, and Mrs. Hope's smile told me clearly enough that the child was mine. The black women giggled and deferred to me.

Other thoughts succeeded each other. Mrs. Hope's breasts and belly were still swollen and there was a flush of pain and fever in her cheeks. She must have been pregnant in Williamsburg, on the night that her eyes held mine through the tavern window; and in the mornings, when Mr. Hope was at the Capitol and that young man ransacked her.

I must have flushed at that because she cocked her head a little, a slow, self-absorbed reminder of her old mystery and cheek, and I thought: I don't know that he did ransack her, but Mr. Hope knows that *I* did. He knows that I am the father of this child because he did not make love to her himself. I thought about our couplings, and wondered which one made the child. Then I realized that if she knew in Williamsburg, so probably did Mr. Hope, and certainly when we rode together in the pack-train, and when he arranged for me to deliver Captain Piquet's report in person. By then the child had been born: my son. I was so sure that it was a son that she must have read that in my face as well.

"We have called him Thomas Lynch Hope," she said, delivering my name and her own before marriage.

I touched the top of the child's head and his faint, silken hair. He kicked and backed off the nipple. The wet-nurse laughed and abruptly put him in my arms. I felt foolish. I wanted to clutch him tightly but dared not. He complained in his throat and his legs stirred. His desires were aimless, but his own. His eyes moved oddly, and I do not think that he could see me properly, but I could see him, and although he had Mrs. Hope's colouring, the shape of his face, the squareness of it, the openness, the creases in the forehead, and the spacing of nose and eyes were like my fathers John and William Derker and by that descent like me.

Then he shifted and complained again, and belched sticky milk over me; it was disturbingly like sperm. The black woman laughed and wiped me, and took the baby back. The room was stifling. Mrs. Hope looked luxurious but worn out. The other children began to argue, and one of the blacks smacked them and then cuddled them impartially. I had both too little and too much to say.

"I must look to my valise," I said, which was as foolish an excuse as any, because the black groom had already taken it to a guest room. But it got me out of that hot female smell and their implacable life that unmanned me, and I stood in the hall and admired once again the elegant curve of the stairs and the gilt whorls round the mirrors, and then I went outside into air that was scarcely less sluggish and oppressive.

I walked past the ice-house and the well where they washed the shirts and sheets so well, having first boiled them up with soap. I passed the schoolhouse and went through the box hedge and stood in the slave quarters, looking beyond it to the open fields and the avenue of poplars, and eventually the towering dignity of the forest.

Somewhere behind me a slave child fell over and began to cry. I turned to pick it up but the mother snatched it away. She glared at me. Some of the first men home from work, round-shouldered and sweaty, stood up to support her. The obeah man did not stand. He did not need to. He lounged back and sipped his rum and touched the dried snake-skin wrapped round his neck. Mr. Hope gave him privileges, so he used the obeah to set the blacks happily to work, and to tell fortunes for the visiting white folks. He had no teeth, and his smile was a barrier of contempt.

I had lived with the slave trade for nearly seven years, and in all that time never had one true and equal relationship with a black person, man or woman, and now it was too late, because I knew too much, and they would always shut me out.

I walked slowly back towards the house, through the smoke of the fires over which they would boil their salt pork and garden greens, past the wooden cabins whose winter fireplaces roared with logs, and on whose hard floors they slept in the blankets that were issued twice a year; their beds and corn-shuck mattresses they made for themselves if they were able. They had their own tumbledown latrines on the side of the huts near the barns, but when they squatted in the fields their shit looked much the same as ours.

I heard a horse behind me and knew that it was Mr. Hope, but I did not turn until he was level with me and had sprung down and given the reins to a groom. He was in plain cotton for the weather and looked hot and stained. He smiled and held out his hand.

"I've brought Piquet's report," I blurted, and yet again he was able to nod in a way that set me at ease.

And then he said gently, as though my sorrow and joy must both be deeper than his, "Have you seen my new son and heir?"

"Yes," I said, and thought suddenly about the fight at the Shenandoah wedding, when the young lover's nose was broken by a blow from a shoe.

Mr. Hope saw the confusion in me, and to reassure it, gestured at the gloomy sky. "It must thunder soon," he said. "When it does we can make juleps and be cool." I compared his vulnerability and self-control with the savage energy of the wedding, and wondered which would endure the longer, and which eventually conquer this unknown continent. For myself, I wanted very much to attain his dignity.

We each stared deeply into the other's eyes, and there, in his unwavering blue gaze, I saw the reflected flicker of the lightning, and then the thunder crashed and rain pelted down. We splashed to the house, and when we looked back, saw running from the fields men and women and utterly bedraggled turkeys, a spectacle at which the house slaves howled with laughter.

Then there was much shouting in the house for windows to be closed, but those protected by the porticoes were left open and it was cooler almost at once. Mr. Hope and I went to our rooms to change, I into my only other suit of summer clothes, and I heard him send a slave through the rain for ice, but when I went to the library it had stopped for the moment, and the trees steamed and dripped.

That evening we supped with Mr. Glashan, the tutor, and the thunder lowered all round the house, so that the reflections of the candle-flames shuddered on the polished table top; but we felt sadly superior to it, and enjoyed the bursts of rain that fell outside, and ate fresh cherries and walnuts, and a honeycomb with our dessert wine, as I told Mr. Hope about the wilderness and he told me what he had heard from the returned Captain Fogg: that my old Antiguan mentor Black O'Riley had died, and Duffy had gone home to Ireland with the sword that he won at the shooting, and Kitty Trash was called Queen Kitty and ruled an empire of nanny-houses.

As for Myrtle Grove, there had been a disaster when one day in the middle of January Young Burwell had discovered that the wheat in his barn was hot and sprouting; it had been destroyed by weevils, and what small harvest he had was useless. He could not pay his debts and was ruined, and his uncle Paul Michieux had foreclosed the mortgage and taken possession. He had sent his silly sister to his own house at Alexandria, married a new young wife, and set to as an improving landlord. Burwell had gone to be an overseer on someone else's plantation, at which Mr. Glashan snorted contemptuously, but of the runaway Walkerton there was no news. I told Mr. Hope about Liddy and Agricola.

He was not surprised, because Captain Cary's sorrel mare had been recovered in Albemarle County, although in a broken-down condition. The Captain and Mrs. Ludwell themselves had agreed on a temporary compromise to enable them to live in the same house: Barnaby had been installed in an outhouse in the garden, and when either of them needed him for purely personal matters they rang a bell. But they could not marry until they had settled his status in relation to the housekeeper, an impasse overcome by Barnaby himself, who had married the said lady, upon which his master and mistress followed suit, and the four had lived for some months in agreeably argumentative harmony.

Eventually, when we had exhausted our gossip, even Mr. Glashan realized that Mr. Hope and I had private Ohio Company business and excused himself. The two of us sat in silence. Mr. Hope passed me the decanter.

"Was . . . Did she . . . was the birth a bad one?" I said.

"She was torn," he said, "and Thomas was bruised. I expect that's faded now."

"Yes."

He watched me shrewdly, and I knew that I must be steady. I withdrew the stopper from the decanter and poured. My hand did not shake. He smiled encouragingly, as if to say that time would set everything right. I lifted my glass to him, and he nodded gravely. I drank, but with the realization that he did not believe that time would set things right, not ever, and he seemed to sense my thoughts because he said that he had decided not to seek election to the House of Burgesses because he had enough work to do to make the plantations pay their way.

He said that England would win the war in the Americas because Montcalm had failed to do so, but that after it there would be difficulties—in trade, and between England and the Colonies.

Then he changed the subject and talked about books, and then suddenly he picked up what remained of the honeycomb and said, "Should we not offer this to Mary?" For a moment, because I never called her that, I did not realize that he meant Mrs. Hope, but then we walked across the passage and knocked on her door.

A black girl opened it and we went in. By the glow of a night-light we saw Thomas in his cradle and the wet-nurse on the truckle bed, and the feather mattress where the black girl had been lying. I heard the girl breathe as she stood near me, and was aware of her femaleness, and then in the big bed Mrs. Hope stirred.

"Uh?" she said. "Uh?"

Mr. Hope wrinkled his nose at the smells in the room.

"We've brought you some honeycomb," he said.

"Mm . . .," she said. "Mm . . ."

Then she opened her eyes wide and from her half-sleep saw the two of us, in our white summer clothes, our shadows vast on the panelling, and she smiled—it seemed to me, with amusement as well as content. I peeped into the cradle, and Mr. Hope set down the honeycomb and for an instant caressed the black girl under the chin. I looked back, but Mrs. Hope's eyes were closed.

Then we went out and stood under the back portico, from which the last shower drops hung and plopped. A dog stood up to greet us. There was a shrilling of frogs and insects. From one part of the sky the clouds had lifted and we saw stars, and from another the thunder still rolled; there was chanting from the slave quarters, and the glare of a fire.

Mr. Hope looked at me and sighed. He was in shadow, but the house and columns were beautiful. I felt anger and loss, an unutterable sense of loss, and yet a notion of justice, too, and the first glimmer of a dream.

"Was atonement to be found in the wilderness?" asked Mr. Hope drily.

"No."

His stare unsettled me. Atonement was here, as he very well knew, because having killed my father I must lose my son. Yet it contented me, and I said so. I recalled William's astounded laugh, and was grateful.

Then the fire in the slave quarters flared up so brightly that it shone on both of us, and we each saw in the other's eyes that there was more; but Mr. Hope was too much of a gentleman to press me, and for all his doubts and irony, too sure that he had won the day, and that the plantation would endure for his lifetime, and that of Thomas Lynch Hope as well.

So was I; and for that reason did not name Henry Dingwall, or Old Howler, or the Shawnee chant for dead souls. I smiled, and Mr. Hope nodded, and with his head on one side said what about a nightcap? He shouted for a black to wake up and fetch it, and as he did so, the sky swirled clear and there was a rush of air, and borne upon it a fresh pattering wetness, and then, heavily and sweetly, the waft of languor and corruption and magnolias; and in my heart I knew that I must seek a northern sky.

Part Five

Patmore Hall

I have lived in far countries abroad, or in the
agitating world at home . . . so that almost all
I have written has been mere passion—passion
it is true of different kinds, but always passion:
for . . . my indifference was a kind of passion,
the result of experience, and not the philosophy
of nature.

—GEORGE GORDON,
SIXTH LORD BYRON

Chapter 43

Landfall

In the wilderness I learned who I was and what I could not change, and at Hope's Landing I made peace with my memory of William; and whereas I will not say that after I had done so I became ruthless, I certainly stood back and observed the way in which I stood back and observed myself. I believed that I had journeyed farther and more dangerously in eighteen years than most people in their three score and ten. I had seen the imponderables of life, and stared into the depths of its contradictions. How could we solve them unless we killed ourselves? And that was not to be done, because, as Mr. Hope would have said, we were the educated minority, the people who struggle with problems and try to tell mankind which way to go.

When I describe myself as educated I no doubt presume, but I had travelled far and seen many different things, and with books I was coming to grips in my own way. One thing I knew firmly was that, in our civilization at least, life could not be conducted in much more than a brutish way without money; among the Jolas and the Shawnees, yes, but not in the world's great centres of energy, where men fulfilled God's notion of progress and decided what was new and, inadvertently, what the savages would want to buy and copy.

I knew only one way in which I could return to England with

money, and that was to buy furs. I had my money from the Ohio Company, and my wages that Captain Cary owed me, and that Mrs. Ludwell—or should I say, Mrs. Cary—could afford to pay. I invested it all in pelts from the Company's warehouse at Shockoe. I arranged through Mr. Hope for the connection to be maintained, and he, perhaps to be sure that I did indeed depart from the Americas, pre-vailed upon a Captain who owed him a favour to give me a free passage to New York and thence to Liverpool, where in September drizzle we made a sombre landfall.

The town was even more of a pandemonium than I remembered. There were more ships, more people, more houses, more wagons, more little factories that belched coal smoke into the damp and smutty air. When I went to Smallshaw's I found that the entire house was used for storage, because old Mr. Smallshaw had died and his son, Edward, moved to a grand new brick residence in Everton, where black boys in turbans opened the doors and Mrs. Smallshaw had her own sedan chair.

Everywhere people talked aggressively about the need to smash the French, to punish them, to show them once and for all that treachery did not pay, and that Britons ruled the waves, and the world, by steadfastness and honest endeavour. When I first saw Liverpool with Mr. Sayer, I thought it a clamorous enchantment; now it seemed a crude and heartless place. It talked tonnages, and percentages, and monopolies, and gross volumes, and debt collection, but never—except in sailors' taverns when men were drunk—the bloody flux, the corpses flung overboard, and the plantation whips; so that its view across the river, its watery sunsets, its lanes that wound into hay-fields, its Hospital for Sick Seamen, and its almshouses and fine walks built by public moneys were a mockery; there was more true caring for the old and broken in a Jola village.

Mr. Smallshaw said that when we had beaten the French the pros-pect was one of limitless prosperity and commercial expansion. He had trouble with his digestion and ate milk slops. He agreed to help my fur business, and when he saw that I was a reserved and industri-ous person, he offered me work in his counting-house, which I ac-cepted. I made it clear to him that I did so in order to tide myself over until my next consignment of furs should arrive.

He understood me. In Liverpool even barbers and pot-boys specu-lated on trade, and he persuaded me, because he knew that I had a few spare guineas, to invest them in one of his slave ships; and I agreed, out of a kind of sombre anger. I disliked Smallshaw, yet he did little that was actually offensive. He even—a bold act for a person as shifty and inconsiderate as he was—made it clear to me that so far as he was concerned, the past was past; my conflict with William had been resolved at the finish by a jury and a court of law, and that was good enough for him. That insincere sincerity, that white, blinking, smiling, slug-like encouragement of a confidence was, I suppose, what I disliked about him and why I felt myself superior. Oh, yes. I did. We all need a person inferior to ourselves, whether it be an African field-hand or a merchant in a broadcloth coat; yet I hated myself for hating him.

Sometimes he would consult me intimately, man to man, deferring, as he said, to my experience in the field. There would be a dispatch from a Captain on the Windward Coast that needed an interpretation of what lay between the lines: Was such and such a dealer behaving outrageously? And what was my explanation for the fact that despite their physique Ibos were prone to melancholy? So far as Mr. Smallshaw could see—and he did go down and stare at them from time to time to reassure himself—the slaves chained to the Goree Piazzas were of a more sluggish and stupid disposition than white men. Would Britons allow themselves to be enslaved? Never. Never, never.

In New York I had ordered a suit of clothes in that distinctive Yankee black, strong and neat and undemonstrative, and it suited my sadness and isolation, and I would put it on when I scoured the Strand Street taverns for Fourfarthings. I never found her. I looked into innumerable faces of girls made old, but there was no answering flicker and no response to the name. Mr. Smallshaw said that she was believed to have finished up there; but that was what people said about all discarded black girls, so I do not know where she went. Perhaps to London. Swallowed up. Buried. Turned somewhere into English mud and worms.

Mr. McBride I met once in the street, but he was drunk and confused me with someone else. A month later he shipped for the Bight of Biafra aboard one of Manesty's slavers, and died there of a fever and was buried at sea. Mr. Partridge I meet once or twice a week, for he retired from the deep-sea trade to work in His Majesty's Customs in Liverpool; before he did so, he had made handsome

profits, and bought a pretty cottage in Walton, and married a wife
who is plain but, like himself, utterly reliable. When we meet we say
little that is not about the business of the day, and he seems content,
in the way that Bo Skerritt was, a man who knows his limits and has
never exceeded them.

I wish that I could say the same for myself. It is now four years
since I returned to Liverpool, and although I have made far more
money than my lodgings and modest clothes would indicate, my
spirit has flown in weary circles. I have set aside more than enough
to redeem the mortgage on High Top, and that is why for the first
time I have returned now to the moors, and write these pages in the
guest room of Mr. Sayer's house.

He is a much shiftier and foxier man than I remembered, yet at the
beck and call of his wife, a woman at least twenty years older than
himself, who married him when he was her widowed father's clerk.
She tinkles a little bell for him to attend her at all hours of the day
and night, and affects headaches and stomach upsets that miraculously disappear as soon as he rides out; then she calls me to her, and
we gossip about the clients, and talk about the books that we have
read.

There is so much prosperity now in the weaving that the value of
the farms as grazing land has not risen like everything else; so High
Top has not proved a spectacular investment for Mr. Sayer, and is
one that he is willing to surrender. Lawyers are always affable when
there is business in the offing, but Mr. Sayer's kindness goes beyond
that, and he still has the knack of making a person believe that he
truly understands him.

We have had many deep talks in which I have described my doubts
about the slave trade, and although I know that Mr. Sayer disagrees
with me, the way in which he puts his ironical comments makes it
seem sometimes that he does not. He is full of sharp questions about
the habits of Africans and Shawnees. He wonders what other worlds
there are left to be found upon the globe, and shakes his head at the
arbitrariness of Mandinka rule when compared to, say, Halifax Petty
Sessions, where the evidence in one simple case of sheep-stealing
would fill as many written pages as the entire history of a savage
continent.

Then his wife's bell tolls, and he rushes upstairs to give her a few
sips of hot water, and on his return praises her uncomplaining na-

ture. Thank God he still has his own health. He asks me confidentially about the kitchen women, because that is his ceaseless worry. Are they to be trusted when he is out of the house? He sighs and stares into the coals. Oh, yes, he would have liked children, he says disconnectedly, and we talk about my relatives.

Crabtree is greyer and older and stiffer, and umpires the wrestling now, instead of taking part in it, and his wife is more squeaky and mouse-like, and tears came to my eyes at the sight of them.

My father's cousin James Derker I met in the Cloth Hall. He at once complimented me on my experience of the world, and asked me for a loan to enable him to set up business in Manchester. His elder son, who when I was a child I hated because he bullied me, now seemed an awkward, untidy man who grinned in his father's shadow. He said that his mother, Kitty, was well and that his younger brother, Edgar, was the brains of the family, but continually quarrelled with James.

Poor James. I remembered how William laughed at him, and imitated his bluster, and one afternoon I walked over the tops to Waterfoot, where my fathers John and William came to court my mother, and I sat in Aunt Annie's kitchen and talked about them both. Aunt Annie had known whose son I was, and now she was fat, and wept, and talked incessantly about days I did not know, days before I was born, days she would never forget, when she was a girl, and men had glanced at her, and what might have been; then her husband, Dawson, came in with yard muck on his boots. He wanted a dish of tea and hardly spoke to me at all. The room, like all the rooms in these valleys, seemed low and dank, and oppressive, until I longed like a child to burst out again upon the moor, but when I did I was bereft.

I had forgotten how the sky came down and how the light blackened; black light filling the valleys; curlews; blown rushes; pellets of sheep dung; sweeping rain and black light as black as my remorse; and High Top so desolate, so tumbledown and empty, that I have no use for it and do not want to buy it, but I will. Not for pride now, not for revenge, but for the dream that stirred in me at Hope's Landing. I will conclude the business with Mr. Sayer tomorrow because I must return to Liverpool and go from there to Bath. This is a new business venture of which I have unclear hopes, but which, as Mr. Smallshaw advises me, cannot go untried.

Bath is a spa in green country east of Bristol, and it is such a centre

of fashion, particularly for absentee West Indians, retired naval officers, and merchants who have made fortunes in the East, that there
may well be a market for my furs. One may also find clean black
women there. The Liverpool whores I do not trust to be free of the
pox, and I need whores, because if I give vent to it from time to time,
my violence can be lived with.

It is a master passion. It is what all men feel in our competitive
Europe, and it has brought wealth and glory in which all have shared,
although few have actually set foot upon the beaches where human
flesh is bought and sold, and taken their feelings to the limit.

I have. I am a wounded person. Even if I marry I will need the
whores. I do not like what I am, but I do recognize it. I resemble one
of those overseers who on the Windward Coast put their black brothers into the longboats: the Captains of the Sands, as they are called,
who send others into hell but save themselves. So I have done and am.
On the moors or in a warm brick house, I am every day a Captain
of the Sands. I wish that I were Henry Dingwall, but I am not brave
enough. I would like to be rich, and to move in society, and learn
everything I can, but there comes a moment when learning for its
own sake must stop, and action begin. We are all pebbles in a glacier,
says Mr. Sayer, and admits with a twisted smile that he heard it
spouted by some advocate. He adds that the world has progressed
more in the last hundred years than in the previous two thousand.

A VALEDICTORY MEMOIR BY DINGWALL DERKER ESQUIRE, GENTLE-
MAN AND MEMBER OF PARLIAMENT, OF PATMORE HALL, IN THE
COUNTY OF HERTFORDSHIRE, WRITTEN DECEMBER 12th, 1864.

My grandfather Thomas Derker died in this house on March
10th, 1820, aged eighty-one. His confessions, as written in five
ledgers embossed "Smallshaw and Hill Ltd.," I found after his
death among a body of papers most carefully indexed and addressed to my discretion. At that time the direct descendants of
many persons mentioned in the ledgers were still alive, and my
own political career was not secured. My decision was to retain
the papers but not to publish them, on account of their lewdness,
and the false light they cast upon the character of a great man
and one of the most influential figures in the history of the
Anti-Slavery Society.

My grandfather gave evidence on the African slave trade to the Privy Council in 1789, and to the Committee of the House of Commons in 1790. He wrote pamphlets and addressed meetings in many parts of the British Isles. In the 1770s he had espoused the cause of the American colonists, and whatever success I may have had in the political arena, both in and out of office, may be ascribed entirely to my adherence to those notions of reform that my grandfather unswervingly proclaimed.

That he is not better known to the public, and was not one of those leaders of the movement who celebrated the final triumph of the abolition of the slave trade on January 1st, 1808, is due to the fact that he had already been afflicted by the stroke which for the last twenty years of his life rendered him speechless and partially paralysed.

To have commemorated the fortitude with which that condition was endured with the publication of a scandalous memoir would have been an act not of piety but of abuse, not least to the memory of my grandmother Lavinia Derker, née Hanson, whose eventual marriage and life-long devotion to my grandfather reads like a calender of true and Christian family love.

When my grandfather visited Bath in 1761, he made it his custom to take a morning chocolate in the Assembly Rooms, where one day he heard a footman shout for the sedan chair of His Grace the Earl of Orrin. The name touched some chord in his memory. He went to the door, and came face to face with a former Antiguan acquaintance, the merchant Mr. John Leslie—but now Mr. John Leslie no longer, since he had been elevated, for his services to the conduct of our policy in the West Indies, and a rambling genealogical connection, to the ancient and long-vacant Scottish Earldom of Orrin.

His Grace, who had come to Bath to take a cure for some dermatological disorder, recognized my grandfather, and invited him to a levee, at which he met many more Antiguans, notable among them Colonel Hanson of Hawksbill and his daughters, Miss Susannah and Miss Lavinia. Susannah had married but separated. Lavinia had never married, for the simple reason that the person she had always loved was my grandfather. This she revealed to him, and a few months later they were married, which transformed his worldly situation.

Within four years they had three children and my grandmother had inherited from her uncle Nicholas Leonard this house in the country, the establishment in St. James's Square, and the plantations at Hawksbill and Mosquito Bay. The seat in Parliament went to her cousin William Leonard, which was just as well, because my grandfather could hardly have proclaimed anti-slavery from one of the slavery lobby's own platforms.

As it was, my grandmother gave unstintingly of her fortune to assist her husband's cause, and lost many of her friends on his account. Her dignity was more than equal to these blows and counter blows, and happily, as that momentous debate has passed into history, our family and those of Leonard and Orrin have amply healed what breaches may have opened between us.

For forty years my grandfather was a sardonic and familiar figure in polite society, a friend eventually of Charles James Fox and of writers and artistic persons of all sorts. For much of that time his pursuit of justice kept him apart from my grandmother, who preferred the charms of domesticity and rural life, and who created the exquisite gardens that surround this house today.

But when the stroke felled him, my grandfather left London for ever and lived at Patmore, with the black butler Grandison to push his wicker wheel-chair and sleep on the truckle bed in his room. I have been a Minister of the Crown in two administrations, and yet I think I can say that Grandison was the most imposing person that I ever met in my life. He was tall, white-haired, as straight as a guardsman, and a stickler for correctness in everything. Woe betide footmen with dirty gloves, or impertinent tradesmen, or those house-guests who did not know their protocol!

I was the constant companion of these two old men, especially in the garden in summer, when my grandfather liked his chair to be wheeled into the scented shade of the cedar boughs. Grandison taught me a game of checkers that I now realize he must have learned himself as a boy beneath some African baobab, and my grandfather watched.

One side of his face and body had been rendered immobile by the stroke, but he had soon taught himself to write again, and was never without pencils and an artist's sketch-block, on which he could write and tear off messages. In that way he expressed a lively interest in all manner of subjects until the day he died, and it is when I recall such scenes that I doubt sometimes the authenticity of the "Smallshaw" ledgers.

We live today in an age in which morals and public conduct walk hand in hand. Even as I write these words, a great struggle rages in America, and in the very forests of Virginia, over the issue of whether men shall live in slavery or freedom. Who can doubt, as General Grant gathers his armies, that men will live free, and that the evils of three hundred years will be banished for ever?

But it was not always so. Public policy was not always informed by public spirit, and the pamphlets and cartoons that accused (alas, from the reforming side) the Earl of Orrin of a form of miscegenation with his domestic staff of which he was indubitably innocent, were among the most vicious statements of a more licentious age.

I knew Grandison, and Lavinia Derker, née Hanson, and her sister, and her companion the charming mulatta woman Miss Hanson, and the Earl of Orrin, and numberless persons of the West Indian connection. I saw them with a child's eye, yet that is no bad thing, and they had a flamboyance about them, as though a hotter sun had entered their natures and made them bloom in fanciful, un-English ways; but they were good people, I swear to it, they were good and true and my grandmother was the purest woman I have known.

My grandfather's love for her glowed in his eyes, and hers for him in the way in which she helped and read to him even when her own ailments sorely troubled her. When she could no longer see to read herself, she had my mother to do so, or my sister, or sometimes the curate from the village. My grandfather liked those passages in which redemption was promised, and the world of light described.

My grandmother was the first to die, followed by Grandison, and it was left to my mother and sister to tend the old man's final years. I am happy to record that I attended his deathbed, and that it was appropriately noble. As I write here now, in my study, with a whisky and soda at my elbow, and in the distant night the whistle of a passing steam train, the age in which he lived seems more distant than its hundred years.

It was a savage, blood-reeked age like that of pagan Rome, an age the like of which I am sure mankind will not see again, because our steamboats and our missionaries take light to the darkest corners of the earth. But my grandfather was entirely wholesome, and a man of faith. His supposed memoirs will not be published in what remains of my lifetime, or in that of my executors.

A LETTER PRESENTED IN RECENT YEARS TO THE DERKER ARCHIVE
OF THE HERTFORDSHIRE COUNTY RECORD OFFICE. IT WAS WRITTEN
BY THE REVEREND JAMES VERNEY, D.D., FOR SOME TIME RECTOR OF
PATMORE, TO A FELLOW CLERGYMAN AND FORMER COLLEGE
FRIEND RESIDENT IN CAPE TOWN, AND DATED MARCH 20th, 1869.

Here's a strange tale for your antiquarian fancy to ponder.
You know that our land adjoins at the stream that of the un-
happy Derker family, and you may well recall that two or three
years ago, when old Dingwall Derker died, the local doctor and
I sat up with him until the end came early in the morning. What
I did not describe to you at the time, for reasons of discretion that
will become obvious, was the extraordinary behaviour of Mr.
Derker's unmarried sister, Miss Mary Derker.

I think you met her once after evensong, a tall woman who
always wore silks, with red hair turned silver-yellow, thin-lipped
and somewhat stooping. She is dead herself now. Do you remember her? Well, the doctor and I had spared her the final night's
ordeal, but as soon as her brother was dead, sent her a message
by one of the servants.

When she neither came to the sickroom nor replied to our
message, we assumed that grief had overwhelmed her. It was not
until we saw smoke and heard shouting and bustling that we
realized that something was afoot in the garden.

We went out there, and found Miss Derker, still wearing her
nightdress but with a shawl around her. She had ordered a footman to light a bonfire near the cedars, and commenced to throw
upon it what were evidently as many of the family papers as she
could lay her hands on.

When we remonstrated with her, because the doctor happened
to know that she was not one of her brother's executors, she
shouted in a hysterical fashion that it was her intention to destroy everything that would add to the glory of men in general,
and of Derker men in particular.

She was clearly not herself, and there followed an unpleasant
scene, at the end of which she broke down and agreed to be given
sedatives. Some papers we managed to rescue, in particular a set
of old ledgers, but most were burned—including, it transpired,
the entire Parliamentary archive of Dingwall Derker himself.

The remnants of the fire glowed for some time, and then a
wind got up and blew them across the garden, where I actually

saw with my own eyes a magpie pick up one large half-charred paper and carry it to the nest that it was building on rectory land.

Now—and here is the point of my story—this present spring was similarly windy, and the old elm in which the magpie built its nest was blown down. Because I was curious I investigated, and found among the mess of twigs and bits and pieces that had composed the nest my half-charred piece of paper.

I have it before me now. It is a letter, dated August 1775, in which Mrs. Lavinia Hanson of Patmore Hall tells her husband not to come there again without her permission, and never in a drunken and violent condition. So much for earthly bliss! Dingwall Derker was wily no doubt, but you and I were brought up to call his grandfather Thomas a crusader, and it seems regrettable, even when history's wrongs have been put right, to be reminded that his wife thought otherwise. How far was she herself undutiful? Decide for yourself from this passage:

"I have compresses for my face and body, but for my heart there are none, and it is that wound I cannot staunch. Why do you strut, why do you cry Captain of the Sands for your excuse, when it is those you claim to love whom you enslave? Either your consciousness says one thing, and your feelings enact another, and you are an ingrained devil, or you are in agony and I love you but will not suffer more—because I cannot but believe that it is what we do in our affections and our common moments that is of influence, not what we say upon the hustings. . . ."

Like me, are you not moved, and persuaded that Mrs. Lavinia was striking—and while we are on that tack, "Captain of the Sands" is a striking phrase, is it not, except that I cannot discover what it means. How about your famous old lexographies? I suppose that the Cape is still sun blessed. Here we have the crocuses, which, as I get older, I seem to find especially welcome.